Spirits of the Black Forest

By: Nia Rose

A Poisoned Apple book
Poisoned Apple Publishing, L.L.C.

Copyright © Nia Rose 2019

Spirits of the Black Forest (Coven Chronicles, Book 3)

Book design by Poisoned Apple Publishing
Editing by Poisoned Apple Publishing

ISBN: 978-1-7348272-2-4

Published by Poisoned Apple Publishing, L.L.C.
www.poisonedapplepublishing.com

Printed in the United States of America

Coven Chronicles series by

Nia Rose & Octavia J. Riley
SPELLBOUND & HELLHOUNDS
SECRETS OF THE SANCTUARY
SPIRITS OF THE BLACK FOREST

Stand Alone Novels by
Nia Rose
SONS OF STARS
KING OF CROWS

Dedicated to: David and Hayden.

Hayden, through all my years that I've been blessed with life, I have found that there is a meaning behind every meeting. Whether it is a dormant lesson that is unlocked through friendship or heartache, or laughter that heals the pain that no words could ever fathom to describe, we walk this life searching for these connections and lessons. Shaking hands with destiny and drinking wine with the memories each wonderful person brings to us. May it be in sadness, pain, laughter, or happiness, there is a moment that is freeze-framed in time that we will often retreat to because it had an impact on our soul. Like so many of these moments collected, your friendship has become not just a memory, but a room — tucked within my heart — that is full of them. You rekindled laughter when I wanted to cry, and you fueled an imagination that refuses to die. I am glad that you and I met and bonded so many years ago.

Thank you for being one of my best friends.

David, you will always be my poetic monster. You are a man that went after my own heart without me even realizing it. We fell in love without meaning to. We have never struggled in love, we've never struggled in supporting one another, and we've never struggled with feeding each other's creativity. From the moment I met you, I knew that I would be defenseless against you. You'd break me and remake me in a way no other could. For all your devotion, for all your love, and for all the creative help, I thank you. But, my love, most of all, I thank you for never letting me give up.

I love you.

Thank you.

DESERT TEMPLE
GAYGHA PESHTPENHVET I ESTVETSYT' AYNNIRUV
HEAVEN'S HAND
DRAGON'S MOUTH
HELL'S H
MOUN
TEMP
RED TIPPED MOUNTAINS
THE GOLDEN SEA
SILVER THREAD
TOLVAD
LORV
BANSHEE BOG
TEMPLE RUINS
JEWELED CA

HAND
NTAIN
PLE
FOREST TEMPLE
SATVIRIYA
THE CURSED
MIRROR
VEMEESE LAKE
THE BLACK
FOREST
HALF HEART
BAY
ADE
VO LAKE
NS
THE GENTLE TITAN
THE DEVIL'S PITCHFORK
ANOPY
AERISTRIA

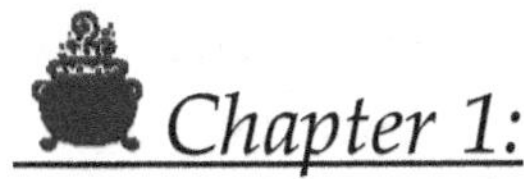

Chapter 1:

The bright rays of the day glittered over the mounds of shoveled snow collected around the outdoor ceremonial stage. Golden illumination was bouncing gaily off the heaps of tiny, crystalized, wintery mirrors. The warm sunlight was amplified by the rolling hills of white and it rose to splash over the worn, sturdy wood of the platform before it burst in a vivid glow against a podium dead center of the rostrum. It was here that the High Priest Torro stood. He gently flattened his notes scrolled out on parchment as he spoke humbly to a patient and happy crowd sprawled out in rows of seats before him.

"It is in light of these valiant efforts that we are here, gathered today, to give way to a new generation of Spellweavers," he bellowed proudly at the end of his speech. Hands outstretched from beneath his spelled blue cloak to clap reservedly with the crowd and then motioned behind him. "Ladies and gentlemen, High Priest Mia shall take over now and present you with the newest additions of the Coven's third rank Spellweavers!" He continued to clap until the female approached the podium and then promptly took his seat.

Vanessa watched it all from the edge of the steps that she, and many others, would climb to claim their new insignia. Silver. She had waited so many years to wrap her fingers around that blessed silver insignia. She looked around herself before dipping a quick hand under her fur-lined cloak and pinching the tender skin on the underside of her upper arm. She made a small yelp, and a few of her neighboring comrades eyed her over as she turned a pretty shade of pink and waved at them awkwardly. Her cumbersome stare steered toward the podium where Mia spoke to the collection of beings seated on the rolling waves of foldout chairs.

Nope. This was definitely not a dream.

This was real and finally happening. She beamed and sucked

in a deep, appreciative breath of air as she puffed out her chest. Today was the day she'd be a Spellweaver. It seemed like it was only yesterday… wait. That was yesterday. Vanessa didn't care how long she had been a Hunter. It was some of the greatest memories that she had, even when she had been knocking on death's door.

Recently, being a Hunter—or any ranked Coven member for that matter—had become a very dangerous thing, indeed. An over-used summoning portal rested beneath Runerite Academy. Because of it, there were scattered hell portals that were like doors to Hell left ajar throughout the main city of Tolvade. Meaning, if the demon could sense the opening, locate it, and had enough willpower, it could crawl right out of the underworld and wreak havoc upon this plane. To make matters worse? There wasn't a soul in Aeristria that had the slightest clue on how to close the summoning portals or de-summon a demon, which had left the jail houses filled to the brim with high-class feral demons that collectively could tear the world apart in a few days if they managed to escape.

Then there were the compromised High Priest Council seats and their Second Chosens. New High Priests had been selected, but their Second Chosen had not yet been announced. It didn't help that after careful consideration, the Council had made an announcement one week prior to the city that Second Chosens were now an official rank, and a proper celebration would be held in conjunction with the oath-binding of the new High Priests. Hex, the formal ceremony to announce the new blue cloaks hadn't even been performed. But it didn't stop them from all being here today.

The cheer from the crowd brought her out of her recollection. Vanessa peeled her vision from blue cloak Mia to glance over the sea of faces. It wasn't hard to pick Leon and Lyx out of the crowd because they were seated next to Bobo. The mammoth-sized ogre dwarfed anything next to him and took up two chairs instead of one, causing a slight hiccup in the pattern of heads lining the row.

It had been two weeks since their incident with the hellhounds had transpired. Since then, the Coven had invoked a semi-permanent partnership between members until the feral demon situation had been fully dealt with. This meant that Leon and

Vanessa's situation was pretty much the same because they were already paired up. Forcefully, but paired just the same.

Most Coven members got to pick their partners. She didn't. But it wasn't all bad for Vanessa and Leon. After everything that they had been through, they wouldn't have trusted anyone else slinging spells at their side. After multiple missions recently, they had grown to be quite the team.

Leon was given a promotion and started training to be a Summoner not two days after Vanessa had woken up from her magic-deficiency coma. It was a position he was already aiming for, so most of his schedules remained the same. The only major alteration was that he now had summoning duties.

Occasionally he could be called upon to do a Dark Market raid, but mostly he was on standby for tethering duty or mission scrolls that were well-above Hunter status. Tethering duty was when Summoners aided a new Coven member in procuring a demon pet from the underworld and helped to tether it to its new master. The chosen Summoner would then blast the demon with an intelligent spell. It took a lot of concentration to focus on keeping a hell gate open while pushing back all nearby demons from attempting to climb out. It also took a lot of focus to tether a demon and master all while being ready to defend those around you if things go haywire.

She was proud he had gone a rank up, even if she was a tad bit jealous. That green with envy soon washed away at the prospect of her finally becoming a Spellweaver. After so many years of toil and struggle and studying, she was finally gifted with the opportunity to be the next rank up. Hunter was grand and all, but Spellweaver?

She could die a happy witch now...

The crowd hailed fervently, and it tore Vanessa from her inner thoughts. She fluttered her eyes free of sunlight piercing her gaze that was still slightly hazy with daydreams. Slowly, she surveyed her surroundings once more. She quickly noted that the soon-to-be Spellweavers were still waiting but were beginning to file into a single line near the edge of the platform where they'd be called forth.

Feeling the first wave of anxiety hit as if an overweight dragon had crashed into her, she rapidly swept her russet hues through the throng of nodding heads, wild clapping, and boisterously cheering beings. All the while, panic played a chaotic melody with the chords of Vanessa's heart. She found them again, Leon, Lyx, and Bobo. They noticed her from afar and instantly gave her toothy, gleeful grins, overzealous thumbs bobbing up and down, and a round of applause that was lost in the swell of excitement pouring out from the crowd.

Leon couldn't stop the smile from splitting his face in two, Lyx took a handkerchief from Bobo and blew her nose in it as she hiccupped, sniffled, and sobbed happily, and Bobo had tears welling in his big, blue eyes that he was trying to pretend weren't there. Vanessa giggled to herself, letting the fear slowly ebb away. This was one of those moments that would be remembered by her always.

Again, she drew in a deep, hearty breath and released it slowly. Her hands were numb with tiny prickles of pins and needles that had been triggered by her growing excitement. Even though her heart felt frantic against her breast, and even though she felt like she wanted to pull the cape around her head to hide from a swarm of strangers, she wouldn't trade this moment for anything.

"Vanessa Peterson," High Priest Mia called the witch's name, and she felt her heart leap into her throat and strangle any hope of calm breathing right out of the poor girl. She swallowed hard, hoping to quell the smothering heartbeat thudding within her esophagus. Otherwise, she was sure to vomit the frustrating organ all over the stage if she got any more worked up.

"You can do this," she whispered to herself as she took a reluctant step forward.

At the first signs of movement, the crowd had fallen a little silent, and it made her heart sink down into her stomach and coil into a knot of apprehension and despair. But there was no reprieve from the muscle's hysterical thudding. It slammed against its bony cage in rapid succession, and she felt her chest tighten as she started to climb up the stairs.

Head swimming in waves of dizzy spells, she focused on the rise and fall of her feet. Each step was like a thunderclap that echoed in her ears and rolled through the crowd. The audience became a winter's night: cold, quiet, and snuffing out the sound for miles. Vanessa was sure she could hear crickets taking up a few of the seats.

Double-dip a candlestick!

She didn't care. So what if they weren't clapping for her? She was no less deserving than anyone else that walked across that stage today. Squaring her shoulders, Vanessa held her head high and mounted the remaining steps until she hit the stage. Her foot slammed down upon its rightful place on the platform.

I deserve this!

She had survived hellhounds, a drunken ogre, being chased by a minotaur, her crippling self-doubt, and a war with backstabbing members of the blue cloaks. She could survive this like it was nothing. But, banish a banshee, was it hard.

All her life, she was ridiculed and taunted by strangers while others whispered nasty, slanderous remarks behind her back. The amount of pain and suffering she had gone through to make sure that those very same people didn't get harmed by feral demons made her blood run cold, her anger bubble over, and it ripped her heart right out of her chest.

Would they ever know the sacrifices and risks that she took to ensure that they could sleep a little better at night?

Did their approval matter to her anymore?

Backbone made of a steel bar, and head refusing to tilt or drop in defeat, Vanessa continued to walk across the stage to gain the silver emblem that she had focused so many years of her youth on earning. Every time the sole of her boots connected with the floor underfoot, it was like listening to someone walking over an empty room lined with worn wooden floors. It sounded lonely, bare, and hollowed. She heard every creak and sigh of the planks, she heard every shuffle and scuff of her buckled boots, and she heard every whine of the beams as her weight was sustained by them. But, still, there was nothing from the throng of beings that had shown up for the ceremony today.

Reaching the podium with dead silence entombing the masses was harder than anything she had ever done. Hex, she was on the verge of crying. But she *wanted* that emblem.

The next breath of air that she drew in was ragged, and her jaw hurt she was clenching it so tightly. Her only saving grace was Mia's warm smile. The High Priest Mia was a stranger to her, but it was a smiling face just the same. Fixed on that smile, Vanessa swam through the splintered wood of the platform to that life raft and bowed out her chest with pride.

That silver insignia was rightfully hers.

Mia snuck a pat onto Vanessa's shoulder and slid her hand down to gently caress a thumb over the young girl's upper arm in a motherly fashion. It was all done so quickly that it was hardly noted before the blue cloak was grasping the front of the witch's cloak and pinning the silver phoenix emblem to it.

"Spellweaver Peterson, we are lucky to have someone so gifted in the ranks. May the goddess bless you," Mia announced as she had with all the others, giving rank and title to Vanessa.

But the words were carried through a hushed collection of bodies. That is, until, the sound of slow, hard, booming applause broke through the spell of silence.

"THAT'A GIRL, VANESSA!" It was Leon, and he was standing up while clapping like he was angry and serious and not going to relent until Vanessa got off the stage or he died. Death seemed like a good idea to her.

What are the chances that a spell could reach him before he'd be able to deflect it?

She flushed crimson so deep she was sure she could melt the remaining snow in Aeristria. From next to Leon, she saw Bobo rise from his chairs with sophistication. The furniture squeaked with the lack of his weight filling them. He tugged at the hems of his tailored jacket and fussed with dusting his lapels before he stretched his arms out, reminding Vanessa of a conductor for an orchestra, and proceeded to clap along with Leon. The cracking sound of his gargantuan hands colliding resonated through the air like trees being harshly snapped in half.

Standing up and fixing her tight, leather skirt, Lyx flipped her illustrious, ebony locks behind her shoulders in a wordless warning of diva-like flare. In action alone, the succubus dared anyone to cross her choice to stand behind the young witch. Goddess help the being that would be brave enough to tell the trio to pipe down. Lyx would snap the whip around their neck so fast their head would spin … literally.

Turning to face the horde of quiet onlookers and take her bow, Vanessa fell forward in a blur of braided onyx hair and flowing cloak ripples as she attempted to rush through the final part of the ceremony with chaotic grace. She just wanted to get the hex off the stage before she broke down. Only, when she dipped into her bend she was immediately stunned.

Much to her astonishment, she could hear it as it happened, the sound of a thousand bodies rising from a thousand seats. Was she really that surprised? She expected them to file down the aisles and leave the ceremony grounds any second, but they never did. Fear gripped her body and screamed through every limb, making it hard to find the will to move.

Were they going to throw rotten food at her? Boo her from the stage in outrage? She feared rising from her sloppy bow so greatly that she remained there a tick or two longer than needed. Feeling like she was chewing her own heartbeat, she raised her head first. And she almost sobbed at the view spanning before her deep, brown gaze.

Every being that had attended the ceremony was folded over with sincere respect for her, bowing to her. Bowing. To. *Her*! The largest screw-up witch on this side of Aeristria, and they were all honoring her with a bow. Rising swiftly, she stiffened and turned to address the blue cloaks and stutter through some half-baked apology. But she was met there again with a sight that made her mind draw blanks.

Fingers rose to her lips to cover their unremitting quivering. Her eyes were wide with awe and amazement. Through her tear-smeared orbs, she saw the Celestial standing next to the High Priest Council members who all were on bended knee to her. And the Celestial, she had her hands married in prayer formation fixed over her bowed head. Vanessa floundered up on the stage for a moment and looked to her fellow Coven members in waiting for answers but found them, too, bowing at her.

Not able to hold it back anymore, a hot tear spilled down her cheek and she wiped its burning trail hastily with the sleeve of her robes before resuming a quick bow to everyone.

"Thank you," she croaked out as new tears rose in her eyes. Lifting from the bow, Vanessa rushed off the stage before they all saw her weeping like a baby.

She was hiding behind one of the beams on the back of the stage. Vanessa was trying to make sense of what just happened while she gathered her composure to face everyone at the afterparty that was to be held within the hour. The resonance of frosted grass and scattered snow piles being traversed through brought her from her confused daze. Turning on a coin, she found Bobo, Leon, and Lyx.

Bobo, the only ogre in all of Raen that could wear a suit and look more refined than an aristocratic farmer—and all farmers were aristocrats—was barely a foot away and holding out a handkerchief. A quick flick of her russet gaze to the succubus madly clutching her own hankie made the beast laugh lightly.

"Remember, dear. I ooze charm and handkerchiefs," he prompted and waved the item about in place.

That was all she needed, a hankie and a laugh. She ripped it from his massive paw with a stifled giggle as she wiped her face and nose. "That was all very unexpected," she said with a voice that hid all the tears she had just shed.

"Well, I expected it," Bobo admitted in a low voice.

"The crying or the bowing or the fact that I'm finally a Spellweaver now?" Vanessa inquired.

"Perhaps, just the Spellweaver bit. Maybe the crying," he teased.

"Darling, I knew you had it in you. I'm proud of you," Lyx chimed in.

"Careful, we'll need her to be able to fit into the coach when we go home. You keep feeding her ego and we'll be walking to *and* from the afterparty," Leon warned his pet with a smile.

Vanessa rolled her red-from-crying eyes and shook her head with a grin. "Green isn't a good color for you, Leon."

"Pfft, me? Jealous? I'm a Summoner, sweetie."

"In training," Vanessa reminded.

He opened his mouth and closed it like a fish out of water before clamping it shut and shrugging. "Give me a week or two and I'll have the pin to prove it. I won't cry about it like some people I know."

That, she had no doubt of. But his reaction was just as she expected, and she laughed at the sight. "Speaking of crying…" she faced Bobo dramatically. "Were those tears that I saw in your eyes when I looked over to you guys?"

The flustered ogre sputtered and flattened his tie one too many times against his white button-up. "Absurd."

"No, I'm pretty sure I saw it," she assured.

He shook his head quickly and violently. "You were mistaken, my dear. Those were not tears of joy. They were tears of dreadful realization."

"Oh, of what?" she pressed.

"Of how doomed Raen is with *you* as a Spellweaver." The mirth in his eyes matched his tone.

It couldn't be helped. Vanessa pouted, huffed, and then shoved Bobo's arm as hard as she could. The meaty appendage didn't budge. It was like slapping a wall with a wet noodle. They all bellowed out boisterous laughter at the hilarity of the action. All the while the poor girl nursed her hand and sucked on her bottom lip as her cheeks flared with heat.

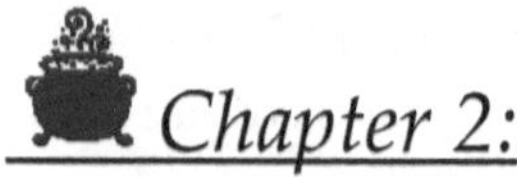

Chapter 2:

Each year, the afterparty for newly promoted Coven members was held at a different tavern or eatery. The bill was generously paid for by the Coven. The fact that the location was constantly changed was because they didn't want there to be a misunderstanding with the public and have them think there was favoritism amongst the contributors of society. Endnote: The High Priest Council didn't want all of Tolvade to think that they preferred Tasgall's Tavern above all other establishments … even if it was.

This year, Tasgall's had circled around and made it to the front of the line once more. This notion made Vanessa's uneasiness a little less unbearable knowing that she would be within familiar walls with an extra familiar face or two.

Vanessa had found herself quite comfortable on a barstool nearest the exit door. This way she wouldn't be lost in the farthest reaches of the tavern while trying to slink out of the party unnoticed. It wasn't that she was not fond of parties. It was that she had gone from zero to hero and she wasn't exactly at ease with basking in the copious amounts of limelight she'd been receiving as of late. So, until the time and day came where she was as fond-with-a-bond-from-a-pixie-wand with the whole ordeal, close to the exit she would remain.

The witch hunched over her drink trying to look less like she was a Coven member and more like she was a common patron of the establishment. Most gave her questionable glances and left her alone, despite knowing exactly who the witch was. Not up for a conversation with someone on that level of weird, most of the party revolved around her and gracefully excluded her. Leon, on the other hand, knew her too well—at this point—to be bothered by her strange likeness to a dark witch in that moment.

"You actually going to drink that, or are you trying to seduce it so you can take it home?" He slunk into a stool next to her with a groan of relief.

"Ha!" She picked up the cup and turned to face him, straightening out her back as though a steel rod were slammed down to replace her bowed spine. "Careful, one might think you were jealous that the cup of ale was getting more action than you," she quipped and took a large victory gulp from the mug.

Leon smirked and leaned in, dangerously close, as he dropped his voice a few octaves and glued his icy blue hues with her deep chocolaty gaze. "If you're into role-playing, I suppose I can play the part of a mug to get a little action. That is, if you can handle me."

To that, Vanessa sputtered into her mug, sending foam flying out from the confines of the tankard and causing herself to go into a coughing frenzy. Gulping in tavern air tinged with pipe smoke and roasting meat, she tried to fill her lungs with anything other than burning ale. Leon threw his head back in unbridled laughter.

Tears were welling in her eyes as the poor witch tried to swallow in anything that didn't have the taint of honey mead on it. A soft, repetitive clap of her back came from Lyx as she came and aided the new Spellweaver. "Take it easy. There, there. And you," the succubus cut her eyes to the bellowing-with-laughter Leon. "Knock it off before you kill her. What on Raen did you say to upset her so much?"

"Aww… come on, Lyx. I was just having a bit of fun. She knows I didn't mean anything by it. Right, buddy?" he stated as he patted her leg. Normally, a male patting her leg would send her into a blushing—or punching—rage (or both), but just then, the way Leon did it, he was so relaxed, so … not into her. The touch lacked so much that it honestly didn't bother her.

Well, not the way one would think. However, it irked her more that he just openly admitted that he didn't care about her like that in front of countless other people. When did she start caring about Leon like that? Who said she did? She didn't care. She didn't care one, tiny bit. She most certainly didn't miss the sound of his soft snoring coming from the couch in the morning. And she positively didn't miss the smell of him brewing coffee for the whole apartment when he woke up. She most certainly didn't miss listening to his stories before they went to bed, and there was no way she missed his banter over trivial matters throughout the day. He had moved back into his own apartment a few days ago, and the peace that was restored within her home was not, in the slightest, bothersome.

Nope. Not. At. All.

Vanessa wiped her mouth and mumbled, "Yeah, sure. Whatever," into her mug before downing the remaining contents. Who would have a thing for a smart and successful guy with long golden locks, pretty, blue eyes, could always make her laugh, witty as a devil, and had a body like …. *Banish a banshee, get out of my thoughts!*

Visibly shaking the ideas out of her head, Vanessa thumped the side of her skull with the heel of her hand. Holding up a finger to hail for another full tankard, she started to recite relaxing incantations to aid in the numbing of her mind. If the Coven was paying, she was drinking. Leon's buddy-buddy talk sort of solidified that notion.

She heard Bobo clearing his throat beside her, although, honestly, he had snuffed the light from Vanessa's personal bubble with his mammoth-sized body long before he'd cleared his throat, and that was the first sign that the well-mannered ogre was at her side. "Right. It is a celebration. Drinks should be had."

Lyx, Leon, and Vanessa all turned on a coin to face the beast with frantic, bulbous eyes. *"NO!"* They barked in a perfect, unified, and horrific harmony.

Bobo was left blinking at them in stunned silence before he waved at the thought and chuckled to himself. "Oh, no. I shall not partake. I had enough to last me a lifetime the last we ventured into this lovely establishment. No. I'll be having tea, myself."

"Thank the goddess," Vanessa breathed the words in a soft, thankful manner.

"That reminds me…" Leon started in a suspicious tone as he whirled his stool ever so slowly to face the succubus that was inspecting the beams that had suddenly become *so* enamoring overhead. "Lyx," he asked with a forced smile.

"Hmmm?" She drew in her lips as she hummed her reply.

Leon tilted his head. "Did you ever apologize?"

"For what, my good man?" Bobo inquired.

"Oh, she knows." Leon's tone said more than his words did.

Lyx continued to eye over the rafters as she tried to avoid every set of eyes from their group that was now resting upon her and awaiting her reply. "I-I… uh… I don't think so," she muttered quickly under her breath. It was hard to hear over all the commotion in the tavern, but Leon heard it just fine.

"Oh, what a fine moment this is," Leon stated while slapping his knee. "Hey, Bobo!"

Lyx snapped her amber gaze to him and hissed, causing the soon-to-be Summoner to throw his hands up in the air. "I'm sorry, I was under the impression that you *wanted* to apologize."

Her heated glare held more fire than the deepest depth of Hell, and that melting scowl was all for her master. "This is hardly the place or time, Leon…*daarliingg*." Her words were threaded with warning. The tips of her hair started to turn from glossy black to a vibrant, burning red.

"It's in the past. Let it go. The lady wishes to seek a better moment for such heavy words. Today is a time for celebration," Bobo cut in, but his eyes were on the bar as if waiting for something. A small ice-touched pixie floated by and slowly placed a full wineglass in front of the gentleman-monster. Gripping the tiny cup in his massive hand, he turned to face Lyx and offered the glass to her. "M'lady?"

Lyx squirmed in place and blushed a hard red, turning her lavender-hued skin a deep purple. The color of her hair returned to normal instantly. She whispered at Leon as she fussed with smoothing out her skirt and bumped her hips from side to side in a short victory dance. "See, he thinks I'm a lady," she murmured. As she spoke, she reached for the glass.

"You're not," Leon blatantly informed.

The succubus almost dropped her glass at his statement. Snapping her hateful glare to the Summoner, she hissed under her breath, *"Yes, I am. Look at the pinky,"* she corrected and pointed to the extended digit sticking out from the side of her glass.

"You're holding it wrong. Oh, and when you blush, you look like an eggplant," Leon spoke over the rim of his almost empty mug before sipping triumphantly.

She was in the middle of sipping and stopped to cut a glower at the man that was filled with daggers and dripping with malice. Ignoring the banter, Bobo reached forward and gently cupped Lyx's elbow, and turned her to face him, bringing the scowl to a screeching halt. The succubus blinked, bewildered at the ogre's willingness to being that close to her.

"It's charming that you hold your glass like that, but… if I may." He let the other monstrous paw grab the side of her glass gingerly and slid the hand on her elbow up to her wrist. He guided her hand to hold the stem of the wineglass and then let go slowly. "There. That is the proper way to hold the glass. Otherwise, the heat from your hand can spoil the flavor of the wine."

As he spoke to the demoness, a fall-touched pixie flew over and placed down two large tankards brimming with mead, and Tasgall herself came by with a, larger than usual, cup of tea for the ogre.

"Well, aren't you a sight for sore eyes?" Tasgall gleefully mentioned to the group, primarily Vanessa.

The Spellweaver spun on her stool and grinned to the red-headed tender. "You weren't closed for that long," she sniggered.

"Any time I've gotta close my doors outside of closing time is too long in my books. Besides, it was long enough for you to go and turn yourself into a Spellweaver. I'd say that's pretty amazing."

"More like a miracle," Bobo muttered with a teacup in hand while Leon nodded in agreement as he swiped a full tankard.

Ignoring the two less than supportive friends, Vanessa turned a joyful smile to Tasgall. "You should have seen it! I… bless my spell, it was such a wonderful feeling to walk across that stage and get this." She thumbed to the silver insignia pinned to her cloak.

Tasgall leaned in and whistled her admiration for the item. Next to her, Me'Glach leaned in to look at the phoenix emblem, rolled her eyes, twitched her autumn-colored wings, and fluttered off to aid another patron. Meanwhile, the lilac-stained irises of O'Glach flitted between the owner of the bar and the proud Spellweaver. The pixie smiled softly, and her voice matched the soft upturn of her lips, "Congratulations, Vanessa." And then the wintery pixie was off to fiddle with coin purses of unsuspecting members of the tavern.

"Order as much as you like, it's on the house," Tasgall beamed.

Leon almost choked on his drink as he tried to laugh and swallow a mouthful at the same time. "*On the house*…hold the crystal ball, isn't the Coven paying for all this?"

The grin practically split the short ginger's face in two. It made her look positively mad. She rubbed her hands together as if washing them in the air. "Yes. Well… order as much as you like." She moved her hands to the sides of her head and wiggled her fingers like spazzing worms. The cackle that pealed from her lips was exactly what everyone expected from the money-grubbing, gossip-hoarding, roguish bartender.

With that, Tassie was off to cause mischief and dig up dirt from other loose-lipped customers. "If I didn't know any better, I'd say she practiced dark magic on the weekends," Leon griped.

"Ha, and miss the craziest hours of business? I think not. Maybe if it was a Tuesday," Vanessa corrected, and they all burst into side-splitting laughter.

The remainder of the evening was spent downing mead and listening to secrets told by the masses that forgot, in their unusually high consumption rate, to ask for a privacy spell. Most of it was harmless and only caused the whole tavern to roar with merriment or gasp in surprise. All in all, the evening was drama-free, carefree, and demon-free… well… save for the demons that were tethered. Maybe just feral demon-free.

Vanessa and her gathering enjoyed one too many drinks, enough to not care about the way they'd feel the morning after. Somewhere down the long line of tankards filled with honey mead, the witch forgot about her troubles, her worries, and her hurt feelings over Leon's solidification of their *friendship*. She also forgot basic math … but, hey, who's counting?

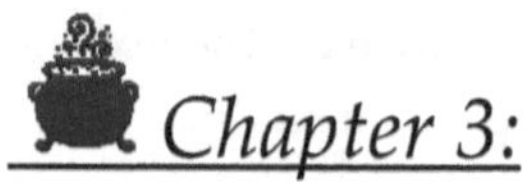 *Chapter 3:*

The next morning, Vanessa squirmed deep beneath the warmth and thickness of her goose down comforter. All the while she hid from the relentless rays of happy sunshine that beamed in through the half-open seam of her bedroom curtains. She heard rummaging outside her door, and she swallowed the urge to expel bile onto her mattress. Groaning, she shifted under the blanket and felt the world continue spinning long after she stopped moving.

"Uugh…I think I'm dying…" she declared, moaning in pain.

"Nice to know I won't be exiting this life alone," Leon's gruff voice came muffled from … *the other side of her bed?*

Vanessa was in the middle of curling into a ball when he spoke, and she froze in mid-motion. Okay, that was just a trick of her ears. There was no way that Leon was in her bed. Perhaps he had passed out on her bedroom floor.

Yet, there was undeniable movement on the other side of her large mattress, and her eyes grew a size too large for their sockets as her heartbeat hammered away under every inch of her skin. She could feel the pulse eating away at each nerve. She could taste it on her tongue, and while she tried to ignore the drumming in her ears, her head spun with the remaining ghosts of lingering booze from the night before. Frantically she sifted through the broken memories of last night's events.

She… He…. They didn't! *Did they?*

She wanted to be sick for entirely different reasons. However, first things first.

Her rich brown eyes drifted reluctantly down to inspect her body. *Still clothed.* Thank the goddess. The weight in the bed dramatically shifted as Leon groaned and—from what she could hear and assume—climbed back onto the mattress. The light from the comforter being lifted caused her to jerk her line of sight to the opening at the head of the bed. She was greeted with his cerulean eyes that could rival the crystal blue of Lorvo Lake and a charmingly, sleepy smile.

"You can come out now. It's safe. I closed the curtains. The cruel sunshine has been eliminated," Leon announced in a groggy voice.

Curse those blue eyes and disheveled hair. Curse them to the lowest pits teeming with hellfire and back!

"I'm fine under here," she cringed as she heard herself speak. She was hiding from him now? *Ugh.*

His carefree expression died abruptly, and he just blinked at her with a face void of emotion. "Really?"

Growling, she relented, still feeling too drunk to want to argue with him, and crawled to the pillow on the other side of the bed. "Happy now?" she grumbled plopping back onto the pillow.

"Not really," he chuckled softly. "I have no idea what happened last night. I was hoping you could fill me in on how," he paused. "You know." He motioned between them. "How we wound up in your bed."

Now she couldn't hide. The moment he asked the question that had been haunting her the past few minutes, she flared a pretty pink from head to toe and stammered as she attempted to collect her thoughts. "I-I… well… F-from what I do r-remember…ummm…"

"Did we?" he trailed off and didn't look upset, just lost as he waited for her to fill in the blanks.

Did they? No. Of course not. She had already checked. She glanced over to him and let her eyes slide down just enough to realize he was shirtless. The red on her face brightened, and she gulped while trying to think clearly. "No. I don't think we were sober enough for that…"

Please no…

He laughed and ran a hand through his sandy-blond hair. "This is awkward. I don't remember a thing last night after Summoner Dean asked me to take a few celebratory shots with him."

Vanessa pondered a moment. "Is that one of the Summoners

that blasted Bobo with an intelligence spell?" *That'a girl. Change the topic!*

"Yeah, him and Summoner Rafe MacBain, I believe," he replied.

"Good, the lovebirds are awake." Vanessa jerked, startled by the unexpected voice. The voice came from Lyx who plowed through the door without knocking and was swishing her tail from side to side merrily as her amber gaze flicked between the two in bed. Her grin seemed to say she knew something they didn't.

Vanessa found comfort in the fact that it was Lyx and not Bobo coming in the room, though he was a gentleman through and through and wouldn't dare open a door without a proper knock or two. Still, it didn't hinder Vanessa from jerking the comforter up to her neck and clamping it down out of pure reflex and utter surprise. The act only made Lyx grin all the wider.

Leon stretched, completely unbothered by the whole ordeal. "Morning," he groaned with a lazy wave.

"Don't morning me. First of all, it's the afternoon. Second of all, you were a sloppy mess last night. Bobo and I had to practically carry the two of you home. I expected that from you, *Leon*, but … Vanessa, you too?" she sighed and shook her head. "What in the name of magic possessed the two of you to get that lost in a tankard last night?" The succubus wasted no time in chastising them.

"Oh, are they finally going to grace us with their presence?" Bobo called from the other room.

"I wouldn't say that just yet. But after a cup of hangover tea, they should be mobile again," Lyx informed.

Leon and Vanessa both cringed as the sound of the two demons yelling back and forth made them feel like they had been walloped over the head one too many times with the orbed end of a wizard staff. The demoness took note of it and huffed, "Serves you both right." Still, the she-demon felt bad for the pair and motioned to the private bathroom in Vanessa's room as she spoke a bit more quietly, "Hurry up and shower and come have some tea and breakfast. Don't worry, it's just toast."

Later on, after their showers, Vanessa stood from the couch and practically screamed at Bobo, "You what!" Her hair was still wet from bathing, and water droplets flung from her mane and slapped Leon across the cheek as she tossed her head from side to side in heated surprise.

"You both were fully clothed, my dear. I hardly see the issue here." He answered, his demeanor unscathed by her fuming outrage.

"He was shirtless," she yipped as she dramatically pointed to Leon.

Leon instantly gawked mid-cleanup of his face and defended his shirtless-ness, "I got hot. Is that a crime?"

"You put us in my bed, without asking," Vanessa steamrolled with the conversation like Leon never made his statement.

"Rude," Leon coughed and threw himself back into the cushions of the couch.

"Well, I wasn't going to have a drunk mess in my bed and you're the one that invited him over, so it was your responsibility, *Vanessa*." The ogre stared at her with an unwavering gaze and a half-smile playing upon his lips. He knew he had her, check and mate, at that moment.

She felt the familiar sting of embarrassment creep through her body over the fact that she was in the wrong. "I-I … I what?" she squeaked out, her aggression immediately deflated at his response.

The succubus came into the seating area with a tray holding a tea set and a few mini cakes. Placing it down, she added her two coins to the conversation. "You invited us to stay the night, darling."

Leon sat up and piped in, "Now that much I do remember." He held up his finger and then pointed it at Vanessa before shaking it enthusiastically. It was clearly something that he just remembered, but he remembered it just the same and wasn't afraid to let everyone else know.

"I… Well… Still, you shouldn't have put him in my bed. The couch—"

"Was taken by me," Bobo interjected the witch's heated outburst.

"But you have—"

"I was sleeping in it, darling," Lyx softly informed before Vanessa could finish her thought.

"Are you done throwing your fit?" Bobo inquired while plucking a single brow up over one eye.

Puffing out her cheeks, Vanessa looked away from the group as she muttered, "…maybe."

Leon chuckled. "Oh, stop your pouting." He then stretched out and leaned forward to grab a cup of tea. Leon was no stranger to the look or smell of the hangover tea and found it easily upon the tray that Lyx had brought into the living room. He wanted to drink it while it was still hot because when cold the drink took on a whole new flavor that was positively repulsive.

Vanessa plopped down onto the couch defeated. Lyx grabbed one of the cups of tea and offered it to the fussy Spellweaver. The witch took it with a sigh and an apologetic glance. "What's on the agenda for today?" The succubus asked, trying to change the mood.

"Aside from recuperating?" Leon groaned his question.

Bobo let a stifled chuckle tickle his throat as he poised the cup of his fire flower tea in front of his lips. Vanessa rolled her eyes as she sipped her own tea and grimaced at the flavor. "I have to report in today," she mumbled over the rim of her cup.

"You really shouldn't have drunk so much last night if you had to go into work today, Vanessa. I'd swear you were trying to drown out something last night if I didn't already know that you weren't the type to do that," Lyx commented. The disappointment was evident in the succubus' voice.

Vanessa instantly forced a smile and tried to not choke on her next sip of tea. She laughed and hoped it would mask her nervousness. "Yeah. I was just too happy with my achievement that I got lost in the celebration." She lied, and let her gaze drop down to the cup in her hands. When she went to take another drink, she looked up and saw Leon staring at her. His stoic features unnerved her, and her heart flipped. She turned away from his unrelenting stare and locked eyes with Bobo. "You should hurry up, so we can go in."

"Want us to come with?" Lyx asked while happily swaying her tail from side to side behind her.

Vanessa shook her head, "No. If anything comes up we'll crystal ball call you."

"That reminds me!" Bobo remarked while standing and gracefully placing his cup and saucer down on the edge of the coffee table with such skill that the contents barely moved within the china. Everyone stared at the monstrous beast as he smoothed out his tie and fussed with his cufflinks. "I need to purchase a new orb on the way to Coven HQ," he announced.

A wicked grin claimed Vanessa's lips and she giggled darkly. "Oh. You mean you no longer want to use your compa—"

Faster than the ogre should have been able to move, he was standing in front of his master and cupping her mouth—or, rather, her face—with his mammoth paw. "Say not another word," he whispered through gritted teeth.

Her hand lifted and gave the okay symbol while her eyes danced full of uncontrolled mirth. The demon's blue eyes squinted, and the witch relented by putting her hands up in the air, signaling that she wouldn't say a thing. Removing his hand, the ogre straightened out his jacket. "As I was saying: we need to stop by the Crystal Ball Emporium on the way to the Coven."

Leon looked like he wanted to ask what had just happened but instead just nodded and stood, placing his empty cup on the tray, and spoke to everyone, "All right, we'll leave so you can get ready for work."

"But—" Lyx tried to protest but was met with a glare that mirrored a poised blade from Leon. "So cranky when you are hung-over," she whispered and turned to Vanessa and Bobo. "Do give us a crystal ball call if you want to hang out or need anything, darling." With that, she and Leon left Bobo and Vanessa to get ready for their day.

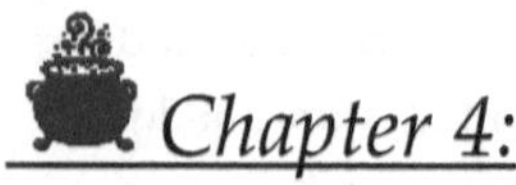

Chapter 4:

The Crystal Ball Emporium was the largest crystal ball shop in all of Aeristria, and it was conveniently located near the heart of Tolvade. If you need a magic mirror, compact caller, crystal ball, or pocket orb, you'd find it at the Crystal Ball Emporium. If you couldn't? Well then, it didn't exist.

The building itself mirrored a massive crystal ball with large, black, lacquered doors that shimmered in the sunlight that showered the busy streets of Tolvade. Morning hours had roused the sleeping city from its slumber and it had become full of life and laughter once more. Shops were opening like the threats that had been pouring through the streets over the past few weeks hadn't transpired. With most of the feral demons locked up in the Zaraltrac Prison, there was a peace of mind that came along with it. Still, the patrons of Tolvade were on their guard with the potential threat of a feral demon looming in the backs of their minds.

Bobo and Vanessa strolled alongside the street vendors as they made their way for the crystal ball shop, stopping at a few stands to make a drink and morning meal purchase. They both were a sight to behold, each gripping an oversized cinnamon bun in one hand and a fresh, steaming latte in the other. They munched on their sticky treats and sipped at their caffeinated brew while they eyed over trinkets and scrolls as they leisurely headed for the emporium.

"I say, those cufflinks were rather dashing. I might need to pick those up on the way back home tonight," Bobo informed Vanessa, who was face deep in her iced pastry.

She nodded with cheeks full of her meal, and he could only shake his head at his owner. "Must you eat like a barbarian chipmunk whilst I'm out in public with you? At least attempt to act like a lady... honestly," he chastised her in a hoarse tone while digging into his breast pocket for a white hanky which he promptly handed to her. "Here, you have a cinnamon bun on your face, dear. You'd best wash it off before the strays eat it off you like you're a walking buffet."

Vanessa snatched the fabric and wiped at her face hastily and then quickly shoved it back into his hand. Wrinkling his nose in disgust, Bobo forced a smile and then chucked the fabric into the nearest receptacle bin along with his cinnamon bun wrapper. "Lovely. You just ooze femininity and charm."

"Why should I even try?" They looked at each other as she spoke with a crazed grin, "You *ooze* enough of it for the both of us."

He rolled his eyes. "Cute…"

Feeling particularly triumphant, Vanessa held her head a little higher and disposed of her morning meal's trash near the entrance of the Crystal Ball Emporium. Bobo fussed with his suit jacket while Vanessa gave her hair a quick tussle and resituated her silver insignia over her cloak. They headed inside, instantly feeling the heat of the building envelope them as soon as they were through the threshold.

"Welcome to the Crystal Ball Emporium. How can we help you today?" A dryad saleswoman asked. She was slightly taller than Vanessa, and the employee gave her best welcoming smile as Bobo and Vanessa eyed her over. She had two bright red pigtails that rose up and twisted through the air like hairy horns around her head. Deep mahogany-colored skin paired well with the bright blue store uniform. The woman's mesmerizing brown eyes had officially locked onto her new targets.

Vanessa thumbed over to the large creature at her side. "He's all yours."

"Morning, sir," the sales representative remarked while instantaneously turning her full attention to Bobo. "How can we assist you with your purchase today?"

He cleared his throat and stood more erect. A position of full control, something he was seldom accustomed to, gave him a more (than usual) regal air. "Ah, yes. I'm in desperate need of a new crystal ball. Maybe a pocket orb or something…"

The sales rep looked Bobo over. Attempting to hide that she was judging the large creature wanting such a small calling device, she motioned across the store to a podium with a plush purple pillow with gold tassels. "You should see our latest model that just came in last week," she exclaimed eagerly as she went on to dodge the isle of pocket orbs, weave by tables of compact mirror callers, and skillfully ignore the rows of magic mirrors on her determined pursuit of the glistening orb atop that pedestal.

"This is the Kristal ICE ball. It comes with magic imprint recognition, MGPS," she leaned forward to whisper to him, "Magic Global Positioning System. Very similar to the great orb in our wonderful Coven headquarters." Then she promptly straightened up, recovered to her usual voice, and resumed her sales pitch. "It also has a new Raenwide chat service, Flitter." She picked up the display ball and turned to face Bobo with it. Her finger glided over the orb and she positioned it so that Bobo and Vanessa could both see. Floating within the crystal ball was four cloudy images. One was a lavender-colored silhouette of a fairy with a wand, another was of a hand-held mirror, the next was the outline of an imp's head, and the last was the image of a crystal ball. All four images floated about the orb in the woman's hand.

"Hmmm… I'm not—" Bobo began, looking rather unimpressed.

"And!" the saleswoman started up again, ignoring his almost dismissal of the item. She turned and put the ball back onto the cushion and stepped back a few paces with a wild smile lighting up her features. "Okay, Kristal," she said, and the orb lit up. "Make a call," she ordered.

"*Okay. Who would you like to crystal ball call?*" a soft, high-pitched voice asked.

The saleswoman looked to Bobo and he was astonished. "I'll. Take. It."

"Me too!" Vanessa chimed in, stuffing her face so close to the orb that she was practically fogging it up with every exhale.

Victorious in her sale, the woman bowed and motioned over to the registers as she continued the last bit of her pitch. "It comes in three colors…"

"Bless my spell, they come in different colors?" Bobo gasped.

She nodded. "Rose gold, silver, or black-tinted glass. All with matching bags."

"Did you hear that, Vanessa? You can get a girly color," Bobo exclaimed.

"I want the black one," she replied dreamily.

"Ooof course, you do," Bobo sighed and then added to the sales representative, "One silver and one black," he said the last like he was disappointed beyond measure.

"All right," the saleswoman sang. She practically skipped behind the register and pulled out two satchels, one being a midnight shade and the other a platinum gray. "Oh, and you get a discount for buying two." Her eyes flicked to the insignia pinned to Vanessa's cloak. The saleswoman's eyes slowly rose and sparkled. "It seems that you will be getting two discounts today. One is for buying two Kristal ICE balls and the other for being a Coven member."

Vanessa looked down at her pin and then proudly squared her shoulders and flipped her black hair behind her shoulders. "That's wonderful." She tried to play it off like she wasn't attempting to show off her insignia even more than usual but failed in a perfect execution of the act.

Bobo nudged her with his—rather large—elbow, and Vanessa looked up to him with an annoyed scowl. "Just pay the woman before you start gushing about how you went from bronze to silver."

"Wh-what? *You're* the one that needed a new crystal ball, not me," Vanessa whined. "Why should my coin purse suffer?"

"Because I have been questioned before the High Priest Council, had a tie demolished with soot stains, ruined quite a number of my best suites, and was chased by hellhounds, a minotaur, and countless other beings because a certain someone I know can't keep themselves out of trouble for the life of them. Besides, instead of getting myself a new suit, I've opted for a better calling device. Now, stifle your griping and cough up the coin."

She pouted and fished around her satchels while grumbling under her breath a few choice words. "Not like it's *all* my fault," she snapped at him and then paid the clerk for their purchase.

 *Chapter 5:*

After magically imprinting their new crystal balls in the store, Vanessa and Bobo headed across the market street to Coven headquarters. The streets were as busy as ever, but the air was full of tension and mistrust. Not toward anyone in particular, but potential feral demons running amuck will have anyone err on the side of constant caution.

Most of the hustle and bustle coming from HQ was due to the fact that there were more assignments than there were able bodies. Low-level Hunters were forced to pull two different jobs—if not more—to enable other, more capable, personnel to venture out on jobs that required more magical abilities. Others were speed trained on how to operate the Great Orb because there was a higher volume of black magic being used. The Coven entrance was one circulation jam away from disaster.

Taking their time to squeeze through the heightened bodies of rushing Coven members, they entered the building and looked for the least cluttered service desk. They quickly located Ell who was hastily stuffing a file box full of scrolls and loose parchment paper. Heading for the desk, Bobo and Vanessa made sure to dodge any rushing members as they headed in and out.

"Hey, Ell," Vanessa called out to the frazzled blonde.

"Oh." Ell fumbled with the box and fussed with her crazy yellow strands as they tickled her freckled face. "...Hi, Vanessa. Morning, Bobo," she greeted a bit out of breath.

"What's with the box?" Vanessa questioned, eyeing over the object.

"This, I … um…" she seemed lost for a moment and snapped her fingers as she remembered what she was going to say. "They need me down in the library. I have to sort out all the new reports and file them away."

The two looked around at the other crowded desks. "Guess I'll just report in at the next desk, then. Need any help before I go?'

"Me? No… No… I'll be fine," she said, waving her hands with a nervous giggle before the box fell over and the scrolls and parchment were sent falling to the ground. "Hex it all!" She stomped a foot and sighed. Before she started to gather everything back up, she turned her attention to the pair. "Don't worry about checking in at a desk, it'll take you forever to get to speak with anyone." She slid the—now empty—box back up onto the wood of the desk. "Besides, I know who has your mission scroll."

Reaching into her side satchel, Ell retrieved her crystal ball and slid her hands over the face of the globe. Her fingers tapped here and there until she found what she was looking for and then smiled warmly as she replaced the ball into her bag. "I just sent you the Hunter's name and location. They have your scroll."

"Ugh… I keep forgetting that Hunters have to hand out most of the missions scrolls now," Vanessa whined.

Ell nodded, "It's only temporary. Summoners and Spellweavers are in high demand right now."

"Yeah. I guess you're right…" Vanessa groaned just as her satchel jingled. She pulled out her new, black-tinted glass orb and said, "Okay, Kristal, show me my last message."

"Here is your last message," the orb replied softly.

"Bless my bits and goodies! Is that the new, top-of-the-line, Kristal ICE ball?" Ell was leaning so far onto the ledge of the desk that her feet were horizontal behind her, and her bright, emerald eyes were glued to the orb in Vanessa's hand. "And you got the black-tinted one…"

Vanessa thumbed to Bobo, "He got the silver one."

"Lucky," she whispered in amazement. Shaking her head, Ell regained her composure. "I have to get down there and start cataloging these reports before the meeting," she reminded herself as much as she was informing the two in front of her.

"Please, carry on." Bobo then started to come around the desk. "Let us help you before we depart."

Ell jumped down from leaning on the desk and almost fell backward right after landing. Wobbling to a more erect position, she turned to face the approaching demon. "Oh, don't worry about it. That mission scroll is a black magic investigation summons; it is faaar more important than helping me pick up my mess." She viciously shooed at the ogre before he could come behind the desk.

Blinking, he frowned and replied, "Well, if you insist, my dear."

"I do. Now… go… go, go, go. There are too many missions and not enough Coven members to go through them," Ell giggled and then went to pick up her mess. "I'll be fiiine." She picked up a few documents and tossed them into the box. Holding a scroll in one hand, she waved at the two as they relented in their desire to help her and made way to their mission keeper.

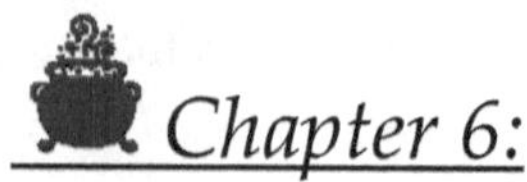 *Chapter 6:*

Zaraltrac prison was located on the shadier side of the Adilith district. It was a place where the population oozed with those attempting to be on the fast track to fame, glory, and gold by rubbing elbows with the rich. As such, the border of Borlimane and Adilith was a blurred line in the sand. One minute everything was flowing gowns, pressed suits, and beings eyeing pocket watches while gasping, "My, my, look at the time. We'll be late for our reservations." and then the next some greasy-skinned, half-dressed imp was hissing, "*Psst*, wanna buy a sundial? I got all da latest modals at half da price." If the above wasn't enough to make you leery of the streets you'd turn down on that side of town, the random passerby patting at his person and groaning about how he'd misplaced his coin purse would make you tighten your belt and hug your pouch with a touch more care.

This wasn't completely the case for Vanessa. Although she was cautious as she strutted with confidence down the streets to her destination, she had Bobo to thank for her lack of worries. Neither a man nor demon would leap out and try to rob a girl who had a creature like him steadfast behind her stride. They would simply jump out with a knife dancing in their hand and predetermined victory glinting in their eyes, take one look at the beefy beast behind her, look at the blade—that now resembled a toothpick in contrast to the demon before them—and cough into their fists before ducking down a street as fast as their feet could carry them.

Bobo would swatch them as they passed and snarl when they got close enough. That was the only cue that the coward assailant needed to spur their speed while making a mad dash for safety. Though, the demon's master seemed to be none the wiser to the numerous posing threats of muggers that had given up before even trying. She was too fixed on her new orb as she attempted to memorize the Hunter's name that she had to meet up with at the prison.

Rolling his blue eyes and giving a corner smile, the ogre shook his head lightly and called to Vanessa. "I think you've whispered his name enough to start writing love letters. Should I assist you? I am quite the calligraphy artist, you know."

"Shhh… I'm a Spellweaver now. I should know all my fellow Coven members, especially the Hunters."

"Oh? Why is that dear?"

"Because…" She straightened up and looked back at him as she said, "I am an inspiration to them. I've come from nothing and become a powerful Spellweaver."

Bobo almost choked, "A what? An inspiration? I wouldn't go that far, Vanessa. Unless you are referring to what they should aspire *not* to be. Then, my dear, you've hit the nail on the head, and you are an inspiration for all."

"Pffft, please, this silver insignia is all the proof I need to confirm my greatness." She puffed up her chest as she spoke to her pet.

"Banish a banshee, you really have lost it, haven't you?"

"Ha!" she countered, but her retort was never muttered as they had finally reached the front gates of Zaraltrac prison.

Their conversation swiftly died off as the rhythmic march of the two suited centaur guards thundered dangerously close by. They veered from the path of the guards as the horse-like creatures circled the massive dome ward surrounding the prison. The duo watched in awe as the guards swapped posts and then resumed their march back around the dome. Two guards remained at the front gates near the intersecting path of the centaurs. Their outside appearance resembled that of little Rikers in training. Each set of eyes were deep and unfeeling, their smiles nonexistent as their lips were pressed into a thin, cold line, and their hair was buzzed in a military fashion. Their charcoal-colored suits were immaculate and free of lint or hair or wrinkle. They tapped their lightning magic enhancing batons (or LME batons for short) on their thighs as their hard glare scanned the road around them.

The apparent nervousness settled into Vanessa… she hated prisons and jails. Not to mention, ever since their encounter with the hellhounds in the underground holding cells, she had a new fear of tight enclosures added into the mix. Attempting to calm her jitters, Vanessa advanced and plucked at the edge of her insignia as she announced, "Spellweaver Vanessa Peterson, reporting for mission scroll retrieval."

The two guards sized her up, and then her pet, only to blanch at the sight of the creature. As they tried to regain their composure, they stepped off to the side and unspelled the gate. Their eyes were ever watchful of the well-dressed monster.

"You may enter. All personal must check-in at the front gate," one of the centaurs grunted, his tail slapping his hip as he informed the two.

She and Bobo nodded as they passed through the front gate and headed toward the doors dead ahead that led into the main prison building. Zaraltrac had an air all its own within the magic barrier. It was a place that exuded darkness and unsettling sadness. Beings of all shapes and sizes were caged up here and forgotten. Vanessa's skin prickled with goosebumps. The low hum of the barrier became background noise that blended with the muffled melody of the monstrous inmates that resided within the prison walls.

Usually, the cells held … tamer beings within them. Blood mages, dark witches, notorious thieves, murderers … but recently they held the evil, soulless beings that only the underworld had to offer. Feral demons and devils were now stored within these cold, enchanted walls. It made the whole place more sinister simply due to that fact alone.

There was less distance between Bobo and Vanessa as they entered the building and headed for the check-in area. Their footwork faintly echoed over the hard granite tiled flooring. The Spellweaver's eyes darted to every square inch that the building had to offer as she made her way down the very lonely path leading to the front desk. She saw a gnome rummaging through one of the filing cabinets in the office area behind the panes of glass with gaping holes lining the bottom half. It was an area used for speaking with personnel and to trade off papers and such.

The gnome wore a uniform that mirrored the prison guard attire, only different in color. It was a deep olive-green shade with blue badges on the chest and arms. Atop his head, he wore a long, deep blue, almost black hat that draped over the side of one shoulder. He peered over to the two as they approached the desk before diving back into the file drawer. Usually, gnomes were the type of creature to run underground herbal shops or were well-known as local medicine men. On occasion, you'd find them running a library or working jobs as filers. They were wizzes with organizing paperwork, but most found their passion within the medical field.

Vanessa found the sight refreshing and some of the tension had eased from her being. That is, until, she saw the bugbear entering the office area and sit down in the small—almost too small—chair in front of the check-in window. She audibly gulped at the sight.

The creature had large, bulbous eyes settled in right under a deep perpetually furrowed brow. Its nose was long and round and covered in warts. Its hair was a collection of tiny braids that eventually became lost in the deep brown fur that covered its body. The creature's fingers were a touch too long and looked unsettling upon the being. The size of it could almost rival that of Bobo!

As the bugbear raised its gaze from the scrolls and papers scattered across the desk in front of it, it locked eyes with the highly disturbed Vanessa. One tawny pointed ear twitched on the side of its head, and the witch *meeped* behind her clenched jaw. In an attempt to quell her fears, the monster smiled. The sharp teeth glistening in two, jagged rows back at her didn't help.

Turning on heel, Vanessa tried to head back to the doors and the safety of the world that lay beyond the prison walls. Bobo, however, intercepted her mid-stride and turned her right back toward the front desk. "Banish a banshee… let's just get the scroll and be done with this, Vanessa," he demanded in an irritated whisper.

She groaned but obeyed. Boogeymen and their very distant cousins, the bugbears, always bothered her. Their long-winded history from the dragon era didn't exactly help. They once hunted children, regardless of them being good or bad. They would eat them up and string their bones from the trees surrounding their homes. Humanoid adults were not hunted because they were bitter tasting, or so the stories go… Around the elven era, many creatures were tamed, spelled, or started to become friendly with the humans. Others evolved through time. Now, these creatures were a part of society and fit right in with the jobs such as Being Resources workers and jail guards or nightclub bouncers. Their dark history took a back burner for most and was completely forgotten by others. She tried to push this silly, personal fear aside and finally smiled back at the creature. The bugbear didn't seem thrilled at her attempt, almost as if it knew that it had been silently judged.

"Can I help you?" Its deep voice snarled to her in a bored fashion.

"I'm here to gather a mission scroll," she managed to squeak out.

It plucked a single brow up and then turned to a stapled stack of papers. "Name of the person?"

She replied proudly without skipping a beat, "Narwhalis Mavrik."

The beast flipped through a few of the pages and then nodded before tapping a single, large digit over the parchment. "Mmhmm. He's on duty today. You'll find him on the second floor of cell block C." The bugbear pointed to the door adjacent to the office. "Wait for the buzzer and go all the way down the hall and then take a left and go up the stairs."

"O-okay. Thank you," Vanessa stammered.

"That's my girl. Now walk over to the door before you pass out," Bobo teased. "Thank you, kind sir, for all of your assistance today."

The creature instantly plucked up and looked instantly less scary from the genuine joy that covered the bugbear's features. There was a nod shared between the bugbear and ogre before its form was snuffed from their sight by the wall separating the office from the side door. As they stood in front of the metal barrier, Vanessa pursed her lips to the side in thought.

"I really need to get better about seeing those beings. You were something dark and evil and far more recently than any of their kind… I really shouldn't judge them based on a past that I never had to live through," she whispered to her partner.

Bobo looked down at her and then sighed as he returned his vision to the large door. "It's something that you will overcome, Vanessa. You were paired with me. As such, you've interacted with me far more than those other beings. One day, with time, you'll rid yourself of any silly notions that you have about them. Until then, just keep trying."

She spared a look over her shoulder to the ogre behind her just as the door buzzed loudly. Bobo gripped the handle and opened it just enough that it wouldn't lock again, and the two stepped into the long stretch of hall that lay on the other side. Instantly, the once muffled sounds of the prison inhabitants intensified with the lack of a barrier between them. Hoots, howls, screeches, and hollers all grew in pitch as they neared the end of the hall and the final obstacle between them and the main prison building.

The low hum of the buzzer ringing dully made Vanessa jump. Again, they passed through the door and stepped onto the other side. The sound on the other end was almost deafening. Murmurs mixed with wordless guttural sounds until they melded into one voice that traveled through the halls in a maddening echo.

Bobo wiggled his pinky finger in one ear as he furrowed his brow in annoyance. "What a bunch of loud riffraff," he muttered as they turned left.

"Let's just find Narwhalis and get the hex out of here," Vanessa tried to be quiet, yet speak loud enough for Bobo to hear her over all the commotion.

As they walked along the main level to the stairs, Vanessa could see countless cells with all manner of creatures caged within. Each safely tucked behind barriers with bars of holy fire. Most of the beings looked weak, tired, and lethargic which didn't exactly surprise her. Inmates were only allowed to drink water spelled by water nymphs and laced with vervain. They are also given the bare minimum for food. A somewhat cruel, yet necessary, precaution practiced by the prison.

They walked up the stone steps to the second floor. With haste, because she didn't want to be there longer than needed, the Spellweaver scanned the area for Narwhalis. It wasn't hard to spot him. He was wearing the same attire as the other guards on duty. His back was facing the duo as he watched the inmates, all while tapping his LME baton on his shoulder. His hair color was hidden under a military beret, and his skin was a deep tanned color. As Vanessa and Bobo neared, he turned to face them, his eyes scrutinized them in an untrusting manner—especially after seeing Bobo—and the look instantly lightened.

"You must be Vanessa!" he called back to them and gave a small smile in greeting.

"That's me," she replied happily.

The young guard reached for a satchel at his side and plunged inside. It wasn't until he was elbow-deep into the bag—which was no larger than the man's fist—that Vanessa realized he had a Bottomless Pit bag from Morgan Le Fay. Her eyes homed in on the vibrant silver embroidery that made up the infamous MLF logo for Morgan Le Fay's exclusive line of bags and satchels.

What a lucky wizard.

Blinking rapidly in disbelief, Vanessa tried to grasp the fact that someone on a Hunter's salary had an expensive Morgan Le Fay bag. She couldn't afford one on her new Spellweaver salary. As the green with envy look took both her and Bobo over, the young man found the scroll and fished it out with a triumphed smile.

"Here it is. Knew I'd find it eventually." Narwhalis chuckled and tilted the wax-sealed scroll from side to side and then extended his hand to Vanessa. "Any mission the Coven gives you should be a cakewalk because of your friend here," he announced with no fear.

"It's good to see a lad like yourself not shrinking away from me just due to my," Bobo lined up his form with one massive paw and held his head high as he finished with, "size."

Again, Narwhalis chuckled and motioned to the cells around them. "Really hard to be intimidated by size or creature when you have to watch over these guys," he admitted. "If you would have approached me two weeks ago, I would have had a much different response."

They all laughed at that. "I suppose you are right," Bobo agreed.

"Yeah, these guys don't look friendly. I couldn't imagine pulling a shift here between mission scrolls," Vanessa replied. She shook her head and looked down at the rolled-up paper in her hand. "Speaking of missions, I best get to it. Coven's been on me to do this one for a while."

"What's been the holdup?" Narwhalis asked.

Vanessa sighed. "There were so many mission scrolls that got bumped up because of their severity that this one was put in waiting. Now that I've gone through a lot of the other missions and aided with a few feral demon captures, I can pour all my attention into this one."

"I see. Well, best not keep the Coven waiting then," the young guard said and then there was a loud buzz sounding all around them followed by a series of bells. "And it seems like it's time for me to get these guys to the mess hall."

Bobo gave a wave to Narwhalis, "Thanks again, lad. You take care."

They all nodded as they headed about their separate ways. Nawhalis to tend to the inmates, and Bobo and Vanessa to tend to their new mission.

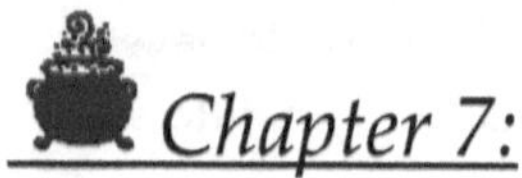 *Chapter 7:*

Once they were outside and back in the safety of the trusted streets of the Lorvo district, Vanessa broke the wax seal on the scroll. Unfurling the parchment, she scanned over the ink scribbled therein. Moments passed in silence.

"Well, what does it say? What mediocre Coven slave work do we have to look forward to today?" Bobo griped while wiping his nose on his handkerchief.

Vanessa's brow was pinched in concentration as she read over the written orders. "There was a massive black spell that went off four days ago. So far, no detailed report has been made on those involved or those that have been to the property." She sighed and rolled up the parchment as she continued, "We are to go and do a follow-up investigation and visit the last known establishment that the pair entered."

Bobo hummed. He was intrigued and, at the same time, surprised that the scroll was as serious as it was. "Any names dropped or are we flying blind, my dear?"

"No, there were a few names. The business we are to visit is the local sanctuary and the Grim Bean. The names listed were Blythe, Cressida, and Sheldon. The mission scroll stated that Sheldon was a portal keeper for the Dark Market, and he last saw the Coven members related to the mission. Also, Blythe is magicless, leaving the Coven to believe that the culprit for the black magic spell used was current the owner, Cressida. We are to thoroughly question them all and, if we find anything suspicious, we are to bring them in to be further questioned by a Summoner." Her robes were tightened, and she swept the busy streets with her gaze before walking across the slushy path.

Stuffing the cloth back into his pocket, Bobo cleared his throat and followed after his master. "Very well then. I would say to be careful, but I doubt that you would listen," he grumbled.

"Hurry up, Bobo, and stop mumbling, I can't hear you all the way back there."

"Perhaps, if you cleaned your ears out every once in a while—"

"I have a feeling that this job is going to be a fun one," Vanessa exclaimed, ignoring her pet's disgruntled mummers behind her and practically skipped down the road ahead of him.

Bobo rolled his eyes. "And here I thought she had grown up a bit. Double-dip a candlestick, I'm doomed. Doomed, I tell you."

"We'll head to the Grim Bean first, since we are so close, and you can get yourself a little something while there. My treat," she called back.

"There is hope for you yet," Bobo switched his tune and perked up to the promise of a Grim Bean delight.

The Grim Bean was a few blocks away from where they had been. That part of Tolvade was where the safe streets of Lorvo became tainted with the riffraff of the Borlimane district, and no one cared as long as the Grim Bean offered them their favorite brew and the café's famous baked treats. The familiar scent of the countless brews that the coffee shop had to offer wafted through the air as it lured unsuspecting victims to its front doors. And none of them were more lured than Bobo. He practically walked on his tiptoes as they traversed the final block before reaching the Grim Bean.

"Delightful," he whispered over and over again as they neared the shop. He needed no prompting from Vanessa. He swung open the door like a homesick veteran returning to his humble abode after a long, grueling war. With the way the beast acted, one would assume that the demon hardly visited the place. When, in all actuality, he visited at least twice a week. However, due to the extra workload, it had been two weeks since he had last entered the café.

Realizing that she had told the ogre he could order whatever he wanted, that it was her treat, and that her coin purse had already suffered through the purchase of two new crystal balls, Vanessa plowed through the door as she hurried to catch up with him. "Try to keep your order reasonable," she yelled to her pet. Only, instead of racing to reach the beast and stop him from ordering everything on the menu, she ran into his backside not but a moment after her comment.

"Oof." Rubbing her nose and peering around the mountain-sized demon, she groaned and muttered, "What is wrong with y —" and her eyes noticed exactly what was wrong with him.

The both of them stared in awe at the sight of the shop before them, did a double-take to the front doors, and then ran out to the streets to crane their neck up to the sign that hung over the awning. Yup. It still said, '*The Grim Bean*' in bright, bold lettering across a worn wooden sign. There was no mistaking it. Scrambling back in through the entrance, they gawked at the inside of the building.

The floors sparkled in the sunlight that poured in through the windows that were free of the usual countless handprints and smudge marks that had been part of the glass for as long as Vanessa could remember. All the tables and chairs were wiped clean of blemishes and crumbs and now sparkled like they were new. A fresh cool gray was painted over the walls, and the red brick accent wall was vibrant and free of grime. There was new tile work on the bar, and the menu board had clearly been updated.

Two gremlins sauntered by, gibber jabbering about something and cackling at their jokes as they made way to clock in for the day. They even took the time to pause, smile, and wave at the slack-jawed gentleman-monster and his flabbergasted Spellweaver companion.

"Rada raaa," they chirped in passing. It was understood that they said hello, though no one could be certain. That is, unless, you were an imp. Of which neither of them were. Slowly, the two confounded patrons waved lazily, and the gremlins continued about their business.

Today, it was slower in the shop. It was the afternoon lull between busy hours for the Grim Bean. Bobo and Vanessa were not only witnessing the shift change, but they were also seeing—what could only be described as—a brand new coffee shop. Even the wood around the windows had been replaced. The light fixtures no longer held a dingy hue due to thick layers of dust. The whole place gleamed with a clean look, and the new paint paired with the fresh atmosphere was both calming and comforting.

It was the sound of some rather grumpy footwork slapping over the glistening tiled floors that brought the two out of their daze. Inspecting the owner of the sad set of feet, Bobo and Vanessa bent their brows in perplexity. An imp wearing a bland pair of khaki-colored leather pants and a size-too-large off-white tunic meandered toward the front doors carrying a box full of files, folders, and random items one would usually place upon a desk, or —in this case—a trashcan.

"Whad are yous two starin' at? Wha', you neva seen an imp lose a jab? Screw dose jaws shut, an' move outta da way."

"My word, Sheldon. What happened to your shop? It looks absolutely fantastic!" Bobo exclaimed.

The imp lifted one drooping ear and perked a single brow over one eye. "You think I did all dis? Nah. No way. Too much work, if ya ask me. Looks too clean." He shivered like the word disgusted him.

"Well, if you didn't do it, then who did? It's great," Vanessa added.

The imp snorted. "Yeah, whateva." He shifted the box in his hands, balancing it with one appendage. He wiped his nose with his, now free, hand and sniffed smugly. "New management," he mumbled under his breath.

"New… new what?" Bobo gasped.

Vanessa, now thoroughly floored, looked around the shop eagerly. "New management? What… I mean… what happened to you?" As she asked, she looked over to Sheldon who was sifting through his box in his hands. While looking him over, she noticed a bronze-colored anklet on him. *That* was a house arrest anklet. A device spelled to immobilize you if you tried to take it off, gave the Great Orb constant updates, and would periodically shock the being wearing it if they were in an unauthorized area.

Snapping her eyes to meet his, she narrowed her gaze. "So, it was true? You *were* a portal keeper?"

Sheldon's eyes shifted about shadily, and he looked like a toddler caught red-handed with their arm elbow-deep in a cookie jar. Swiftly changing his tune from scared and scatterbrained, he resumed his usual demeanor. "I ain't tellin' you nuthin'. Yous two are wid da Coven. If you askin' questions, zilch is comin' outta my mouth."

Bobo and Vanessa exchanged glances. Sheldon was never too keen on Coven members, but he never outright disliked them. It made them wonder what had transpired to change his outlook on those wearing an insignia lately. "So, it was the Coven that fired you?" Vanessa pried.

"Ha!" Sheldon barked a short, mocking, burst of laughter at the Spellweaver. "Like da Coven could do dat. I'd still own dis establishment if it weren't for dose two picky, double-crossin' beings posin' as custamers. Curse that honeybadger and mousey guy for comin' into my respectable place of work and forcin' me to open up a portal. Next thing I know? BAM! I have health inspectas swarmin' all over dis joint and a Coven memba chattin' wid dem. They had tha audacity to say *my* place won' clean and said it was my final warnin'." The imp went on to grumble a few things under his breath before shifting the box in his hands and sniffed again.

"Whateva... not like a knowledgeable imp like myself can't find a job 'round dese parts." Resuming his walk, he grumbled a bit more and then shuffled past the ogre and witch on his way for the door.

"Whoa. Whoa. Wait a second." Vanessa ran to cut off the imp's path. "You said you were forced to open a portal? I have some questions that you need to answer before you can leave." She shook her finger at Sheldon. "You were the last known contact before two

Coven members were found on the site where a massive black magic spell had been cast. I need you to answer a few questions."

Sheldon scowled. "Black magic? I dun know nuttin'. And questions? I ain't answerin' none of your spell flingin' questions."

"Oh, yes you are," she stated matter-of-factly.

"Oh, no I'm not. And ain't nothin' you can do about it, there raven locks," the imp snapped back.

Vanessa smiled, and it was as devious as ever. "I think you will answer them."

"Pfft. What could you possibly do ta get me ta spill da magic beans? Huh? Nothin'. Dat's what. Get outta 'ere," Sheldon went to take a step forward and a monstrous sized shadow swallowed his stubby form whole. His imp eyes crawled up the line of a towering being looming over him. Bobo crossed his arms over his chest and stared down at the tiny demon with a rather cross look fixed upon his features. Sheldon's ears drooped, and he audibly swallowed hard. "Y-you're a big fella…" With no care or finesse, Sheldon dropped the box from his grasp (which, in reality, didn't have far to fall before hitting the floor). "Okay. Look. Let's not get hasty or nothin'. You hasty, Raven Locks. Calm down. I neve' said I'd neve' answer your questions. You have questions? Fire away!" he paused and held up a hand at the ogre as if to stop the large beast from doing the small imp any harm. "Not real fire, big guy. Just sayin' the girl can ask questions. Keep the flames in your pouch. Okay? Okay."

Vanessa spoke up, bringing Sheldon's attention back to her. "You said you were forced to do something. If the Coven isn't responsible for you giving over the ownership of the shop, then what did the Coven do?"

Sheldon pointed to his foot with wide-eyes and a mocking smile. "You think dis is a fashion statement? They put me on house arrest. Considerin' what they could've done, I'll count it as a blessin', but it still doesn't sit right with me. They were pretendin' to be payin' custamers, and then I get insignias in my face not too long after. I'm tellin' ya, something won't right wid dose two. They were Coven membas, I know it." He shook a finger at Vanessa. "And what they did, that's false advertisement, I'll tell ya. I would know."

"What do you mean they forced you to open a portal? Last I checked, the Coven doesn't blindly slap house arrest anklets on people that open random portals. Where did the portal lead to?" The Spellweaver watched as Sheldon shifted in place and looked around nervously. He acted like he hadn't heard her, and she started to speak louder. "Where did the—"

"All right. All right. All right. I heard ya. Sheesh," Sheldon griped. "It was to…" he looked around again, and then dropped his voice down to a whisper. "Da Dark Market."

Bobo and Vanessa both shouted out in surprise, "The Dark Market!"

"What… what's wrong with yous two? You couldn't keep a secret if your life depended on it," the imp groaned. "You'd think I was whisperin' for da fun of it. Sheesh."

"So, the reason you aren't in a holding cell right now?" Vanessa pried.

Sheldon shrugged confidently and said, "What can I say? I'm a respectable citizen of Aeristria. They cut me some slack."

"Ha. I'm sure that the portal opening in conjunction with your poor managerial skills led to you handing over the title of this establishment," Bobo grumbled.

"Hey. I was a great manager. If it weren't for that honeybadger and mouse man, I'd be runnin' this place like a well-oiled machine."

Bobo grunted, and Vanessa sighed. There wasn't going to be much else that they could get out of the imp. He was forced to open the portal, which meant he wasn't given a reason why. And it was most likely not tied to the black magic spell that went off at the sanctuary. Though, it was something that would need to be noted in her report for further investigation later. "You're free to go."

"Of course, I am. I ain't done nothin' wrong, after all," Sheldon mumbled as he retrieved his box from the floor. Strutting like he had no fear at all, he squeezed between Bobo and Vanessa and sauntered to the front doors once more. As the bell rang dully, announcing Sheldon's exit, both Vanessa and Bobo looked at each other as they mouthed, *Honeybadger? Mousey man?* Who those two were in the Coven, and their potential ties to Sheldon's relinquishing ownership of the Grim Bean, baffled them both.

As the wave of confusion lingered, they prepared to approach the counter to make their order when an imp came flying out of the manager's office. She had a long, violet side ponytail that came down to her upper chest. She wore a pumpkin orange chiffon skirt that flowed around her feet, hiding her black slip-on shoes. Her deep, mossy green tank top had a cute, crotched, off-white cardigan that hung around her shoulders. The freckles kissing her sage skin made her small round face even more adorable and complimented her skin tone with a hearty brown spackle around her button nose. A set of wide-set, hazel eyes searched the main room of the coffee shop.

"Sheldon!" she cried out, pausing momentarily to smile and wave to the gremlins returning to their workstation. It was when she looked back to the main walkway that the imp was brought to a sudden halt by the sight of Bobo and Vanessa. "Oh, my." Her heart-shaped mouth unhinged for a second. Slowly, she cupped the item in her hands a little closer as she slowly scaled up the monstrous size of the ogre. "You're gonna want a large," she whispered to herself.

Sensing the ogre's possible protective stance on his weight, and attempting to defuse a misunderstanding before it started, Vanessa cut into the conversation with, "Sheldon already left."

The imp's ears drooped in a disheartening fashion. "Oh," she sighed woefully.

"What do you have there, my dear?" Bobo inquired at the imp.

She looked from the demon to her hands and smiled, "This? Oh." The female imp opened her hands, revealing a perfectly shriveled, brown plant. It was possibly dead if not currently banging relentlessly on death's doorstep. There were green thumbs and brown thumbs and then whatever Sheldon was, and from inspection of the plant that the young female imp had… he was a *black* thumb. The thumb of death. The thumb of no return. Silently, Vanessa hoped that Sheldon wouldn't find a job at a florist while she muttered a prayer for the poor potted plant.

The female imp toyed with one of the leaves, and it crumbled to dust. "I think it fell out of his box when he was packing up," she explained with a sad expression tugging at her sweet, almond-shaped eyes.

"More like fell out of the trash bin," Bobo mumbled.

"Hmmm?" the female imp hummed.

Vanessa leaped to the rescue and stumbled over her excuse for her demon companion. "H-h-he was just saying that maybe he left it behind for you. A sort of memento to remember him by."

The imp tilted her head. "He did?"

Bobo cleared his throat and assisted his master. "But of course, he did. By the way, are you the new manager that he spoke of?"

She was standing on her tiptoes—although it did little to aid in looking for Sheldon—and she visibly shook off whatever she was thinking and smiled sweetly. "Yeah, that's me. Name's Freeda," she let one hand slip away from cupping the tiny plant and extended her hand to them. "I'm the new owner of the Grim Bean," she beamed.

Bobo looked impressed as he took her tiny appendage into his gargantuan paw. "That explains a lot about the recent upgrade of the establishment's appearance. Bravo, young lady."

Freeda giggled, "Aw, shucks. I'm just doin' what comes natural to me."

"You've done a fabulous job with the place so far," Vanessa added in.

The sudden sparkle from the sun's rays bouncing off of the Spellweaver's insignia caught Freeda's attention. "Oh. OH! You're wid da Coven. Oh, my. Where are my manners? Come, order up somethin' and I'll tell ya anything you wanna know."

"I would rather enjoy some new company and gossip," Bobo nudged his master and she rolled her eyes. "Fiiine, Bobo," she whispered and smiled at the manager. "Sure thing. We'd love to."

"Oh good!" Freeda clapped her hands excitedly and almost dropped the plant. She fumbled with the poor thing before cradling it in her hands with a thankful look in her bright eyes. "Phew. You guys order and I'm gonna go find a sunny windowsill for this guy." As she turned around, Freeda commenced cooing to the plant. "Who's gonna be the biggest, prettiest plant? That's right, you are. You're going to be so big and pretty…"

While Freeda shuffled off to water and put her plant in the perfect spot, Vanessa and Bobo fussed over what to order. They were stuck between the option of tea and lunch or a more breakfast-like meal with a cup of coffee. Around the time that they finally agreed upon having lunch, Freeda was making her way back toward the ordering station, stopping occasionally to fix a napkin holder or talk to an employee. With her actions alone, she made it abundantly clear that she was the backbone of the Grim Bean. The gremlins were all perky and upbeat, the place was clean and tidy, and the overall atmosphere of the coffee bar was joyful. It was as if they were in a whole new building.

Bobo rubbed his thumb over the bottom of his chin while deep in thought while Vanessa griped at his side. "Ugh, just order something already."

"I do say, it is quite difficult, Vanessa. The choices are so abundant, and I always did wish to try the blaze petal tea."

"Then just get that."

"But I did feel like the blend would go well with unicorn milk. Though, I can't be for sure as it has been such a long time since I last had the stuff." He uttered feeling completely lost.

Overhearing the conundrum the poor gentleman-monster was having, Freeda dove into the rescue. "Go ahead and order unicorn milk."

Bobo and Vanessa both darted their eyes in the imp's direction. "Oh, I couldn't possibly be a bother." But as he made the remark, he slowly took notice of the fact that none of the gremlins looked worried or frightful.

"It's fine, it's fine. Don' worry about it," she pressed.

"I-I'm not suure," he stated, sounding a little less certain of his reply than the first time.

She nodded, understanding the giant's plight, and waved a hand at him. "Just order da milk, I'll handle dis." She pointed to the gremlin at the register, "Unicorn milk in whateva he orders." The gremlin grinned and gave a thumb's up before returning its attention to Bobo.

"Well, I suppose…" the ogre replied sluggishly.

Freeda giggled again. "I insist!"

"Very well, then. I shall have the blaze petal tea … *with* unicorn milk," he announced proudly.

"Wait… I want unicorn milk in my order too," Vanessa piped in as she practically climbed on top of the counter.

The gremlin didn't seem concerned at all as it made the adjustment to her order and put in the ogre's as well. "Rad ra raada ra," it gurgled while dropping the coin into the register and pointed to where the two could wait.

Meanwhile, Freeda came to the door that had once been decorated in countless warning signs in various languages. She rapped lightly on the wooden barrier and waited a few seconds before opening it. Surprisingly, there was no flying barrage of coffee beans, no cackling back and forth banter, or any shrieking retorts from the other side. Only the soft sounds of a content horse-like creature and Freeda's gentle voice.

"Hey, Bernard. How are you doin' today?" There was a pause and a whinny from within the room. Freeda's face lit up. "Oh, that's good to hear. Look, sweetie, I know you are supposed to be on break, but dere's a couple of customers dat haven't had unicorn milk in a while and dey would like to have it with their lunch." There was another pause followed by a series of knickers. Freeda giggled. "Sure, sure. You can have an extra five tacked on to your break." There was a loud whinny and Freeda laughed. "You too sweetie. Keep up the good work." She closed the door and walked back to Vanessa and Bobo. "You wanna sit down? I can have da gremlins bring your order to ya."

"Yes. All right. That would be quite convenient," Bobo uttered as he marched over to a window seat.

"Can you bring me a dandelion root tea with two teaspoons of honey when you bring the order to their table?" the female imp asked sweetly. The gremlins just nodded quickly and rapidly spoke gibberish to the other workers.

The three of them sat down at a clean booth on the far side of the coffee shop. Outside, the light peeked between two buildings and lavished that portion of the café with splendid, warm, golden pools of illumination. Bobo basked in the delicious glow while the two ladies got situated.

Vanessa broke the silence with her usual blunt nature, "I noticed that your accent is different. You don't sound like your accent is as thick as other imps that I've met."

The imp blinked a few times and then gave a gentle smile that made her small round cheeks even rounder. "Oh. Yeah." She laughed under her breath before continuing. "That's because I'm not full-blooded imp. I'm half brownie and half imp."

"I say. I did not expect that," gasped Bobo as politely as he could.

She nodded, seeming to understand both of their surprise. "Not a lot of people do. My Ma was an imp, and my Pa was a brownie."

"Well, it certainly explains your level of cleanliness. I shall say that," Bobo declared.

Vanessa pinched her brow in thought. "But aren't imps and brownies natural enemies?"

Freeda's face lost some of its luster, and she looked down at her clasped hands resting on the tabletop. "Yeah. They've come a long way over the years, but there's always been a real hard segregation between the two breeds. Ma and pa didn't actually care for one another at first." She gave a short, nasally laugh. "They got stuck in a cellar lined with iron. Five days straight. They were so hungry and thirsty on the second day that they started searching through the storage bins and barrels. Found some fruit and grain, but things didn't get strange until they found a couple skins full of wine that they mistook for water." She cracked a smile. "Both of dem are such lightweights." She tried to control her laughter. "And here I am!" She burst out into an uncontrollable fit of laughter and Bobo and Vanessa could do nothing but join her, albeit a bit nervously.

They all took a moment to regain their breath. As Freeda wiped a few stray tears from the corner of her eyes, she added, "They love each other like there ain't nobody else in da world, though." Her face was so loving and sweet, and her eyes twinkled so brightly as she drifted off in thought. "I wouldn't trade them for anything on Raen."

"So, how did you get this place?" Vanessa had been dying to ask since Sheldon had stated that the Grim Bean was under new management.

"Oh, the Grim Bean?" Bobo and Vanessa nodded in unison while silently waiting for her answer. "Ma actually put in a good word for me."

"It's good that your mother could pull some strings and get you a job like this," Bobo stated.

Freeda waved her hands back and forth in front of her face with bug eyes. "Oh no! Not my ma. Ma, Ma. You know, Leslie's mother."

Vanessa had to stop and wonder out loud, "Is there anyone that woman doesn't know?"

The manager was quick to reply, even though Vanessa wasn't really expecting an answer. "I don't think so." There was an undeniable truth that rang with the statement.

The Spellweaver looked around once more. "I have to say that everything has really changed here, and I like it. Everyone seems really happy."

"The gremlins weren't that happy before. Sheldon ignored their requests to clean as often as they would have liked because he said that it slowed productivity down." Freeda frowned slightly. "It's really sad, ya know? Gremlins are neat freaks, and it really made them upset that they were denied a simple request like cleaning."

"Wait. Wait. Wait. If it was that bad, then how did this place pass inspection?" Bobo aggressively butted in.

The female imp batted her lashes as she looked utterly confused. "It didn't."

"What?" Vanessa shrieked.

Freeda nodded again. "Yeah. Sheldon lost the place because he kept enchanting the health inspector's signs. Made the 'F' look like a 'B.' He even paid off a few of the guys to keep quiet about everything goin' on here."

Both master and pet blanched at what the imp stated. Vanessa practically had her eyes bug out of her skull and shivered multiple times as she repressed the urge to gag. Bobo seemed to struggle more than her because his usual calm demeanor was replaced with an expression that resembled a battlemage haunted by a flood of war memories. Freeda waved at them like she was shooing away their bad thoughts. "Don' worry about it now. The place is now a solid 'A' plus." As if reading their thoughts and knowing that they had slight doubts about the framed grade on the wall behind the counter, she giggled to herself and added, "I couldn't spell my way outta a paper bag."

Shortly after, their order was brought to the table and lighter conversations were had as the two Coven members got to know the new owner of the Grim Bean. After a nice lunch, they excused themselves and departed, stating that they'd be back again soon. Leaving the café with full bellies and wearing large grins upon their faces, the duo headed back to work.

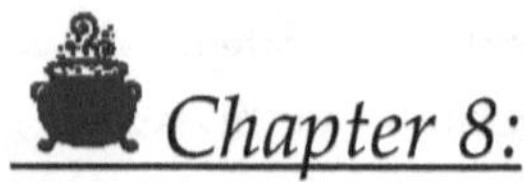 *Chapter 8:*

The sun glinted off the edge of the orb in Vanessa's hand as she fiddled with her new device, while Bobo fidgeted with his glasses and inspected the mission scroll. "It says here that we are to report to the sanctuary, Srbeveara." He dropped the parchment from in front of his face. "That is on the eastern side of the Vemeese district."

Vanessa nodded with a low, "Mmhmm," while her slender fingers continued to glide over the glass ball.

"Shall we teleport there, then? Or continue hiking our way there on foot?" He prodded his master with questions, hoping she would get her nose out of her orb long enough to produce a respectable answer.

She let the object drop from in front of her face as she pondered over their options. "I am sort of enjoying just a slow day today. What do you think? Is walking all right with you?"

Jutting out his lower lip as he rolled up the mission scroll, Bobo seemed to think it over. He was a touch impressed with his master's response, and he was trying to shed off a few pounds that had been sticking to his bones rather relentlessly from all the winter feasting he had partaken in. "I am in desperate need of a good walk, honestly," he admitted finally.

"It's decided then, we shall walk!" she announced joyfully before resuming having her face practically pressed into the glass of her new calling device.

Content with the Spellweaver's reply, the ogre pulled out his book and spectacles from his satchel on his hip and started to read through his newest literary find. The sanctuary in question was at least another hour's walk from where they were. Even with the snow almost melted.

The ground outside of the sanctuary, Srbeveara, was soggy and covered in patches of slush and scattered patches of thin ice. Vanessa's russet eyes revered the stone platform that served as a flat, dry welcoming mat to any being that would come up to the massive double doors to the two-story cottage. Smoke plumes rising out of the chimney snaked up into the air before falling like a fog to kiss the ground that surrounded the building. It was homey. In a quirky sort of way.

"It seems rather small to be a sanctuary," Bobo remarked quietly.

Vanessa furrowed her brow and nodded. "Yeah." Then the idea hit her. "Betcha it's one of those spelled cottages. You know, the ones always featured in the Cottage and Fairy Garden magazines that have more room on the inside than they appear."

Bobo's face widened with understanding and nodded slightly. "I suppose that could be the case," he agreed. "I've never been inside one myself. I'm rather excited to see what the inside of a sanctuary looks like."

After that, they both trudged over the sloppy soil to the front doors. Wet, squishy sounds echoed through the clearing that made the enormous ogre cringe in abhorrence. Bobo sucked at his teeth as he looked down at his shoes that were quickly becoming covered in muck. "Thank goodness I didn't wear my good shoes today." Then the beast revered his slacks that were spackled in mud and dirty snow. He groaned, annoyed at the mess he was so casually wearing.

Although the demon was most displeased with the way the mushy ground was affecting his attire, Vanessa seemed to have a hardened countenance twisted with determination. Looking up from his muddy loafers, Bobo took notice of his master's unusual expression, and it sparked curiosity in the beast. "I say, Vanessa. What is with that peculiar look upon your face? Is there something the matter?" He sniffed the air, trying to find traces of possible feral demons or the potential use of black magic. "I don't sense anything amiss," he muttered while waiting for his master's reply.

"I've been thinking the whole way here," she started.

"Oh, dear. I do hope you didn't hurt yourself," Bobo replied.

Ignoring his jab at her intelligence, she continued with, "There was a massive black magic spell that went off four days ago and four Coven members haven't reported back to HQ with a proper report. The whole thing stinks of a cover-up, and I'm going to figure out what they are hiding," Vanessa snarled.

Bobo widened his eyes. "Oh, you will, will you? Well, I suppose I shall sit back and watch the show. You're such a big, bad Spellweaver now—"

"I am," she cut in proudly as she stuck her nose in the air. The ogre only rolled his eyes in a silent response.

Only the cringe-worthy squelching filled the air as the two came to the front doors to the sanctuary. Slowly, Vanessa reached up to place her hands on the smooth, wooden door. Bobo spoke up before the Spellweaver could attempt to open them. "Aren't you going to knock?"

She blew at a stray strand of ebony hair and gave her pet a confused look. "I'm with the Coven. I don't need to knock. I'm here to investigate."

"Well, I mean… we aren't seeking refuge, so I would stand to think that it would only be polite to knock first."

"And give them a chance to prepare a lie? I think not!" Vanessa barked. Just as she finished her comment and lifted her hands, there was static dancing over their skin and the feeling of suction that tugged at their clothing and made Vanessa's hair lift toward the sanctuary's entrance before everything returned to normal.

Quickly exchanging a glance between one another, they spoke in perfect unison, "Teleportation spell."

They hurriedly returned their sights to the doors, and the young witch pushed with all her might against the massive wooden barrier. The doors felt like lead and hardly moved when she tried to open them. Seeing his master struggle, Bobo reached up and pushed lightly on the seam between the two doors and they swung open effortlessly, causing the Spellweaver to stumble inside and fumble with her footwork in order to try and stop the oncoming tumble to the floor. Bobo's massive paw jutted out and snatched the girl by her cloak's hood, aiding her to swiftly stand upright.

Like the incident never took place, Vanessa propped her balled up fists onto her hips and cleared her throat. "I am Spellweaver Vanessa Peterson. I demand an audience with your sanctuary owner, Cressida Katsaros." She waited with her head held high and her chest puffed out, properly displaying the silver insignia over her breast with pride and authority.

Bobo leered around her side and inspected Vanessa, even took his rather large digit and poked her cheek with it. She swatted it away with an annoyed expression. "Stop that. What is the matter with you?" she whispered heatedly.

Blinking quickly, the beast managed to maintain a rather deadpan look that matched his monotone voice as he said, "I was just seeing if you were real or an illusion. You spoke so well just now."

"I'm capable of speaking properly," she huffed.

"I beg to differ," he mumbled under his breath as he stood back up to his full, monstrous size.

She let her jaw unhinge in disbelief. "I can—"

A voice cut through their bickering as the owner of it came out of the office room to the side. "What's all dis racket? There are customa's tryin' ta sleep. Not every being is a daywalker, ya know."

Both Bobo and Vanessa whipped around to see Ma standing in the lobby. They blinked, flabbergasted at the imp before them. "Ma?" they shrieked.

"Ya. In tha flesh," she said with a grin.

Her eyes twinkled as brightly as the double-wrapped pearls that she wore around her neck. Short, stubby fingers were adorned with rings that glimmered in the light as she smoothed out the wrinkles of her black, long-sleeved, velvet dress. White lace traced the neckline, cuffs, and the hem of the dress, and the color matched the snowy, braided pigtails that bobbed atop Ma's head. The lively imp flashed a few poses and pointed to her feet. "Like my red slippa's?"

She giggled as she twirled in place before adding, "I got them from Wicked West Avenue. They just opened up a few days ago, and their shoes are ta *DIE* for!" she gushed.

Bobo opened his mouth and then forced a smile as he looked to the shoes. But, truthfully, the duo could only stand in silence as the confusion continued to consume them. Ma's warm smile was the last thing that they thought they would encounter within the walls of the sanctuary.

Shaking her head in an attempt to clear away all the new questions that had popped into her brain, Vanessa knitted her brow at the female imp. "We felt a teleportation spell." The witch's tone alone insinuated that she suspected foul play and that those she needed to question were attempting to make a run from the Coven.

Ma tilted her head, appearing flummoxed for a moment before laughing lightly and waving her hand up and down at the duo standing by the front doors. "It was a customa relocating. They were all better, but still needed a day of rest. So, I suggested that they drop by the southern stationed sanctuary that was closer to their home in the bog." She stopped explaining and looked at Vanessa with a peculiar expression. "Why? Is there a temporary ban on teleportations?"

Bobo attempted to smooth over the misunderstanding. "Not at all, my sweet lady. We were just inquiring the source because—"

"We were making sure that the culprits in question weren't turning into fugitives by making a run from a Coven member seeking to question them." Vanessa didn't seem to care whose toes she was stepping on. She blurted everything out and didn't even sugarcoat the blunt statement.

The ogre threw his hands in the air. "Why do I even bother?" he grumbled to himself.

Ma could only look like she was slapped in the face as she stiffened up and batted her mascaraed lashes in rapid succession. "Wait… what?" she sounded so lost.

"I'm needing to question Cressida Katsaros. If she has attempted to flee, I have no choice but to brand her as a practitioner of the dark arts, hunt her down, and bind her magic until her court hearing." Vanessa was determined. Resorting to throwing her Coven status around, she made it known that she was serious and would not back down. The law was the law, and she was here to enforce it.

Nodding, Ma looked to the floor and pursed her lips together while silently thinking. "All right," she said finally and motioned with one of her thickly ringed fingers for Vanessa to come closer. "C'mere."

Vanessa deflated a touch as she looked around her and pointed to herself. Ma nodded again with a warm smile. "Mhmm. C'mere." With a single digit, the lady imp continued to beckon the witch closer.

The Spellweaver inched nearer. Ma still wiggled her finger, as if the digit had a mesmerizing spell being cast from it, guiding Vanessa closer still. Awkwardly, the girl came to the imp's side and paused when they were practically toe to toe. Ma's sweet smile was still thickly painted in place as she waved Vanessa to come down to her level. Considering the short stature of Ma, it was a bit of a dip for the Spellweaver. The witch obliged uncomfortably by bending down until both she and Ma were eye to eye.

With a speed no one would have expected from the older imp, Ma's hand snaked out and took hold of Vanessa's ear in an unforgiving grip. Surprised, Vanessa yelped only to have the hold on her appendage tighten. "Customa's are restin' ya know. Let's keep it down." The female imp cleared her throat and continued, "I'm normally an understandin' imp. I have a bubble around me that's a judgment-free zone." She tugged Vanessa's ear, pulling the poor girl closer to her as she dropped her pitch to a darker tone the Spellweaver and ogre hadn't heard before. "But Imma step outta dat zone for a second." She brought her voice back to a higher pitch, but there was a harshness threaded into each word as she spoke. "How's about you follow me, big, bad Coven memba, okay?"

Without warning, Ma started to drag Vanessa through the sanctuary by the witch's ear. All the while, the Spellweaver tried to make her painful hisses less audible than she desired, for fear that the louder sounds would only bring Ma to rip the blasted thing off the side of her head.

Meanwhile, Bobo only sighed and looked skyward. "It's a lesson learned, ol' boy. Let her learn. Can't save her all the time." The sloppy footwork of his master assaulted his ears. "Can't save her all the time," he whispered again to himself before following after them.

As they walked, Vanessa could only focus on her footwork rather than which corner they were turning or the direction they were heading in. Being hunched over while being guided through unknown territory with a throbbing pain in her ear ever-growing made it a little more difficult to pay attention to where they were heading.

Stalking with purpose down a dark hall, Ma came to a sudden stop in front of a closed door. The female imp opened the door, revealing a bedroom on the other side. She then jerked on Vanessa's ear just enough to force the young girl to look inside.

The dim room was only illuminated by the dying halo of a candle burning upon a bedside table. The orange light cast its glow over the writhing body of a female whose dulled red hair was plastered to her face with sweat. The thin, stray strands of hair became lost in the black webbing of the woman's veins that stretched out under the skin that held grayish hues. She looked sickly and thinner than what her frame would suggest was healthy. The only thing Vanessa had ever seen to compare it to was a blood-fevered vampire that had not been properly staked. It was left to teeter upon life and death. This woman in the bed before her was no vampire, and no piece of wood stood out from her chest.

Ma relinquished her hold upon Vanessa's ear, and the girl didn't even think to cradle the red, pulsing body part as she registered what it was that had hold of this woman. It *must* have been a stage of Medusa's Kiss that most never laid eyes upon. A stage most wouldn't *want* to lay eyes upon.

"There's the owna. Cressida Katsaros. Ask her anything dat ya want." Ma's voice didn't sound angry anymore. It sounded sad.

"How… how much longer until…" Vanessa couldn't even bring herself to finish the thought. She could only stare and pity the sorceress that was a husk of the person she had once been. The person she had never met.

"I don't think much longer," Ma whispered.

Bobo grimaced and looked away. "What a horrid way to go," he assessed with a deep frown.

"Momma!" Cressida's voice croaked out followed by muffled moaning.

Everyone cast their eyes to the floor. "So, if there's nothin' you wanna ask…" Ma said.

"No. I'm good." Vanessa didn't even stop to think about it. She answered and turned back to the door and walked unsteadily through the threshold. Ma nodded as she reached into the room, grabbed the knob of the door, and slowly closed it.

Slow footsteps brought Vanessa to the end of the hall where she stood looking forlorn. Bobo approached a moment after, looked down at his master, and searched his mind for a way to comfort her. He was saved by Ma, as the imp came to her side, reached up, and gently took hold of Vanessa's hand in her own. Patting the top of the witch's appendage, Ma spoke softly. "There was no way you could've known, hun. The spell, it *was* black magic. There ain't no denyin' that. But she was tryin' to get rid of her magic… so … so she could escape it."

Bobo spoke in a surprised, hushed tone. "You mean the spell was an attempt to get rid of Medusa's Kiss?"

Ma only nodded, but it was Vanessa that spoke next. "I just thought…"

Her thoughts were cut short by Ma squeezing the young lady's hand. "You thought you was doin' somethin' good in this world. That ain't nothin' to be upset about. But not everything is so black and white, Vanessa, baby. Sometimes, the world needs those shades of gray. Without them, the black and white don't seem so stark, ya know?"

Vanessa looked up and then into the soft gaze of the older imp, and she seemed to realize something. Nodding to herself, she took a deep breath, knelt down, and hugged Ma. "I'm sorry."

"Me too, suga. Me too." Ma then giggled quietly as she tightened her embrace around the young witch. "You gotta stop lettin' that emblem go to your head."

Vanessa couldn't help but smile because what Ma said was the truth.

 *Chapter 9:*

After some much-needed self-reflecting and a quick cup of tea, Vanessa inspected the rest of the sanctuary and found nothing out of the ordinary. The black magic inflicted area had cleansing magic residue left behind, meaning the proper protocol for eradicating potential lingering black magic had been performed. Leaving Vanessa to believe that perhaps just a slight hiccup in the paperwork was the only real culprit here and not some massive cover-up sprinkled with unlawful deeds by trusted members of the Coven. The incident from a few weeks ago still had her trust in all members serving within the Coven rattled. Still, there was a nagging feeling that she was missing an important piece to the puzzle.

However, knowing that the sorceress responsible for the black magic spell was now magicless (and writhing in pain as she slowly faded from this life), Vanessa thought it best not to take Cressida into custody. Besides, any unanswered questions that Vanessa had wouldn't be answered by the woman. At least, not in a clear manner…

So, the young witch left things as they were and left to head back to headquarters to make her final statements on paper. Besides, she was told that she had another assignment to tend to after she finished filing her report.

Outside of the sanctuary, Bobo sighed heavily and scratched at the back of his head. "That was nothing near what I expected we'd find."

"Oh?" Vanessa stopped walking and turned to face Bobo. She wondered if he had thought that something was off about the whole ordeal as well.

"Yes," he said. She instantly perked up. Being well acquainted with his owner's looks, he instantly raised a finger and ticked it from side to side. "No. No. That's not what I meant. I am only stating that, usually, things don't go that smoothly for you. You tend to get into a lot more trouble before we exit a building."

Vanessa rolled her eyes and resumed marching, now in a huff, to headquarters. Bobo could only chuckle as she stormed through the soggy lawn.

Back at the Coven, Vanessa was continuing to ignore her pet as she headed for the usual service desk. All the while, she attempted to sidestep a rush of Summoners as they hastily made way for the departure pads. It seemed that there was something big that they needed to tend to. Vanessa chalked it up to the Coven locating a new feral demon as she headed for Ell's usual desk.

A pixie flew by, replenishing the old inkwell on the counter with fresh ink before fluttering off to do the same to the other remaining inkwells. The dust left behind was waved at as the witch burst through the sparkling cloud in her rush. The service desk was clear of bodies. Ell must have been running an errand, and all the other desks were full... again.

Vanessa groaned. She didn't want to have to stand in line. She turned and leaned her back against the edge of the desktop. Suddenly, from behind her, a white cat leaped up onto the countertop and meowed. Dramatically throwing her arms into the air, Vanessa squealed and ducked into a ball to avoid the imaginary attack.

All those in the vestibule turned to face Vanessa after her outburst. Some were even reaching for their wands just to be safe. After everything that had happened in the past few weeks, it was clear that the Coven, as a whole, was still uneasy within the walls of the building. It was Bobo that defused the masses with a smile and gentle, "Nothing to see here, folks. Just a witch having a nervous breakdown, that's all. Move along. Move along."

Without warning, Vanessa jumped to her feet and slapped at the ogre relentlessly. "Ow. Ow. OW! D'all right, Vanessa," he barked, causing a few more to turn their gaze upon the fussing duo before casually returning to their work. "Banish a banshee, was that really necessary?" Her hand raised ready to strike him once more, and he pointed a finger at her with a glare. "I have an ax. Don't make me use it."

She growled at him.

He growled at her.

And from beside them came the soft rumbles of a happy purr. They quickly put a lid on their quarrel. Slowly, both of them turned to see a white, longhaired feline with big, bright blue eyes staring back at them. Its long puffy tail floated around behind it as if it were an apparition, and its ears had long tufts of white protruding from the tips. It sat straight and proud like an alabaster statue upon the service desk. The tail was the only dead giveaway that it was very much alive.

"Do you need to file a report," its eyes flicked down to Vanessa's emblem and then back up to lock gazes with the witch as it continued, "...Spellweaver?"

Vanessa's jaw unhinged, and her pet's eyes swelled in surprise. "Bobo. Bobo. It's a-a-a... a familiar," she said in a hoarse tone.

He could only nod in reply.

"I can still hear you." The familiar seemed unamused.

Visibly shaking her head to snap out of her daze, Vanessa stood tall and tried to collect her thoughts. "I—um. Yes. I need to file a report. But..."

The cat flicked an ear and tilted its head. "But what, Spellweaver?"

"Well, for starters, might we have a name to address you by? I think kitty wouldn't be fitting or proper considering your role," Bobo interjected.

The cat's tail seemed to pause in its seamless, floating, flickers before resuming its quiet, mesmerizing role behind the animal. "Hmmm... yes. You are right." It shivered in a way that made its fur all puff out before the creature sprawled out, lying down flat and calm out on the countertop. "Pristine," she said simply.

"Who's familiar, are you?" Vanessa inquired.

The cat sighed. It wasn't moving its mouth when it spoke, but they could hear the words clear as day. "I am Ell's familiar, if you must know." Pristine sounded unhappy about admitting that point.

Bobo and Vanessa both exchanged a look. It was well known that the amount of concentration and sheer willpower it took to astral project was so great—and rare of a trait most magical wielders possessed—that the Coven deemed it too great of an occupational hazard, and removed the option of choosing between a demonic pet or a familiar. If one so desired, they could request a familiar after they summoned their demon pet. However, they were required to fill out a form that absolved the Coven from any family members attempting to hold the Coven responsible for any personnel who has an early demise. For if that member could not relocate their form within the allotted time necessary to reclaim the vacant body, they perished from the mortal realm. With that said, both Bobo and Vanessa were floored at the fact that Ell, who possessed very little magic, had managed to accomplish such a difficult task. Honestly, it made them view the young lady in a most respectful light.

"My word," Bobo gasped. He then looked down at his master. "Vanessa. Look. There is hope for you yet. If she could find her familiar, you—"

"Say another word and I'll bind your taste buds from being able to savor anything for the next month," Vanessa cut in and stated through gritted teeth.

Closing his yapper rather abruptly, Bobo shrugged and turned back to the cat. "I'm just saying that it is rather remarkable, that's all."

"Trust me, I'm just as shocked as you both," Pristine said in a smooth voice. She then lifted a paw to lick at it as she asked Vanessa, "Are you reporting an incident or filing a completed mission?"

"Oh. Yes. I am filing a completed mission," Vanessa answered, snapping back to the task at hand.

Pristine twisted in a way that only a feline could and veered over the edge. After a second, a paper floated out from one of the many filing cabinets behind the service desk and gently flew over to the top of the counter. "There is fresh ink and a quill to either side. Please fill out the form and return it to me to be filed away," Pristine advised and then resumed lying down as she cleaned herself, the long puffy tail occasionally flicking in the air and dancing from side to side.

"Thank you," Bobo and Vanessa both whispered. They stepped off to the side so that the next Coven member could advance and make a request.

After a few minutes, Vanessa read through her finished report before she rolled it up and manifested a ribbon and wax seal with a bit of her gold dust to ensure the contents wouldn't be looked at by anyone other than a Summoner ranked member.

She smiled as she turned and started to hand it out to Pristine when a hand, from over her shoulder, reached out and snatched the scroll from her grasp. Whirling around, Vanessa shot out, "That is a highly classified report. I demand you return it at once, or I shall be forced to—" she stopped dead in her sentence and gulped as she stared at the gold emblem pinned to the cloak of the woman in front of her. "I'm sorry, Summoner... I didn't know."

The woman wore a knowing smile, and her lips seemed to be half-puckered, as though she were always deep in thought or like she was about to correct someone. Her silver eyes gleamed with a pool of secrets. The slightly taller woman had her ashy brown hair in a neatly woven, tight braid that stiffly hung like it was fastened with weights, and it zipped down her back like a second spine. Her dark green cloak hid most of the high-end leather tunic that held gold plated prongs and shimmering embellishments. The whole thing probably could pay Vanessa's rent for a month. And she honestly had to wonder how someone could fight in something like that. Though, the appearance of the woman portrayed a more book intelligence that graced an office desk than that of a field worker.

The woman's lips curved into a smile and she gave a gentle nod to the stumbling Spellweaver before her. "I'll take the report from here, Spellweaver Peterson."

Vanessa's eyes darted around, half expecting Leon to jump out and cackle like a mad man over some harebrained prank. But nothing happened. Except for awkward silence, that is. "You know my name?" She stopped to think about the fact that the ceremonies had recently taken place. "Of course, you know my name," she whispered to herself. There was a short pause. "And you are…?"

"Second Chosen Winona," she answered without a hitch.

Vanessa tried to not die at that moment. The woman wasn't a Summoner, she was a Second Chosen! She could almost feel Bobo go stiff and lifeless at her side as he tried to, in all ways that an ogre of his proportions could, not gain attention. "S-second Chosen Winona," the young witch stammered. "I see the scroll is in good hands then."

"Indeed, it is," Winona agreed and tucked the scroll away into a pocket under her cloak. "As for you, I believe there is a second mission that you need to tend to before the day is through."

Vanessa nodded wildly. "Yes."

Winona's smile widened. "I believe that Ell is in possession of your mission scroll. I sent her down to file away some of the overflow of reports in the Coven's library."

"Ah. Okay. What section should I find her in?" Vanessa questioned.

Holding up a finger as Winona searched her pockets, she pulled out a corked, miniature glass jar and handed it over to Vanessa. "It will glow blue when you get to the correct rune door. She had many different cases and she tends to be a bit… scattered…" she trailed off. "So, she could be in various places down there. This would be the most suitable method of locating her."

Holding the teensy, tiny jar up to her eyes, Vanessa revered the dull orange glowing orb that was suspended within the glass container. "When it glows blue," she recited.

"Yes," Winona confirmed. "Now, I have much business to attend to. I hope you can forgive me for going about my way."

"No. I understand," Vanessa said, lowering the jar and giving a slight bow as Winona parted ways with them. When Second Chosen Winona was out of earshot, Vanessa tipped back and was caught in the expecting embrace of Bobo.

As he looked down at her, he spoke quietly, "I don't think my heart can handle another scare like that, today."

Vanessa nodded her head, agreeing with him. "That was unexpected, to say the least."

"Yes," Bobo said, watching the Second Chosen walk away. "It was very odd, indeed. Wasn't it?"

Following the instructions of Second Chosen Winona, Vanessa and Bobo headed for the Coven's library doors. They kept a careful eye on the jar as they awaited the blue orb to glow. When it did, they noted the rune marked doorway and headed downstairs.

Lighting their way with a simple spell, Vanessa took the lead for her and her pet through the dungeon-like tunnels that made up the Coven's basement library. Walls of texts, shelves of books and scrolls, randomly placed desks with blank parchment and half-dried inkwells lined the endless halls. All the while, they kept gazing down to the jar as its blue light pulsed brighter and brighter as they advanced deep into the catacombs.

"Ell!" Vanessa called.

Bobo jolted and stifled a scream between a tightly screwed mouth. Slowly, he gave her an annoyed look as he composed himself. Quietly, he chastised her, "Let a man know before you go bellowing out into the dark like that. You sound like a wailing spirit."

"Ugh. I do not!" she scoffed. "It's not my fault you're afraid of the dark," she snapped back.

It was Bobo's turn to scoff. "I beg to differ. Who dragged me down into winding tunnels below the academy, got us lost, run over by a minotaur, and chased by hellhounds? How could I not develop a fright when enclosed in small, cramped areas with the likes of you?"

She waved the thought away like a swarm of annoying flies. "It was all a matter of bad luck," she said in her defense.

"Well, bad luck follows you," he retorted.

Just as Vanessa turned to fuss with Bobo even more over the matter, there was a mousey voice that caught them both by surprise.

"Vanessa? Bobo? Is that you guys?" the voice asked from behind a thickly stacked bookshelf to their side.

Bobo craned his head as he inspected the heavily shelved cases where the voice had come from. "Ell, my dear. Is that you?"

"Yes, it's us, Ell. Where are you?" Vanessa called out.

A hand poked out from betwixt a few boxes of scrolls on one of the shelves. It pointed down to the far end of the bookshelf. "Meet me down there," Ell exclaimed and then retracted her arm to the other side of the bookshelf.

Cautiously, they made their way through the cobwebs, dust, and darkness to the other end of the shelving unit and smiled when Ell's head popped around the corner. "Hi, guys. I was wondering if you'd be able to find me down here," she said, sounding exasperated and then giggled as she dusted off her hands. "I hope I wasn't too hard to find," she expressed with worry in her eyes.

"No. Not at all," Bobo said with a cheery look and pointed to the jar in Vanessa's hands. "Thanks to a little trinket that we were bestowed with, finding you was a breeze, my dear."

"Oh good!" she then eyed over the item in Vanessa's grasp. "Oooh. What is that?"

Vanessa shrugged. "I'm left to guess that it is a newly developed locator spell, but it seems to be linked with you specifically."

The look that washed over Ell's face was not one that neither witch nor demon would claim to be normal. It was serious and calculating and seemed to weigh heavy with thoughts that didn't quite match the Ell that they had always known. But she bounced back to her usual self and reached for the jar. "May I?"

Blinking and looking at the jar that had little use to her now, Vanessa shrugged and handed it over. "Yeah, sure. I don't need it anymore. I know you like to look at new stuff like this, so, why don't you keep it, Ell?"

Ell perked up and looked from the jar to Vanessa back to the jar and giggled excitedly. "Really?"

"Yeah. We used it to find you. Kind of don't need it anymore," Vanessa admitted.

"Oh. Thank you!" Ell reached to the glass and the moment she touched it, the orb burned a bright, vibrant blue before sizzling, popping, and then dying into a heap of ash at the bottom of the jar. "Fascinating," the girl whispered, holding the jar so close to her eyes that she went cross-eyed.

Bobo made a sound, "Mmm," and then pulled his attention away from the strange antics of the young lady. "The Second Chosen mentioned that you had our next mission scroll."

Dropping the bottle from her view, Ell lit up with remembrance and nodded. "Yes. I do. Now…" she turned around and then turned around again and again until she was spinning in place while searching the empty floor. "Oh. Oh no," she murmured while biting at the tips of her fingers.

As if she already knew, Vanessa asked, "Did you misplace the scroll?"

Cringing in horrible despair, Ell turned slowly and nodded with a deep frown.

"Don't worry, my dear. I'm sure that it can't be far," Bobo stated with a smile.

Vanessa chimed in, "Where did you last see it?"

Ell thought for a moment before snapping her fingers and pointing to the other end of the bookshelf. "I left my stuff down there when I told you guys to meet me down here. Hold on." She went bounding down the aisle to retrieve the box full of files, reports, and (of course) Vanessa's mission scroll.

Bobo and Vanessa slowly followed after Ell while eyeing over the dusty shelves lining either side of them. Stopping at the box, Vanessa peered over one of the shelves and grimaced as a spider skittered over the worn bindings of forgotten books. When Ell rose up from the box and turned to face Bobo and Vanessa, she froze in place, her eyes bulged, and she let out an earsplitting scream. Turning swiftly on heel, Vanessa reeled to face whatever lay behind them and her hand fumbled for her spell pouches. Two faces lit up in an eerie green glow stared back at them from the darkness and Vanessa screamed. Ell screamed again. Bobo jumped and shouted, swept up in the excitement. Then Lyx screamed. But it was Leon who broke the repetitive screaming in the room.

"Why are you all screaming?" he roared in confusion.

Lyx whimpered and threw her arms around Bobo's neck. "It's so creepy down here. Hold me, Booboo!"

"Get a hold yourself, woman. You're hell-born. If you're scared, I'm a runesmith!" He fumbled with where to put his hands to remove the succubus before Leon rescued him by peeling his pet off the ogre.

"Calm down, Lyx. It's a library, not a dungeon," Leon muttered. "And you," he pointed to Vanessa. "Why were you screaming?"

She swallowed hard and put a hand over her frantically beating heart that thundered like wild unicorn hooves within her chest. "I'm just a bit jumpy today," she lied. In truth, she was screaming because it was Leon, and she wasn't prepared to be face to face with him so soon, and so surprisingly.

"And you," Leon rose his pitch as he turned his attention to Bobo. "Why on Raen where you screaming? You're... the scariest thing in here!"

Bobo reached out and grabbed a hold of Leon's cloak and pulled him close. He leaned in and whispered into the Summoner's ear. "First of all...Do you not see the vixen behind you? She'll be the death of me, I can feel it. How can a man not be frightened when staring down his own death?"

Leon looked back to Lyx who blinked innocently and then turned to face Bobo as he whispered, "And the second thing?"

The ogre shifted in place and twitched his lips before saying, "And secondly, words hurt, Leon."

Leon rolled his eyes and groaned. "Oh, come now, Bobo. You know that you are one of the most respected and handsome beasts in the whole Coven!"

The gentleman-monster let go of Leon and straightened out his tie. "Yes, well... it can be forgotten from time to time. Egos can be fragile things, you know."

Vanessa giggled and took the scroll from Ell. "Well. As fun as this was, I want to get my job done so I can go home and rest."

"Agreed," Bobo chirped.

Unfurling the scroll, Vanessa slowly took the time to read over the scribbling therein, only to have her heart sink with each written word she uncovered and read. She found herself frowning hard at the unrolled parchment. While she attempted to not cry out in outrage over, yet another, boring mission scroll.

"Oh, it can't be that bad, Vanessa. Let's have a look," Leon tried to comfort her as he snatched the scroll from her grasp. Three faces buried themselves behind the paper as they read the contents of the mission.

Bobo broke the silence first by yelling out, "Success!" and fist-pumping the air in a bizarre manner that had everyone staring for a moment in complete awe of the ogre's actions.

"I don't get it, why is searching the Coven library for clues on the elves and de-summoning rituals a good thing?" Lyx whispered to Leon.

Bobo threw the parchment into the air and skipped away from it as it landed on the ground. "Because, my dear lady," Bobo practically sung as he took the succubus up in his arms and danced in a circle. "She can't get into trouble in a library." He chuckled loudly to himself until the booming laughter filled the halls.

"Laugh it up. Go ahead. But I'll find a lead and be out of here in no time, you'll see," she snapped heatedly.

"I'll help you," Leon offered.

"Thanks," she started, and she fought with what to say next. Did she tell him that she didn't need him again? It didn't matter because he seemed to have an idea hit him that tore his attention away from her.

"Wait a minute, Bobo. Didn't you say that you thought you might have a lead on that? You even showed me a book…" he then snatched the scroll up from the floor and rolled it out flat on a vacant shelf. He scanned the writings and pointed to it. "Ah-ha! I was right. They want you to find clues because Bobo listed the lead in your report! You do have a lead, and the Council thinks that it's credible enough to look into," Leon announced.

"Spill the magic beans, Bobo," Vanessa demanded.

The ogre's disposition shifted into great sorrow. He went limp and stopped chuckling and dancing and left Lyx to pout. Hanging his head in defeat, he claimed, "I had forgotten about that. It's true. I am my own worst enemy."

"Bobo," both Vanessa and Leon yelled in perfect unison.

"Yes, yes. I hear you! Just a moment. Let me recall it all in detail."

While they all waited for Bobo to wrack his brain for the information, the rest of them helped Ell with putting away some of the reports and scrolls, making the poor, overworked girl grateful that her work had been lessoned for at least a little while.

"Ah, I remember!" remarked Bobo, loud enough to jolt the group from their work. "*When the phoenix is made of metal, and old treasures are guarded by those with dragon's blood, the ancient ways shall be found again, and a darkened place will be brought to light.*"

"We didn't ask for a poetry session, Bobo," Leon muttered.

"You're too uncultured for one. However, that wasn't a poetry reading. It was a passage from Darion Black's complete works. Specifically, *The Fairy Fall*, if I'm not mistaken."

It was Vanessa that spoke up next, "You mean to tell me that was the lead you were talking about?" She sounded bored.

Bobo groaned and held his forehead in the palm of his hand. "I'm doomed to have such an ignorant master. How can you not see all the great leads that were listed?" Everyone stared back at him with blank faces. "Oh. Oh, you can't be serious. None of you caught onto the hints? They are hidden in plain sight."

"The de-summoning spells?" Lyx questioned with a tilt of her head.

"N-no. The hints," Bobo sounded exhausted.

Leon held up his hands and motioned for everyone to calm down. "Let's just take a step back here and have you explain it, all right big guy?"

 *Chapter 10:*

After calming down, Bobo, Vanessa, and the others all went to one of the large oak tables that were in the center of the hall between the endless rows of shelves. Everyone chose a seat while Bobo stood at the end of the table, leaning on its surface as he explained.

"There are a few who believe that Darian Black knew secrets about the elves and magic of this land and wrote hints into his works. Most picked it apart, but no concrete evidence has ever been looked into or researched past theories." Bobo lifted to his full, monstrous height and rubbed his thumb and pointer finger over the smooth line of his chin. "When I was reading, I found a few lines that really stuck out to me." He paused to think for a moment.

"What are the others?" Leon asked.

Bobo looked like a fish struggling to breathe as he opened his mouth, closed it again, and repeated the action a few times more before he exhaled loudly. "I cannot recall."

"Do you still have the book?" Vanessa asked.

The ogre shook his head. "I returned it a week ago."

It was Ell that spoke up next, "I can get it for you. Or at least the next best thing to the book itself." She beamed with pride at being able to be helpful and drew in a deep breath before she called out, "Seshat. Seshat. Where could you be? Your endless knowledge is required by me!"

The air around Ell shimmered with the power of the spoken spell. It was a simple spell, but the whole table was awestruck at the amount of practice and dedication the almost magicless girl had to put into obtaining this ability. Soon after, the glittering specks turned into an orb in front of Ell. It shot up toward the ceiling of the library and then burst into a million fragments before spreading out through the vast, limitless corridors that made up the library.

The spell was searching for the librarian, Seshat. An all-knowing being (when it came to the written and documented word) that resided within the underbelly of the Coven. If you had a question based on the vast knowledge that was listed in the confines of the limitless library, Seshat knew the answer. She roamed the halls and scoured new scrolls and books that seemed to always be stocked away down below. If her eyes read it, she remembered. A safety net that the High Council developed after the fires consumed the previous Coven building that resulted in the loss of countless books and priceless knowledge that none remember to this day.

A rush of air howled softly before a being started to materialize in front of them. Ebony, shoulder-length hair framed the sharp, angular features of a woman with deep, brown eyes and olive-colored skin. The female, still materializing, swept a handful of hair behind her shoulder and scanned everyone around the table. As the last of the glow dissipated, it revealed a spotted feline print dress with a golden, sheer material layered over the fabric. Her hand went to swipe away a few gold flecks that lingered from the magic that aided in producing her presence. Her body held a translucency to it like she was caught between being a ghost and a complete being of Aeristria.

"I was summoned." Her voice was silvery and laced with hints of a smoky accent.

Ell proudly raised her hand and swayed it from side to side energetically. "Oh. Oh. Me. I did. I summoned you!" she announced proudly.

The being, Seshat, turned and faced Ell before bending in a slight bow. "How can I be of service?"

Ell, proud of herself and making no effort to hide it, sat up straight in her chair and she motioned to Bobo. "My friend has a question about a book."

The mammoth-sized beast stood tall and dignified while he cleared his throat. "Yes. I'm in need of all of the passages that speak of dragons from Darion Black's epic poem, *The Fairy Fall*."

The being went still as it searched through the immense knowledge that it had stored away. After a moment, Seshat blinked repeatedly as she resumed movement and listed the information that Bobo had requested. *"When the phoenix is made of metal, and old treasures are guarded by those with dragon's blood, the ancient ways shall be found again, and a darkened place will be brought to light."* Everyone nodded, as Bobo had already recited. She continued without skipping a beat, *"Those with the blood of the ancient ones, will have the tongue and bare the horns, but their bodies have altered and changed form."* There was silence as Seshat finished with, *"His father an old one, his mother a fair maiden born, he is the perfection of both dragon and human, for his kind the world is full of scorn."*

"Thank you, my dear," Bobo said with a slight bow of his head to the librarian.

Lyx pinched her brow while expressing her, very understandable, worry. "Are you saying that the dragons have the information that we need?"

The sound of Leon's chair scraping over the floor as he stood up brought everyone's attention to him. "Welp. Count me out. Dangerous missions, sure. Feral demons, okay. Battling the strongest members of the Coven and saving Aeristria, can do. Dragons?" He shook his head. "That's where I draw the line," he admitted without care of what anyone thought of him for it.

"Well count me in," Vanessa chirped.

"Why am I not surprised?" Bobo grumbled under his breath.

"Over my dead body!" Leon barked heatedly.

"Leon! That is bad luck. Don't say that!" Lyx chastised her master.

"I'll do whatever I want. If it saves Aeristria, then I'm doing whatever needs to be done," Vanessa expressed with flames licking at every word she spat at the red-in-the-face Leon.

The Summoner's eyes narrowed at Vanessa, and he leaned over, letting his hands bare the weight of his upper body as he firmly planted them upon the face of the table. "A dragon would gobble you up long before you would get even a sliver of information on how to de-summon a demon!"

She mirrored his stance after standing so fast that her chair flew backward and slammed against the ground. "I guess that is a risk I'm willing to take for the people of Aeristria!"

"Double dip a candlestick… why are you two so upset?" Lyx asked as she looked from one to the other.

Bobo spoke up, and his tone alone dared anyone to try to speak over him or try to let the banter float over to his end of the table. "You two can lay to rest your petty squabble because the hints aren't telling us to go to dragons…well, per se."

Everyone faced the ogre with confusion scrolled all over their faces. Except for Vanessa, she seemed to almost be upset over the fact that they wouldn't be hiking it up the mountainside and potentially facing the fire breathing flyers before the day's end. In a huff, she turned and picked up her chair and practically slammed it right-side up. Both she and Leon hastily sank back down to their respective seats while avoiding direct eye contact with the other.

While they resituated themselves, Lyx leaned over to her master and whispered, "What is wrong with you?" But he only replied by waving her away from him and ignoring the question as he faced Bobo and waited for him to further explain the situation.

"The hints are all pointing to dragons that have changed their form. A breed that has both a human and dragon parent. They indicate that it will be one that specifically has a dragon father and a human mother. Further into the writing, it mentions that this breed will not be respected or liked," the ogre informed.

"Oh!" Lyx yelped. "Dragonkin!" she bellowed proudly.

Leon furrowed his brow and stared at the smooth surface of the table. "But Dragonkin are so few in Aeristria, and if there are more, they are hidden for fear of being treated poorly or worse by those residing in Tolvade."

Everyone seemed to stop and think. Vanessa added in a sunken tone, "And finding one that fits the criteria listed by Darian Black's work is slimmer than that."

While playing with a lock of her hair, Lyx seemed to be lost in thought, calculating things she was saying nothing about while the silence swam through those seated at the large table. She lifted her head and took a moment to let her gaze rest on each being around her. "I wouldn't say that it's impossible," she said finally.

Bobo raised a brow over one eye. "Pray tell, what do you have in mind, my dear?"

Lyx faced Bobo and said, "Not what, but who," she corrected. "I know of a guy that might actually fit the bill. If he isn't the one we are looking for, he would most definitely know what direction to point us in or at least know a name to toss our way."

Everyone asked Lyx in a unified harmony, "Who?"

She blinked, taken aback by the tidal wave of voices crashing into her. "Uh," she scanned their eager faces. "He goes by the name of Vice." They all stared back with muddled expressions. None of them had heard of that name before. She shifted uncomfortably in her seat and started to blush in the cheeks a bit. Her usual strong and sure voice was strangely replaced with a quiet whisper-like tone. "He works at the Flustered Dragon."

Everyone's jaw unhinged.

But none of them were more flabbergasted than Bobo. "Th-wh-g-n-ch…" he stumbled so thoroughly over his speech that he couldn't produce more than scrambled sounds of, what one could only assume were, the start of a string of words. But his thoughts were too addled by the fact that this creature was stationed at the Flustered Dragon to be able to finish the word, much less properly put it into a sentence. "I-I-I beg your pardon!" he shot out finally.

"Oh, thank goodness. I thought that she broke you," Vanessa teased.

He shot her a dirty look and then turned that glower right back to Lyx who sunk so far down in her seat she was practically sitting on the floor under the table. "And how, might I ask, would you know that he works there?" The ogre awaited an answer.

She fidgeted with her fingers, turning the pale lavender skin into a blazing white shade as her newfound meek voice informed him, "I pick up a few shifts there every now and again." If it were possible, she slipped further down her chair.

Once again, everyone managed to make sounds that would put mating cerulean blue monkeys to shame. Except for Ell, who covered her mouth and turned brighter than a cooked apple as she giggled into her palms, "Oh my!"

"Why on Raen would you work at the Flustered Dragon?" Leon managed to bark out.

Tired of being judged, the succubus shot straight up in her chair and faced her master with a fiery look in her eyes as she held up both of her manicured hands. Making sure to show off the nails glistening with immaculate polish, she wiggled her fingers as she kept her heated stare locked onto her master. "Do you think you can pay for these? Or the spa trips? Or my polished hooves? What about my filed horns, hmmm? Do you think you can pay for those… on your salary?"

He lost some of the puff in his chest and pouted slightly. "Maybe not on my Spellweaver pay, but I'm a Summoner now." As he spoke, he seemed to regain confidence that her barrage of questions had stolen.

"Oh goody." She gave him a mock grin while she jerked one hand out of the air and shoved it under the table and thrust the other out in front of her. "You can at least afford this one, now," she snipped.

He pouted harder. "Still. Working the…" he paused and looked cautiously around the dead library before dropping his voice and resumed speaking. "…working the steel down at the…the…"

Lyx looked bored as she finished for the man in the most lifeless voice, "The Flustered Dragon."

"Yes," he hissed.

"It doesn't matter," she said with a sigh. "I'm not talking about my side job," she cut a look to Leon, daring him to say anything more on the matter.

He looked across the table to Vanessa and begged for her help. "Don't you have anything to say about all this?"

"Who, me?" Vanessa laughed mockingly.

"Yes!" he yelled.

She motioned for him to quiet down before flipping her hand in Lyx's direction. "She's a grown demoness. If she wants to 'work the steel,'" she gave air quotations, "in her time off, who cares? I think it's pretty cool that she does."

"Thank you, darling," Lyx purred to Vanessa. "And Leon, I don't dance. I serve drinks at the bar." She gave a quick smirk. "Who would have thought that you had such a perverted mind, hmmm?"

"Behave," Bobo ordered in a hoarse tone.

She giggled and leaned ever so slightly across the table, her wings flapping energetically behind her. "But I'd give you a dance if you asked," Lyx whispered.

Poor Bobo went stiff as he seemed to forget how to breathe which—of course—sent Lyx into a laughing fit that could wake the dead or at least disrupt the undead from a nice nap.

Waving her hands in the air, Lyx gained everyone's attention. "Like I said before, it doesn't matter. My side job isn't the focus here, ladies and gentlemen. It's the fact that who we might be searching for works there. Vice." Lifting her pointer finger to tap at the bottom of her chin, she raised her sight to the ceiling and thought for a moment. "I believe he's on the schedule tonight." She laughed then. "When is he not?" she giggled again to her own joke, "I'll just pop in and ask him a few questions."

"I think not," Bobo sputtered with sureness that no one was willing to defy… except for Lyx.

She practically crawled on top of the slab of wood, "Are you saying that you are going to go into that floozy-stuffed building without me and ask him yourself?" Her voice was playful and pouty.

Beads of sweat were growing along the lines of the ogre's brow. "I-I-I… wouldn't dream of it."

She jumped up to her feet and clapped excitedly. "It's decided then. We shall *all* go to gather intel!" she exclaimed.

Bobo swallowed hard. "Oh dear," he muttered under his breath.

"Banish a banshee," Leon cursed.

"Welp. First time for everything. I suggest we head out before the late-night riffraff shows up and make gathering Information a bit difficult," Vanessa said in a chipper tone.

Leon raised his hand. "Might need to wait for me and Lyx. We have summoning training before I'm free."

Throwing a quick, silent tantrum in place at being hindered again, Vanessa groaned, "All right. All right. I'll go watch you train. But then we leave."

They all looked to Ell.

She beamed. "Oh. Don't worry about me. I have Seshat." All eyes went to look to the ghost-like woman that was rummaging through a box of scrolls. Ell giggled nervously. "There's always work to be done too," she said. "Besides, this was fun." Lyx looked a little embarrassed as she tried to laugh off her unease over the silly blonde knowing a very personal detail about her private life. Picking up on it, Ell waved her hands from side to side. "Oh. I won't tell a soul, Lyx. Promise. I've always looked up to you and Vanessa, so I wouldn't want to break your trust. I don't see anything wrong with what you do once you're off duty."

The succubus raced over, and half glided to the girl, and slammed into her with a big hug. "You are just the sweetest!" the demoness squealed.

 *Chapter 11:*

The summoning training grounds were outside the main Coven building. After having high volumes of summonings go wrong, it was best to have the hell gates placed outside rather than indoors and constantly needing to rebuild walls that had exploded into rubble by hellfire. It made it easier to maintain, watch, and was a lot more stress-free than the tight, stuffy rooms that they used to summon in years and years ago.

The courtyard had a massive dry water fountain in the dead center, and the cobblestone walls were lined with training dummies for all ranges of Coven members to practice slinging spells at. Two main summoning circles were used to tether new demons to their masters with to the eastside, and to the westside, there was the training summoning circle that had chalk infused with salt and sage to prevent anything unwanted from coming through. Around each circle was a protective barrier dome that encased the summoning ritual and those performing the ritual.

Along the building's walls were scorch marks that would never wash off and signs that there used to be unruly ivy vines growing up the face of the stone before they had been turned to ash by repeated waves of hellfire. The once green grass was now brown, and patches of hard dirt from being subjected to the magic and relentless heat of the underworld for many years scattered the courtyard.

But none of these were as scary as the five-foot-four-inch woman known as Willow Penelope Barnes, the Coven summoning instructor. She had a long, thick, and graceful braid that hung behind her like a silver pendulum. It swept across the back of her ankles as it ticked from side to side while she watched those practicing holding open a hell gate. All the while, she paced with her eyes locked on those that were finishing up the incantation to keep the portal steady. Her lavender hues gave silent hints to her fae bloodline that most of the Coven presumed she hailed from. Though, no one was for certain. The lines on her face told the tale of age that most assumed to be around her seventies, but, yet again, no one knew if that was correct or not as well. However, what everyone *did* know was that she was as strict as she was swift. Someone that looked to be as old as Willow shouldn't be able to move with the speed and grace that she possessed.

Oh, but she did.

Mess up your incantation? She was on top of you like a siren to a song. She could manage to correct you, do the spell herself, and back up from the area before you had a chance to register what happened. Accidentally break formation and all of the underworld's untethered beings start to try to rise up from the hell gate and kill everything in sight? Not on Willow's watch! She'd whip out her weapon (a yardstick with a half-burned smudge stick woven like a cocoon around the far tip) and—in a heap of horrible smelling smoke—she'd whirl through the air like a deadly pinwheel and slap the head of the beasts trying to escape. They'd be sent yelping back down to the underworld as she said a banishing prayer and cleansed the out-of-control magic before it spread beyond the protective barrier. She was a capable and scary woman that no one in the Coven, not even the High Priest Council, wanted to test their magic against.

Mrs. Willow, as everyone respectfully called the summoning instructor, was standing outside of the barrier protecting the hell gate. Her yardstick was rhythmicity tapping against the same shoulder of the hand that bore it, while the other reached out to pet her demon pet werewolf. As if the woman wasn't scary enough, she had a six-foot-tall werewolf always parked at her side. Her name was Asha, and her fur was clean, well-groomed, and a mesh of whites and deep grays. Asha's golden eyes were always watchful of everything her master wasn't keeping an eye on. If a shadow moved, the wind blew, or a threat was about, the werewolf knew everything about it.

Vanessa eyed over the ancient woman as her hand disappeared into the fluffy collar of her demon pet. "Go pet it. You know you want to. It's dangerous. You naturally want to do it. You gravitate toward the obscure and deadly, it's… sort of your thing, my dear," Bobo whispered to the gawking witch.

The Spellweaver jumped and looked to her pet as she snipped back in a low tone, "And lose a spell-slinging hand? No thank you."

As soon as the words left her mouth, Asha turned and faced the duo with a scrutinizing glare. It made the pair hush up and look at Leon, anything that wasn't that penetrating golden stare was better. Though, as she watched Leon focus on the incantation when it was his turn, she didn't feel like it was better than the yellow gaze of the werewolf. The witch eyed over the Summoner's every motion as he strained to keep the portal open. Her mind traveled through so many memories while she was lost staring at him. She felt her chest lock up and a stab of pain in her gut as she remembered what he said back at the bar. They were just friends. She didn't want to admit why it bothered her so much. And now that she pretty much was sure that he didn't care about her that way, there was no point in telling him and getting rejected. That would just add insult to injury. Sure, she had reckless moments, but she wasn't a glutton for punishment. And rubbing salt into her own emotional wounds was not at the top of her to-do list.

Noticing the odd look on his master's face, Bobo sighed to himself and nudged at the girl. "Is everything all right, Vanessa?"

She slowly blinked back to reality and looked up to Bobo as she contemplated telling him everything, only to be a coward and back out the next minute. "Yeah. I'm fine. Just anxious about gathering that information from Vice." It wasn't a total lie.

One point for avoiding telling the truth with telling a different truth.

Bobo nodded. "Yes. That is going to put all of us to the test, I'm afraid." He didn't sound happy about it.

"Are you upset?" Vanessa asked.

"About?"

"Lyx working at the Flustered Dragon," she pried.

Instantly, he went a bit red in the cheeks before he blew out a puff of air he had been holding. "Why would that bother me? I just find that an establishment like that isn't fit for a lady to be in."

"So you *do* think of Lyx as a lady," Vanessa expressed with a grin.

Naturally, the ogre became flustered and stumbled around his words a bit before he sniffed and stood straight and proud. "Nothing of the sort. I just don't want to be seen associating with someone that comes meandering out from the likes of a risky hole in the wall such as….as…. *that* place."

"Whatever you say, big guy. But when you are ready to talk about matters of the heart, you can come to me, all right?" She slapped him on the back for good measure.

He opened his mouth and whispered, "Preposterous. If that isn't the cauldron calling the kettle black." He then looked from Leon to her and said without skipping a beat, "Likewise, dear girl. Likewise."

It was not the reply she was expecting, and she went from giggling as quietly as she could to choking on her own saliva. The roaring coughing fit caused Leon to break his concentration. That was all it took for the spell to crackle. "Ah, hellfire," Leon whined.

Dirt dryer than the Golden Sea flung up from behind Mrs. Willow's feet as she darted to the Summoner's side. She waved her sage embellished yardstick and yelled out, "I banish you back to the abyss. You are not permitted to the world above, fall back and remain in the underworld until you are called and tethered!"

A series of wild howls permeated the courtyard air. "Where is your head, Summoner?" she seethed at Leon. "Your concentration is the most important part of the ritual. Get your head out of the clouds and back in the spell!"

"I—yes, ma'am," Leon sputtered as he attempted to get the incantation right before reciting it again. More yowling shook the ground all around the etched markings outlining the hell gate. The calming yellow and green hues faltered as red crackles of power pushed through the barrier. Hellfire lapped at the edges of the darkened void where Mrs. Willow was waving her smudge stick around and muttering a banishing spell.

"Hurry up, lad. It's a smudge stick, not a Celestial tied to the end of this thing!" Willow bellowed over sinister, cackling laughter and a series of howls rumbling from deep underground.

Leon's brow furrowed as he concentrated. "I'm trying. I'm trying!" he wasn't one to yell, especially at authority figures in the Coven ranks… but he was pushing himself as hard as he could. Beads of sweat collected across his brow before sliding down his face that was lined in stress.

"Summoner Zvěrokruh!" Willow barked.

With a growl, Leon managed to recite the incantation, "From deep below we call to thee, and drag you through the fires, to be above with one who calls and whose spirit you will be tethered, until their voice is heard and their hand pulls you through your layer of hell, your anger is quelled, your hate is silenced, and your spirit shall not pass, through this void or any looking glass." His hands slapped together loudly as he reached for a clearer mind, his memory attempting to repeat the segment over and over until he was lost in nothing but those words.

Mrs. Willow pulled back with her yardstick, a sigh on her lips and shaking her head. "A rookie mistake," she mumbled as she passed him. It was evident that Leon had heard her and that the comment had been a blow to his pride, but he didn't screw up a second time.

Bobo and Vanessa were battling their own demons as Asha had flown across the courtyard and slid to a halt right in front of them. Plumes of dirt clouds ebbed, revealing a very disgruntled werewolf sizing them up on the other side of the wall of dust while growling lowly. Bits of saliva dripped from its black, leathery lips as those golden orbs held the two responsible for breaking the Summoner's concentration.

"It'd be in your best interest if you took other people's studies seriously in this courtyard. Being a small-time hero in the Coven won't save you from the destruction that a hell gate can release if not properly maintained open," Asha's guttural voice rolled awkwardly out of the beast's mouth as it scowled at Vanessa like she was a nuisance.

The duo could only nod relentlessly as the werewolf looked them over like they were a pair of perfectly packaged snacks. "Of course," Vanessa squeaked.

"Asha," Willow called to her pet. "Don't give them a hard time. That one has had issues with concentration all week."

As soon as she said those words, Vanessa darted her worried expression from the hulking werewolf to Leon who was closing up the spell and wouldn't make eye contact with her or anyone. He had always been so good with concentration… or so Vanessa had thought. So, why was he having issues now?

"This is the only warning I will give you," snarled Asha as she turned and padded away to her master's side.

Leon strolled over, looking less lively. "Terribly sorry about that my good man," Bobo tried to take fault for something that he couldn't shoulder complete blame for.

Leon knew it too, and his lackluster expression accompanied by his drone tone made it very apparent that he did. "Not your fault," Leon grumbled.

Vanessa tried to make a joke out of it. "I was just slightly choking, no big deal. Didn't need anyone to come and save me." She laughed nervously and hoped that it wasn't *too* obvious.

The chilled glare that Leon shot from his icy eyes toward Vanessa made her body go still. Slowly, she started to hug herself like it would chase away the sensation that the look made her feel. The silence skulked in and no one really tried to break it.

"Come on. Lyx is waiting," Leon said and walked off. Vanessa sighed as she watched him walk away. She didn't know if she should apologize, try to cheer the guy up, or just forget that it all took place to begin with.

"I can see the smoke plumes puffing out from your ears, Vanessa. What are you thinking?" Bobo asked in a quiet and curious voice.

She ignored his little insult and watched Leon as he dragged his feet toward the courtyard exit. "I can't help but feel like something is bothering him."

"Why don't you talk to him about it?" the ogre wondered why the logical answer escaped her… and then realized who he was talking to.

She groaned. "Things have gotten—" She paused mid-sentence, and a sigh soughed from her lips. "Nothing. It's just been weird trying to talk to him lately. We seem to always fight now," she admitted finally. The sound of the truth hurt her a lot more now that she was saying it out loud to virtually anyone. She could have been talking to air and the comment would have been like a dagger falling out of the sky to plummet deep into her chest. It hurt. It hurt more than she wanted to admit.

Bobo waved at the air like the idea was absurd. "So, don't you two always bicker?"

She shook her head. "That's just it. Normally I am on the verge of laughing when I fight with him. Sure, we pick at each other, but it always feels like I'm talking to an old friend. It usually doesn't feel like I have weights hanging on my every limb and like we are trying to escape each other at the first possible chance, but here lately it does." She frowned hard as she spoke.

The beast nodded as if he understood but only hummed in reply not knowing how else to aid his master. It didn't matter because if the ogre had a thought it was snatched away by the sound of Leon calling back to them.

"Are you two coming or not?" he asked as annoyance tugged at every portion of his handsome, tired face.

Vanessa fussed with her spell pouches dangling around her waist and nudged Bobo with her elbow. "Come on. I'll figure something out. I'll talk to him. Okay. But let's get this job over with so I can sort some things out, first."

"Very well. As you wish, my dear." The demon made no attempt to fuss with her over the matter. Both Vanessa and Bobo made for the courtyard exit where they met up with Leon, and they all headed over to Lyx before leaving the comforts of Coven headquarters.

The first stop was their homes for a change of attire. Vanessa didn't want to go into a place like that sporting a Coven seal and Lyx agreed. Leon changed into basic trousers, boots, a crimson-colored tunic, a black leather vest, and his sage-dyed street cape. Lyx remained in her usual leather skirt and corset. No one objected. Vanessa chose her own street clothing; fleece-lined and skin-tight suede pants with a loose-fitting cream-colored tunic. As for her cloak, she only had the one and unpinned her emblem from the front of it. Bobo opted to stay in his current suit, saying, "I fear whatever I choose will be ruined before the night is over. I can bear to part with this one. Besides, I am most certain that the mud from the sanctuary has stained the pant legs."

And with that, the group headed out and on their way, albeit, some more reluctant to leave than others.

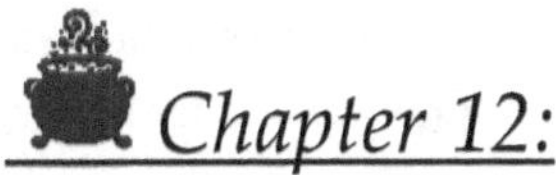 *Chapter 12:*

The Flustered Dragon was located on the perfectly darkened corner of a perfectly silent street that was perfectly placed in Tolvade's riffraff-ran roads of the Borlimane district that bordered the snobbish Adalith district. Not that Vanessa was at all surprised about that. The posh and proper residents of Adalith might have enough coin to please a dragon, but they had questionable tendencies just like the rest of Tolvade's residents, and the rest of Raen, for that matter. So, there was no amazement over the fact that those that resided in the Adalith district couldn't get the unsightly building relocated to a more "proper" place. Perhaps gold couldn't buy everything… or perhaps those with more of it were responsible for finding ways of keeping the building just where it was.

Either way, the building remained in its perfect little spot regardless of what the good people of Adalith had to say about it. And it was on that very darkened street corner that Vanessa now stood, staring at the glowing business sign as it flashed between bright, neon colors that splashed over the dusky block. Thick stones of varying tans and whites made up the face of the building while deep, brown-stained wooden beams covered the structure in a pleasing pattern. On the second floor, a large balcony jutted out just over the entrance door and rose up like a tower looming over the establishment's second-story roof, its own pointed peak stabbing at the inky night sky. Along either side of the building were winding steps that traveled in a dizzy path, some branching off to merge with bridges that adorned the archways leading to other buildings and roads on the second level of the district. As people walked to and fro, paying no mind to Vanessa and the others staring at the building before them, the young witch realized she had never felt so out of place.

While she started to lose all of her confidence, she swallowed hard and attempted to mask the gesture. But no one was louder in voicing their diminishing resolve than Bobo.

"I don't think I can do this. Shall we all take a rain check for the next day of Satur, perhaps?" The ogre tried, yet again, to deter the group from going through with their plans.

This, naturally, gave Vanessa a burst of confidence. "Oh, don't be such a killjoy. What's the worst that can happen, big guy?" Vanessa stated as she threw her hands upon her hips.

Ocean blue eyes slowly stepped down a flight of unseen stairs in the air between beast and Spellweaver. "Come again?"

"What?" she asked, motioning to the building in front of them.

As she gestured to the building, a broom gang flew up. Brooms, the flying sort, specifically, were hard to come by. It didn't take a lot of concentration to ride them, but they were a very dangerous thing to own. They held slivers of spirits that once belonged to magic wielders. As such, they had a mind of their own and typically rejected anyone that tried to own them. The few that exist are passed down through families. Most that own them now are part of broom gangs. They were rebel Coven members that broke away from the Coven in order to deal a justice of their own. They usually carried it out in ways that caused a lot more damage because they don't follow the laws of Aeristria as much as many think that they should.

The broom gang members cackled and dismounted their brooms. Propping the flying, glorified, magical dust sweepers against the outside wall of the Flustered Dragon, they adjusted their attire, elbowed one another while grinning wide, and walked toward the front door. Meanwhile, the smell of pipe tobacco wafted through the main entrance and carried through the faint breeze as a set of patrons left the building while laughing merrily. The two groups veered out of each other's walking paths politely, waving as they passed.

From the street corner neighboring the Flustered Dragon, a nearby cart vendor offered the busy street side patrons a tiny dragon. "Light your fires, your cigars, and your pipes. These babies do everything from roasting and toasting to igniting those torches to light your way." The little scaled, lizard-like creature zipped up the merchant's arm, perched on his hand, and blew out a small puff of fire into the air overhead with a gurgling purr. "They're also great at aiding in sniffing out treasure in those tucked away dungeons or left behind by greedy family members!" the seller added enthusiastically.

Lyx looked intrigued. "Oooh."

"We're not getting one," Leon muttered to her. She instantly pouted, but Leon would have none of it and ignored his pet's disappointed expression and irritable tail flicks.

Vanessa's eyes were glued to the gleaming, iridescent scales of the tiny dragons as their skin twinkled under the light of the street oil lamps. Bobo leaned down close to her ear and spoke in a low tone, "You're not getting one either. I'd be the one to clean up after it, and I refuse to do so."

Shooting him a look, she got ready to protest—or at the very least claim that she didn't want one—but chose to not lie and crossed her arms dejectedly. Jutting her chin in the opposing direction, she avoided the gaze of her demon in a huff.

Leon gave a lifeless sigh and cracked his neck before addressing everyone, "Come on and let's get this over with."

"After you," Vanessa chirped happily and shoved Leon's back, causing him to stumble forward and scramble to not eat pavement as his muddled footwork righted itself gradually. Awkwardly, he gawked up at the undeniably intimidating Molionids, who was manning the establishment's entrance.

The giant (literally) had two sets of scrutinizing eyes fixed inside two separate skulls. Their gaze beat down at Leon from above his hunched over body as he attempted to straighten himself out. The creature was not only large but had multiple appendages attached to its gargantuan sized body. Four legs with four feet, four hands attached to four long, muscular arms, and two heads resting on a set of beefy, broad shoulders. Collectively, the being was known as Molionids.

Molionids leaned over, and as one head atop the creature's shoulders eyed him over with an inquisitive stare, the other head giggled as Leon gulped at the two-headed giant that loomed over him.

"Are you going in?" the first head, Eurytus, asked seemingly annoyed.

The other head, Cleatus, cracked a grin. "Hehehehehe. Yeah. Are you going in or what, hmmm?"

Both heads waited while Leon attempted to dust himself off and look somewhat presentable. Shooting a positively livid look back to Vanessa, Leon coughed lightly and straightened up to his full height. "Yeah. They all dragged me here. So, we all need to get in," he said while thumbing back to the rest of the group.

The bouncer eyed them over with a muted growl. Vanessa instantly looked off to the side as she twirled a long lock of her raven hair and tried to not look nervous. Bobo looked like he was about to die from holding his breath, and Lyx just sashayed up to the front doors as she wiggled her fingers in greeting to the giant. "Hello, Cleatus and Eurytus, darlings," she said with a smile.

Two sets of eyes blinked as they saw the lavender skinned beauty approach. "Working tonight, Lyx?" they asked in dreamy unison.

She giggled and blew them a kiss. "Not tonight, boys. I'm just a girl having a night out on the town," she purred. "Mind letting me and my friends in? The night isn't getting any younger."

Cleatus raised one of the four hands closest to his half of the body while a second hand closest to Eurytus's half also reached for the door handle. "I'll do it!" Cleatus bellowed and then gave a goofy burst of giddy laughter.

But his outstretched hand was swatted away by the two arms controlled by his brother, Eurytus. "No. *I'll* do it!"

"I think you're mistaken, *brother*, because my hand was here first," Cleatus stated while jerking his brother's hand off the door and reaching for it with his own free hand.

A very disgruntled Eurytus put one of his hands over the handle at the same time. "I said I would do it," he informed through gritted teeth.

Suddenly, a flurry of slapping hands began as they boomed back and forth about who was going to open the door. In a fit of rage, Eurytus stomped on one of his brother's feet, causing the poor conjoined brother to hop about while stifling howls of pain. As the two wrestled, Lyx sighed and pulled her whip off of the side of her hip and cracked it against the top of the building. Bits of dust and rubble rained gently down over the two giant's heads.

"Boys. Boys. Boys! Fighting like that is cute and all, but I really would like it if you two could work together for little ol' me and open the door up. Momma needs a drink." She spared a wink at them and Molionds was butter.

"Okaay," they drew out the one word in songlike harmony as they each took hold of the door and opened it up for Lyx and the rest of the crew.

"Impressive," Vanessa whispered to the succubus.

Lyx giggled and muttered back, "Men are quite easy, darling. Just crack a whip, say something sweet, and make it seem like you need their help and they are all over it."

"I beg your pardon," Bobo managed to say after being stunned into silence.

Sweet, blissful silence.

The demoness grinned wildly and slunk back to his side and wove her limbs around the crook of his arm. "Oh, you're not like the rest of them." She buttered him up as she tugged him further into the mouth of the Flustered Dragon.

Although he was sated with the compliment, Bobo was far from blind. His words became caught in his throat as he attempted to speak, but only found sputtered half-spoken words as they ventured through the entrance doors. "Wai-coul-sto—"

Leon rolled his eyes with a groan before frowning hard and followed the others while Vanessa giggled and lightly jogged to catch up. She waved at the—still—fussing twins as she passed. "Thanks, guys!"

The halls leading up into the main event room were dark and splashed with deep plums and vibrant reds. The bouncing orbs of charmed lighting spelled to illuminate the halls were an electric yellow that gave a cheery feel to the quiet space. Drifting pipe smoke filled the halls and laughter mixed with mummers of multiple conversations followed soon after. The cramped space was doing nothing to aid Bobo's nerves.

The ogre turned on heel, his bulbous, frantic eyes told the story of how distraught he was, but the quick hand of Lyx spun him back around before he knew what was going on and tugged him along the remaining stretch of the corridor into the main event room.

The hall opened up to a large room. It was fixed with random seating areas throughout and had a massive bar that was made up of a carved onyx slab. The bar itself was tucked in the corner and then proceeded to wrap around the far wall. Multiple enchanted stools lined the black slab. It was the sort of spelled seating that shifted height and size depending on the being that sat in it. A rather convenient feature when you served more than just the average human.

On the opposite side of the room was a large stage where different shows were performed by various groups. Across from the main stage was an enormous enchanted tree that grew up from the floor of the showroom. Its leaves sparkled as the bright light that enveloped the tree like an aura bounced off of its crystalized vegetation. The bark was a luminescent white, and dangling from its branches were jeweled fruits. The fruit itself was edible, but the skin had no value. As soon as they were plucked from the limbs, the fruit altered into a more easily eaten treat with soft skin and juicy centers.

Around the tree were plush, purple cushioned booths and deep brown oak tables. The lute player near the stage called out to the crowd with, "Lords and ladies, we now present Mad Mary's Mirthful Menagerie!"

Lyx clapped excitedly with the rest of the crowd. "Oooh, this is going to be good. I thought I already missed their show for the night."

"Oh no," Leon gasped to himself.

"I'm not ready. I'm not. I'm… I'm leaving. I wish you all luck on your endeavor. Goodbye," Bobo blurted out loudly before he tried to retreat with haste, but Lyx only giggled and clamped down on her hold of his arm.

Flipping her hair with her tail, she flicked her golden gaze up to the ogre with a positively wide grin. "Oh, no you don't. Trust me. They are the tamer show that they put on here, Booboo," she purred.

Meanwhile, Vanessa had her eyes glued to the stage as curiosity drove any embarrassment right out of her system. The sheer, lavender curtains adorned with vines and flowers were peeled to one side, allowing a satyress to saunter through. She ruffled her multilayered skirt dyed in various colors of green and winked at the crowd as she smoothed over her short, white, form-fitting blouse. "Hey boys," she called out right before she fluffed her long, rich auburn hair and slowly rose her searching fingers up through her mane to rub over her curved ivory horns. "Matilda here and you know I can take good care of you!" The crowd boomed in approval while the next performer in the group stepped forward on the stage.

"Hello, gents. Lady Marisa here," a harpy chirped. Where her nose and mouth should have been, a small beak protruded from her long, angular face. From her elbows down, she had long, glistening, purple and blue feathers fanning out to brilliantly display her beautiful wings. Black talons extended from her hooked hands and jutted out from her bird-like legs. Soft, puffy feathers covered her naked body as she bumped her hips from side to side. "I hope you enjoy our show!" she seductively squawked.

Suddenly, from behind the harpy, a dryad with hair like a weeping willow and skin with flowers and moss creeping over the bend and curves of her body emerged. Bark covered her fingers, wrists, and arms like wooden gloves. She waved at the inhabitants of the room. Her sheepish voice sent the crowd into a frenzy of hoots, hollers, and whistles as she said, "Mavis here to entertain you all."

To her side, a wereleopard with long, straight, pearly hair that brushed over the small of her back draped an arm over the dryad's shoulder. The creature's pure white coat was spotted with coal-colored dots and it shined under the glow of the spotlight cast down onto the stage, giving her already lustrous fur an ethereal glow. "Meredith boys and I *know* how to entertain," she announced and then flashed everyone a sharp-fanged smile before licking Mavis' cheek affectionately.

From behind the veil of hanging flowers, a tall beauty emerged. Blonde hair in wild curls bounced around her oval-shaped face. Bright, green eyes scanned the floors beyond the stage with the prowess of a predator. Black leather hugged every inch of her body, from her boots to her pants, to the corset synched as tight as it could muster around her thin waist, wide hips, and generous bosom. Flicking a thick wave of collected curls behind her shoulders, she snapped her fingers and the girls fell in line at her side. In this one's gaze, there was an unbridled mirth that bordered the insane. She didn't have to say her name; Vanessa already knew who she was. "And you all know me," she purred confidently to the audience.

The mob of drooling onlookers bellowed out in perfect unison, "Mad Mary!"

A deep, smoky laugh erupted from her throat like molten hot honey. "That's right boys and girls. Mad Mary here, and mmmm… do I have a show for you." She waggled her eyebrows before giving a quick wink.

It was at this exact moment that Vanessa tore her eyes away from the stage. She would have nightmares of Leon poking fun at her flustered features if she continued to watch and pretend that she was unabashed by the performance that was about to unfurl on the stage.

Quickly, before the others could notice, Vanessa slipped away through the masses and snuck over to the bar to order a drink and collect her thoughts.

She slipped up onto a barstool, waited for it to adjust to her weight and height, and rested her cheek on the palm of her hand as she propped her elbow up on the surface of the bar and sulked for a moment. She tapped at the wood under the pads of her fingers nervously as she pondered over what the implications of finding the de-summoning spell would hold for Aeristria. *If* they found it, that is. Streets could be safe again. Businesses would thrive without fear of curfew. Families could venture closer to the edge of the woods for picnics and herb collecting without worry, and secluded villages tucked away within the neighboring forests would no longer fall victim to the atrocities that they had already endured. The loss and death over the past few months had slowly climbed into numbers that made her heart weep. Although they had recently slowed, it didn't take away the sting of loss that lingered for those left behind.

Her mind swam through a sea of doubts as she mentally listed each and every threat that her world would have to endure if they couldn't manage to get this all under control. The Coven was hiding their fear well enough and was doing a great job of giving the people a sense of security. But how long would that last before hysteria broke out? How long before the demons overtook everything?

Something tickled the side of her face as she felt a lock of hair being tucked behind her ear. With lightning reflexes, she slapped whatever was near her face away. "Don't touch me," she snapped. The last thing she wanted was someone in this place putting their hands on her. Besides, there weren't a lot of beings out there that were big on someone breaking the boundaries of personal space, and she was rather fond of her bubble not being breached by random strangers. But the breed of strangers that this place could produce was the kind that made your skin crawl, and, as such, made the desire for touching far, far less than usual.

"Whoa, whoa there, broody princess. Don't cut off my tail. I was just tryin' to get a look at those pretty eyes that you're hiding with all that hair while you're pouting at my bar." The voice came from a male behind the bar that was nursing his wounded tail.

She eyed over the man in question with a scowl fixed on her face. He was tall, almost as tall as Bobo. But he lacked Bobo's refinement and good taste. The man pulled on his black leather vest and cleared his throat into his fist. A well-defined, corded chest, which was the color of an apricot, spasmed with the owner's forced coughing. Aside from the vest, his upper body was bare. His lean figure loomed over the edge of the bar as his tail reached across and caressed a nearby woman's face right before it replaced the giggling customer's drink. His deep green eyes burned a hole through Vanessa as she took him in from the plum-colored leather pants all the way to his hair that resembled quiet layers of flames resting upon his shoulders. Crimson soaked strands flowed down from the top of his head until it slowly faded to orange and finally bled into a yellow down at the tips. As he dipped his head to one side, the lighting from various candles lining the bar and the enchanted tree glinted off two ridged horns that rose from the top of his head. He was very much aware of her lingering eyes on his body. "If you're wanting more than a drink, little lady, I'm going to have to charge you extra…" He slid closer, his movements fluid and graceful like a prowling predator. "Unless," he began as he fixed himself in front of her and planted a hand on the bar to support his weight as he glared back at her and continued, "…Unless you're a screamer. Those are my *favorite*. I'd never charge if you were a noisy one." His voice had a guttural sound that made Vanessa shiver. Already she was sure of one thing: she didn't care much for this lusty bartender. The sooner they got the information and left this place, the better. She was thankful that at the very least, Bobo would back her up on that. For now, she wanted to teach this cocky man a lesson. Her hand dipped down to her wand at her hip, already her mind was reaching for the perfect spell to fling at him that would—hopefully—not get them kicked out.

"Vice, you dog. I was hoping I'd find you here!" Lyx called with a bright smile as she slammed into the bar. Giggles poured from her like a string of tiny, chiming, silver bells. Straightaway, Vanessa's eyes bulged and her hand at her side went still.

Coming over to the bar gradually, Bobo slowly sunk into a seat with his back to the bar and took out a handkerchief to wipe his brow that was coated red with embarrassment. "My word. I shall never recover from the incidents that took place on that stage tonight. I'm a wounded man."

Leon shrugged torpidly. "It wasn't that bad, big guy. Stop your fussing."

"B—wh—well, I—tha—nev—" Bobo was too flustered to put a proper sentence together for a moment. "Did you see what they did with their skirts? And the dancing was so… so…" he cringed and wiped his brow again. "Such provocative creatures," he mumbled. At that precise moment, a scantily clad naga slithered by, paused to look Bobo over, and winked at the winded ogre. "Dear goddess, no," he whispered and hurried to turn around and face the safety of the bar top.

Vanessa peered around the growing group now surrounding her and looked at Lyx in surprise as she did a double-take to the barkeep. "This—" she thumbed to the flaming-haired man, "is Vice?"

Lyx looked over the man Vanessa was thumbing toward and nodded slowly. "Yes. Have you two met?"

The male Dragonkin chuckled. It was deep and hearty as he used his tail to grab a nearby glass to hand himself before he started to clean it until it shined under the dim lighting. "Not until a moment ago, Lyx," Vice admitted.

"Oh, thank the goddess. It speaks common." Bobo fussed with his tie and tried to ignore the fact that he was sitting at the bar inside the Flustered Dragon.

"Oh, no," Vice grumbled. His eyes dimmed as he realized that they weren't here to play, but something else. He took into account each face that seemed to make up the group gathered around Lyx. "I know exactly what in the name of magic is going on here. You look like a group of ragtag misfits setting out on a quest and looking for information, and *I'm* your last resort."

"Funny you should say that," Leon started, but the man was met with the Dragonkin ticking his finger back and forth while shaking his head slowly.

Vice turned suddenly to the succubus with mock hurt glinting in his emerald eyes. "Lyx, baby. Come on. Why do you have to treat me like this, huh? Why do you gotta do this to me? Am I not good to you? Don't I treat you right? You know I care about you—"

With his head bowed down, Bobo growled and rose slowly from his seat. "I. Beg. Your. Pardon?"

The male Dragonkin blanched and raised his hands, dropping his towel and the cup he was cleaning—which his tail skillfully caught before it shattered on the bar floor—from his now vacant appendages. "Heh, no need to get territorial there, fella. I'm just asking if I don't pay her well. That's all. Swear. As the owner, it's kind of my thing." Rushing, he put down the items with his tail and then plucked a wine glass from the rack with it before he bent down under the bar and returned with a bottle in his hands.

"You look like a fine—" he eyed over the ogre hungrily and made a satisfied sound in the back of his throat, "*very fine,*" he muttered, and then cleared his throat as he continued, "—man. Yes, a fine man, indeed. The kind of man with exceptional taste, I might add. You should unwind with a glass of this. Three hundred-year-old rose wine made from blackberries and with accents of cocoa beans. It was aged in the Pools of Time that are nestled in the Red Tipped Mountains."

With a raised brow, Bobo leaned over as he hummed with interest. "Hmmm. Three-hundred-years old, you say."

Three hands jutted out and tried to push the bottle away from the face of the ogre that was slowly being bought over with the presentation of the drink. Lyx, Leon, and Vanessa all eyed each other over and laughed nervously. Vanessa was the first to speak. "That won't be necessary. Right, Bobo?" she looked over her shoulder to him as he seemed to think about trying a glass. "Need I remind you that we are still on duty?"

To that, Bobo rose to his full height and sighed. "I fear not, dear fellow. I am here on business."

Vice playfully pouted and slowly replaced the items. But it was apparent that he was happy that his fast thinking had snatched him out of the angry, galloping centaur's path that was Bobo's wrath. He exhaled audibly and reserved himself to appearing defeated. "All right, all right. Follow me. Looks like I have no choice but to help you guys. *Destiny* and all that."

"Don't you want to know what we are going to ask?" Vanessa asked.

The bartender smirked devilishly. "My dear maiden, when you have seen the things I have, lived as long as I, and acquired vast amounts of knowledge, you don't wait for folks to ask questions. You know what they need before they ever ask."

With the crook of his finger, Vice beckoned the group to follow him around the bar. They walked by a table of vampires enjoying the evening show as they sipped at glasses of O-type Bloody

Mary's. Their eerie, glowing gazes fixed on the sashaying vixen's walking the stage. As they passed, Vanessa took notice of the fact that Bobo was trying—desperately—to not look in the direction of the show. She giggled to herself while continuing to follow Vice to the back of the main room with the others.

At the back of the building, there was a door that led into a small hall. A few doors decorated the walls as they passed by each one in silence. At the very end, there was an oversized oak door bearing a heavy iron lock. Vice turned once they reached it and addressed the group. "This leads down into the special wine cellar where I've accumulated most of my finer alcohol and most of my treasures."

"Treasure," Vanessa mumbled to herself. So, it was true, even half-breed dragons enjoyed their treasures. Not many Dragonkin existed and even less lived in the heart of Aeristria. Most lore about them were guesses at best, but one thing was for certain: they were from unwanted breeding between a dragon and a human. Through-out time, the dragons forgot how to shift into their human forms, and thus mating between species ceased. Unfortunately, they left behind a small and undesired species, the Dragonkin. Immortal beings with all the flaws of humans and all the desires of dragons. Most beings ignored them or ostracized them which left the Dragonkin very few comfortable options within society. And even fewer choices when it came to reproduction and finding an accepting spouse. Though, Vanessa was starting to think he had little issues getting what he wanted from women… and men. Vice had, however, made quite a nice business nestled between the two districts of Tolvade. He found a way to live with what he was, regardless of what others thought, all while thriving in the business world to boot.

Vanessa shuffled her weight between her feet and sniffed in thought. "So, uh… you know… how old are you exactly?" she blurted out casually.

Bobo turned with flames dancing in his blue, ogre orbs. "Leave it to my master to ask the rude questions."

"What? Everyone is thinking it…" Vanessa snapped.

There wasn't a single objection in the hall to her statement. It was at this time that Vice chuckled as he unlocked the door. The sound of old iron squeaking with disapproval to being disturbed echoed through the empty hall. Hinges moaning regretfully as the door was unhurriedly swung open while Vice replied with, "I'm old enough to know what cities lie beneath cities, what temples have been forgotten, the names of the world's creators, and what number of beasts and magic resides within the mountains." The grin plastered to his face widened as the door did. "But today, let's stick with the treasures I've collected."

The creaking door silenced as it came to a stop, and staring back at them was a yawning cavity of pitch speckled with the flickering orange light of torches deep within the shadowed abyss. "All great adventures begin with a single step into the beckoning unknown…" Vice whispered mystically. His voice returned to normal, and he shrugged his shoulders nonchalantly, "Or so I've been told."

With that, the male Dragonkin turned on heel and descended down into the depths of the Flustered Dragon's underbelly. As he delved deeper, his tail curled and ticked from side to side before it plucked a torch from the cobblestone wall as he went deeper still. The rest of them remained up top staring down the long, spiraling stairwell.

Why did all basement stairwells seem to spiral?

"Are you guys coming or what?" Vice called up.

"Welp. We came this far. Might as well keep going," Leon suggested and stepped forward.

Lyx sighed and flipped her hair behind her shoulder. "I suppose we won't be leaving empty-handed."

Nodding to Vanessa, Bobo eyed over the entrance as the succubus slipped out of sight. "I'll bring up the rear. You go first. This is your crazy adventure, after all."

Vanessa smiled. "It's not going to be an adventure, Bobo. I'm sure that we will get some information and take it back to headquarters in the morning. A quick and simple task," she said, patting the ogre's back as she stepped in front and took the first step down.

Bobo rolled his eyes with a tired groan. "When has anything been quick or simple when you are involved?"

She peered around the wall with a wild grin. "Oh, come now, Bobo. You know you love it."

"There are many things I love, Vanessa. A long book, a rich cup of cappuccino, a nice high-quality tea, or a freshly cleaned handkerchief, but, rest assured, that the crazy antics that I must put up with on the regular coupled with the trouble you often find yourself in when the job should be quick and simple, are not things that I *love*," he corrected with a pronounced frown bending his lips aggressively.

All that he could hear was Vanessa's cackle-like laugh as she quickly headed down the steps to catch up with the others, leaving Bobo at the top of the stairwell shaking his head with a soft smile slowly replacing his frown.

 *Chapter 13:*

The cellar air wrapped around them like a cape drenched in bog water. Natural, yet musty, smells lingered as they permeated through the underbelly of the Fluster Dragon. It wasn't a bad smell, but it was hardly a pleasant one. Silently, they all shuffled through the basement as they followed Vice to another locked door.

"A locked door within a locked door, isn't that a bit much?" Leon griped.

Vice chuckled then and ticked the iron key in his grasp from side to side as he said, "You can never be too careful protecting something that is important to you. Don't you think, Summoner?" his words were chased with a pointed look in Vanessa's direction and then a knowing smile splayed over Vice's lips. Leon looked embarrassed and said nothing as he let the male Dragonkin carry on about his task.

A few seconds later and they all piled into the room. Barrels were stacked all over the floors and were pushed up against the walls, there were crates filled with cloth or bottles, and there were trunks hidden between the rows of barrels with large locks keeping their treasures hidden. Further in, there were baskets with jewels, odd gold coins, or crowns spilling over the top of the heaps of glistening mounds. It wasn't until they reached a wall at the very end that they stopped. A small cubby space was built into the cobblestone wall with two large torches on either side. Vice lit them slowly as he spoke to everyone behind him.

"I never thought I'd ever bring anyone down here… again, at least. But I honestly never would have guessed that of all my treasures, this beauty would find a meaning outside of my growing collection."

His hands reached into the tiny space and when they emerged, they were cradling an intricately carved box. One of Vice's hands glided over the sides and top of the box as he traced the object into his memory. No dust coated the tiny treasure. "I found this buried beneath the rubble of the first Coven," he stated with his gaze fixed upon the box.

Everyone in the room widened their eyes to his comment. "That box had been under the building?" Leon remarked, loudly.

Vice nodded his head softly. "And I can't be for certain when it had been buried there, but I'm sure that it was around the time that the first Coven had started its construction."

"Outstanding," Bobo whispered. "To think that it could contain something that even the Coven thought needed protection is within the realm of possibilities." He took a few steps forward. "What is inside? Don't keep us all in waiting, my good sir."

The Dragonkin peeled his eyes off of the ornately engraved wooden container and shrugged his shoulders with a small chuckle trapped within his throat. "Oh. I wouldn't know. I could never open it," he admitted.

Everyone couldn't help but blink in astonishment. "But you've kept it so safe, and I can tell you've been taking care of it for as long as you've possessed it… how could you not have figured out how to open it?" Vanessa cried out.

Shrugging again, Vice sighed and patted the top of the object. "This thing, ever since I've found it, I've known that it held an important secret that was for me to keep and never to know. The spirit of the dragon deep within me can feel it. It plays across the cords of my being like a long-lost song. I was to guard and keep this treasure, but it would never be mine. There are some valuable items out there that not even a dragon can stake claim to without it tarnishing their soul. If it has a master, we must yield to it."

Leon, almost unsure of how to speak at first, asked, "Then why would you give it up now? Why give it to us?"

The Dragonkin let his eyes hold the treasure in his gaze the way you'd return from a long journey to a faithful lover. His smile was soft and warm as his hands searched every dip and curve of the wood. "It's like it's telling me, whispering that it is time to let go." He looked up to the group and held it out. "It's asking for you." His hands were outstretched to Vanessa and those surrounding nearby parted like they were opening up a path for her.

"Me?" she asked in quiet amazement.

Bobo rolled his eyes and laid a massive paw on the small of the witch's back and ushered her forward. "When a Dragonkin offers you a treasure from their hoard, you do not hesitate, my dear."

Lyx's sultry voice carried through the enclosed space. "He's right, ya know."

Hesitantly, Vanessa meandered over to Vice and gingerly took the box from his hands. With all eyes now on her, the witch felt a little uncomfortable under the limelight and hunched in on herself. "Uh, so…" Her orbs scanned the box as she flipped it over and then rattled it next to her ear. "What now?"

Vice looked like he was about to jump out of his skin when she rattled the carved item. "Could… I mean… Just be careful, would you?" he griped in a half-whine.

Waving her hand at him, Vanessa nodded repeatedly and said, "Don't worry. I've got this. I can get this bad boy open, no problem."

"Oh dear," Bobo stated in a hardly audible tone and looked to the rafters overhead. "Every nightmare starts with those words."

"What words?" Lyx whispered.

"Don't worry,'" Bobo informed the curious succubus.

Leon stifled a roaring laugh and pretended to cough into his elbow while Lyx slightly pursed her lips to the side as she gave a faint nod in agreement to her master. The demoness, however, recovered quickly from her internal thoughts and slapped at Leon's shoulder. "Hush up," she snipped.

Again, they all looked to Vanessa, but she was now a few feet away and was using one of the wine barrels as a table. She seemed to have been trying to open the box for quite some time with brute force and was now standing with her hands on her hips as she glared at it. "Maybe…" she said to herself while digging around in her assorted bags dangling around her hip.

A few plunges into a couple of pouches later, she was sprinkling a concoction of gold dust, will powder, white dust, and lizard tail herb over the top of the box while she chanted, "Loosen the grip, let go of your hold, let us see what you're keeping, and give up your treasures to the bold."

The spell sizzled and popped like a tiny firework show, and plumes of smoke billowed around both witch and treasure. Wheezing and fanning the growing clouds away, Vanessa quickly located the box and tried to open it. Again, to no avail. "What sort of sorcery is this?" she yelled heatedly.

"Let me give it a try," Leon announced, coming over beside her.

"Gladly," she grumbled, stepping off to the side to let him work.

Lyx, Vice, and Bobo all inched closer to watch the two work at opening the box. Curiously, they wondered what could be inside, and, also pondered over what could potentially open it up.

Two hours had come and gone and still the box remained unopened. Several frustrated faces loomed around the object. Vice was the first to speak to the sea of disgruntled beings surrounding the gift he had given to Vanessa. "I told you it wouldn't be easy to open."

"No, you didn't," she bit back at him.

"Oh, I didn't?" Vice looked off in thought and shrugged. "Well, I thought it. And you know what they say, it's the thought that counts."

Lyx knitted her brow and turned her attention to the male Dragonkin. "I don't think that's what that phrase means, darling."

He waved at her with a smirk before running his hand through his hair with a charming expression. "Of course it is," he stated overconfidently.

Bobo couldn't peel his eyes away from the Dragonkin and Leon leaned over to whisper, "What are you thinking?"

"I'm thinking," the ogre started, "that it's like seeing a male version of her." He thumbed dramatically over to Vanessa, and she was so focused on the box that she didn't take notice of *any* of the conversations that were going on around her.

Her hand snuck down to the belt strapping a small knife to her thigh and pulled the blade free. While everyone was lost in conversation, Vanessa was still bound and determined to get the box opened. One way or another. Touching the blade to the seam, she tried to wedge the flat end between and pry open the box.

Vice's eyes widened, and his tail pushed Lyx out of the way. "Don't do that!" he yelled. But it was too late.

The box started to jostle about in Vanessa's grasp, and the blade slipped, slicing open the tips of her fingers on the opposing hand. Instantly, Vanessa cried out in pain and dropped the knife. "What in the name of magic?" Leon spat and raced around the barrel to inspect her wound.

Embarrassed, Vanessa jerked her injured hand and turned away from him. Dropping blood over the top of the box as she waved it over the item in her attempt to get away from Leon, she tried to clamp down around the sliced skin. "I'm fine," she hissed in pain, clearly lying.

"No, you're not. Stop being a baby and let me see," Leon grumbled and reached for her hand. Yanking it back over to him, he attempted to inspect the wound, but the bright, blood orange light rays coming out from the box had regained everyone's attention.

Shielding his eyes, Bobo grunted in an annoyed tone, "Wonderful. She's managed to break it."

Vice couldn't stop grinning. "I wouldn't say that at all," he murmured.

All of them watched as the box shimmered while the light bleeding through intensified until it softly pulsed before dying off. The lid then made a sound as it popped open, and a wisp of cobalt-tinted smoke slowly trailed up out of the cracks. It was an ethereal, baby blue, swirled puff cloud with milky white light, and from it a tiny creature formed in midair. It cradled its knees to its chest. There was no sign of fingers, toes, or feet. Just points like someone had drawn a stick figure and filled it in until it was plump and cuddly. Wide, round, hollow eye sockets peered up at the group. Its oval-shaped head tilted to the side. Smoky tendrils and bubbles of magical light wafted around the tiny being. It blinked, and a small black mouth opened to yawn before it stretched out and came to stand upright.

"*Rrrggg*," it cooed.

"I want to keep it," Lyx whispered with a hand starting to reach out to touch it.

Leon slapped her appendage with a cross look spreading over his features.

The wisp did a flip in the air and made motions like it was giggling, but no sound escaped its inky mouth. Again, it looked them all over and fixed its eyes upon Vanessa. "*Qu'rrrggg*," it gurgled in its native tongue. Though, to everyone there, it sounded like nothing more than soft, garbled murmurs.

She blinked back with an expression that said how sorry she felt, as well as how confused. "I-I don't understand you," she admitted.

The wisp looked down. A nub reached up to touch its mouth while it seemed to take a moment to ponder. The silence stretched, and just when they thought it was all they'd receive, it spoke. "Did. Did it open the box?" the wisp asked in a tiny, meek voice.

Bobo exhaled loudly, making the wisp jump and look in the direction of the sound. Upon seeing the ogre, it turned into a cloud-like stream of glittering dust, and it swiftly slipped back inside the box that it had emerged from to hide.

"I was worried that I was going to have to brush up on my Wispin. I haven't touched that language in ages," Bobo mused.

Ignoring her pet, Vanessa dipped down and sweetly coaxed the creature out of hiding. "Come on. He isn't big and scary at all. Come on out. We won't hurt you. What were you trying to say?"

Leon looked to Vanessa and then to Bobo as he whispered, "You know, if she spoke like that to most of the people at the Coven, she might make a few friends." They both started to laugh until they heard a hiss and turned to see the narrowed golden gaze of a very cross succubus. They both coughed and cleared their throat while turning their attention back to Vanessa. All the while, they were quietly hoping that Lyx wouldn't think to use her whip on them.

"Come on, little fella. Come on out. I just want to talk," Vanessa continued to speak to the wisp.

"*Qu'ruu ru*," Bobo chirped, and the language made everyone turn to face the beast with a judgmental gaze. The ogre blushed lightly. "I taught myself one summer. The r's a bit difficult to manage, but I think I did all right remembering how to speak it."

Any comment that they were going to say was forgotten the minute they saw light coming from the box again. Its tiny arms pushed open the lid enough to peek out through a small crack and it eyed each one of them over. "No hurt?" it whispered questioningly.

She shook her head. "No. I won't hurt you. None of us will. Could you talk to me?" Vanessa asked. The wisp nodded, and the witch smiled warmly. "What were you doing in the box?"

The magic bubbles floated and popped around the wisp as it thought. Turning to inspect whatever lay within the confines of the box, the wisp seemed to think on whether or not it should answer. Facing her once more, it spoke through the safety of the box. "Guarding something," it said softly.

Inch by inch, Vice had tiptoed his way over to Vanessa's side and was now crouched down next to her like a mesmerized child at a puppet show. His tail was weaving and curling energetically behind him as his eyes were wide enough to be the same size as the wisp's head. "Guarding something, eh? What were you guarding?" he asked in a voice thick with curiosity.

The lid sunk down as if it were about to close again when the wisp noticed how quickly the new being was within touching distance. Again, the top gradually rose as the wisp regained a bit of courage. "I was guarding the secret. Only one can open the box," it said in a quieter tone.

Everyone's face came closer to hear it speak, and it froze with a small squeak. "Go on, little one. Who is the one you speak of? What are you guarding?" Bobo asked in a gentle voice.

Smoke-like swirls of light started to emit from the creature as the box lid was lifted a smidgen. "Its secrets. I wait for the special one—" As soon as it said the last word, a bright light engulfed the creature, and the box lid flung open. The wooden container and wisp both rose in the air as the light around it trickled out like water falling and disappeared into nothing but gold dust on the top of the barrel underneath.

Suddenly, the wisp's voice was booming and proud, reciting something that it had been enchanted to remember. "By the blood of the daughter, this box shall be unsealed. Not by water or fire or earth shall it be broken or harmed. When the spell is broken, she'll inherit the charm." The light dispersed and the wisp began to fall out of the air in a daze.

Without a second thought, Vanessa outstretched her arms and caught the spirit in her cupped hands. There, the tiny being shook its head and whirled in place for a moment. "Are you all right?" Vanessa asked concerned.

It nodded in reply.

"Strange," Bobo muttered to himself while he scrutinized the box that was still slowly lowering back to the barrel. All eyes strained to peer inside the teeny chest. Therein, a smooth stone with strange etchings rested at the bottom.

"A rock." Leon looked less than impressed at the findings.

Vice smirked and gave a small chuckle to himself. "Not everything that glitters is gold, and not all treasure shines, my boy. Not all treasure shines…" He reached forward to touch the rock and the wisp grunted angrily before springing out of Vanessa's hands and flew over to the Dragonkin's appendage. Latching on, the spiritual being gnawed at Vice's fingers aggressively. "Hey, hey, hey! Whoa there, little buddy. Calm down would ya? I was just going to look at it."

It spoke in its own language, "*Rrggg qrrrggg!*" Removing the flesh from its mouth, the wisp spoke in the gentlest angry voice Vanessa had ever heard in her life. "Not yours!" It bellowed protectively.

"All right. All right. I won't touch it, okay? So, you don't have to bite me anymore," Vice stated with a huff. Clearly, he was not thrilled about the fact that he couldn't touch what he had safeguarded for so long.

Vanessa stood up and leaned over the barrel, looking at the contents of the engraved box before slowly reaching out and plucking it from inside. It felt warm to the touch, and its surface was unnaturally smooth. Even the carving on the top seemed smooth, and the carvings themselves appeared almost too perfectly etched within the object. Flipping it over in her hand, she noted that the other side was not blank but had what appeared to be a map. "It's a map," she gasped.

"What in the hex?" Lyx yelled out and then jerked Vanessa's hand over toward her so that she could look at it without touching it. "Well. By the goddess, she's right. It is a map."

Everyone was so bewildered by the item that they didn't notice the wisp starting to fade away. Vice frowned and pet the top of the being's head. "You can sleep now. Your job is done," he assured.

Vanessa looked over her shoulder and pouted as she noticed the wisp swiftly fading. "Thank you for keeping it safe for me!" she cried out.

The last thing that they heard was the wisp saying, "*Qruggg.*" The sound was like a happy purr as the last remaining magic that made up its body faded into a pile of dust in Vice's hands.

A digit extended and a sigh soughed from the Dragonkin as he poked at the pile of gold dust in his open palm. "If no one should object, I'd like to keep this little guy's remains."

"I don't mind," Vanessa gently replied, and the whole room nodded their head as they silently agreed with the Spellweaver's decision.

"Is there anything else in the box?" Lyx asked. Leon peered over and then shook his head 'no.'

Bobo straightened out his tie and cleared his throat. "Vanessa, let me have a look at that, could you?" he asked.

Just then, overhead, the floorboards from the Flustered Dragon shook and a series of fancy footwork stomped over the space above. "Sounds like the last show of the night," Vice informed thoughtfully.

Bits of dust and dirt sprinkled through the cracks and fell all around the group, causing them to duck and cover their heads and move closer to the door they'd originally came through. Something darting behind a stack of crates caught Vanessa's attention. She stopped suddenly as she watched the pile of trunks and packages where she had last seen the movement.

Lyx looked from the girl to the corner she was fixated on. "What is it, darling?" she asked quietly with worry tugging at her features.

"Someone is in here," Bobo answered for the young witch while he reached for his battle-ax.

Vice looked around and started to say, "There couldn't possibly—" but he saw it then. A cloaked figure popped up from behind the pile of treasures and sprinted for the door. "Well... I'll be a witch's toad," he grumbled just as the door slammed shut and the lock sliding home sounded through the room.

"Oh no you don't," Vanessa muttered angrily. "Bobo!" she called out.

Bobo grunted as he ran. "Already on it, my dear!" he bellowed before smashing through the door like a wrecking ball. Wood sprayed out everywhere and chunks tumbled over the floor as splinters rained down around him.

Lyx made a sound and seemed like she was going to melt where she stood. "What an ogre," she mused, fanning at her face.

Leon pointed to a figure that had stopped to look back at them as the crash had unquestionably gained the culprit's attention. "There! Get them!" Leon ordered.

Sniffing the air, the Dragonkin recoiled and peeled back his lips, revealing a menacing display of teeth. Vice snarled, the sound like a reptilian tiger growling from the confines of the caves deep in the Red Tipped Mountains. "Careful. They are tainted!" he advised in a boisterous yell as the group piled out of the room.

Great. It was a black witch or wizard. If a single spell went off in the building, the space would have to be cleansed or the black magic would infect the whole building. There was a strange sound and then a plume of green smoke followed by a wave of magical backblast.

"Watch out," Bobo roared as he grabbed Vanessa and Leon and threw them behind a wall for cover. Lyx grabbed Vice and dove behind a few crates of apples stored in the cellar.

"Banish a banshee, Vice, you're going to need to call in a cleanser," Leon barked and then peered around the corner.

Vice coughed and choked as he tried to sit back up. "I'll get right on that. I won't have black magic putting my baby out of business," he said and searched for an orb. "You guys hurry and catch them. I'm calling in for a cleanser now!"

Lyx ran over to them. "It was a teleportation spell!"

There was no time. They needed to pinpoint the caster's location before the spell's residual imprint faded. Pocketing the rock in her spelled satchel, Vanessa then dipped her fingers into will powder and then threw it out at the steps. "Leon," she said his name and held out her hand. Without question, he took it. Bobo knew that this was going to be a spell that was going to test the witch's abilities, so he took her free hand and poured every bit of his thoughts into acting like a magical conduit for the incantation.

The sound of Vanessa's chant prickled in the air with a hum of power. "Their magic aided them in their flee and hidden their location from me; show me what is veiled and unknown, show me where they have flown."

Crackling magic spread out like stretching ivy searching for a trunk to claim. It wove its way through the air that they had last seen the perpetrator, and the lines of magic dove deep into the space between the seen and the unseen. A seam was ripped in the remains of the black magic, and a portal was revealed. It wouldn't remain open for long, and the spell was empowered by the three of them to the point that they didn't have to keep holding hands. They just had to keep their concentration on each other in order for them to jump through the portal and come out in the same area.

"Quickly, before we lose them," Vanessa ordered everyone. And they all raced for the opening without a second thought.

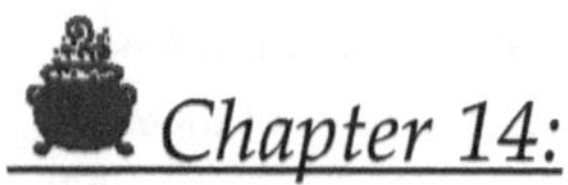 *Chapter 14:*

One by one, they all piled through the other side of the portal that dumped them out into a vast meadow. Dingy, goldenrod grass arched over the field, bowing their flowered heads to the muddy ground below. Dusk had splayed sharp pinks and oranges over the horizon that bled into murky purples and blues with whispers of stars twinkling across the deeper shades. Trees were in the distance and swayed in the faint breeze as they blackened under the darkening sky.

Vanessa turned around and focused on trying to spot the cloaked figure as Bobo and Leon passed through the magic that forced the previous teleportation spell open. The gateway crackled and the spell diminished, leaving without a trace behind them.

"Wait," Leon stated in a gasp. He spun around for a moment and then balled up his fists in frustration. "Where is Lyx?"

Vanessa spun around, confusion knitting her brow. "Didn't you concentrate on her when you passed through?"

"Does it look like I did?" he snapped and motioned aggressively to the empty space around him that was very much lacking a certain succubus.

Bobo clamped his hands down on Leon's shoulders and spun the Summoner around to face his serious expression. There was a moment of silence before the ogre quickly drew Leon into a tight hug, to the point that the man could hardly breathe. Instantly, the demon pulled Leon away from his embrace and shook his shoulders lightly as he said, "You don't know the service that you've done for me this day. I owe you. On my word, I shall grant you whatever favor that you ask of me in the future."

Vanessa rolled her eyes and resumed scanning the darkness for the cloaked figure. "Shhh," she snipped. "They couldn't have gone far," she stated. With her comment alone she was trying to remind them why they were there.

The haunting quiet that they received was deafening. A moment ticked by before Leon came to Vanessa's side and whispered to her, "Check the ground for footprints."

Still wet from recently melted snow, the ground could have easily picked up the being's tracks. Nodding, she pulled out her wand—the only weapon she had on her since she left her staff back at the house along with her insignia—and spoke an invocation. Her mouth blew a faint breeze as she over annunciated a few of the words. "With this whisper, I light my way." The tip of the wand had a glittering light sparkling from the tip, and she held it low as she gently waved it from side to side over the soggy ground below.

Meanwhile, Bobo scanned the darkness to see if the perpetrator would try to make a run for it while his master used the light spell. He was met with stillness and shadows. His eyes narrowed. "Something isn't right," he whispered to the other two.

They could feel it as well. It was like there was an electric charge lingering in the air. It was almost palpable. Continuing to sweep the wand from side to side, Vanessa scavenged for the fresh set of footprints that would allow her and the others to catch up to the person that had been in the cellar. At first, it was just strange that they had been watched, but after the black magic spell went off, there was no way that they could let the perpetrator go. They put multiple innocent bodies at risk when they cast the dark spell in the basement. Thankfully, there was some space between the magic and those still enjoying the last show of the night upstairs. Still, one had to wonder what they were doing following them down there and lurking in the shadows.

"Do you think they were after the box that Vice gave you?" Leon whispered as he had his own light spell glowing over the ground a few feet away.

Vanessa looked confused. "What? Why wouldn't they be down there for the heaps of treasure?" She sounded irritated like it should have already been known why the being had followed them down into the basement to start with.

It was Bobo's turn to bring to light a morsel of information. "They didn't seem to care about anything else in there except for what you had."

"Almost like they were trying to listen in to what the wisp or the rest of us were saying about the artifact that you had," Leon added.

She thought about what they were saying, and it did seem like a legitimate reason. Why else would they not have tried to hide so they could steal what was down there or snag some priceless piece before making a run for it? They were clearly sticking around trying to hear what was going on, right? But why?

"Over here!" Bobo called and then pointed toward the tree line. "They headed northeast."

"Come on," Vanessa commanded in a hushed tone and darted off in that direction, all while trying to keep an eye on the footprints to make sure they didn't shift in direction. Leon was close behind with a magic-seeking talisman out, making sure that whoever this was, they didn't make another leap in order to escape.

There were faint sounds of crickets chirping their lazy song through the chilled night. Even though spring was around the corner, the nights, on occasion, still frosted the ground with winter's goodbye kiss. Tonight was no different. Though it wasn't cold enough to freeze the sloshed-up ground below, it was still cold enough for Vanessa and the others to see their breath as they ran in pursuit of the black witch or warlock.

Wispy puffs of soft gray surrounded their heads as they panted while running for the tree line. But as they ran, not a single pair of eyes saw the culprit weaving through the trees. It was like the perpetrator had vanished into thin air. It didn't stop them from searching as they slowed in their approach.

Bobo had reduced his footwork into a languid trot as he scanned the area with a tightknit brow. "Something is still off," he mentioned again.

Leon replied, "Yeah. It's like there is something in the air and it's just getting stronger as we head in this direction." He paused while thinking to himself. "Vanessa. Don't get too far away," he called after her.

"I'll be fine. Just keep up," she said hoarsely. "I'm not a child."

Grumbling, Bobo added beneath his breath, "Could have fooled me."

Leon ignored the ogre's comment and shot out in a quiet hiss, "It has nothing to do with us treating you like a child. We can't protect each other if you are out of our spell's reach, and if you are out of sight. Just … stop being such a stubborn, proud witch that runs around acting like she doesn't need anybody."

She stopped and turned around with her jaw unhinged in flabbergasted awe. "I do not act like that."

Bobo caught up with her first and stated in a low tone, "Don't try to deny it. We'll be here all night if he chooses to start listing the mountain of evidence against you, and I'd rather like to make it home before the morning hours."

She scoffed, Bobo laughed, and Leon lurched forward to grab both of them by their clothing and jerk them back before they headed through a collection of bushes.

"I say, dear boy. Why the sudden tug?" Bobo griped, brushing off the wrinkles on his suit jacket.

Vanessa was slapping the Summoner's hand away like it was the most annoying thing on Raen. "What's the big deal?" Her voice sounded as cross as the look plastered to her face, and it was angrily fixed on him.

Quickly and silently, he planted a finger in front of his lips. His brow furrowed in annoyance and then pointed to the clearing beyond the bushes that the two had gotten ready to pass through. There, on the other side—and much to their disbelief—stood guard three beings that made Bobo look on the small side.

Gargoyles.

They were enormous creatures with stony hides and wingspans that could blot out the sun. They had big, bat-like ears protruding from the sides of their skulls, and their large, yellow eyes were scanning the surrounding forest for intruders. Their muscle looked like it had been chiseled from a massive stone and it rippled over their arms, legs, backs, and abdomens in a display that would make even the greatest of bodybuilders pale in comparison. Stone, talon-tipped toes sunk into the mud-caked patches of grass underfoot. Each one looked like they were just what they appeared to be—stone statues—but it was the faint rise and fall of their chests, the shifting of their yellow eyes, and the occasional twitching of their clawed hands that alluded to the life that stirred beneath the hard surface.

Suppressing a gasp, Vanessa covered her mouth and flattened herself against Leon, forcing him to become a pancake against the tree they sought refuge behind. "Gar-gar—," she took a moment to swallow hard before attempting to squeak out in a hardly audible tone, "Gargoyles."

Bobo peered around the trunk of the tree and sneered at the beasts. "It would appear so, my dear."

They all sat quietly for a moment. Tapping Vanessa on the shoulder with insistence, Leon looked like he was dying to fill his starved lungs. She scrambled away with a half-apologetic glance in his direction.

Recovering quickly, Leon made motion to the creatures. "There's no way we can take on those things," he rasped, his voice sounding like paper tearing.

"I don't think that the black practitioner even came this way. If they did, I doubt they are part of the land of the living anymore," Vanessa stated while trying to watch the three creatures. Her eyes narrowed, and she scooted a little closer. "Hold the crystal ball," she grumbled. A slender finger pointed out to the other two something on the ground. There, under the feet of the granite giants, was a summoning circle.

"You've got to be kidding me. Is that what I think it is?" she asked.

"What is it?" Leon hissed trying to see over the foliage.

Bobo saw it first and sighed unhappily. "They didn't kill the practitioner… they were summoned by them."

"Ugh," Leon groaned hoarsely and threw his back into the tree. "That's why the air was so charged when we got here," he noted with understanding. "Not because of the teleportation spell but because he summoned those things."

Bobo and Vanessa could only nod quietly. Any chance of pursuing the culprit was going to end in death or heavy maiming. Neither an outcome Vanessa was willing to achieve. For once, the witch thought a tactful retreat would be better than risking life and limb on an endeavor that would wind up with them all six feet under.

"We should head back before they spot us," she advised, remembering every academy professor stating that gargoyles were highly territorial and would kill upon sight. Only two things to do: (a) run until they reached a point that they are deemed out of the line of their territory and (b) try to hide. But above all, don't get caught, because being caught would unmistakably result in death.

Weighing their options carefully, they nixed the plan on an evening run and started to turn to head out of the woods. Vanessa led them away while internally patting herself on the back for sidestepping danger for once in her life.

Without warning, Bobo slammed a hand down on Vanessa's back, pushing her face-first into the mud. Twisting at the last possible second—and feeling the layers of fabric clinging to her backside become soaked in muddy water—she landed flat on her back. She had a split second to view the stars that took the sky captive, the pale glow of the moon that remained half-hidden by the canopy of ageless trees nearby, and a blazing firebolt zip by a mere foot from her face.

Wide-eyed and confused, she rose up, feeling heavier with the mucky, waterlogged cloak dragging behind her. Bobo already had his ax pulled out and was scanning the area, but not a moment after the shadowy culprit dipped back behind a collection of trees, there was a tremendous roar piercing the air. Heavy wings flapped, causing the bushes and grass to sway and bend in its wake.

"Looks like the quiet retreat is a bust," Leon griped.

Just then, from behind them, one of the gargoyles darted up into the sky and then looped around, aiming for the ground below. As the being landed, they could all feel their legs rumble as the quake from the impact shook the ground. Effectively, it had managed to cut off their escape route in one fell swoop. Another gargoyle broke through the trees, and that was when the group realized that it wouldn't be long before the third would be in hot pursuit as well.

"By the goddess…RUN!" Vanessa cried, and they all turned and fled for the only open space not harboring a threat.

Leon stopped to fling a few spells, but Bobo plucked him up and tucked the man under his arm without breaking a sweat. "As much as… I admire… your bravery… I think we best… focus on… getting the hex away," the ogre informed between panting breaths.

"You're crazier than me! Stopping to fling spells at a trio of gargoyles. Do you have a death wish?" she barked and dove through the thick foliage of the forest.

"Oh, come on now!" Leon snipped while being jostled about in the demon's grasp as the hefty creature hurdled over a fallen tree. "No one is *that* insane."

She cut him a look that promised she'd spell his mouth shut if he said another word, but the sounds of the gargoyles plowing through the trees like they were toothpicks tore her vision from him to assess the dangers behind them.

In the distance, she could see the creatures breaking limbs like they were twigs and shredding through the bushes and vines like they were paper. She gulped and turned her attention back to her footing. "Not good," she squeaked and then heard one of the stone beasts take to the sky. "They are in the air, Bobo!"

"I'm thinking, woman. I'm thinking," the ogre hissed.

"I have legs you know," Leon reminded in an aggravated, sing-song tone. "I can run on my own."

Without breaking stride, Bobo set the man upright, kept hold of the Summoner's upper arm, and let Leon catch up to speed before letting him go. "We just need to get far enough away that they'll no longer see us as a threat," Leon tried to remind them in hopes to calm them, but the howling that echoed through the night air shattered those hopes in an instant. "Or, you know, we could panic. I rather like that idea," Leon confessed with a gulp.

"No. You're right," Vanessa said.

"I am? I mean… of course, I am." The look that came over Leon's face as he tried to appear confident made Vanessa smirk despite the life-threatening situation they were all in.

Her eyes tried to look through the darkness, but the moonlight provided little light through the thick branches and dense needles of the trees. There was another howl and her skin crawled. "Wait, Leon! Do you have any light runes?"

"Light runes?" he asked perplexed and ducked beneath a low hanging branch. A second later, understanding registered. "You're going to do a solar flare spell." He sounded elated at the prospect of a plan.

Grunting as she hurdled over a patch of briars and slammed into a tree, she paused to catch her breath. "Not if you don't give me the runestone," she huffed while pushing off of the trunk and racing around the tree and instantly tripped over a thick root sticking up out of the ground. Stumbling forward through the underbrush with no grace, she tried to regain her footing as quickly as possible.

Overhead, there was another howl and a stone spike impaled the tree where Vanessa's head was a moment before she failed in righting herself and plummeted to the ground. The sound of projectiles thrusting at high-speed through the air ripped through the night, and then a series of spikes pummeled the ground, staking a path right for the frightened witch. Frantically, she crawled over the leaf-caked floor as she came to her feet and ran for the cover behind a thick tree. The rapid succession of stone sinking deep into the wood of the tree vibrated through the trunk and thrummed over Vanessa's spine. Wearily, she peeked her head out from behind her hiding spot and examined the damage with a grimace. "Leeeooon," she called in a worrisome tone.

From a few trees away, she heard him reply, "I'm working on it, okay?"

A large mass crashed through the canopy. Twigs, bark, and needles rained down on her, assaulting her relentlessly and skewing her vision of the gargoyle rushing down for her at a breakneck speed.

Double-dip a candlestick!

Her breath caught in her throat as she felt the need to run slam throughout her nervous system and made her heart leap in her chest before slamming down into the pit of her stomach. A high-pitch howl rang in her ears until she felt them pop. Scrambling as she turned around, Vanessa—in a panic—followed her instinct and made a run for it. Another core-rattling cry from the beast fast on her heels gave her indication of how close it was. She could feel the energy bouncing off of her like waves of chaotic magic—a type of energy that consumed a caster rather than power controlled by one.

In a frantic need to survive, Vanessa dove forward toward the ground and tried to shield her fall by catching herself on her hands. A small, broken tree stump slammed through her palm and poked through the other side. The white-hot pain blasted through her appendage before she felt the warmth of her blood rushing to coat her skin. The scent of copper clung to the air. She managed to bite down on her lip to silence her wail of pain, but a muffled cry hampered by the back of her teeth still pierced the wooded area. A split-second later she felt the air of the gargoyle as it flew inches away from her form. Its talon reached out to graze against her body. The sharp, stony claw raced like a razor blade over her back. Her cape was slashed, the garment beneath it hardly stood a chance, and the skin below that wasn't any better. As soon as the gash appeared, Vanessa cried out in anguish while the creature pulled up and looped around in the air and weaved through the trees as it came back to finish the job.

Jerking her hand free of the trunk she had impaled herself on, she grunted in pain and threw herself out of the beast's path. "Leon!" she yelled, but there wasn't a reply.

Panting, she listened to the stillness that had suddenly descended down upon the forest. Pulling out her wand, she winced in pain and pointed the tip at her injured hand. Blood had turned it a deep crimson that bordered along black, and she felt lightheaded just looking at it. Licking her dry lips, she steadied her breathing as she ignored the sweat running down her brow and dripping off her chin. Concentrating as best she could, she tried to think of the spell, but her mind drew a blank on all healing spells. In a panic, she whispered, "Scorch mark!" It was typically a spell used for wood burning art or ways to mark bone runes, but, today, it was a method for cauterizing her wound. The smell of burning flesh assaulted her nostrils as her skin sizzled, and heat flared deep into the wound. She writhed against the trunk of the tree, feeling its rough surface scratch and irritate the long gash on her back. There was no way she could reach it to heal it even if she did remember a healing spell. The edges of the inflicted area pulsed with fiery pain and the ridged gash itched with a dull heat. Bending forward, Vanessa fought past the urge to hurl as her head swam in sick pain.

With each breath, slowly, the feeling ebbed.

She lightly leaned back against the tree and scanned the woods. Hazel hues relentlessly searched the shadowed foliage for the gargoyles. The sound of tree bark cracking under the pressure of a tight grip came from over-head, and the cruel melody of long nails sinking into wood played over the cords of her nerves. The fearful song drove her heartbeat to trip over itself as the tempo became chaotically unrhythmic.

A low, guttural snarl made the witch and her heartbeat freeze in place while bits of bark pebbled her neck and shoulders. Hot tears pricked her eyes and blurred her vision. *"Banish a banshee, I'm not going to cry,"* she told herself between gritted teeth. Just as the creature howled, its hand reached around the trunk and slashed its hooked fingertips through the air. At the last second, Vanessa dove toward the beast, dodging the attack and putting her face to face with its yellow eyes and stony head. The jaw unhinged as it lurched forward, and she jerked to the side, slammed into another tree, hit the ground, scrambled to her feet, and took off running. All the while, she could feel the blood gradually streaming down her back and starting to soak her britches.

From behind her, the Spellweaver could hear the creature tumble through the leaves before quickly correcting itself and rushing in her direction. Her limbs burned with fatigue, and her body flared with heat. Her lungs felt like they were breathing in sandpaper as each inhale scraped over her throat. She didn't know how much more her body could endure before it would just give up on her.

Thunk!

The enormous, thick body slammed into the ground unexpectedly, and a deep roar pierced through the night. Turning on heel, she saw Bobo on the gargoyle's back and his ax braced under the creature's neck, choking it while his legs straddled the beast's abdomen. It flopped and flailed as it tried to take flight, but it wasn't going anywhere with Bobo's weight anchoring it down.

The ogre's ocean blue eyes rose to look at his master, "You fool! Go!"

Her heart ached as she watched her pet intercept to save her. She wouldn't leave him behind. All of a sudden, Vanessa was jerked to the side, and she screamed out in fright. Without thinking, she balled up her fist and threw a punch. Much to her surprise, she didn't land a hit onto a humanoid bolder, but—instead—it met its mark on a soft-skinned meat-bag.

"Hex it all, Vanessa, it's me!" croaked Leon in pain.

Cringing, she tried to reach out to the side of his face that was already starting to swell up. "Sorry," she whispered apologetically.

"Don't be. If you can punch like that, I'm the one that's sorry for your future husband. I was hoping you had at least one soft bone in your bo—" Leon started.

Cutting him off by slapping his chest, Vanessa yelled hoarsely, "This is hardly the time for your jokes, Leon."

"Right," he admitted.

Holding out her hand expectantly, Leon dropped the rune in her awaiting appendage. Holding a chiseled stone never felt so good. Double-checking the rune, she made sure that it had the simple sun-like drawing etched onto its surface. As she inspected it, Bobo's strained voice carried through the woods, "Are you daft, woman? Run! Don't worry about me."

Again, she felt hurt piercing her heart. Sure, she was used to the jokes about her incompetence, and yeah, she was used to the cracks about her messing up spells and her knack for getting in trouble, but after all these years she had yet to master getting a tough enough skin to handle her own crippling self-doubt and her ghastly ability to verbally cut herself down. But the fact that Bobo thought that she was selfish enough to leave him behind to battle this on his own shadowed any internal berating that she could deliver herself. Her fingers curled around the rune stone as she searched through her pouches.

"I'm not leaving you, Botobolbilian!" She meant every word of it. After all they had been through, she wasn't going to leave him behind to save her own skin. She might be a lot of things, but a selfish coward wasn't one of them.

A screech pealed from up above, and all three of them directed their attention to the swaying branches overhead. The second gargoyle located them and darted up into the night sky before it changed direction and swan dived for the forest floor. There wasn't enough time. She looked at the rune in her one hand, and she fumbled the dust as she tried not to drop the wand she had cradled in her fingers. Sucking in a quick breath, she tried to quell her fears as she focused on the spell at a speed that astonished even her.

"When the night's moon does not glow, shine for me and let it show, bring the beams and let the shadows be undone, by your light like a flare from the sun!" The rock warmed in her hand. She could hear Bobo growl as he prepared for the impact from the second gargoyle as he struggled with the first. "Bobo, move!" she ordered. Vanessa turned her head from the light, unable to shield her eyes from the piercing rays that emitted from her hands as the spell took over.

Darkness graced her vision as Leon drew her head toward him and held her against his chest to shield her eyes from the storm of white overtaking the forest. He growled while shielding his own eyes with his free arm from the onslaught of powerful illumination. Hisses of pain filled the air as the gargoyles met with their impending demise. As the blinding white raced through the surrounding area, shadows were swallowed up and there was no place for darkness to hide. It was like day had visited the night. Every inch of the creatures that were once covered in stone instantly charred into black like they were being burned from the inside out. Bits and pieces crumbled off of their bodies until there was nothing left of them but a pile of rubble and gray sand.

The light from the evocation sputtered and then halted, the rock dropping back down into Vanessa's hand with the symbol etching now gone. She pocketed the item in her rune pouch. When, and if, they made it back to Tolvade in one piece, she'd visit a local runesmith and get the etch mark reapplied for Leon.

Hearing the sophisticated ogre coughing brought Vanessa back to reality. Racing over to his side, she ignored the blooming pain that consumed her spine as she hit the ground next to him and inspected the demon carefully. Scratches covered his body, but none were too profound. Thankfully, even though they had claws like a sphinx, none of his wounds were deep.

"How you look like you were only scratched up by an owlcat instead of a gargoyle, I'll never know. But I'm glad that you're okay, Bobo," Vanessa expressed before crashing into the ogre's chest.

Bobo hugged her back tightly. "They are all from briars and unforgiving branches, I assure you, my dear," Bobo admitted with a soft smile while hugging the young witch in return.

Leon coughed and they both turned to note the Summoner's presence. Quickly pulling away from each other, Bobo sputtered and coughed before patting Vanessa's head awkwardly. "Good job on not getting yourself killed. The gold star is awarded to you. I shall purchase you some cheap trinket when we return for your grand efforts."

"You mean thanks for saving your hide with that spell?" she corrected.

"Speaking of hide," Leon stated, gaining her attention. "I spelled him with a dragonhide spell. It wouldn't stop anything, but it would help if he got close to one of them. And we were trying to catch up to you… that's what took us so long."

Impressed, Vanessa nodded. "Good thinking," she said with an approving smile.

With a chuckle, Leon brought to light her own quick thinking. "You weren't too bad yourself. That was pretty crafty of you, using a solar flare spell to recreate sunlight. I'd almost forgotten it is one of the few things that can actually do any real damage to a gargoyle."

"Indeed," Bobo chimed in. "However, I'd suggest we get a move on before their friend catches up with us."

"You didn't lose it?" Vanessa asked.

"Well, I'm not willing to linger to find out if we did or not," Leon said while holding out his hand to help Vanessa up.

When their gazes met, Vanessa grinned and then froze in mid-motion when she noticed something dark lurking within the forest. Her eyes trailed ever so slightly to the side and remained fixed on *something* that drained all the color from her face. Bobo's hand was immediately gripping the battle-ax without mercy as he, too, stared off behind Leon.

"It's behind me, isn't it?" he inquired lifelessly.

Turning slowly, he was greeted by a dark, hulking form. A towering wolf the size of a small, one-story hovel glared at them with piercing gold eyes. It easily dwarfed the trio as it slowly stalked closer to them. Its glossy coat mirrored a starless sky at twilight, and its claws were as if they'd been dipped in oil. The fur bristled along its back in warning. Glistening, white fangs dripping with saliva were bared aggressively in their direction. Their newfound victory was obliterated in the shadow of this beast.

"I think I'd prefer the gargoyle," Leon whispered.

Vanessa fought past the fear that strangled her voice and managed to squeeze out, "What do we do?"

With a nasally snort, Bobo grunted in reply, "Well, my dear, I wouldn't suggest petting it and calling him Fluffy Bottom the Third."

Noting the eerie silence that draped the forest, Vanessa turned her head gradually to one side and then the other. "Well, this thing would definitely explain why the third gargoyle didn't attack…" But she berated herself inwardly for the spell that she had cast at the gargoyles. She had saved them from one danger only to call forth another foe with the blasted solar flare spell.

"Snap out of it, Vanessa," Bobo hissed, knowing that his master was lost in her own mind. "To the right. Do you see it?" Bobo asked them both in a hardly audible tone.

They dared not move more as they traced the area with their eyes. Nothing but thick trees, thorny brush, and thinned out bushes filled their vision. But at the last moment Vanessa saw it. Cascading down jagged rocks were a series of twisting roots that flowed over a small ledge. A tiny stream of water trickled over the mossy, vine-like wood as it crawled up the rocky shelf. Within its twisted roots, it cradled a deep opening beneath the trunk of the elder tree. A smaller, and very dead, sapling was nestled within the winding gnarled fingers of the ancient tree and marked the opening to the cavern.

As they noticed what the ogre spoke of, Bobo informed quickly and quietly, "I don't know how deep it is, but, at the moment, it's our best shot at safety."

They all agreed. But the real trick was evading the giant wolf. A thing of legend. A thing that should not exist. And, this thing that should not be, was glaring at them all. It alone confirmed one very important detail.

They were in the Black Forest.

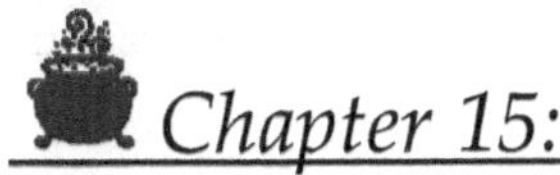 *Chapter 15:*

There wasn't time to make a plan. The only course of action was quick battle spells and—if luck permitted them to—a flash spell to blind the wolf. Doing so would enable their much-needed escape to be all the more successful.

Darting her eyes between the two at her side, she gripped her wand and prepared to dip her hand into a pouch at her hip. Every nerve was singing with fear. One quick move and the wolf would pounce and devour them all like they were nothing. The beast snarled and jolted in place as it gave a short, deep, and guttural bark. Together, Vanessa and Leon flung a bolt of magic at the creature's face. The spells connected flawlessly and the giant animal was stunned in mid-attack. Yelping out in pain, the wolf brushed the remains of the spell from its snout with its paw as Vanessa dipped her hand into a pouch. Removing a pinch of will powder, she raised her closed fist to her mouth as she concentrated and yelled, "Blind!" before tossing the spell at the wolf just as it came out of its daze.

It couldn't even run more than a few feet before it crashed into a tree. The weight of the large animal slamming into the object caused the base of the trunk to snap and splintering wood creaked through the forest while it started to fall toward Bobo, Leon, and Vanessa. Not waiting for a second longer, they darted off for the cave and to escape the deadly falling lumber.

The wolf staggered behind, the short-lived blind spell starting to lift, but not enough for it to see more than blurred movements between shadowed lumps of collected shrubbery and rows of trees.

At the bottom of the roots that dangled from the ledge, Bobo slid to a stop and turned around with his arms and hands outstretched awaiting Vanessa and Leon. "Leon first. Then pull up

Vanessa when I toss her to you!" The man leaped into Bobo's waiting grasp and, as if the Summoner weighed no more than a sack of potatoes, he was thrown through the air.

Yelling out in fear as he started to plummet back down, Leon flailed as he tried to grab hold of the roots that snaked over the ledge. "Hnfff," air escaped his lungs as he made contact with the hard surface a bit harder than he had anticipated. Gasping for air, he gulped wildly to fill his lungs all while trying to keep his grasp on what little holding he had. His nails bit into the wood and he hoisted himself up. Turning around, he called down to Bobo. "All right!"

The ogre looked down and put his hands gently around Vanessa's waist. Her hands instantly covered his as the wolf shook its head in the distance and sighted them fully. Angrily, the beast snarled at the soon-to-be victims.

"What about you?" Vanessa asked gripping his hands.

"It's my job to protect you. You meddlesome thing," he tried to joke, but the tears misting in his eyes made her open her mouth to tell him to wait. That she would find a way for both of them to get out safely, but Bobo would have none of it. One moment she was safe and sound on the ground, and the next she was flying through the air. Vanessa screamed out of impulse and looked down at Bobo, and a deep frown set on her mouth as she watched the ogre prepare to stand his ground.

Leon dove his hands out over the ledge and grasped her arms before pulling her in. Seconds later, she landed on top of him with a grunt of pain. Clambering over the Summoner, she raced over to the edge. The wolf was too big; its pursuit was more of a lumbering sprint through the heavily dense forest.

"Dust. I need dust," she frantically patted her person down and located more will powder.

A bolt of blue darted out from behind her.

And then another.

And another.

Leon assaulted the creature with a barrage of orbs. Some connected with the animal, making it growl in annoyance or yelp in pain. Others smashed into trees before exploding, the burst of light causing minor setbacks that equated to fractions of a second. But it was enough. Anything was better than nothing. Grabbing gold dust in her free hand, she held her arms out to either side as the giant, black wolf lunged into the air. His jowls open, ready to devour, and its golden hues fixated on the battle-ax-bearing Bobo.

Narrowing her eyes at the creature, Vanessa inhaled and felt a swarm of warmth prickle across her skin. She wanted nothing more than to protect, and that thought rang out like a bell in her heart.

But would it be enough?

"Shockwave!" Both hands swept through the air and she clapped her hands together. The two opposing dusts collided into one another and the clap of her hands intensified like a tangible sound wave. A blast of magic emitted from her, throwing her back into Leon who caught her as she was flung back by the force of the spell. The wolf yipped as it was tossed into the forest. It went crashing through a few thick saplings before slamming into the ground below. There was the sick snapping sound of bones breaking and a long-winded howl of anguish ripped out of the beast's throat. Whimpering, the wolf rose and sniffed at its body, lapped its tongue over its side, and then retreated deeper into the forest with its mournful cry clinging unnervingly to the void of the night.

Vanessa groaned as she felt her backside throb with pain. Her spine felt like it was on fire and it hurt to breathe. But the warmth from Leon eased some of the tension out of her shoulders and limbs.

Leon's mouth was close enough that she could feel his breath playing over her neck and ear as he asked, "Are you okay?" Her body involuntarily shivered and the action tore a moan of discomfort from her mouth. "Where are you hurt?" he asked, his words breathily grazing over her again.

"Stop talking!" she burst in a strained voice. It took everything in her not to rip out of his grasp, but the adrenaline was fading out of her system and the throbbing ache that emitted from the slice along her spine was excruciating, and her injured hand wasn't much better off. To make matters worse, her body felt unusually heavy.

Had she used too much of her magic?

Just then, a sophisticated voice traveled from the ledge. One giant hand grasped desperately to the knotted webbing of the elder tree that snaked over the rocky floor before rushing over the edge like a waterfall of roots. "No, no. Don't worry about me. I only stared…" he paused and grunted while pulling himself up. "…down the face of my own demise and managed to survive by the grace of the goddess and my good fortune." He huffed and pulled himself up chest high to the ledge and lay over it to rest before he'd resume his clambering up the stone facing. His blue eyes scanned the area and landed on Vanessa resting in Leon's lap.

The ogre blinked astonished and turned a bit pink in the cheeks. "I mean… I realize that we've encountered many close death experiences in the last hour, but… don't you think that now isn't quite the time—"

Not caring about the pain that flared throughout her back as she threw herself off of Leon's lap, Vanessa scooted away while shrieking out, "It isn't like that!" However, there was more pain than there was defense latching onto her words.

"Well," Bobo started. "In that case, you won't mind lending me a hand, my dear man?"

Rushing over, Leon spoke as he went to aid the demon. "Sorry about that, big guy. That blast really did a number on us."

"I'll say," Bobo grumbled.

"That reminds me." Leon turned to face Vanessa. "What the hex did you do back there?"

Vanessa looked lost and defensively snapped back, "What? What did I do now?"

"Ah. She finally has realized that she is accident-prone and a magnet for trouble. There is hope still yet," Bobo clipped sarcastically.

Shooting him a look that held the same heat as a forge, Vanessa pursed her lips and, with a look, dared the ogre to make another snide remark. Dialing down her anger, she turned her attention back to Leon waiting for him to answer her.

He instantly pointed out to the forest floor beyond, where they had stood when they attacked the gargoyles. "That solar flare spell was three times more powerful than what it should have been and," his finger jutted down, the digit indicating where she stood during the second spell, "that shockwave spell was equally overpowered. What did you do?"

Both males faced Vanessa expecting an answer. Their inquisitive stares burrowing deep into her and she squirmed under their scrutinizing gazes. "I-I don't know," she admitted in a hasty, high-pitched whine. "I just cast the spell. So it was overpowered, what's the big deal?" She gestured toward Bobo, "It's not like I have never done something both powerful and out of the ordinary before."

Though her statement was true, even she didn't believe what she said. Ever since the fight between the blue cloaks had broken out and she turned all golden, glowing, and mega-powerful, she had felt a shift in her spiritually. It was like a flood gate had been opened that day and when the connection to … whatever that was, was severed, she hadn't really closed the gate all the way. It was left cracked, and she could occasionally feel the power trickle out of her bit by bit, overtaking everything from simple spells to the enchantments she had performed all evening. But she could never seem to call upon it like she had that day.

"Did you figure out how to tap into that power?" Leon asked flatly.

Her mouth opened and closed as her mind floundered for a response. "No?"

Leon's gaze narrowed. "Vanessa," her name was said with a thread of warning lining the Summoner's voice.

She sighed heavily. "Look, all I know is I was scared out of my mind and wanted nothing more than to protect the two of you," she shot out in a huff. "That's all I know that I did differently. I've been trying for weeks to see if I can tap into it again and I come up empty-handed and my spells lacking the extra boost," she stated and threw her hands in the air, only to instantly wish she hadn't. Wincing in pain, Vanessa doubled over and then regretted that move as well. She stiffened her back straight as she screwed her eyes shut and rode the waves of agony that raced up and down her spine. Warm liquid trailed down her back under the shredded clothing that held its shape by a few threads that weren't going to last for much longer. Her head swam in a dizzy spell and she felt like she was going to get sick as her stomach clenched in painful knots while she tried to steady her breathing.

In a panic, Leon rushed over to her and caught her as she swayed in place. The moment his hands were on her, she flinched and started to scoot away from his grasp. Pain was evident in the man's face as she did so.

"Am I really that repulsive to you?" he snapped in a low, harsh tone.

She blinked and looked back at him confused. "What?" she breathed the question.

He motioned to her. "You flinch whenever I'm near you and even when I try to help you recoil. I get it. You don't like me like… romantically and all, but if being your friend is even hard for you then, just say it."

She searched his face trying to figure him out like he was suddenly Raen's most complicated math problem. "I don't …" her face felt hot. "I don't dislike you," she practically croaked out the words.

"You sure have a funny way of showing me that," he grumbled.

It was her turn to narrow her eyes at him. "I don't know what you're talking about. But you sure do assume a lot for someone that never put themselves out there or even tried to tell me that you even liked me!" Why was she so mad? Why was she yelling? She didn't even know. Her ears were ringing and she felt dizzy, but banish a banshee if she didn't find the energy to snap back at him.

"I didn't? I've been dropping hints for weeks, Vanessa," he thundered as he suddenly rose to his full height.

"When? When did you ever try to tell me?" she snapped back anxiously. She refused to believe that he even tried.

"The ceremony party back at the bar, the next morning in your bed, both times your reaction shot down any attempt that I wanted to make. Double-dip a candlestick, take your pick anywhere between before and after we've been around each other these past few months—and all the moments in between—and tell me you didn't feel it, Vanessa!" he yelled at her and that was when she saw it, all of the hurt, rejection, and lost hope swimming in the pools of his azure gaze like mournful, lingering ghosts of unrequited lovers.

Her mouth unhinged as she tried to find something to say, but she came up empty-handed. Her mind was racing with every incident that had transpired that gave unmistakable hints that she had somehow managed to overlook or chalk up to him just being kind, friendly, or teasing her. She forced herself to remember every single shred of truth she had attempted to deny because she'd rather self-sabotage any chance of happiness because she doubted, for a moment, that she could be loved. For so long she had been alone that she had long ago reserved her heart to sit on a shelf, never expecting someone would dust it off, hold it close, and treasure it even more than what she did.

"I didn't know." That was all she could muster. Her mind was lost in a sea of emotions and trying to figure out which one to grasp a hold of. She went to stand and go to him. But the moment she moved her legs they felt like they were stuck, heavy, and hurt tremendously. She remembered why she felt so weak. The room spun for a moment. Throwing herself onto the stone floor, she dry heaved and then focused on not moving. Even the lurch of her stomach as it attempted to retch up whatever remained inside from that evening's meal caused pain to sear its way through the wound along her spine.

Again, Leon tossed his emotions to the side and closed the small distance between them. "Vanessa, what's wrong?" He tried to look her in the eyes, but the moonlight spilling in through the mouth of the cave washed over the torn garments, and her white flesh slathered in deep, dark red caused him to go hauntingly still. "Banish a banshee. What happened?" he barked out. "Bobo! Bobo!" he desperately called for the ogre.

Coming around the corner, the demon ticked a finger from side to side as he spoke, "I shan't be pulled into your emotional affairs. This has been a long time coming and you two need to work through this without the meddling of outside—"

"Vanessa's hurt!" Leon interjected. His voice was a mix of fear and agitation as he looked lost at how to touch or hold the poor girl.

The ogre needed not another word. His playful expression died away and was rapidly replaced with the need to aid his master. "Blast it all, girl. What stunt did you pull to earn your backside a bruising this time?" he stopped and gasped at the gaping wound that stared back at him. The skin trailing the rippling cord down the center of her back was a mess of torn flesh and caked, black blood. But the most concerning detail was the edges of the torn tissue that looked like granite stone had merged with her body.

Bobo's face was inches away from the inflicted area, inspecting the long, angry gash with a determined glint in his eyes. A massive paw went to remove his spectacles from his pouch and fixed them upon the bridge of his nose as he came incredibly close. "Well. It seems that the venom in the gargoyle's claws has infected you," he stated in a cold, lifeless tone.

"Infected?" Vanessa rasped.

Leon sucked at his teeth and shook his head. "This isn't good. How long do we have?"

"What do you mean infected?" she squeaked out.

Bobo removed the glasses and tapped them on his bottom lip while in deep thought. "I'm not sure," he said, finally. "It could be a few days before she starts to show all of the signs. But she is already starting to shift."

Vanessa drew in a deep breath, her lungs expanding painfully as she did, and yelled, "What do you mean I'm infected?" she bellowed and felt like she had been sliced open all over again. She knelt on all fours on the ground and panted between groans of pain.

"Gargoyleism is a disease, my dear. Much like any strand of zoanthropy, you are infected either by bite or scratch. Some shift within days, others weeks. But you're already showing a morph in your DNA as you've started to have the stone skin manifest." Bobo drew in a slow breath and released it even slower. "We'll need to get a sample of the venom in order to create an antivirus," he said calmly to Leon. But there was nothing calm about the situation at all.

Heat rolled through her back and it felt like lava was dripping along her spine and seeped further into her being. Droplets of pain tapping over her stomach in a nauseating reminder of the suffering that was taking hold of her as the adrenaline slowly left her system. "Anything, just… make… the pain…stop," she expressed torpidly.

Leon's hands were searching through his element pouches before they were glowing a mint green as he hovered his appendages over the blood-soaked laceration that ate up Vanessa's skin under her cape. But anywhere his hands were, the skin refused to heal. "Bobo," he said in a shaky voice. "It isn't working." There was a quiet hysteria to the man's faint voice. It was a sort of spoken dread that traveled through the air and decimated any hope that things were going to be alright in the moments to follow.

"Drat," the ogre hissed. "I was afraid of this."

Vanessa's voice was strained and riddled with a stinging ache, "What?"

"The venom is deep in your system. Probably from your immense power. Instead of it repelling the toxins, it is accepting them at a rapid rate."

"You said… that there was … an antivirus," Vanessa felt each word struggle to leave her mouth as she felt beads of sweat form over her brow.

Gently, Leon rolled Vanessa over onto her side and swiped away strands of stray raven locks that were plastered to her cheeks. "Don't talk," he whispered, his heart eating away at itself as he looked down at her and noticed every line and strain that made up her agonizing expression.

Bobo slowly knelt down next to her and cupped the side of her face. His voice was low, tender, and apologetic. "We need a living gargoyle for that."

Her eyes squeezed shut and tears started to stream out through the cracks. She was going to change into one of them. She would no longer be Vanessa. She would become a mindless, feral demon. Rolling her lower lip between her teeth, she bit down hard to repel her desire to cry out in despair. It wasn't fair. More tears blazed their way down her face as she came to terms with the undeniable truth of what her reality would be in the next several hours.

Labored breathing filled the confines of the cave as she blankly walked the future that she would live within the safety of her imagination. Opening her eyes, tears blurred her vision as she found the strength to speak. "Kill... me," she rasped.

Both Leon and Bobo gasped in unison and knitted their brows in defiance to her request, but not a word left their lips. It was like they were staring down at someone living out their final moments. You did not deny their dying wish... but it didn't mean you had to accept it either. The silence stretched out painfully. Only the desperate attempts to fill her lungs sounded through the stone-walled cavity.

"No," Leon shot out without a tinge of remorse.

"My dear man—" Bobo started to say calmly.

"No!" Leon snapped, interjecting. "I refuse to comply with this outlandish plea." His stoic and steadfast face peered down to Vanessa. "We will find a way."

She hurt. All over, she hurt, but the pain in her heart as she stared up into his mournful eyes was ripping her to shreds. "But... if you... don't," she wheezed, her lungs feeling like they had weights tied to them. Each breath had become such a tiresome act.

"We'll find a way," he confirmed, disregarding anything she was saying. To Leon, there was no other option aside from her living. Snapping his blue-eyed gaze at the ogre, he asked, "Do you think we could find the third gargoyle? Maybe it went back to the summoning circle."

Bobo pressed his thumb and pointer finger to his chin as he hummed thoughtfully. "Perhaps. Though, finding our way back may be the most problematic portion of this equation."

"It doesn't matter. We will figure it out. We have to." At this point, Leon's voice was a woven tapestry of worry and panic.

Shaking his head with a sigh, Bobo searched the shadowed walls of the cave while trying to decipher the best course of action. But there was no answer lying within its murky depths. "Leon." He stopped and swallowed hard. There was no simple way to speak the truth.

As if he knew what was coming, the Summoner shook his head and stifled a mad cackle. "We always do crazy things and pull through, am I right?" His gaze madly urged the gentleman-beast to agree with him, to put his nerves at ease. He closed his eyes for a moment and when he opened them the pools of water collecting in his turbulent orbs were all the proof they needed to know how much he was fighting the reality of Vanessa's situation. "Remember when you went in those tunnels even though I told you not to?" he choked back tears and forced a smile. "Hex it all, you took on a pack of hellhounds. This? …" he drew in a shaky breath. "This is nothing." The more he spoke, the more he tried to convince himself that there was a light at the end of the tunnel.

A dawn to their growing, endless night…

Reaching out a comforting hand, Bobo clasped Leon on the shoulder and the man shook un-expecting of the touch. When their eyes met, the demon would simply shake his head with a hard frown. The threads hardly holding Leon's façade together started to rip at the seams. He was quickly being undone. Turning his attention to the witch that was so still in his lap, he inhaled sharply as he noticed how quickly the virus was coursing through her.

Patches of gray-white stone stretched over half of her face, leaving the stark contrast of smooth flesh melding sickly with the harsh blotches of stone skin. One of her eyes had turned completely black and was like an endless inkwell staring back at him. Two, sharp incisors had started to descend from her upper gum line, and a tiny bump—the start of a horn—obstructed the smooth surface of her forehead. She blinked, but the black eye seemed to move slower and there was a strange grinding sound of rocks emitting from her as Vanessa's chest rose and fell. A stone plagued hand slowly reached up, attempting to touch Leon, but no words left her gasping mouth. His stomach churned at the sight and he held back a tidal wave of emotion as he snatched her hand up and pushed it hard to the side of his face. Despite its rough, rigid texture, it felt so warm against his skin. It was a vague sign that she was not completely gone and still there with him.

But not for long…

"I love you, Vanessa. I'm such an idiot to have waited this long to tell you. I was afraid of rejection… I was so afraid… but…" he gritted his teeth and squeezed her hand resting on her stomach. Sniffing, he regained some control. "I fear a world without you more than anything," he blurted out. "Please," he begged. Every word tugging with his mournful plea, "Please stay with me," his voice cracked. "Please?" The word was barely a whisper; he didn't have much strength left in him. Could pleading be its own form of magic? Could it pull her from the disease that was trying to claim her?

The corner to her mouth twitched. Her lips moved but only guttural sounds rolled out. She smiled. And the image of it was like slamming a stake through his chest. The tears rose in his eyes with a vengeance. Death would feel better than the torment of watching her fade from this world.

Just then, from outside, a rather large crow took perch on a low bough of the half-dead tree surrounded by the knotted river of roots. It opened its beak, singing its bleak song that almost sounded like dark, drawn-out laughter.

"What a pesky little vermin, that bird. I shall shoo it away at once," Bobo stated gravely, sorrow swimming in the depths of his ocean-blue eyes. The way the giant rose to his feet lacked its usual grace. He even wobbled to the side as he tried to find his footing.

The world that they all knew was shifting and altering at such a rapid pace. Concrete things that had been so well-established in their life only moments ago were now being smashed and harshly removed piece by piece. They all remained in silence as they tried to wrap their heads around it. All the while, Vanessa's rasping made it abundantly clear that her lungs were slowly turning to stone. Leon bent over her body, forehead to forehead, and hugged her. "I'm so sorry. I'm so sorry, Vanessa," his voice cracked as he whispered.

From outside the cave, he heard Bobo struggling and he looked up from Vanessa to see what all of the ruckus was about. The crow was hopping about the branch while the ogre pointed energetically at it and then off into the forest. The bird only replied with loud cries that sent the demon into a frenzy.

"Won't listen to reason, will you? Well then, don't blame me for the actions I must take to get you to comply, you feathered *devil!*" Bobo roared and pulled out his battle-ax.

The bird flapped about, bits of bark raining down as its claws scraped over the branch as it went from one end of the branch to the other. Loud, mocking caws echoing through the cave. It was all loud enough to make Leon wince. "Bobo, what are you —" but he stopped in mid-sentence as he noticed the moonlight seeping in through the canopy and glinting off of tears that ran down the ogre's face.

Bobo sniffled and tried to mask his quivering lip. "Stay still you mangy beast," he commanded in a growl, but all that anger was an attempt to hide the pain that was cascading down his face at that moment. The soft glow of moonbeams had betrayed his river of tears.

It hurt to watch the ogre carry on like that. "Bobo, stop," Leon pleaded. His tone was careful as he tried to get the attention of the ax-waving demon.

Tired, or spent to the point that he just couldn't carry on the façade any longer, Bobo hit his knees and punched the base of the tree. Wood splinters flew out around his fist as he slumped in deeper to the cold, hard ground below. "For all my strength…" Bobo's breathing shuddered and his hulking body shook with the attempt to inhale so that he could finish the thought. "…It wasn't enough to protect her," the words drifted like the final sigh of a dying warrior. The fight gone, and the acceptance seeping in so deep that there was nothing left but letting go of the fading spirit within.

Flapping wings filled the air as the crow came down to the ground and glided around the dead sapling before fluttering to the solid ground underneath. Hopping once, and then once more, it inched closer before tapping its beak over the blade of the ax and then lunged back, wings beating madly, as it had expected the demon to move and swipe at it once more. But the defeated ogre just remained there, crying into one, massive paw as he let guilt and sadness consume every fiber of his being.

No longer interested in the demon, the crow bounded happily over to the entrance of the cave. But, strangely, the closer it got, the larger it became.

"Oh no," Leon groaned expecting the worst. He searched his person for the closest weapon while Bobo looked over his shoulder and instantly snapped out of his woeful state. Snagging the ax, he roared protectively and rose to his feet to rush at the creature with purpose.

But he stopped and stared in awe before he could get close enough to land a killing blow.

Right before their eyes, the crow transformed.

Its feathers grew out and shifted from black as it slowly turned a bright, plant-like green. Spongy moss started replacing the appearance of feathers. The crow was no longer a bird but was some large being that was hunched in on itself. The strange creature was covered in a cloak that had been pieced together and colored by nature. The vibrant moss covered the entirety of the cloak, and patches of autumn leaves piled near the shoulders and upper back before spreading out in a fading line over the greenery. Twigs and sharp quill-like bones were jutting out from the pile of leaves and they twitched and moved like they had a mind of their own.

From beneath the leaf-woven cape, a mesh of tattered, faded garbs flowed out and dragged over the cave floors as the creature took slow steps toward Vanessa and Leon. The robes hung from its darkened form and nothing but a swell of shadows were seen beneath the fabrics. A thin, bony, black hand was grasping a staff that widened up at the peak like a caribou horn, and the being rested its weight on the trusty weapon as it came deeper into the cave. The being walked to a jittery beat. *Step. Step. Slide. Step. Step. Slide.* The strange gait of the monster was closing the distance between them as it did not relent in its approach.

"A Crix," Bobo whispered in astonishment, his ax lowering sluggishly to his side.

The Crix stopped for a brief moment and turned its head to look at the ogre from over its shoulder. Ebony feathers adorned the elaborate headdress of the being like a thick, wild, mane of glossy hair. Bark was interwoven around reeds and made a crown around the forehead that dipped down into the more macabre elements of the ornate mask that was attached to the headdress. A giant crow's skull jutted out from the being's face, hiding the true visage underneath. The large, bony, off-white beak hooked forward almost in a menacing fashion. The deep-set eyes of the mask were hallowed out and revealed glowing, orange eyes therein. But the oddest thing of all was underneath the fabric and mask, and wherever the shadows should have lived, the darkness was more than pitch-black. It was the night sky shrouded by elements of nature. It was as if the being carted with it the very heavens beneath its mask and cloak and its body swam in the dusting of starlight swimming within the onyx sea of space.

Leon opened his mouth to speak when it stopped to hover, silently, over them. Its head craning to and fro chaotically like that of the bird it had once been. Bones and gourds jingled with a soothing hollowed sound as it reached within the hidden space of its attire and rummaged about. A second later, a vial was brought forth and the stopper was removed. The staff was gently laid upon the ground, and wordlessly the creature went to cradle Vanessa's head. Her features covered in even more patches of stone and signs of the virus rapidly taking her over.

The hand holding the vial started to dip down toward the witch's lips and Leon spoke quickly, "Is that going to hurt her?"

It halted completely in movement. There were no signs that it was living, just a prolonged stillness that made Leon's insides knot with worry. Instantly, the head snapped to the side and locked eyes with the Summoner. Gradually, the Crix shook its head in a calm fashion. The sound of the feathers brushing over the leaves of the cape filled Leon with a tranquility that steadied his heartbeat and quieted his mind. Focusing its attention back on Vanessa, the Crix brought the vial to her mouth and tipped it, forcing her to drink it all down.

At first, nothing happened. The little hope that Leon had allowed himself to grow started to escape him. But then, suddenly, Vanessa's eyes darted open wide. The young witch began to shift from side to side. Violently, she stiffly rolled and contorted in sharp, fast movements. The whole display had Leon conflicted on whether or not he should scoot away so he wouldn't be harmed or hold her so that she wouldn't hurt herself by thrashing about. She whimpered and her breathing quickened. Then everything dramatically came to a sudden stop.

Vanessa's bulging eyes slowly drifted closed.

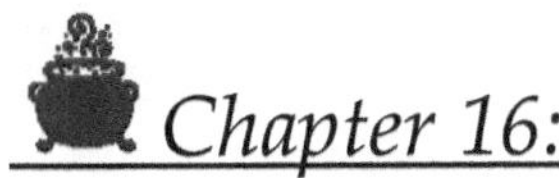 *Chapter 16:*

Leaping across the little distance between them, Leon snarled as he took hold of the Crix's cloak and robes in his fists, ignoring the freezing chill that enveloped his fingers as they were submerged in jet-black under the cape. He shook the being with a vengeance.

"You killed her!" he bellowed out in a voice that was laced in pure rage. "Bring her back," he demanded fervently as his face went dark. His tone dropped into a pitch the matched a villain as he drew out the word like a command, "Now." There was a threat in that single word, a threat that would be carried out if his demand was not met.

But the Crix did not speak or cower. Instead, it pointed back behind the Summoner. Leon's eyes walked the floor until they rested on Vanessa. The shallow rise and fall of her chest indicated that she wasn't dead, she was deep asleep. Turning back to the being, Leon looked confused. "Yo-you didn't kill her?" he questioned quietly.

The bone-faced creature shook its head 'no' and then lifted its hands to pat affectionately at the Summoner gripping its attire. Even though Leon couldn't see anything, he felt like it was smiling at him, telling him everything was all right. It rang like a hollow bell within the deepest corners of his fractured mind.

"Let him go, my good man. I think he helped her in a way we never could," Bobo's voice broke through Leon's haze.

"Oh. Right," Leon said softly and nodded while letting go of the creature and taking a few steps back. Looking apologetically to the Crix, the Summoner took another step back and frowned. "Sorry," he mumbled.

The being was unbothered by Leon's outburst and didn't seem to care about his apologies either. Instead, it was focused more on the passed-out witch. The strange soul bent down to pick up its staff and swiped a hand over the top of the girl's body and then nodded to itself before turning to the others. Churning its hand in the air, it called both Bobo and Leon over to it and motioned to the girl.

"Uh… What?" Leon asked, but, when he turned, he was staring at the big blue eyes of Bobo instead of the lifeless bird-bone mask of the Crix. Turning on heel, Leon saw it already near the mouth of the cave. "Wait," he called. There were so many questions that he had. What it had given to Vanessa being at the top of that list.

Without skipping a beat, the being turned and motioned to the girl, both men, and then beckoned them to follow. Again, the ogre and Summoner made eye contact. "I suppose we should follow. I'll get her, you hurry and catch up to him," Bobo said softly and leaned down to pick Vanessa up. "*Oof…* All of her insides must be stone because she feels a lot heavier than usual," the ogre grumbled.

"Careful. Deep asleep or not, if she hears you talking about her weight like that she might wake up and toss an iron punch spell at you," Leon warned as he jogged to catch up with the Crix. Though its stride was strange, it was far from slow.

The two of them followed the creature down the tree's roots, careful not to drop Vanessa on the climb down. All the while, the jingling of bones and gourds rung like a dark wind chime clinging to the porch of a grave keeper. The gothic instrument peacefully hummed as it swayed in a breeze that carried countless souls to rest. It was both creepy and beautifully soothing.

As they walked, they worried over the possibility of coming upon another giant wolf. But the being seemed to know the path that it was taking and did not falter in its destination. Leon had asked once if they should quiet down, fearing the hollow sounds of the Crix's strange items adorning its person made too much noise and would gain attention from one of the various dangers of the forest. But the being only shook its head 'no' and waved for them to keep following.

Falling back a little ways until he was at Bobo's side, Leon whispered to his friend, "I'm not too sure about this. I don't think we can trust it…"

The ogre hummed and watched the Crix while deep in thought. After a long stretch of silence, he whispered back, "I don't think we have any other choice at the moment."

They both revered the hopping creature as it made its rhythmic way toward a small opening in the side of a jagged, rocky hillside. The opening was not even visible at first as the mouth of it was densely covered in thick, snaky vines that veiled the face of the rock like an elaborate curtain. Gnarled hands that told a tale of a life lived, that far exceeded anyone present, reached out and drew the strands of creepers to the side. Its bone-masked head tilted to and fro as it craned its head this way and that, darting the glowing orange eyes about the thick forest cautiously. The Crix frantically urged them forward without a sound, and they complied. They understood all too well that the threats that lay within the woodland didn't need to find this haven within the Black Forest. Or, at least, they were praying to the goddess that this was a safe haven.

One by one, they slunk inside the darkened space behind the vines and awaited their guide to follow them in and then lead the way. Small patches of moonlight that had managed to break through the thick canopy outside trickled in from the small needle-like seams of the trailing plants. The Crix brushed by them before standing still. Hands dipped and searched beneath the robes, its dark skin searching the ink blotted space beneath its cloak that twinkled with faint glowing starlight and distant swirls of galaxies. Leon could almost get lost in that vision. But the robes closed again, and the creature held half of an amethyst geode in its hand.

They could hear it, yet they couldn't see the being's mouth move, but there was air being blown onto the geode cupped within its palm. The sound was like a breeze rustling through the summer trees. A perfume of ripened flowers swirled around them, and there was a song-like hum lacing the air. It was like they were being embraced by all the lazy, happy moments of a quiet summer day. One filled with soft winds trailing through the tall grass that held a melody of its own and could gently coax a resting body into a mild nap under the warm sun hanging high in the clear, blue sky.

It was the light that started to grow in intensity from the amethyst that broke both Bobo and Leon from their entranced daze. The ogre visibly shook his head while the Summoner rubbed his eyes and patted his cheeks to wake up.

The Crix was already deep within the tunnel and had stopped to wait for the two to gain their senses. The amethyst slowly pulsed with bright, brilliant, lavender rays that lit up the walls of the structure. Scattered clusters of crystals twinkled and reflected the beams of light, further illuminating the once dark space. The bone face was less shadowed and foreboding now. Strangely, it had taken on a more comforting appearance under the surrounding brilliance.

Leon urged Bobo to take the lead and looked over to the sleeping Vanessa draped in his massive arms as the ogre passed. Some of the stone patches on her face had receded, bringing a lively pink hue to her once colorless features. He breathed a sigh of relief before following after Bobo and the Crix.

They traveled the passageway for about twenty minutes before the walls widened and spilled out into a massive cave. The jagged gems that lined the surface of the walls now refracted two light sources. One was emitted from the Crix's glowing geode. The other was the soft, milky beams of the moonlight coming down from the mouth of a giant hole in the ceiling over a small water hole on the far side of the grotto.

The constant flow of trickling water pitter-pattered into the crystal-clear pool below from above the hollow opening overhead. The sounds were a natural tune of a forgotten world. Large stalagmites surrounded the spring like a rocky crown. Great big patches of soft soil surrounded one side of the cave-bound waters, and they were filled with vibrant green sprouts of various sorts. The tilled soil had a simple, rickety, wooden fence stretched out over the length of the small field and it rested against the side of a stone cottage with a thatched roof. Plumes of gray clouds rose up out of the chimney and floated near the rocky ceiling before crawling toward the opening over the nearby water.

"Can we lay her down inside?" Leon had a million other questions to ask, but right now he just wanted Vanessa comfortable and to watch over her until she woke up.

Assuming that the cottage belonged to the Crix, they were both surprised when it hobbled up to the front door and knocked. Deafening silence was all they heard from the other side. When they thought that no one would answer the door, they heard scuffling about inside. The Crix nodded to Bobo and Leon who stole a glance at each other, questioning whether or not they should be concerned for their safety at that given moment.

Without a word, the black, boney hand reached inside its cloak and rustled the many dangling gourds and bones, washing the confines of the large enclosure with the symphony of mystical, hollow sounds. Whatever was within the home stopped for a moment by the door and tapped on it lightly with a series of rhythmic knocks. In turn, the Crix lifted a blackened claw and rapped gently a reply onto the wood of the structure.

Quiet enveloped the cave. Only the distant melody of crickets mingled with the dribbling water collecting in the pool were heard. The door opened slightly, just enough that the seam was aglow with the orange light of the home's fireplace. Bit by bit, it opened, and a face emerged from the other side.

The owner was a female. She was around the same height as Vanessa but with skin tinted with the hues of a stick of cinnamon. The sound of her large, tooth necklace jingled as they rhythmically tapped against her robed breast when she widened the crack in the door. Her hair was the shade of starlight and complimented her dark, tanned skin. The woman darted eyes that were stained black, through and through, like a clear, winter's sky submerged in the twilight hours. But in the murky depths of the void, there were glittering, twinkling lights that mimicked the celestial orbs that hung deep within the night sky.

Threading strands of pearly, white hair behind her sharp, pointed ear, she let her blackened gaze roll over the group resting on her doorstep. When she noted the Crix, the door widened all the way, and the long bone dagger she had been hiding behind the wooden barricade was revealed, though she didn't seem ready to wield it any longer as she dropped her hand to her side.

"Raka, where have you been all this time? I was worried sick." Her eyes flicked to the ogre holding a girl and the blond male at his side. "Who are they?" she asked like they weren't even standing there next to the being she referred to as Raka.

The Crix looked at the three and then to the white-haired female and pointed to the girl in Bobo's arms, then its blackened, clawed index fingers extended in front of the creature while jabbing them twice toward each other before the digits fell back to the Crix's side.

The female drew in a slow breath. "Oh, really?" she turned to face Bobo, but her inky eyes were fixed on the girl resting in his arms. She sighed when she noted the color on her face and pursed her lips to the side. After a quiet moment, she spoke again to the creature. "How long has she been like this?"

Raka lifted his left hand and held it straight up and flat. With his second hand, he made a fist and extended his index finger. Placing the right hand against the left, he circled it clockwise once and then rested his appendages once more.

"I see," she whispered. "In only an hour she got this bad?"

Raka nodded in reply.

She hummed before asking, "And you administered the antidote?"

Again, the creature nodded. She sighed and moved off to the side. "Bring her inside quickly. The worst is yet to come. Follow me," she stated hurriedly and turned into her cottage.

The Crix entered first and rolled its wrist at the others, indicating they should quickly follow. They didn't need more prompting than they already had. Squeezing in through the threshold, Bobo entered the home with Leon in tow and followed after the female and Raka.

While Leon navigated the home behind Bobo, he took in the atmosphere. On the far wall was a large fireplace, and next to it was a small wooden table with enough chairs to seat four arranged neatly around it. Along the top of the walls and hanging from the rafters overhead were various assortments of dried herbs, plants, and flowers. Bottles and jars were littering countless shelves and bookcases that took up most of the space in the home. As they walked by a tiny seating area, they turned down a small hall. A few paces later and they turned the corner into a room with a large canopy bed fixed with red and gold curtains nestled into the center of the room. A large, fluffy quilt lay at the end of the mattress, and a giant chest was pressed up against the foot of the bed.

The female addressed the Crix, "Prepare the bed, Raka." Before darting out of the room and disappearing further down the hall. Both of the men entered the enclosed space cautiously.

The Crix stepped away from the nightstand after lighting an oil lamp and faced Bobo while touching the side of the bird bone mask with the palm of its hand twice. The demon understood it wanted him to lay Vanessa down on the bed and he did so gently.

"Will she be all right?" Bobo asked in a grave voice.

The female reentered the room and spoke as she put a pitcher of water, several cloth strips, and a large bowl on the nightstand next to the lamp. "I'm sure she will be fine once the fever passes."

"I…" the demon seemed perplexed. "I didn't realize that she had one," he admitted while looking down at his hands, wondering if he possibly hadn't noticed it while carrying her.

The woman shook her head as she leisurely braided her white hair over her shoulder. "It hasn't come yet," she explained simply. Her night-sky eyes looked to the two new faces in her home. "I'm Raven," she said softly.

"Bobo," the ogre introduced with a light bow.

Waving awkwardly, the Summoner added, "Leon."

"I'm sure this would be a pleasure if the given situation wasn't so dire… but I will need you gentlemen to leave for now. I have to attend to your friend."

"Is… is everything okay?" Leon asked.

She smiled sympathetically. "What is her name?"

Leon licked his lips and spoke less frantically. "Vanessa."

Raven's smile widened. "Vanessa will be fine, Leon. Especially with me keeping watch over her. My friend Raka and I know what to do. But the fewer bodies in here would be best. There will be a strange air coming into the home soon. A mix of magic and fever is about to battle around her body, and I will need to concentrate to assure your friend comes out of it alive… and the way that you remember her."

The Crix ushered the two toward the still open door. "There is soup and freshly baked bread in the kitchen. Help yourselves," her voice spoke chipperly and without a care in the world. Then the door was shut, and it was like every fear was locked into the room but also all the answers to every question dancing about Leon and Bobo's mind were in there as well.

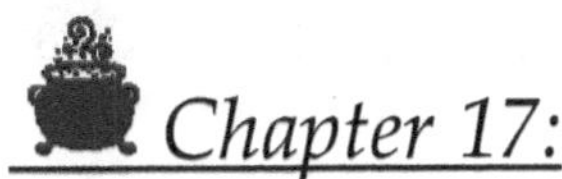 *Chapter 17:*

They found their way into the kitchen, but their appetite had abandoned them for the time being. Instead of feasting, the two men pulled out chairs and sat in silence as the worry gnawed at their minds. The quiet was thick and enveloped them in an embrace that harbored all the charms of misery. The uncertainty was slowly sinking in as they stared off into the lapping sway of the flames within the fireplace. They knew that it was going to be a long night. They were tired and hungry, but neither cared to move somewhere to rest or open their mouth to speak to pass the time.

It was Leon that broke the silence first as his eyes remained glued to the undulating flames dancing over the charring wood. "I know that she will pull through. She has to."

Bobo blinked and peeled his orbs from the fire pit to look Leon over. The Summoner was a mess. He looked beaten, soiled, bruised, and sleep tugged at eyes that refused to cave into the desire for rest. His usual lustrous locks were dulled with dirt and bits of leaves that still clung to his strands. Dark circles hugged his lower lids, and the demon knew what the man was going through without saying anything.

"I couldn't help but overhear what you said to Vanessa, Leon," Bobo skirted delicately around the tender topic with the grace anyone would expect from the gentleman-beast.

The young man stiffened in his seat and refused to make eye contact with the ogre. Instead, he fought the rising tide of red that threatened to overtake his bruised face and coughed into his fist. For a long moment, he was conflicted about how to reply. Should he ignore what Bobo said, or make light of the event, or should he just confess and get it over with? "Suppose you sort of always knew, huh, big guy?"

Bobo gradually nodded and sighed heavily. "I did, my good man. I did. Perhaps before the two of you did."

"You know, I never thought I'd fall for someone like her," Leon whispered and then gave a short burst of laughter.

"Most that fall in love never plan or expect it to be with the one that captures their heart. It just happens as it should, like an unexpected storm rolling in through a rain-starved terrain. It shakes up the trees, it drowns the grass, it thunders about making its presence known, and when absent the world feels too quiet without it." Bobo nodded and sat back in his chair, the wood creaking as he did so.

Leon smirked, "Sometimes I think you'd be better off a poet." He chuckled then and the ogre joined him.

"It'd be a dream come true," Bobo mused.

Shaking his head, Leon said, "I was raised all my life to be the best of the best. I was expected to be top of my class, to excel in every study, and to perfect every magic I came into contact with. Coming from a family of money and power, my parents made sure that I had the best tutors and was groomed to be both a gentleman and the next in line to take on the family business. That is, until Sara was born. At first, she was to be the one to join the academy and be set on the path to be titled as a Second Chosen within the Coven." He rose from his seat and exhaled through his nose while he fussed with the fire and fed the flames a few choice logs. "But that was before we found out she was born magicless. When she turned ten, both of my parents put into motion our new future plans. I was to become Second Chosen, and Sara was to take over the family business. Which is best, if I can state the truth."

"Why do you say that?" Bobo asked.

"Because Sara was always better at the business stuff. Even when she was younger, she was able to help me with my studies and grasped them better than me. I was always better with magic, even without a teacher." He sighed. "By the time I made it to the Coven, everyone knew who I was. Women treated me like I was some sort of prize to be won, my superiors treated me like a treasure to be claimed, and my peers acted like I was a status symbol instead of a person. I was valued, but in ways that made me feel sick to my stomach. Friendship was nothing more than a masquerade party… and I was the reluctant host." He chucked the last piece of wood into the pit aggressively, and the blazing fingers ensnared the lumber greedily. Embers stirred chaotically before gradually dying off.

The chair creaked under Bobo's weight as he shifted in his seat. "That doesn't sound like you enjoyed what you were doing with your life or the path that had been selected for you."

"Not until later. At the start I loved it. But that love slowly died when I attended the academy and, eventually, the Coven. Everyone treated me like I was nothing more than a pretty face and sought to gain what my last name could offer them," Leon admitted. "But when I met Vanessa and she didn't treat me like everyone else, it was… hellfire. It was so nice to be treated like a person. I was so used to being loved and liked without me opening my mouth or expressing myself. Not with her. She would stand toe to toe with me and fight with me if she didn't like or agree," he chuckled.

Bobo smiled and shook his head. "She isn't afraid to tell anyone that she disagrees with them. Headstrong little beast, that one."

Leon nodded with a wide grin. "For me, it was like a breath of fresh air. Cliché, right?" He snickered at himself and pushed an ember back into the pit with the toe of his boot. "I actually felt like somebody. And she got such a bad rap for being careless and loud and crazy, but I saw what everyone was really trying to mask over. Their jealousy of what she was capable of. She had raw power, and for whatever reason, so many within the Coven couldn't stand it." The fire popped loudly. "I think I just wanted to try to help her out at first. The rest came so… unexpectedly," he said, turning back to his chair and plopping down into it.

"She does have a way with people, doesn't she?" Bobo teased. Silence descended once again.

Bobo questioned, "I do wonder, my dear man, about… how many beings have you… you know…?"

Leon blinked taken aback. "Bobo! I hardly think that that is a suitable question—"

The ogre's eyes widened in horror as he waved his hands back and forth frantically. "Oh. No! I would never. I didn't mean…" He took a moment to collect himself. "I was simply curious as to how many beings that you've… you know," he stopped and made his finger mimic the act of slicing a neck and shut his eyes with his tongue lolling dramatically out the side of his mouth.

The Summoner calmed down and laughed nervously. "Oh. That. I'd say about thirty or more. Hard to say. I stopped counting, really."

"I see," the gentleman-beast replied with a nod.

"And Vanessa?"

"Hmmm? Oh, she hasn't."

Leon looked confused. "Ever?"

Shaking his head, Bobo replied with, "Not once."

Leon was astounded by the fact that Vanessa hadn't, not once, killed a being while working for the Coven. It was such a common thing that most assume that you've killed at least ten or even fifteen reckless beings while in the line of duty. But she hadn't. She was still green. He didn't know if he should be happy for the witch or ashamed that he hadn't tried to keep his numbers lower.

Another lull in the conversation stretched out for a long moment…

After a while, Bobo spoke up again. "What if she doesn't remember what you said when she wakes up?"

Leon didn't skip a beat as he replied, "I am not entirely sure."

"Surely you won't miss the chance to confess to her again."

Shrugging, Leon leaned back in the chair and lounged lazily while deep in thought. "What about you?"

"I beg your pardon?" the beast questioned, baffled by the reply.

"You and Lyx," Leon stated plainly. "I've noticed you two getting along recently."

Bobo sputtered and coughed. "Preposterous," he mumbled. "I'm merely trying to be a gentleman. Both of our masters are paired for specific job assignments. It would only make sense that I would try to get along with her," he added quickly.

Looking over to the rattled ogre, Leon cracked a grin. "So, are you trying to deny your emotions?"

Sitting up straight and true, Bobo cleared his throat. "I see that this conversation has come to a standstill."

"That it has."

"Indeed."

Crackles from the fire filled the home as they stared each other down. "Very well then," Bobo griped. "I see that you won't share unless I open up as well, and I…. I'm honestly not sure how to answer you," the demon explained.

Nodding, Leon grinned knowingly. "Take your time, big guy. I understand if you don't have your own emotions figured out just yet. It's serious stuff. Not something you fly into without thinking."

"Quite," the ogre said.

"Mind if I ask you something off-topic?"

The demon eyed Leon over cautiously and murmured, "What would that be?"

"I thought ogres could use hellfire," Leon stated plainly.

The ogre went still. Too still for a creature that size. His ocean blue eyes held the Summoner in his gaze as he weighed many things silently. Finally, when silence was the only thing Leon thought he would receive, Bobo answered with, "I had Vanessa seal it away."

Leon managed to choke on air, and he stood from his seat in surprise. "You what? Do-do you know how helpful hellfire could be? Could have been? Against—"

Bobo raised a hand and cut the man off. "I know how impetuous my decision sounds."

Leon nodded vigorously in reply.

The ogre continued, "But I've already beaten myself up over it tonight. More than you know. And past occurrences coupled with tonight's happenings have painfully reminded me of my short-comings due to my… handicap, shall we say." He sighed and rubbed his hands together as he clasped them on the top of the worn, wooden table. "I've started to wonder if I should have her lift the seal I had put on me. You see, it isn't using hellfire that is the problem. It's that …" The pause was staggering. The ogre's eyes lifted and crashed into Leon with a sadness that ate away at the man's being. "When I first awoke, I was a mess. I couldn't really help the poor girl. For a solid month, I lived and breathed in despair and hated every ounce of my being for things that I had done when I lacked the morals and intelligence that I now have. I didn't like myself, Leon. Most of us don't when we are pulled out from the underworld. But I *really* didn't like myself... At least not the parts of me that were demonic still, or that reminded me of what I was and what I was capable of. I struggled daily with the reality of who and what I was. I felt torn between two existences. One that I had lived, and one that I was just starting to live. After a long, healthy dose of self-loathing, I made a choice. And, so, I had her seal it away."

"You swept your magic under the rug to escape dealing with the fact that you are what you are, a demon," Leon tried to make Bobo see how horrible of a choice that was.

"It's not like you don't hide from your own emotions in your own ways, Leon. I'm just forward about my methods."

Again, they both went silent.

No matter what Leon thought, Bobo made the choice that was right for him during that time. Even if Leon didn't like or agree with it. The magic would have been helpful, but there was nothing that they could do about it now. You can't change the past. You can only shape the future. Again, he plopped down in his seat and focused on the dancing flames.

The Summoner ran a hand through his dirty locks and picked at the tangles that consumed his mane. Realizing he was fighting a losing battle, Leon relinquished the knotted strands and let out a long, drawn-out sigh. "What about now?" Leon asked in a low voice.

"Hmmm?" Bobo hummed. The ogre blinked his attention away from the flickering hues within the fireplace and let his gaze roll over Leon who slowly met the ogre's stare.

Clearing his throat, the man scooted the chair closer to the table and leaned his arms on the flat surface. "Do you like yourself now?"

"Ah, that." Bobo sniffed and rubbed a massive paw over his upper arm while he searched for the right words. "I don't think that I could say that I dislike myself anymore. Just, I fear what I'm capable of becoming. I feel like I've been freed from a darkness that I was not aware I was living in. The last thing that I want is to return to the place that Vanessa saved me from."

Nodding his head, Leon said, "You think having the hellfire ability will make you power-hungry and turn into a flesh-eating monster?"

"I fear, Leon…" the ogre started, his eyes going dark and his voice dropping an octave or two, "that I will hurt someone that I care about and no amount of magic will be able to repair the damage that I have inflicted."

Instinctively, both males shifted their gaze to the hall that led to the room that Vanessa was in. There wasn't a doubt in Leon's mind that if hellfire touched her, she would forgive the gentleman-beast, Botobolbilian. However, the chances of the demon forgiving himself were slim to none. And that he understood more than words could ever say.

About an hour had passed with the two sitting around the table while watching the flames grow and dim before adding more wood to the fire. There was a terrible grumble that had enough bass to make the wood nestled between the two men shiver.

"Hungry, big guy?" Leon asked with a smirk.

Blushing, Bobo nodded. "Indeed."

"I think that gal, Raven, said something about soup and bread. Let's go find ourselves some bowls and have at it. I think we'll need the nourishment and strength," the wizard advised.

"Yes. I believe you are right."

They both rummaged around the cabinets, avoiding knocking over the many jars and vials full of questionable things as they searched for a set of dishes. Upon locating them, they served themselves the meal and sat back at the table to eat. The rest of the home was dark. Unnaturally so with the home being in a cave. The fact that it was night did little to aid in the matter of shadowed spaces. The fire's glow provided enough illumination for them to feast by, but their eyes constantly walked the corridor that led to the room where Vanessa was and were greeted with nothing but blackness.

It had been so quiet for so long. The paranoia from so many unanswered questions coupled with being in the home of a stranger started to birth anxiety in the two males as they slowly ate their meal.

The sounds and sensations that suddenly came did nothing to quell the rising worry in their minds. Inside the home, the air suddenly felt heavier. It was followed by a low wail. Like a distant ghost had come to haunt the cottage. The sound was lost, detached, and mournful. As if it were keening over a forgotten soul, yet there were distinct sounds of anger washing through each wave of dull whimpers. The air started to feel colder. The roof and walls creaked and moaned like they were moving. A teeth-chattering chill consumed the once warm cottage. But it was the ear-splitting scream coming from the room that Vanessa was in that peeled the males out of their seats.

Scrambling through the halls, they tried to ignore the webbing frost that surrounded the walls and floor of the corridor and painted over the bedroom door in a foreboding white. Bobo didn't knock. Normally, the gentleman-beast would. But given the circumstances, he didn't give thought to proper manners. Gentlemen or not, he was a protective beast. The spiritual ties that he and Vanessa shared tugged at him, yanking at his metaphysical form with a silent plea to be saved. He was her pet, tethered by soul and magic alike, but he was also her friend, and that wordless cry for help had him splintering the door like it was made of twigs.

Needless to say, the door was pulverized into tiny bits.

"Vanessa!" Bobo roared her name as he barreled into the room. Showering wood particles rained down over the floor as he stormed inside with a warrior-like purpose.

Leon crashed into the room behind the demon, panting as he scanned the tiny area. Before him, he saw Vanessa slightly elevated off the bed, and the Crix was standing behind Raven with its hands placed on the white-haired female's shoulder blades. Plumes of dark, inky smoke speckled with vibrant dots of light poured out from the Crix's cloak. The tendrils of night-shaded essence were weaving and flowing like they were a living, breathing being, and they wrapped themselves around the creature's onyx arms before being absorbed into Raven's back. The woman seemed to pulse with a milky white glow as she attempted to maintain a charcoal-tinted, amber barrier around the floating witch.

Black magic.

Without thought, Leon reached for his wand and pointed it at Raka and Raven. "Don't!" Raven hissed without looking at the Summoner. "If you want your friend to survive the night, don't," she advised.

A howl broke his attention from the female with hair like moonlight, and he pointed the wand at the first threat his eyes laid upon. A shadow. Or, rather, a spectral swam through the room and then sped for Vanessa. Slamming into the barrier that Raven was maintaining, the being bounced off as sizzling pops exploded around the ward, and the entity gave a wailing cry of dissatisfaction before flying up toward the ceiling to circle above the girl. Raven groaned as she struggled with the magic, and a second spectral mirrored the first's attempt.

"What in the name of magic is going on here?" Leon gasped, not knowing where to point his wand all of a sudden, and chased one shadowed apparition with his lacquered stick.

Raven faltered as two spectrals slammed into the dingy-colored dome. Raka steadied the woman before humming softly. The power from the singular sound radiated through the room, calming everything in it except for the ink-blotted ghosts. Feeling more mentally stable than a moment before, Leon spoke to Raven while he followed the darting shadows as they circled the room and slammed repeatedly into the barrier. "Well? What in the hex is all this?"

Groaning, Raven answered through gritted teeth, "Sorry, I was… a little…" she growled and pushed more power into the spell, sending the spectral whirling in a dizzy pattern about the room. "Busy!" she huffed and blew at hair that fell in front of her view. Turning swiftly, Raven set her heated glare upon the bewildered Leon and pointedly looked to Bobo, "I thought I told you two to leave earlier. This is a delicate process that could cost you your friend's life if handled wrong!"

Jutting his wand out in her direction, Leon snarled while stabbing the air energetically, "That's black magic! How are you saving her with that? This whole place is contaminated now. She's in more danger in your care than she was with the virus!"

Raven scoffed. "Ha. You *must* be a Coven member," she shot out with disdain dripping from every word. "Not really surprised with your lack of magic knowledge and waving a wand at people trying to help your friend that clings to the edge of death. By all means, twirl your stick in my face some more. It really helps me keep this barrier up."

"Leon," Bobo attempted to calm the Summoner down.

"No!" Leon barked. "Exactly how is black magic supposed to save her? Hmmm? And these spirits all floating around seem pretty drawn to your power source."

Sneering over her shoulder at the blond-haired man, Raven replied in a miffed manner, "If you have no knowledge of black magic outside what the mindless Coven taught you or those half-baked academy's professors then I suggest you hush up and let me focus."

"There is no telling what sort of damage that spell is doing to her," Leon yelled.

"If you don't have a shred of elven blood in you, I suggest that you kindly put a seal on your lips," Raven stated, matching Leon's tone.

"If you don't have any elven blood in you, miss, I kindly ask you to let me put up a light barrier instead," Leon countered.

"I am elven!" The dominating roar that bellowed from her throat rolled through the room like lost thunder. Both Bobo and Leon were left speechless. "My arms are getting tired, there are far more spectrals than usual, and her fever is at risk of getting worse. Instead of being another enemy added to the room, help me or kindly remove your presence from here!" she shouted.

"I can aid in grounding you," Bobo offered quickly and went to stand behind Raka. Meanwhile, Leon remained at a loss for words. He did, however, lower his weapon. Even if it was involuntarily done, he stopped pointing the wand at Raven as she had asked.

The ogre placed his hands on the Crix's shoulder blades, mirroring the pose that it had with the white-haired female in front of him. Together, they channeled, and when the power flowed through Raven, her chest bucked forward like she had been spiritually pushed from behind. Gasping for air, the woman regained her bearings and grinned wildly. "Now that's how momma likes it!" Her feet pushed into the floor as she centered herself, focused on the spell, and metaphysically pushed the flow of power out through her palms, willing the dark orb of light to grow, pushing back the shadowed creatures that were now swarming about the room.

"You!" Raven shouted to Leon. "I need you to wake her up."

He blinked, confused. "How am I supposed to do that?"

"Right now she is on the edge of life and death. This spell drops and she's gone. Gargoyle, spectral, or death, whichever comes first, it will have her. I need her to wake up. She is caught in a dangerous sleep. One that is between this world and the other side. Call to her and wake her up."

"Oookay," he replied slowly.

"She is calling for someone," she mumbled. "She is confused and calling for someone. She thinks she's lost this person. I can hear her." A grouping of night-shaded spirits slammed into the barrier in rapid succession, each time they connected, the barrier seemed to shrink in size, and all those powering the spell appeared as though they were being pummeled with punches. "Hurry!" she ordered.

He needed no further prompting. His hand wrapped tightly around his wand, and he rushed through the remaining space and collided with the ward. Slipping through with little resistance, he half fell onto the bed, and his face was inches from Vanessa's levitating body. The stone and horns had all melted away, but her skin looked like it had been washed in grays, her eyes had deep, black circles under them, and there was a light sheen of sweat coating her that glistened under the light of the oil lamp. Reaching up, Leon let the pads of his fingers trail from her forehead to the side of her cheek and felt his heart stop beating. He retracted quickly and the next few pulses from his heart made his chest tighten in pain.

She was so cold.

Why was she so cold? He remembered that Raven said she was on the edge. It wasn't a lie after all. For a moment, all Leon could do was stare in disbelief. Every bead of sweat, her pain riddled features, and the lack of color and luster to her youthful skin were all committed to memory as he noted the state she was in. Even though he knew it was not his fault that she wound up like this, he couldn't help but blame himself for not being able to stop the torment that she was going through. No one wanted to see the people that they cared about suffer. No one.

Licking his incredibly dry lips, Leon tried to find the words that he hoped would bring her back. Not just to him, but to everyone that cared about her. "Vanessa," he whispered to her. "I need you to wake up," he continued. "Bobo won't stop being worried about you. He'll never admit it when you wake up, though." He stopped and laughed at his own joke.

"Try… a little… harder," Raven ordered with strain soaking every word spoken.

Bobo added, "I know you can do it."

No pressure.

Clearing his throat, Leon nodded and scooted closer to Vanessa. "Hey. Come on now, Vanessa. You're making me look bad. I need you to wake up. You…" he stopped again and just admired her. Even sick and ghastly, she looked beautiful. His face softened, his heart felt lighter, he smiled, and his voice became a gentler tone as he tried again. "You are so much stronger than this. You don't need me, and you don't need Bobo because you are so amazing. We will never leave your side, but we need you to *wake up.*" He swallowed past a lump in his throat. "*I* need you to wake up. Please."

Vanessa's fingers twitched, and her eyes moved behind her closed lids, but she still didn't wake up. Raven yelled as she held off another assault from the swarming spectrals taking over the room. In a panic, Leon turned around and placed a hand on the side of Vanessa's face. "Vanessa. Come back to me!" Still, nothing happened.

Was this the part where … you know, prince charming would kiss the girl? Is that something that still happened? Weren't fairytale curses old school and banned in most parts of Aeristria? He gulped. Well, he needed to try something because talking clearly wasn't working.

Dipping forward, Leon prepared to do the age-old 'True Love's First Kiss' which was nothing more than a kiss from someone who cared about you enough to risk causing a witch or wizard to seek revenge for breaking their curse on their selected host.

Right when his mouth was kissably close to hers, Vanessa's eyes flew open and immediately went wide as she noticed how close the Summoner was to her face. She fell from the air and onto the bed with a gasp.

"Thank the goddess!" Leon sighed and then yelled, "She's awake!"

The swirling, murky shadows had paused in their attacks on the barrier and their circling had slowed tremendously. "Prepare yourselves!" Raven's warning was bellowed seconds before she started her spell chant. Power thrummed over the floorboards rattling them, the bed quaked with its otherworldly hum, and the rolling waves of magic set everyone's teeth on edge. An ogre and a Crix were grounding her own elfin magical capabilities, and the damage she was about to produce was sure to leave a hole in the wall if she didn't know what she was doing.

Bobo and Leon really hoped she knew what she was doing.

"I invoke the forces of nature and fire, I command the chaos and ruin, within my sight, you will be no more, set forth my magic and wreak havoc!" Like a towering tidal wave, the magic built up in the room. The black barrier grew and grew, the sparkling edges teeming with dark power like an iridescent, onyx stone twinkling under the moonlight. One moment Raven's voice was like a prayer soaked in power, the next that wall of magic came crashing down over everything around them.

"Banish a banshee!" Leon cursed and rubbed his fingers over the ring on the opposing hand. His talisman instantly activated from his touch. Just before the sonic boom of the spell hammered down on the home, a protective ward flew up and encased them all. Glass shattered, exploding out into the cave ground just outside the home. Curtains fluttered violently, chairs flipped top over end, and endless items flung themselves off of dressers and shelves. The wailing cries of the evil spectrals shielded and clawed at their eyes before becoming nothing.

Slowly, the home returned to normal. Or, as normal as it could get with shattered glass decorating the cave cottage yard, a bunch of toppled furniture, and a group of spell-spent creatures panting on a bedroom floor.

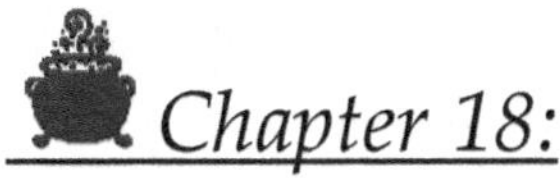 *Chapter 18:*

The amulet's spell dissipated from them as they all lay motionless, only their haggard breathing showing signs that they had not perished from the powerful spell.

"We could have died!" Leon shot out angrily.

"Yeah, well… we didn't," Raven said between breaths.

"Cutting it a bit close, don't you think, Leon?" Bobo asked.

"I-You-What?" Leon stumbled and attempted to quickly gather his thoughts while pointing dramatically at Raven. "She was the one casting the spell. How is our almost death my fault?"

Groaning, Raven rose from the floor slowly. Very slowly, and dusted herself off. "I did say prepare yourselves."

The Summoner narrowed his eyes at the white-haired female. "That isn't exactly a clear order telling me—or anyone—to get their talisman spell ready."

She sniffed. "Hmmm… you seemed smart enough. I was sure you'd figure it out."

"Leon…" Vanessa's strained voice came from under the Summoner.

Frantically, he faced her and looked her over for any signs of injury. "What is it? Are you hurt?"

She winced as she shook her head. "No. You're heavy. Get… off…" she wheezed.

Realization registered across his features, and he instantly rose from the bed. Her deep inhalation sounded through the room as she gulped in sweet air into her starved lungs. Licking her lips, she furrowed her brow and turned her attention back to him as she asked, "We-were you about to kiss me?"

Flushing red, Leon stifled a burst of nervous laughter. "No. Don't be silly. I was trying to speak to you and wake you up. I was just trying to get close to your ear for you to hear me better."

She pointed to her ears on the side of her head. "They are over here," she then pointed to her mouth, "not here."

"You must have imagined things. A lot was going on," he fumbled for an excuse and frowned for being too embarrassed to tell the truth.

"Is it—" She sounded weaker with every word she spoke. "Is it hot in here to you?"

With those final words spoken, she closed her eyes again. The fever! Sure enough, as soon as the spirits left, the fever that Raven had promised wasted no time in making its grand appearance.

Raven sighed and turned to Raka. She threw her index finger out in front of her, then clawed her hands and grasped at the air as she tugged the nothingness back into her chest with balled up fists, and, finally, she held up three digits to form a 'w' and pressed the index finger twice to her lips.

The creature nodded and stepped out of the room. Its nature-drenched cloak rustled through the hall as it disappeared into the shadowed length. She then turned her attention to everyone else. "Now comes the easy part. In a few hours, your friend will be fit as a fairy."

Hours passed, and they all took turns through the night and well into the following day breaking Vanessa's stubborn fever. It was early afternoon, and Leon had taken over after Bobo's watch. The fever had broken during the ogre's turn an hour prior to the Summoner entering the room, but Vanessa was still fast asleep. Leon sat in a small, wooden chair next to the bed. But endless hours of chaos fueled adventures had finally taken their toll on the man. His upper body draped over the side of the straw mattress in a light slumber. Occasionally, he'd wake with a jolt and reach to touch her arms and forehead to ensure that the incessant fever had not returned. Each time, a breath he'd held while worry coursed through his veins was quickly released with a smile before he would collapse on the bed and fall fast asleep once more.

Through the yawning cavity outside the home, the golden rays of the sun bounced brilliantly off of the rippling water at the base and illuminated the once dark and dismal cottage with a warm, inviting glow. Fractured beams of light caught by the trickling spring water falling off the edge of the cavern ceiling splayed tiny rainbows in a vibrant display over the drab, barren surface of the rocky hollow.

The wind blew and circled through the open space, rushing through the broken windows and gently caressing Vanessa's cheek. A faint voice whispered sweetly, *"Welcome home, daughter of Saellah."*

Shocked by the voice, Vanessa's eyes fluttered and fought back the blinding beams of light that poured in through the bedroom window. For a cottage nestled in a cave underground, it was sure bright. Her hand ran over the quilts layered on top of her, and she stretched lightly, only stopping when the pads of her fingers brushed over the skin of another being.

Jolting with a gasp, she retracted and sat up quickly out of sheer reflexes. Realizing that the culprit was nothing more than the slumbering Leon, she felt the tension in her melt away. Tilting her head, she tried to inspect his sleeping face. He looked so sweet and innocent like this. Then again, even imps looked like little angels when they were fast asleep.

Still…

Light played over his sandy locks, and the beams warmed his naturally tan skin. Without thinking, she did nothing to resist the urge to lean forward and run her fingers freely through his wild and matted mane. A soft smile painted her lips as she toyed with the strands and combed through them. She was half attempting to fix the tangled tresses and half petting the resting Summoner.

He started to stir, and she retracted her hand like he'd bite her. She positioned herself to look like she was looking out the window the whole time and didn't even notice the Summoner waking from his nap. Rubbing his eyes, Leon yawned and sat up straight in his chair. His eyes trailed over the bed until they rested on Vanessa who was sitting up and gazing out the window. Her messy, raven hair gently billowed in the breeze wafting through the broken window.

He groaned as the sudden urge to stretch overtook his limbs. "When'd you wake up?"

The smell of damp stone floated in the breeze, mingling with the deep-rooted scents of dirt and the forest above. Now that her fever was gone and they weren't being chased by one sort of beast or another, she could appreciate the smell of the forest and not see it as such a cursed thing.

"Not too long ago," she admitted in reply.

Nodding, Leon looked around the room. There were still pieces of toppled over furniture, but most of the glass was swept up, and a few books and knickknacks were littering the floor. It looked like a disaster zone. But most of them had been too focused on trying to catch small naps between watching over Vanessa's fever to worry about cleaning up. Hopefully, Raven wouldn't mind the mess for a little while longer.

"How do you feel?" he asked cautiously.

She looked her body over and realized that she felt the same. There weren't many signs that the previous night had taken place. Only the dull aches that blossomed all over her body were remaining. Smiling and hugging herself, she said, "I feel fine." It wasn't a lie, but she was feeling a bit strange. Nervous, more than anything. Her heart was picking up in tempo, and she was cursing the fact that it wouldn't listen to her demands to slow down and remain steady.

"Do you know where you are?" He looked worried for a moment. "Do you remember anything from yesterday?"

"I've been out of it for a day?"

"Almost," he stated with a nod.

She looked down at the quilt and picked at the brightly colored patches. "Oh," she whispered as she swam through the murky depths of her hazy memories. Finally, she shook her head. "I don't know where I am or how I got here," she stated finally.

Again, Leon nodded. "I didn't think you would, but I thought I would ask." There was a long pause while he collected his thoughts. "We brought you here after you passed out back in the cave. A Crix found us and gave you a strange potion." He stopped and clasped his hands tightly together while he spoke. "What-What was the last thing you do remember from last night?"

Vanessa took a moment to think. *What was the last thing she remembered?* Licking her lips, her brow scrunched while her mind tried to navigate the complicated paintings of what had transpired the night before. Her frontal lobe throbbed with pain as she tried to remember. The pain was spreading the more she pressed for memories that were hidden behind sleep, spells, and sadness.

Finally, she shook her head. "I remember the wolf," she whispered. "I remember using more magic than what the spell should have granted me," she continued and then shook her head while cupping her brow. "I... I... I can't remember anything much after that."

There was an unnatural stillness from Leon that had her worried. It ate away at the room like an angry disease and set her on edge. She started to feel like she had done something wrong, so very wrong, by stating what she had. But when she thought silence was the only answer she would be met with, he spoke.

His voice was calmer and more collected than she had expected after so much silence. "You don't remember anything after that?" He waited to see her shake her head before he seemed to be lost inside his own mind once more. After a moment, he spoke. "You had Gargoyleism take you over. The magic in you... it was causing it to take you over rather than help fight it off. I ... *we* thought that we were going to lose you." He paused and took a breath before continuing. "I confessed things that I should have spoken a long time ago. But I was more worried about rejection. I realized, in those final moments, that I feared a world without you more than I feared you telling me that you didn't feel the same way. So, I told you the truth." Slowly, he lifted his head to look at her. "I told you that I love you."

She felt herself catch her breath and hold it captive as she read his face. But he was unmoving. The lie came crashing down around her sooner than she had expected. "I know," she said and clutched the blanket to feel something of this world tie her down as she continued to speak. "I just wanted to see if you would back out if given the chance to."

"Excuse me?" he spoke the words, but the emotion was sapped from them.

Turning red, she coughed and repeated more in-depth, "I know that you confessed your feelings for me. I just wanted to see if you would... do it again... or use this as a way to forget that it ever happened."

"Why would you pretend to forget?"

"Why would you hold back your feelings?"

"Because your actions have done nothing to make me think that I even had a chance!" he cried out.

Her mouth opened and closed several times, her actions mirroring a fish gasping when pulled out of water. The more that she tried to process what he had said, the more lost she felt. "When did I ever make you feel like I didn't care for you in that way?"

"Oh, I don't know. Should I start listing them again now?

"Yes," she commanded angrily.

"Fine!" he bellowed, his tone sounding vexed. "The bar, in your room the next morning, me trying to help you on your missions, the way you act when I arrive unannounced, you pulling away when I touch you..." his voice raised in pitch with every point of reference listed. "...Need I continue? I'm sure I can come up with more," he finished calmer.

The bar. The moment he said it, she relived that moment. The one where he called her buddy and gave her such a cold pat on the thigh. "I'm pretty sure back at the bar you made it clear that you only thought of me as a friend."

"How on Raen did you come to that assumption? I hit on you, remember? And your reaction didn't exactly announce that you were interested." He sounded exasperated as he spoke.

She blushed a bit and fumbled over her jumbled mind for a good excuse. Nothing came to save her quick enough, though. The only thing that she could even remotely come up with was the truth.

"Well, it seems that I am not so great at picking up on your hints," she muttered.

Silence ate up the space between them.

"So," Leon started. "…do you want me to just go on being your friend, do you need space, or do you want something like a Forget Me Knot spell?"

To the mentioning of the spell, Vanessa raised her head from staring down at the intricate patterns of the quilt. She had found herself playing with the fabric and lining the designs with the pads of her fingers while the argument lost its heat. But that spell. It wasn't a spell someone just cast every day. It was the sort of spell you cast when something is too ugly to remember or too painful to keep around. There are cases, however, where it is cast on someone who can't unhear what they've heard. "Why would I even entertain the thought of something like that?" she huffed.

Leon slowly rose out of his seat and fussed with his hair. Hurt and agitation pulled on every line under his tired eyes and made the young man seem far older than what he was. "Because I wasn't sure you'd be able to be around me if you knew how I felt. I am not aiming to make you feel bad. I'm prepared to make you forget this moment or even walk out of your life if you ask it of me. But I can't change how I feel. I—" He knit his brow as he paused to think. A memory struck him then. Not a second later he added, "What were you trying to say?"

"When?" she asked, her voice sounding more lifeless than she wanted it to.

"Back in the cave. Right after I confessed. You tried to say something after I told you that I … that I love you. What was it?"

Vanessa nodded and turned to face the window as the breeze played with the curtains. She tried to quiet her thundering heartbeat galloping like a herd of wild unicorns within her breast.

Leon sighed, and grumbled, "It doesn't matter. Don't worry about it, Vanessa. Think about what I said, and we can figure it all out after your mission." With that, he started to make his way out of the bedroom.

Closing her eyes tightly, she muttered a silent prayer to the goddess and turned to look at Leon before he could even make it to the door. "I said, I love you too," she blurted without restraint.

Again, there was a stillness that descended over them. Like the hush that enveloped the forest at night. The kind of quiet that was unnerving. The confusion was clear in his voice just as it was plain on his face when the Summoner turned around to her. "What did you just say?" he breathed.

She drew in a breath and felt like she was about to burst. A dull ache rose in her chest. Even drawing in more air in preparation to repeat her confession had been painful. Her hand rose to rub the pain in her breast away as she sat up a little more proudly, a little surer of herself, and said once more, "Last night, while we were in the cave, the words that I tried to say were: I love you too," she admitted.

"Please," Leon started.

"I'm sorry that I pretended to forget and made you confess to me a second time. I was worried, and I let my own issues get in the way of making a good decision. You didn't deserve that."

He could only blink in reply for a moment. "So, does this mean…?"

She held up her hand, "It means that we have a long talk waiting for us when we get home." He smiled at that and nodded. "But, for now, let me focus on my mission, and let's get the hex out of here before we start mapping out a future together."

He raised his hand and smiled even wider. "As the goddess as my witness, you have my word that I'll wait until we get back before we talk about this again."

"Thank you," she said softly.

 *Chapter 19:*

Vanessa had asked if there was a chance that they could each bathe before they talked about anything that had happened last night and what their plan of action was going to be today. The elf woman agreed with a crinkle of her nose that they all needed a nice, long, hot bath with plenty of soap. Raven even threw in the fact that they needed to try to heal themselves up as best they could, reminding Vanessa that she had used a scorch spell on her hand. Cauterizing the wound was a smart move and healing it would be far easier now. However, her hand would forever hold a scar. Magic can only do so much. Scorching a wound was always grounds for scarring if not looked at within a few hours. Not that it was going to be a big deal, but it had reminded the witch of all that transpired the previous night, and it always would.

After a much-needed washing, the trio was seated in the living room. The elf sat in a tall back chair while Raka stood behind her, entwining Raven's white locks into tiny braids while she spoke to Vanessa, Bobo, and Leon seated on a couch across the tiny coffee table that separated them. The smell of the fireplace, bubbling stew, and spiced herbs dangling from the rafters overhead filled the room while they conversed.

"I don't need to see an insignia to know where you all belong. What exactly is the Coven doing this deep in the Black Forest?" Raven asked casually.

Vanessa had been daydreaming about going home. Back to her soft bed, her hairbrush, and all the comforts that she had that were free of all the horrors that lived within this forbidden woodland. "Well," she started, feeling at a loss while wrapping up in a blanket. Fixed between Bobo and Leon, her body was pressed between the two rather tightly. If it wasn't for the fact that she was cold, she would have opted to stand instead. Being hip to hip with Leon had her running circles in her mind, and he being as comfortable as he was with their bodies pressed against each other wasn't helping the matter. But at least she was warm.

"Yes?" Raven pressed.

Vanessa shook her head and got back on topic. "Oh, uhm… it is all so chaotic." As she recalled the events that led up to that moment, she realized just how crazy it all was. She wove the tale as best she could, all while making an attempt to not leave out a single detail. Shortly after, Raven pressed her thumb to her bottom lip and thought.

"Do you still have the stone on you?" she asked after a long moment.

The witch nodded and wormed her hand under the blanket and dug into her satchel. A second later, she had the stone removed and was presenting it to everyone in the room.

"May I?" Raven asked and waited for Vanessa to nod before she turned around to face Raka and flung her index finger out and pointed to the object in the Spellweaver's grasp.

The Crix bobbed its head and walked over the worn wooden floors to retrieve the item, cooing when the smooth stone caressed its long, black fingers. Clicking sounds escaped from under the mask as the creature inspected the object. Its cape scraped over the ground as it returned to Raven's side and laid the rock in her hands.

She smiled, lifted her right hand to her mouth, pressed the pads of her fingers to her lips, and brought the hand down toward Raka.

The creature hummed happily, washing the room in a feeling of joy. Raka then mirrored the elf's hand motion with his left hand's fingers touching the bird beak of his mask and bringing the hand down toward her.

The Crix quietly went back to playing with the woman's hair as she inspected the item curiously. Turning it over in her hands, Raven's eyes widened. "This is a map to the Altar of Offering," she gasped.

"The what?" Bobo, Leon, and Vanessa asked in unison.

Raven lightly waved the rock in one hand at the group as she explained. "This map gives the location of the Altar of Offering. It is a sacred place within the forest where you make an offering to the qilin. Once your offering is accepted, the qilin will emerge and answer one question for you."

The astonishment was scrolled over all of their faces. Qilin were creatures that, to all those residing in Tolvade, were … well, myths. As some legends had it, you could make an offering and if you pleased it with your gifts, it would show itself to you and grant a wish. Most lore depicted them as a chimera-based creature that held infinite knowledge, but descriptions beyond that were lost. It was also written that they also could only be summoned once a year.

With a grin that could put a devious imp to shame, Raven stood from her chair and came over to Vanessa. As she plopped the stone into the girl's hands, she said, "If you want to know where this de-summoning spell is, the elves are sure to know, along with everything else your people may have lost from them cutting ties with the humans two-hundred years ago."

"My word, they still live, don't they?" Bobo whispered loud enough for everyone to hear.

Raven turned, her smile a touch softer and far less insane. "Yes. Though, no one is sure where."

"But, aren't you…" Leon trailed off feeling lost.

"Not the same kind and definitely not on friendly terms," she said with a sniff and hard frown. "So, I most certainly do not know where they would be. It was years before I was born when the divide happened."

"I bet a qilin would know," Leon said with a smirk.

The white-haired female nodded gently, "Oh, there isn't much it wouldn't know. But it can only be called upon once a year."

They all looked crestfallen. "Well," Raven added. "No one knows where it is anymore. The Altar of Offering, that is. I doubt anyone has called to it this year, much less any year before that. The Altar of Offering is heavily spelled, indestructible, and timeless. No sound from outside can be heard therein and none therein can be heard outside. But once you make an offering, the qilin will come, and it will answer whatever you ask."

Vanessa stood up quickly, dropping the blanket to the couch. "What are we waiting for? Let's go! If we find the elves, we can get the spell and get the hex out of this forest."

She started for the door, but Raven clearing her throat made Vanessa pause in mid-stride. "If you don't mind, I know my home isn't much but, it is still mine." She pointed a single digit at the heap of blanket piled messily on the couch.

Oops.

Everyone took a few moments to help straighten up the elf's home. After all, it was the least that they could do after she had helped them. Once everything was as orderly as it could get, Raven grabbed her dual bone axes and packed a small satchel full of various items. Slipping on a red hooded cloak, she then hung the packed sack on her shoulder, stepped out of the home, and turned to Raka on the front porch. Pointing at the Crix, Raven made two fists and then extended out only the pinky finger and thumb. Her right 'Y' hand jutted forward and down. Lifting the right hand, she made a 'V' with her pointer and middle finger and brought the digits to touch under her eyes, and then swept her hand up to the cottage. Finally, she made a roof with both of her hands.

Raka bobbed its head understanding and then jutted a night-dipped digit in Raven's direction. Then taking both hands, the creature made a 'V' with its fingers, placed the thumb between the split, rested the left hand over the right hand, and made a circle that spun out from the body a few times.

The elf smiled and wrapped her arms around Raka's body. The sound of gourds and bones chimed all around them as she drew the creature in close to her. "You be safe as well, my friend," she whispered while giving Raka a final squeeze before letting the being go.

They made their way back up through the tunnels and stopped just outside of the vines that hid the entrance to the small, carved out pathway. "Be careful. Though it is day, there are still many dangers," Raven whispered cautiously to them.

Leon jutted his chin in her direction as he said, "And should things go south?"

She gave a corner grin and looked down at the weapons strapped to her hip. "I assure you that they are not for show, and I can hold my own in battle."

Bobo leaned over, his blue eyes curiously inspecting the axes. "I do say, those are magnificent specimens. What are they made of?" he inquired while reaching out, pausing to flick his gaze up to the female with a silent 'may I' glimmering in his ocean blue hues. Raven gave a single bob of her head, and the ogre reached forward to test the edge of the ax's head. Bobo's face lit up instantly with a proud smile. "Sharp as an enchanted blade," he mused.

"Made them myself," she stated. "From the remains of one of those monsters."

"You mean—" Vanessa began, but Raven cut her short.

"The wolves," she snapped with a look of disgust twisting the edges of her lips into a snarl. "Those creatures are abominations. A crime against all beings, magic, and nature," she seethed.

Leon looked around and then back to Raven with concern in his eyes. "Did they take someone special from you?" he wondered out loud.

Her black eyes seemed to shift. One moment it was the night sky holding heaven's sparkle, the next was a shower of meteors blazing over the ebony surface of her twilight gaze. "They took everyone," she whispered. "I'm the last of those that stayed behind." Her frown deepened. "There is only me and…" she trailed off before shaking her head, and her features hardened. "No," she hissed in a hardly audible tone. "There is only me and Raka left. Most of his kind went into hiding underground, scattered throughout the forest when those things came into being. They destroy everything within the forest. To them, nothing is safe, and nothing is sacred."

Vanessa looked worried for a moment. "Would the Altar still be intact?"

The harshness that had eaten away at Raven's softer features lost some of the chill as she looked at Vanessa. A faint, yet confident, smile washed over her lips. "There are things older than the wolves, and those items and beings are blessed by the goddess herself. Not even the wolves can destroy or harm them."

"Oh," she sighed, relieved, and then bit the side of her lip. "I'm sorry that you have been alone for so long," she said finally.

Raven gave an airy laugh and shook her head. "I have a few things that hold my heart together in dark times. They are my moon in my night, my torch within shadows." She motioned for them all to stay close to her. "Come now, we will be safe at the Altar, so let us move swiftly," she stated, her voice resuming its hushed tone from earlier.

"Wait," Vanessa called out in a quiet panic. "I know that they can sense magic, but they still rely on sight. Let me do a chameleon spell."

Bobo pat Vanessa on the head, "Look at you being all safe in the face of possible danger."

She slapped his hand away with an agitated look and gritted her teeth. "Nothing will hide that stom—"

Leon's hand instantly went to cup her mouth, and he forced a smile as he gained everyone's attention. "All right. That's enough banter for one afternoon. Don't you think, Vanessa?" He dipped his lips low to the cuff of her ear and whispered, "We saved you from almost certain death. Could you not go staring down lady death a second time? Hmmm?" he motioned with his gaze to the very disgruntled ogre standing in front of them, and Vanessa groaned from behind his hand and rolled her eyes before tapping his appendage.

He released her, and a sigh exploded from her mouth. "Stand still so I can cast the spell," she advised, ignoring her urge to finish her previous thought.

A chameleon spell didn't cost much, and it would enable them to move through the forest more freely. It wouldn't mask their heavy footfalls or conversations. Those would be reliant on their stealth abilities. Anything that would give them the upper hand was a blessing, though. Grabbing bits of herbs and dust from her pouches, Vanessa concocted the spell and sprinkled it over everyone in the group before making her chant.

"The eye of newt is to mask our form, the crushed devil's cap is to mask our scent, we seek secrecy and stealth, to travel and blend, we want to be like the spirit of the chameleon."

The spell was cast, and they were set.

One by one, they shrank out from behind the dangling vines and scanned the area from floor to canopy before they inched quietly through the woodland. They slunk along the forest floor, carefully maneuvering through the thick trunks of trees and avoiding the prickly caress of wildly woven briar bushes.

The Black Forest looked different during the day. It wasn't in the slightest the nightmare that they had remembered it to be hours ago. As they traversed cautiously through the foliage, Vanessa noticed the birds singing overhead. She could see the sun turning the canopy of budding branches into tiny jewels fixed upon the sturdy boughs with the golden wash of the early afternoon light showering every bit of exposed bark.

Though there were softly painted buds peeking out, and the melodious chirping of gay birds flying hither and tither, there was an anxious mood sweeping through the party. Even during the day, there were dangers in this place, and nothing would save you if you were caught off guard. Their eyes all darted about like a herd of skittish deer roaming through the forest. They were trying desperately to miss leaves or frail twigs from gracing the soles of their feet while they walked.

Occasionally, they would stop, and Raven would ask to look at the stone again. Quietly, she would inspect the deeply etched map before narrowing her gaze to the surroundings, noting the placement of the sun in the sky and locating moss on a tree. After a quick glance, the white-haired female would point in a direction with a surety shining in her eyes, and she'd pronounce, "This way," before pressing on through the dense woodland.

Hours later, they emerged in a clearing, and the moment they stepped into the small, perfectly laid circle, the anxiety and fear that they had carried throughout their journey melted away from them. This was a sanctuary. A safe haven within the nightmare-riddled sea of towering trees and twisting thorn bushes. Peace freely took them over and replaced any worry that had laid claim to their being. The tension that had been built up in their shoulders was obliterated, the panicked pacing of their heartbeat found a soothing rhythm, and their clammy skin gradually dried in the gentlest of breezes that encircled the vibrant space surrounding them.

The Altar of Offering was more than a tranquil clearing, though. On the far side of the clearing, there was a stone altar. But it wasn't one that was made out of the usual stone that you saw in the more well-known areas of Tolvade. It was made of a deep black rock that was swirled with milky white ribbons throughout its surface, and it appeared as though it had been polished to a high shine, although it was hidden under a thick layer of debris and pollen. On either side of the table were two, massive hands cupping matching black liquored bowls. The containers were meant for fire but were still and lifeless and filled with years of decaying leaves.

How long had this place been untouched for?

The warm light filling the clearing poured over the surface of the table and gold carvings, sending beams of light bouncing off of the shiny surfaces and glittering through the air all around them. A shadow of a bird fluttered through the crisp, neon green grass under their feet, and Vanessa looked up just in time to see the creature pass. Long, fluffy tail feathers flowed in the breeze, and its vibrant purple and blue coloration was as beautiful as its song that belted from its beak.

This place felt safe, peaceful, and like you didn't want to leave it. It felt like home. "How do we carry out with the ritual?" Vanessa whispered the question, her voice showing traces of the awe of the place that still held her entranced.

Raven hummed in thought, "Mmmm… trying to remember the stories that the elders and my mother and father used to tell me. It has been a while since I last heard them."

She walked past them all and ran her hand over the surface of the offering table. Twigs, leaves, and nutshells fell to the ground as she gently swept the surface free of nature's mess. Her eyes were a mix of shame, pride, and sorrow. Her mind was dancing with the memories of ghosts that the rest could never understand. She hummed again, but the sound slowly transformed into a melody. She smiled, though she looked like she was on the brink of tears. A single digit tapped the center of the table as she sang softly.

"I bring my questions and prayers laced in magic,
I light the fires for the spirit to see,
May my offerings call to you,
And bring you swiftly to me.

In the sacred place, we gather,
With fruit, wine, magic, and incense,
May our offerings call to you,
And guide you with smoke of the frankincense.

We give to you that which is sacred,
And kneel for the wisdom that you give,
Through smoke and forest, you travel,
Within our spirit, you quietly live."

Everyone watched her as the song ebbed away, and she blinked past the jet-black tears threatening to fall. A lifetime of remembrances encircled Raven's mind, people that had filled her life and had been ripped away, moments of songs and story-telling by the fireside that was teeming with security, laughter, and love. Every soft beat of the song had carried with it a moment she had almost forgotten and was interlaced in a time long ago.

There was a pause that was soaked in grief. Gently, Vanessa broke through it as she said, "I don't have any of those things on me." She was almost upset that she had spoken. Like she was interrupting some important moment the elf was having.

Raven, shaking off the depressed look that had slowly consumed her features, returned to her usual self and gave a wry smile. "Then it's good for you that I packed a few things before leaving the house." She patted the satchel nestled against her hip.

Bobo leaned over to Vanessa and whispered, "Oh! Look, Vanessa. Someone that you could take notes from. She is well-mannered, hospitable, tidy, and plans ahead. I say… you've hit the mentor jackpot!"

The look that the witch cut to the ogre was enough for him to straighten up and mask his chuckle with a false coughing fit. Ignoring her pet, she slowly closed the distance between her and Raven as she spoke. "So, an offering is like a ritual?"

Raven blinked, confused. "Have you… have you never done an offering?"

Vanessa could feel the heat rising in her cheeks. "I have… It's just. Only once a year for the Wild Hunt, and I've never really paid much attention to it all."

The white-haired woman walked closer and inspected Vanessa. Her nostrils flared while trying to breathe in the scents surrounding the Spellweaver. Raven's black eyes narrowed at the girl. Suspicious of how truthful Vanessa had been with her, she gauged the girl's response and reaction silently.

Finally, she nodded slowly. "Very well." Motioning to the table, Raven urged her to follow. "You will need to take out the items, bond with them, give them some of your magic, and pray at the altar for wisdom and guidance. When the qilin comes, it will answer whatever question you have. But only one." The last three words hung in the air with a lead weight tied to each and every one of them.

"Vanessa, are you sure you should be the one to—" Bobo started.

"I'll be fine," she cut in before he could finish.

"Should I be concerned?" Leon asked.

"No," Vanessa shot out.

"Yes," Bobo replied not a second later.

"I need to know what he is talking about, Vanessa. This question we are supposed to ask involves us all. If there is something that Bobo thinks you'll ask instead—"

"I won't," she snipped.

"I just need to know what it could possibly be. If it is that important to you…" Leon pressed.

"It isn't," she said without skipping a beat.

Bobo glowered at his master and huffed. "I beg to differ."

"Drop it, Botobolbilian!" she warned with pepper in her tone.

"Vanessa," Leon tried to reach out for her, but she pulled away.

"I said drop it," she turned and tried to focus on anything but all the eyes that were watching her so intently. Marching over to the bag, Vanessa tried to focus on taking everything out of the satchel while she kneeled next to the altar.

Stiffening, Bobo let his voice roll out flat and lifeless as he spoke to her and everyone around them. "You can hate me if you want, Vanessa. But they deserve to know the question that, to this day, keeps you up at night."

Vanessa paused and hugged a corked bottle of wine to her chest. "Please don't," she pleaded softly.

"There is a chance that she will ask—" Bobo started.

"Bobo, please. Don't," she whimpered and turned around with tears that mingled with the angry flames in her eyes.

"—Who or where her parents are," he finished.

The question seemed so normal. So mundane. Yet, for her, it was so much more. For her, it was years of questions that had not diminished through the stretch of time but grown. She didn't have an affectionate family take her in and buffer the loss of being given up when she was a baby with the love of a family that picked her, just her, out of a house full of parentless children. No. Instead, she spent years growing up and having countless meetings that all turned sour because she wasn't what the family wanted. But all the other children came and went. They came with tears clinging to their eyes, and she'd spend nights by their bedside making them feel at home and at ease.

Things that she would have wanted someone to do for her, but they never did. And then they left with smiles as they walked hand in hand with new caring moms and dads.

Her chest tightened, and she looked away from everyone while the tears threatened to burn their way down her face. Traces of them were clinging to her eyelashes and blurring her vision.

Why was she never good enough?

Why didn't they keep her?

Why didn't they give her to an aunt, uncle, grandmother… someone…

Why didn't they love her enough to keep her?

The unexpected hand of Raven caressed Vanessa's shoulder like a feather skimming over the surface of a placid pool of water. It was almost unnoticed. Her touch continued until her fingers glided over the jawline and tilted Vanessa's face to look at her. Night eyes speckled with starlight stared deeply at her as the elven woman cupped both sides of the Spellweaver's face. Obsidian orbs searched every inch of Vanessa while Raven's brow contorted in confusion. But in the depths of that black gaze, there was an understanding that painted those heavenly onyx hues in sadness.

"You are loved," she whispered. "*Vall l'ae mintis,*" she whispered in her own tongue and repeated in common tongue, "You are loved." Her hands squeezed, ever so slightly, on the sides of Vanessa's face as the first tear blazed down her cheek like molten lava. "Your worth is not defined by being kept, given up, money, or power. Your worth is echoed in the spirit of every being you help when you are lost and by what you give when you have nothing. It ripples through time as the spiritual and material riches grow and you keep giving. Even if it breaks you. You are a treasure, Vanessa. No one ever gave you up because they didn't love you." Something pooled in the corner of Raven's eye. "Sometimes giving up a child is the one way to save it and the one way to love it," her voice sounded brittle as she spoke.

As soon as the words left her mouth, Vanessa lurched forward, dropping the thick wine bottle from her grasp and letting it roll down her lap to the grassy ground below. Wrapping her arms around Raven, Vanessa wailed into the slender neck of the elven woman. Every doubt and hurt she had harbored in her soul came rushing to the surface. Climbing higher and higher, the emotions clambered to find release from the quiet chambers of her soul where Vanessa kept her darkest secrets hidden.

Safe from everyone.

Safe from even herself.

A black tear streaked down Raven's face, and she tightly wrapped her arms around the sobbing girl. "*Fi'a nunn. Fi'a nunn mei, tuel,*" she cooed into Vanessa's ebony locks. Her voice was a tone none had heard until now. It was silvery and wrapped you up in a warm hug that penetrated past skin and bone.

For a long while, only Vanessa's weeping could be heard throughout the clearing as she let go of pent-up hurt. Without warning, Bobo thudded on the ground behind her and hugged them both as he whispered, his voice straining to keep his emotions together, "You are *my* family, Vanessa. And I won't let you feel alone anymore. I love you."

Warm hands managed to snake their way in and wrap around her waist. Leon's face was buried into the side of her neck, and he nuzzled with a sound that reminded her of when he thought he was going to lose her. "You've always felt like home to me," he breathed against her. "You are my home, Vanessa."

She then cried for entirely new reasons. A mix of happiness and sadness burned in her chest. The sensation was threatening to snuff her from the inside out. But, instead, she felt a weight being lifted from her with each tear. It was a bittersweet moment that would be a part of her, now and forever.

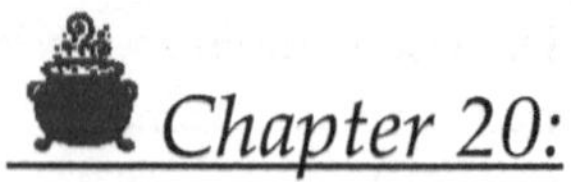 *Chapter 20:*

Leon had done a small cooling spell on two runestones and let Vanessa roll them over her eyes as she tried to erase some of the puffiness and soreness she had unwantedly accumulated. She sniffled for what felt like the hundredth time and smiled, handing him the rocks. The redness of her eyes had significantly gone down, and all that remained was some slight congestion and a mild headache.

"Thank you," she said meekly.

He smiled and nodded. "I'm just glad I could help."

Her digits brushed over his palm, resting on his hand for a moment longer than intended after she'd dropped the runes into his outstretched appendage. Slender fingers ran over the edge of his palm while she braved the urge to touch him without shying away, and she felt her body hum with life. "I really need to get this ritual started," she whispered. "But... I wanted to apologize."

"There is no need," he tried to convince her.

Vanessa shook her head. "No. I do." She sighed. "I need to learn that hiding my problems doesn't fix them. And it won't let anyone get closer to me if I don't find ways to admit the things that I try to keep locked away. I'm sorry that I tried to hide it. You guys had every right to be worried. My strongest desire has always been to know who they are, where they are, or why I was given up. Being presented with a way to finally have an answer is..." she stopped and shook her head a little. "I could have jeopardized so much for everyone."

For the second time that day, Leon hugged her. His strong arms reached out and drew her into a tight squeeze. "We would have understood. But you're right," he said.

"Vanessa," Bobo called.

Leon let her go and jutted his chin toward the altar. "Go on. They need you."

The Spellweaver wiped a bit of moisture from her eyes and nodded with a faint smile curling her lips. "Thank you," she said softly and headed over for the ritual table.

Just like before, Vanessa picked up each item and tried to bond with it. Reaching out metaphysically, she embedded her magical essence into each piece that she'd put up for offering. The wine, fruit, bread, and incense were all fused with these little hints of her. With tiny fragments of her magic.

Raven explained that the action of giving magic with the offerings was a sign of respect to the one being called to and trust in the balance of the world. That everything given freely is one day returned. Because in the waking life, anything of value or worth was not obtained without first giving something away. You had to show the spirits, the elements, and yourself, that you were willing to give up something you treasure in order to gain what you were trying to achieve.

Tips of the frankincense were burned, and the small flames dimmed into embers. Tendrils of smoke danced as they twisted up toward the sky, mingling with each spiraling, ascending strand until they blurred together and dispersed overhead in a woody perfume that held hints of spiced fruit. The solace that was held in that scent washed over everyone present. Next, the fires were lit in the large basins that the carved, golden hands cupped on either side of the altar. The cup of wine was poured, the bowl of fruit and bread were positioned carefully, and Vanessa bowed her head and knelt to pray.

Minutes passed in a strange silence.

The birds that had been chirping within the clearing had all gone silent. They no longer flapped or fluttered through the many boughs and branches. Instead, each feathered body had gone motionless within the trees. They had all gone still as statues and their little, beady, black eyes were fixed—unmoving—on Vanessa's praying form. Their engrossed stares were ever watchful. Unwavering. With hardly a notable rise and fall of their brightly colored feathered chests. There was just a quiet that was so consuming that it ate its way through sound and action alike.

"That isn't disconcerting in the slightest," Leon muttered to Bobo, who was already cupping the top of his ax for comfort.

"Mmmm… indeed," the beast grumbled.

Raven smiled unaware and nudged the ogre. "Look at that form," she said, motioning to Vanessa. The elf's chest swelled with pride. "It's almost perfect." Her arms crossed over her breast. "Her concentration is sound. It's astonishing," she continued to praise, ignoring the men as their attention was clearly torn between the devilishly eerie, unmoving birds and Vanessa's praying form.

"Considering what she has had to pray and spell her way through, I wouldn't believe she was not capable of it," Bobo mumbled under his breath.

If she had heard him, she made no indication that she had as she continued. "With a form like that, we may not have to wait very long," she said with a light laugh.

With a groan, Leon's light, azure eyes scanned through the webbing of tree branches lined with quiet, motionless birds all staring down at Vanessa. "Let's hope so," he added sotto voce.

Rising, Vanessa steadied herself on the altar and waited for her eyes to adjust to the bright afternoon light once more. Wasting no time, Leon crossed the clearing, coming to her side and offering her aid to stand without fear of falling. "You all right?"

She nodded lazily. "Yes. I'm just a little tired from infusing my magic with the offerings and praying for so long. I should be fine in a few minutes," she stated groggily.

"I do believe I have a bit of biscuit and a few pieces of jerky stashed in my pouch," Bobo admitted, his massive paw rummaging around the bag at his hip. His usual spectacles, a book, and—finally— a package tied with twine were removed. He removed the string, opened the thick, wax-covered paper, and presented the contents to Vanessa.

The witch did not turn a nose up at the meager offering. In fact, she braced herself on Leon while hurriedly turning to fully face

Bobo and his bits of biscuit and jerky. Surely, it would have been a snack for the massive demon but to Vanessa, it was a small meal.

Stuffing a few bits of bread into her mouth, she chewed ferociously before popping a few select pieces of dry meat into her mouth. Raven tapped Vanessa's arm with a gourd full of water. "Drink," the elf urged softly. "You keep stuffing your mouth like that and you're going to choke."

The Spellweaver needed little persuasion, and she eagerly reached for the water, uncorked the top, and gulped down several mouthfuls of cool, refreshing water before returning it to the elf.

"It's been a while since I've felt like that after using my magic," she said while panting to catch her breath.

Raven smirked and nodded knowingly. "It is a different kind of spell casting. Those that don't do it often feel like you did. The need for food and even resting are common side effects."

"A different kind of spell casting," Bobo repeated the phrase, but his features begged for the woman to divulge in more detail on the matter.

After fussing with her white mane, Raven turned a palm up to the table as she spoke, "This is spell casting too. It's just a different kind. Instead of powders and enhancers, or elements to produce more precise magic, you use your magic to fuse with the offerings. You give with the chance of a payoff, but there is no guarantee..."

"Wait, so there is a chance that the qilin won't come?" Leon half-whined the question.

Raven looked bewildered at him and then the others. "How is it that these simple rituals and exchanges elude you all? What about the Wild Hunt that you all perform each year?" she barked, her eyes wide with surprise.

But no one was paying her any mind. For far off in the forest, something was approaching the clearing. She did a double-take from them to the woods, a bit annoyed, and then froze in place. Just a few yards away, the qilin stood watching the group around the Altar of Offering.

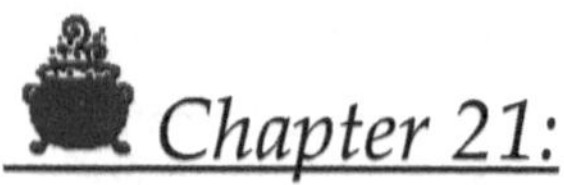 *Chapter 21:*

The qilin held its head proudly in the air as it locked its eyes on everyone dead ahead. Its long tail whipped languidly behind the being as it contemplated its next course of action. Another soft breeze wafted through the dense forest, rustling leaves and bushes lightly as it swept through the woodland.

Big, bright, blue butterflies were gently beating their delicate wings in an attempt to keep them circling the strange beast. Their bodies were almost twinkling in the afternoon glow that peeked between pine needles and budding limbs overhead. Like flower petals that had been dusted in iridescent glitter, they fluttered about the qilin, giving the animal an air of gentleness that, otherwise, its appearance lacked to invoke.

The majestic beast itself had a large, muscular body. Soft, tawny fur mingled with luminescent, golden scales covering the back and inching over its rump and hindquarters. But a long, flowing tail undulated as it rode a magical current all its own. The colors of the tail's hair caught the sunlight and it glinted off of the lustrously bright green, deep turquoise, and midnight blue that faded into a charcoal black in a magnificent display. Under its belly, the tan fur from its hips, sides, and legs turned into a hard, lizard-like hide that rippled into a soft yellow color. The hooves were like that of a horse but engulfed in flames that neither grew nor dimmed, only remained one constant shape of dancing flames. A thin line of clouds circled around the ankles just above the flickering tips of the fire, and beneath the hooves, the ground was a fusion of life and death. Trailing up from the chest, the beast had a massive mane of hair that hid the qilin's long, elegant neck and mirrored the coloration of the tail with the green, blue, and black hair and it hugged the edges of the creature's face. A long snout that was a mix of feline and deer with large protruding fangs and a set of deep, yellow eyes faced the group with a profound sense of wisdom and intelligence that, honestly, scared Vanessa. A great number of the butterflies had taken perch in the creature's massive entanglement of antlers that far exceeded anything that could be perceived as a natural occurrence.

With a snort from the beast, the delicate winged insects all took flight and flittered slowly around as the qilin began to walk forward. The eyes were solely fixed on Vanessa as it took its time in approaching, giving her the ability to watch the ground around its hooves burn and char into ash before tiny, curling vines, patches of clover, and small bell-shaped flowers exploded out from the soil underfoot. It was a cycle that she was mesmerized by but not nearly as captivating as the eyes of the qilin. They kept her rooted in place even though she wanted to run away from the beast. There was a fear and a strange sense of tranquility that loomed around the ancient creature. She could feel it even from this distance. But that distance was quickly being shortened with each passing second.

Vanessa's mouth opened to speak, but nothing came out. She felt it coursing through her veins like an old and forgotten power, humming its way through her body, waking her up… making her remember things she didn't even know she had lost. It was like a wall was knocked down in her mind, and the knowledge that flooded her was flowing through her in a way that made Vanessa feel like she was drowning. Unless she looked into those yellow, cat-like eyes, she *was* drowning both in power and in knowledge. But just a single look from the creature made her feel like she was breaching the surface of the ocean after a series of waves had pushed her underwater. The world felt like it was fading around her and all she could see was the qilin. Sound had even disappeared. It was haunting and beautiful at the same time.

The only thing that existed in that moment to her was the beast slowly coming toward her.

The fires lit behind her at the altar turned green and wildly danced about the golden bowls that now hardly contained them. The sweet, nature-filled scent of frankincense wafted and swirled by the stone slab and encircled her. The qilin wasn't just a knowledgeable creature. It was a timeless being that thrummed with power and magic that made the blue cloaks look like ants in comparison.

Her mouth felt dry, and her heartbeat hammered like a thousand galloping unicorns trying to outrun the wind.

"Vanessa." The voice made her think of warmth and pure happiness, but the tone was calm, deep, and loving. "You called upon me, yes?" The more it spoke, the more that the voice made Vanessa want to sit down and listen to it speak for hours. To drink in whatever words it had to say. To soothe her into a long and peaceful sleep.

She nodded, not sure she trusted her voice to speak.

"Ask me," it urged her softly.

The witch's mind felt muddled. Thoughts, conversations, everything before that moment simply slipped away. Her stomach flipped in excitement, and she licked her lips. She could do it. She could ask about her parents. She could ask and have the peace of mind that she had always wanted. So what if the qilin could only be called upon once a year? What was one more year in a holding cell for those demons?

Demons… wait. That's right. The demons would keep flooding this plane of existence if she didn't get the de-summoning spell. How could she have forgotten? The de-summoning spell!

Ah, there was another temptation. She could ask for the de-summoning spell and they would be done. They could all go home. But… what they would lose if they lacked the audience that they needed with the elves could cause damage too. If they located the lost elven city, then they would have knowledge of so much forgotten magic. So many answers could come from just that one question.

She had to sift and search to remember things that had been so clear to her a moment ago. Like the waves of knowledge that pounded against her mind had eroded thoughts from her memory. It wasn't trickery of the qilin. It was the overwhelming presence of power. But now she had steered through the chaotic mess of her own mind. The question to ask was simple.

"Where is the lost elven city?" she whispered.

For a second, she thought she saw its black lips curl into a smile before the being crossed the remaining distance that lay between them. The nose of the creature sniffed around her and then laid a gentle kiss upon her forehead. The press of its wet nose was cool against her skin right before she felt the growing tingle of heat spread from her brow, to her head, and then it exploded through her body. There was no warning as the magic coursed through her painfully.

Her jaw unhinged to scream, but her throat didn't produce a single sound. In her mind, she felt the seed being planted. The answer then blooming, and each petal that intersected with the reply unfurled, revealing the paths that looped and webbed together to make up the information that she had requested.

She hit her knees and slammed her hands firmly on the ground in front of her as she panted, desperately trying to catch her breath. The throbbing in her head matched the dull pulse that enveloped every limb and nuance that made up her body. And she felt like she had run miles while standing in place.

"You gave more power than needed, Vanessa. For your generosity and for your ability to put selfish questions off to the side, I leave you with a gift," the qilin informed before shaking its head, causing the hair of its mane to fan out and the surrounding butterflies to disperse slightly before returning to the creature's side.

Slowly, Vanessa lifted her head and spoke, but—just like before—her voice couldn't go above a whisper. "May I be so bold as to ask what you have so generously given, qilin?"

There was the soft, rolling laughter that roamed through the air as if a distant storm were announcing its presence. "You are so in touch with magic, yet you fear it. I simply opened your mind and freed you from your shackles. The power that you have is not a burden, Vanessa. It is a gift. And gifts are meant to be shared. Fear not the power that you have. Fear not the magic you wield. You are the vessel of a lost world. It is my duty to see it flourish once more."

Looking up into the creature's gaze, she knew that it had to leave, but she didn't want it to. "Would it be rude of me to ask you to stay?" she asked.

Again, it laughed lightly. "It would be rude for you not to."

She cracked a smile, even though she felt her heart ache at that thought of it leaving. There was so much she wanted to know. The questions tugged and pulled at her, whispers of possible answers for things that she always dreamed of finding out. But she knew she couldn't ask a single one aside from what the qilin had answered.

"Thank you," she said, her voice sounding small.

"Do not be sad, Vanessa. Look to the dawn. I am always on the horizon. Speak to me, and I will hear you. Though I cannot promise an answer," the being explained.

Dipping its head down, the qilin's snout nuzzled into Vanessa's cheek, and she encircled her arms into the creature's massive mane. Her eyes screwed shut, and she squeezed it tightly while she felt the desire to sleep take hold of her. "But I will always hear you," the qilin finished softly.

When Vanessa opened her eyes, the qilin was gone, the world had returned to normal, and they were all spread out on the grassy clearing. One by one, they woke, groaning as they held their heads and tried to make sense of the time that they had lost. Overhead, the sky could be seen, and it was no longer clear blue heavens with warm sun cascading through the canopy. It was night. Deep and dark like the bottom of an inkwell and fixed with a large, glowing moon dusted in orange hues.

"Looks like tomorrow is going to be a blood moon," Leon said with a groan as he stood up and stretched, cracking his back.

"How long were we out?" Bobo grunted.

Raven rubbed her forehead as she said, "Well, if tomorrow is the blood moon, then we were only out for a few hours."

Bobo looked up and tried to read the sky. "It isn't that late in the evening, and the moon is so full. Why on Rean is it so dark?"

Raven chuckled, "Welcome to the *Black* Forest." She then motioned around them. "Where the days are dangerous, and the nights are filled with nightmares."

"Well, I suppose I shouldn't be surprised with its reputation and all…" Twisting from side to side, Bobo stretched and hopped to his feet with more agility than Raven had expected the ogre to display.

She held up two hands, her black eyes dancing with mirth, as she splayed out all her fingers and made them dance in place as she giggled. "Ten out of ten. Good form and an excellent landing."

Blushing, Bobo cleared his throat. "I do try to stay fit and in shape," he admitted confidently.

"You are a prime specimen of your species," she flattered the gentlemen-beast.

"Finally, someone that appreciates me," he stated, standing proudly.

Leon turned his attention to Vanessa as he held out a hand to her. "Need a hand?" She took it, even though she was capable of standing up on her own, after doing it for a lifetime, it was nice to be asked instead of having someone assume that she'd take care of herself.

"Thanks," she said softly.

"So, what did it say?" Leon asked.

Instantly, all eyes were on her. The memories of what had transpired came rushing back to the front of her mind. The sound of the qilin's voice and the sensation of the kiss to her forehead all overran her senses, causing her to gasp and take a step or two back before catching herself. "It… It didn't tell me," she started.

Bobo looked concerned as he inquired, "What do you mean, Vanessa?"

"The qilin, it… showed me, somehow. It gave me the answer." She then looked around them and took note of every tree, sapling, bush, and rock. "I know where we are."

"Well, that is good. Jolly good. I'm so proud of you," Bobo teased.

"No. I mean I know where we are. I know the whole forest. I can get us to the elven city. No problem." She laughed and shook her head. "It's so weird to have information just planted into your mind like that. But it gave me the location."

Raven searched the forest for a moment and then the sky. "I suggest we move out as soon as we can. The dangers of the forest grow as the night goes on."

They all surveyed the inky night that coated the woods outside the Altar of Offering. Midnight hues dug deep into every nook and cranny as nightshades etched their shadows over every dying leaf. The winds that had been gently blowing all day toyed with the foliage of the forest, making the woodland seem like a living, breathing entity. The sway of the branches and vines made it appear like the world outside was a predatory creature that was circling them all. Watching and waiting for its opportunity to pounce and devour them.

Shivers ran up and down Vanessa's spine like an icy dance from a frost fairy sent to entrance her bones to their chilled touch. The whispering winds that trickled over her skin did nothing but aid the dark, ominous feeling that had consumed her mind and body at that moment.

Raven looked up in the sky, her black gaze scanning the stretch of stars hanging within the heavens directly above the sacred circle. "The moon hasn't reached its highest point. We should take this as luck doing us a favor and make haste to our destination," she advised more adamantly than before.

And none disagreed with her. For when they looked out into the woods, they felt what their eyes could not see. A looming darkness that spread with the shadows, breathed with the breeze, and filled every part of their minds with fear. Nodding, they all turned to gather their belongings before lining up near the edge.

Bobo nudged his master and pointed with his chin out into the vast stretch of trees. "Lead the way," he said with a smile.

 *Chapter 22:*

Stepping back through the protective barrier felt so very daunting. One moment, it was a tranquil peace with spells of worry as they watched the forest. The next, it was a deafening silence that was accompanied by the soft sounds of nightlife scurrying throughout the Black Forest. As they passed through the wards, the magic prickled over their skin, leaving them humming with life and renewed magic.

Vanessa inspected her hands inquisitively. "Wow. That is a cool feature to have in a ward," she whispered.

"Even the sacred place nestled within the forest knows the dangers that lurk outside the Altar of Offering. They recharge the spirit and body so that none are left defenseless," Raven informed near the witch, but her onyx orbs were scanning various points of the forest. "Tap into whatever the qilin gave you, girl. We need to hurry."

The Spellweaver made a sound that implied she understood the severity of the situation and closed her eyes and willed her mind to focus. Opening her hazel hues to the night-washed world splashed with pools of milky white, she looked at all the trees and rocks that had once appeared the same to her but were now landmarks on an unwritten map in her mind.

"This way," she whispered to everyone. "Follow me."

Every time one of them swore they were lost, Vanessa urged them otherwise and pressed on. In her mind, there was a path that was etched into the world itself that only she could see. It took them through the thickest portions of the woods, had them scaling boulders covered in moss, and had them weaving through briar patches. But they steadily made their way through the foliage.

"Vanessa, my dear, are you sure this is the right way?" Bobo asked in a hoarse whisper.

She rolled her eyes. It was not the first time he had asked her that, and it was surely not going to be the last. "I told you, I know where I'm going."

Bobo grunted. "Yes, well... pardon my doubts. This is the first time you actually *do* know where you're going." He looked to the side and did a double-take. "There! That stump. I swear we've passed it twice now," he said sounding panicked. Theatrically, he laid the back of his hand over his brow and gave a quiet wail of worry. "Lost. We are lost," he claimed fervently.

"It's the woods, Bobo. You're going to see a lot of stumps. Besides, how can you be so sure with how dark it is," Vanessa hissed in return.

Leon laughed through his nose as he tried to stifle his chuckling. "I mean, the big guy has a point, Vanessa. I feel a bit strange following after you for this long and us *not* being lost..."

"Leon... by the goddess, I have gold dust and a wand, and I'm not afraid to use them," she snapped angrily.

Raven's face contorted as she tried to listen but couldn't hear the sounds over the bickering of her party members. "Shhhh," she sounded like an angry snake. "You'll get us all killed if you don't hush up your yapping," she whispered. The next question was directed at the Spellweaver, though the starry-eyed gaze of the elf was scanning through the infinite void that ate away at the endless pillars of trees surrounding them. "How much further?"

"Not far," Vanessa informed.

Just as the witch turned, there was the sound of a twig snapping. Everyone went still as distant bushes rustled. Raven hit the ground. Her toes dug into the dirt, and her palms held up her upper body from the forest floor. She looked like a lizard about to scurry away to the safety of a nearby tree. The rest of them didn't look much different from her. They had all crouched or bent down to hide. Part of Vanessa thought that it was just an overactive squirrel or feisty creature hunting down its prey. But that part of her quickly died when they heard the sharp cry of an animal being devoured by something larger. Much larger. The sound of bones snapping in multiple places echoed all around them, almost taunting them with a fate that they'd all meet if the creature crunching away loudly found them.

Waving to gain everyone's attention, Vanessa jabbed her finger in a specific direction and then motioned for them all to follow her quietly. No sooner had they all taken a few, carefully laid steps, did they hear a low growl. It was closer than the cry of the dying animal had been. And what was worse was the fact that there was a second, deeper growl that accompanied it. But the most unsettling matter was the immense, ear-splitting howl that soon followed before a chorus of mirroring howls joined in.

Raven's eyes bulged, her face seeming paler than before, as she whispered in horror, "The wolves."

That was the only prompting Bobo needed. Slowly, his large paws reached down, freed his ax from his hip, and held it firmly in both hands. The elf, though shaken, had hardened her features while she pulled forth her two, small, bone axes. Leon prepared a spell and searched the woods before locking eyes with everyone one by one and then turning his attention to Vanessa. He nodded to her, silently telling her to lead the way.

Not willing to be caught without a weapon or means to save herself, she too had prepared a spell and had her wand drawn, and she was suddenly missing the comfort of her staff. It happened so fast. They could hear it all around them. The sounds of the wolves searching the forest floor as they sniffed frantically, trying to find the source of the enticing scents that mingled in the stillness of the underbrush.

Each snort that carried through the air brought Vanessa's hairs on her skin to attention, her skin humming with electric jolts all while attempting to swallow her urge to scream. Her body felt like she was walking in a pit full of poisonous snakes and hazardous spell vials, and all of her senses were screaming at her. Her heart picked up in tempo as her blood rushed through her body, drowning out her precious hearing. But nothing could drown out the sounds of the cursed wolves. Wherever a paw landed, saplings snapped like twigs underfoot, and leaves were crushed in a mind-numbing harmony.

Each sound entangled itself in the panting and sniffing as the pack of giant beasts weaved through the abundant vegetation.

Mid-step, Vanessa paused as she heard the chaotic inhalation of one of the beasts uncomfortably close to them. More specifically, close to her. It grunted and dug at the ground, its claws scraping over a root of a tree that the witch was hiding behind. She could feel the nails drag over the aged wood and reverberate through the trunk of it. The feeling was setting her teeth on edge. Her body seized for a moment. She didn't move. She didn't breathe. She stood motionless, and the others instinctively followed suit.

The wet, charcoal-colored nose peeked around the tree as the beast lifted its gray snout and searched for the source of the smells it had caught a whiff of. Carefully, it tracked the unknown intruders to its forest. The black, rubbery lips peeled back as the monster growled. The quivering skin raised over the beast's jowls to reveal two rows of pointy teeth. They had been found, and—after realizing this fact— Vanessa gulped with a deep frown tugging at her mouth.

As soon as the beast bellowed its cry to the rest of the pack, Bobo snuffed out its howl barely a moment after it had begun. A sharp yip cracked through the air. Yanking back on his ax, the ogre whipped the weapon off to the side to sling the blood free of his blade. The Spellweaver watched as crimson sprayed the nearby trunks with droplets of deep red before rising to her feet and taking the lead. "Quickly, this way!" she cried out to the others.

She could hear the other wolves howling as she spoke, calling out to each other and letting them know that the hunt was on. Darting from her hiding space, she ran for a spot that called to her in her mind. They were so close to the elven city. She could feel it. The entrance was close by, but those creatures were blocking the path. Now, they had to focus on not being prey before they could bother with locating the entrance to the hidden city. Branches scratched at her face and body as she slapped multiple thin limbs from her path while she barreled through the forest like a crazed goblin.

Double dip a candlestick!

As they ran, the ground underfoot thundered with the crashing paws of the wolves that were fast on their heels. Vanessa led the group through a narrow passage of enormous trees that grew clumped together. One by one, they darted through the small openings that were large enough for them but too small for the larger animals.

No sooner had they leaped through the tight space, they heard the heavy thudding of several bodies crashing into the trees. Their paws were lashing out through the cracks, and sharp talons desperately searched for flesh to sink into instead of bark and soil. Gnashing teeth pushed through the trunks as the wolves snarled at their escaping prey. Noses rose to the air and lowered to the base of the trees as they tried to find another route to Vanessa and the others.

"Do you have a plan, dear?" Bobo asked windily.

Her eyes darted about as she dogged the shrubbery. "I'm… sort of making it up as I go," she admitted.

From behind them, two massive bodies lunged from the trees and hit the ground running. The impact made the whole ground shake, and Vanessa screamed as the excitement that was building up inside her exploded, involuntarily, out of her mouth. "RUN!" she commanded in horror as the third broke a young tree in half and fell in behind the other two wolves.

Snap.

Crack.

The tree whined with splintering crackles as it leaned and descended upon the leaf-blanketed floor below with a thundering *crash!* A howl erupted from behind them. The chorus of cries was building higher and higher. The howls became shorter and shorter as they mingled with the guttural sounds of triumph that quaked within the beasts' throats.

They were gaining on them. Up ahead, there was a dip in the land. There was no telling how far down it went. Vanessa spared a look over her shoulder, and her eyes widened at the image sprawled out before her. The massive, furry creatures were angrily snapping at the air and slamming their bodies into the bothersome trunks of trees that hindered their fast approach as they ran.

Turning her vision back to the ledge ahead, she furrowed her brow and let her mouth set in a hard line. She was going to do it. It was this or lingering where they were to see how long they could outrun the beasts. And, considering their large, speedy gait, it wouldn't take much longer for her and the others to be lost under the claws itching to pin them down and the teeth that longed to have flesh between them. No. They either tried this daredevil escape or died.

Dying wasn't an option Vanessa was willing to make today. "Leon, you blind them. Bobo, the trees. Raven, give me a hand!" The commands were short, clipped, and filled with urgency. There wasn't a lot of time to explain and trying to do so while out of breath was a hassle in itself.

Nodding, Leon turned around and stopped dead in his tracks. His hands were already holding the spells that he had prepared. "See your servants suffering, guide your hand to the tormented place, open the sky with your glory, and all evils that are upon me, by the light of the goddess, BE BLINDED!"

White glowed in his hands before shooting out in a massive ray of golden illumination that pierced the veiled darkness. The fur of the wolves glittered. The forest bloomed in a magnificent, splendid light that held warmth and comfort before exploding with a bang around the faces of the beasts.

Short yips echoed in the air as the three wolves ran into trees, stumbled over themselves, and rammed into one another as their eyes were blinded by the spell.

"Bobo," Vanessa reminded.

His powerful arms drew back, ax in hand, "Already on it, my dear!" he growled and let a monstrous heave of his arms crash his blade into the body of a tree. The force of the blow caused the ax's edge to land deep into the bark and deeper into the meat of the wood.

Vanessa slid to a stop and faced her pet. Her arms raised up, and one hand rested under her elbow, the other was held straight up. Her thumb lined with her third eye, her pointer and middle finger extended, reaching for the sky above. She closed her eyes and focused, whispering a chant.

"Do it!" Vanessa roared, breaking off in the middle of the chant.

Taking in a deep breath, Bobo felt his eyes prick with tears. He looked to his master as he watched her keep her eyes locked on him and smiled, "You are more than an ogre to me," she said it quietly, but he felt the words deep down. They awoke the need to protect others, and himself, but they also fanned the flames of self-love that he harbored within the depths of his soul. It flared through him like a wildfire and traveled through his blood like tiny rivers of molten lava. Growing until he felt the parts of him that he thought he had buried so far down that they could never claw their way out of their grave. The part of himself that he denied. The part that he feared. The part that he hated. That portion of his being that was him no matter what he said or did and was always there no matter how much he tried to deny it. For the first time since he had been summoned, he found that part of himself and did the one thing that he never imaged he would do.

He let it break him and remake him. He embraced it and made it bend to his will. He accepted that part of himself and all its horrors and drew in another deep breath.

Vanessa's chants were whispers, but they built up in pitch. Just the mystical sound of words that were spoken but their names unheard. Until, finally, she said clearly and with command, "The seals that I have made, the binds that I have placed, let them lift from the body, and forever be erased!"

Metaphysical chains became brittle and weak before shattering their bonds like ropes made from dry leaves. Bobo's mouth opened, and he felt it welling up like the tears that threatened to spill from his eyes. He roared. Like a battle cry filled with all the pain that Aeristria had to offer, he roared monstrously and let the forgotten power flow through him.

Green flames engulfed his forearms and shot out through his ax, the vermilion fires slicing through the trunk and exploding out of the other side in a brilliant lime and yellow flare. The tree split clean in two upon the hellfire's impact. Silence consumed them all before crackling cut through the quiet. Snarls from the wolves emerged from behind them as Leon flung a few spells at them before rushing over to Vanessa and Raven's side.

Leon looked from the wolves that were shaking off the last lingering effects of the spell and rising up with menacing growls. "Ladies and gents, I do believe that we should move on to the next part of the plan if there is another part… or start running…"

"Wait," Vanessa whispered, and she pulled out a bit of dust from her pouch, caressed her wand with it, and snapped her wrist as she cast a spell over the tree. "Fall for me." She looked to the wolves and saw them set their eyes on the group.

"The spell won't last long," Leon said.

"I don't need it to," she said with a smirk. "Raven. Your turn." She pointed to the ledge ahead.

There was a very clear drop-off, but there was no telling how far it went. With luck, it was a tremendous drop. The land rose up on the other side, but even the massive beasts couldn't make a leap like that unless they could sprout wings and fly. "We are going to feather fall to the other side," Vanessa informed.

Her ludicrous plan took root in all of their minds, but it wasn't accepted without resistance. Just then, the spell lifted, and the wolves scattered as they attempted to dive out of the way of the falling lumber. Only one went still beneath it.

"Are you mad? There are too many of us! That is a far fall, and you'd even need to use power to steer how we'd all fall. You could deplete your magic," Leon barked.

"There isn't another choice," Vanessa snapped.

"I believe in you," Raven said quickly, grabbing Vanessa's hand.

"Do you believe in me, Leon?" the Spellweaver asked, but there was so much more to the question as she held out her hand to him.

The wolves were running for them again. "I do." He grabbed her free hand and Bobo came running over just as the other three started to dash for the edge. "For the record," Leon shouted as Vanessa cast the spell, Bobo laid a hand on Vanessa's shoulder, and they all jumped into the air. A rocky, yawning cavern greeted them below with deep shadows hiding how far the drop stretched just as the spell began to manifest below them. "…you're crazy!" his scream echoed through the depths of the drop below their flailing bodies.

The bubble of safety enveloped them, however, they didn't feel safe as they could now make out the jagged rocks lining the river flowing between the narrow passage. In the distance, a massive waterfall roared as the plumes of white mist billowed around the cascading waters. Vanessa grunted and shifted hard to one side as she tried to maneuver the bubble. Sweat had started to collect on her forehead as she twisted to the other side. As she steered the bubble, they could all see that the young witch was not having an easy time with the spell.

It wasn't until her eyes drooped and her head lulled for a split second that the panic had started to rise.

"She's sputtering," Leon growled.

Raven started to feed more magic into the Spellweaver as she yelled, "I'm giving her all I've got."

"Hold on!" Vanessa roared as the manifestation of the orb around them flickered and waned. The ledge was so close. Just a little closer.

Just a little closer. . .

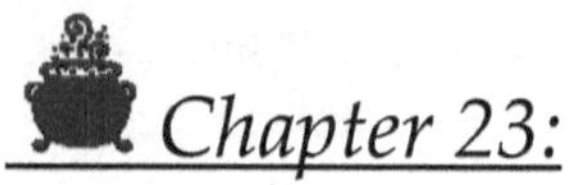 *Chapter 23:*

The wolves cried mournfully as they paced the ledge from afar and on high behind them. Had they not just been trying to eat them, Vanessa might have felt bad for the creatures. However, they had, and the whining only confirmed that her plan had worked.

For now.

Raven was grinning like a madwoman. "That was fun," she announced.

"Remind me to never go anywhere *that* woman says is fun," Bobo expressed while panting.

Vanessa laughed. She laughed until her sides hurt, and her body tingled with fatigue. "I used a lot of power," she said in a weak voice. She didn't even notice that she was falling.

"Okay. I gotcha," Leon announced swiftly, catching her before she hit the ground. "This is why I didn't want you to do this," he said with worry threaded into his voice. "Had it been a little further and—"

Vanessa's hand cupped the side of Leon's cheek, and he stopped speaking. "I'm fine. You aren't the only one willing to risk yourself to save the people you care about."

All the worry and anger melted from the Summoner's face. The sculpted features turned into something else. Something that was softer and fixed with understanding. "All right, Vanessa. You win. You're right," he said softly.

"Mark me, you're starting a habit that she will never let you give up," Bobo declared.

Limply, Vanessa curled her lips and then pointed to the side. "Over there," she said meekly, her eyes being tugged at with sleep. "The entrance ... it's over there."

"Stay awake, Vanessa. Just a little longer," Leon begged as he hoisted her up in his arms and started to walk, passing Bobo who held out his arms.

"I can—" the ogre started.

"I have her," the Summoner muttered in a tone that left little room for argument.

Lowering his arms, Bobo nodded to himself. "Very well. As you wish."

They hadn't gone far before there was a set of towering, mossy, aged stones blocking their path. Violet morning glories crawled over the base of the stones and climbed up the edges to frame the rocks in a flowery wreath.

Leon looked down and lightly shook Vanessa. "Vanessa. Vanessa. Wake up, there are stones blocking the path. Where do we go now?"

Blinking, Vanessa woke and turned her head sluggishly. She pointed to the stones with a lone, tired finger, and whispered, "Through the stones." With that said, she shut her eyes once more and her arm fell.

The wizard looked lost and shook the young witch in his arms. "Vanessa. Vanessa!"

Raven stepped forward and eyed over the stones. In the distance there were howls. Where they had left the wolves was bare. They were on the move again. Without a doubt, the blasted beasts were trying to find another way to get to them. "She has depleted a great deal of her magic. Let her rest. I have this. They will find us if we just sit here all night, and Vanessa did her part. We are here," the elf said quietly.

"You've been here before?" Leon questioned.

She shook her head. "I was only a twinkle in my father's eyes when the city had been hidden, remember?" Her eyes traced over the stones. "But there is strong elven power permeating from these stones."

She didn't say anymore as she looked the large stones over. Her hands roamed over the soft, soggy moss as she tried to find some sort of etching or hidden mechanism that would give them passage.

"It's spelled. I can feel it. I just need the words to unlock it," she whispered with threads of excitement woven into her hoarse tone. "*A filla scin tu men veye monone*," she hummed the words and they glided off her tongue like a song. The tune brought the stones to light as they softly glowed with a dim, powdery-blue light. The howling grew closer, and the ground beneath them held faint rumbling tremors of paws thundering in the distance.

"We're running out of time," Leon informed. Though, it wasn't needed.

"*Monone! Monone!*" Raven spoke more frantically as excited yips from the approaching wolves tangled with their short howls. The stones started to glow brighter. "Now," she yelled. "Go through them now!"

Excited barks and short growls reverberated off the stones as the wolves were fast approaching. "Now!" Raven reiterated, reaching out for Leon as he came to his feet, Vanessa held fast in his arms, and the elf clamped her slender fingers around his arm to drag him through the unseen opening. Bobo turned his back to the glowing rocks and held his position, making sure all passed through before he, too, disappeared into the entrance.

The wolves rounded the corner and searched the area with whimpers and whines while sniffing at the ground all around the stones. Finding nothing but the scents that the group had left behind, they faced the stars overhead and howled mournfully before moving on.

The air and sounds all around them were different. The Black Forest had held a foreboding presence the whole time that they had traveled through it, but this place, it didn't hold the same darkness to it. Instead, it felt lighter within. Not like the Altar of Offering, but similar to it just the same.

All around, tiny creatures twirled in the air near the bushes and gardens surrounding the hidden entrance to the city. One landed on a large leaf near Leon and began to glow a soft orange. Its body mirrored a cross between a salamander and a bug while its iridescent wings fluttered nervously on its back before taking flight to loop about the air with the others of its kind.

They had found it. They had found Satviriya, the hidden city of the elves. "Bless my spell," Bobo whispered, his ocean blue eyes slowly drinking in the finely groomed gardens that were sprouting splendid flowers that held thick, honey perfumes mingling with the soft scents of wet grass kissed with dew. It was like the city was stuck forever in spring. No signs of winter lingered here, and even the air held a slight warmth washing over their heavily garbed bodies.

Bobo fussed with his wrinkled collar and sighed at his haggard appearance. "This is not the way I wanted to show up here." The grumble left him but none acknowledged it. And no one could truly fault the ogre for his fretting.

The lost elven city was a perfect union of city and nature. The homes were nestled inside of massive trees and hills, and swaying bridges filled the canopy overhead. Small huts jutted up from the ground in tiny groupings like they were giant mushrooms sprouting. A large tree grew along the side of an enormous boulder and the roots that hugged the edges gave the effect of the two natural monuments hugging, married, and timeless. From within the great rock, warm light and merry music was pouring out. All around them they saw the perfect union of a city within a great forest, where one did not disrupt the other.

Leon looked around the garden to the saplings hugged with flowered vines that dripped down from the boughs and brushed over the vibrant grass surrounding their slender trunks. Slowly, his eyes drifted until they landed on the elf girl who'd been quiet ever since they passed through the stones.

Raven looked like she was both happy and sad as her hand quivered, reaching out to caress the petals of the neighboring blooms.

"We are here. We've made it to Satviriya," she stated in a voice that lacked any real emotion. Her eyes were following the dancing ebon glows that were dizzily twirling about the garden. Ebon glows were the critters that were a cross of insect and small, flat-faced dragons that had luminescent bellies that would glow, as their name suggested. The gentle glow of the tiny creatures gave a soft, peaceful light to the surroundings. The white-haired female extended her digit and one landed, danced in a circle atop her finger, and then fluttered off to the white flowers to enjoy their sweet, fragrant nectar.

"They are coming," she said softly, watching the ebon glow at the edge of the garden. Before anyone could inquire what she meant, a grouping of beings came rushing over.

The hasty mass of creatures took the formation of a wall, lining the stone path that led out of the garden and blockading the group from heading further into the city. All of them were tall, slender, and beautiful. The beings had large eyes and long ears and skin that glowed in an unnatural way. Silky robes of various colors and design floated behind them as they came to a stop at the edge of the garden, authority oozing from their posture.

A few of them had war scythes that stood a foot taller than the beings themselves. The sharp edge was glinting in the moonlight while the blunt side held a beautifully sculpted angel wing that seemed to contradict its deadly other half. Untrusting glares were fixed upon Leon, Vanessa, Bobo, and Raven. Near the middle of the group, a female guard stepped forward, and her eyes scrutinized every inch that made up the adventurers sprawled out in the gardens. The guardswoman's finger pointed out aggressively at them all as she spoke in a rushed manner, "*Viela mina eh torme alise tullia?*"

Raven stepped forward and spoke heatedly, "*A'ah lenna e` filtos min qilin falle na ose.*"

Bobo bent down and took Vanessa from Leon and let the young witch lay in his lap. "I need you to sling spells without fear of her being left behind or hurt," he whispered softly.

The movement had slightly woken the witch up, and she peeled her eyes open after much effort. "What is going on?" she croaked out groggily.

"Hold on," Leon whispered while the elves spoke. His hands were steadily searching his person for something in particular. In one of his many spell pouches, the Summoner pulled out a small vile and uncorked it. Placing his finger over the top, he wet the pad of his digit with the clear oil within the container. Dabbing one ear and then the other, Leon repeated this process for Vanessa so that she could hear as well. Before he corked the bottle and placed it back in his bag, the Summoner then put a few drops into the palm of his hand. The remaining oil was then pressed against each of their mouths.

It was barrier breaker oil. An oil made up of juniper oil and enchanted elder tree sap that could enable those who used it to hear any language spoken (as long as it wasn't Dragconian or a demonic language) if the user applied it to their ears. If rubbed over the lips, it could enable them to speak the tongue of whomever they were speaking with. Unfortunately, Bobo couldn't use it so the others would have to translate for him...

The moment that the oil was applied, Vanessa could hear the angry exchange of words being tossed between the female guard and Raven.

"No one has entered through these front gates in two-hundred years. How did you find this place?" the female guard asked.

"I told you, we completed the ritual at the Altar of Offerings and had an audience with the qilin. It gave us the knowledge on how to get here." Raven sounded upset that she had to repeat herself.

The guardswoman narrowed her eyes. "That doesn't explain how *you* made it through the forest alive and to the front gates."

Raven stiffened at the statement. "Watch yourself. These walls can't save you from my wrath if I am trapped within them with you," she snarled with malice lacing her words. Her fingers stretched and curled, longing to reach for the familiar blades and caress their comforting hilts.

In retaliation, a few of the guards reached for their war scythes, ready to defend themselves if the need arose. But the sound of Vanessa's tired voice broke through the growing tension. "Uh. Hi?" The elves all turned to face her.

"Who are you?" The guardswoman asked, her expression suspecting that Vanessa was of suspicious background with a mere glance.

"I'm Spellweaver… Vanessa Peterson." She paused to draw in a breath and force herself to remain conscious. "I come from the Coven in Tolvade," she sounded winded as she spoke.

All of the elves went wide-eyed and glanced between each other. "By the goddess… your kind still exists?" the female guard whispered.

"Is …there an issue …with us coming… here?" Vanessa cautiously asked, her words dripping with the desire to close her eyes and just sleep. She was so tired, and talking seemed incredibly difficult all of a sudden.

The female guard shifted uncomfortably in place as she turned to clear her throat. Looking Bobo, Vanessa, and Leon over, she spoke with less pepper in her tone. "No. It was just…" her eyes trailed over to Raven. Disgust settled into the guardswoman's eyes. "…unexpected," she finished.

"Oh. That's…goood," Vanessa whispered right before her eyes rolled in the back of her head and her body went limp in Bobo's arms.

"Vanessa," Leon gasped. He instantly rose to his feet and shook the witch, trying to rouse her from her sleep. Worry tugged at every inch of his face as he checked to see if she was still breathing.

Bobo was already at her side and checking over her eyes by gently pulling them open. He laid a massive hand over the side of her neck. "She's magically fatigued," he reminded Leon and Raven.

"Quickly, aid them!" the guardswoman ordered. The throng of elves scattered like petals in a rainstorm. Their flowing, colorful robes trailed behind them like thin, wispy clouds. The elves fell all around them at a speed that made Leon feel anxious, even though he knew that they meant no harm. It didn't help that he was territorial about them touching Vanessa, and he instinctively tugged Vanessa out of Bobo's arms and pulled her closer to his body.

Bobo let the man take the Spellweaver from his grasp before he swiftly rose to his full height, his hands instantly going to his ax. "What did they say?" he growled, ready to defend his master and friends.

Leon was quick to reply, "Don't worry. They said they're going to help us." He half had to remind himself of that fact as he spoke it.

Instantly, the gentleman-beast relaxed. "Ah. Very well, then." He stepped back a bit, giving more room for the elves to move freely about. He was a rather large being, after all.

One of the elves waved a hand over Vanessa's body. A wispy trail of smoke-like, milky light was left behind where the hand had once been. He nodded to another and said, "Her essence is faint. We need to get her to the lunar pools to help her regenerate."

The other elf laid a gentle hand on Bobo's arm as he looked to Vanessa's slumbering form. "Follow me this way, underworld lord. The pools will help her heal and regain lost magic."

"What did she say?" The ogre asked, feeling bad that he couldn't understand the elf.

Leon gave a light smirk as he rose and handed Vanessa over to the ogre. "She said to follow her, underworld lord."

He blinked, shook his head, and then … there was a glimmer of pride washing over the beast's features. Saying nothing, he cradled the young witch and followed behind the elf.

While the elves fussed with Vanessa and the others, the guardswoman informed two other guards by her side, "Seek the Allatari. Tell him that outsiders have entered the city. I'll stay here and make sure that they are not a threat."

They bowed lightly and saluted with their elbow out straight and poised and their fist over the heart while stating in unison, "Yes ma'am!" before marching off to do as instructed.

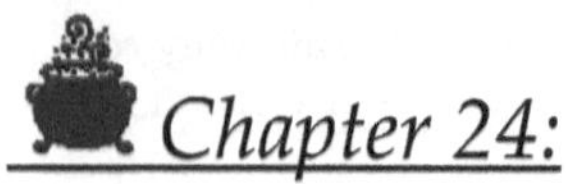 *Chapter 24:*

Several placid pools of silver water glittered beneath the night sky and the soft light that it provided. All around them were large, smooth stones stained in muted tones of browns and grays. The still waters rippled as the elves took Vanessa from Bobo's grasp and submerged her, fully robed, into the lunar pools.

She floated for a brief moment before her body sank down. They positioned her head upon the rocks and made sure to keep a hand on her, making sure she wouldn't slip completely in and drown.

"Will she be all right?" Bobo asked while pacing in a nervous circle around the pool that Vanessa was soaking in.

The elves replied, but the ogre's features contorted as he couldn't understand them. Turning to Leon, the ogre waited for the wizard to explain what had been said.

"She'll be fine. They are keeping her here for about an hour. After that, they said she needs to sleep. Then it will be like it never happened. They did state that she would need to be more careful with her magic casting." Leon informed.

Bobo nodded. "We all know she won't." He sighed and watched the young girl in the silver water. His eyes softened as he did so. "A lot has happened in the past few days. I'll admit, I'm surprised she isn't worse than this."

Leon had to agree with the demon there. They were lucky that the worst of the damage was her having a magic deficiency. Taking the blessing with little complaint, they went quiet and watched the elves fussing over the young witch.

They stayed by Vanessa's side for the next hour. Raven had met back up with them, and, after the wait, they followed the elves to a small hut. There, they gave Vanessa dry clothes and laid her down in one of the spare beds.

"Meals and water will arrive shortly. Try to let your friend rest," said Fielan, one of the elves that had gone to help Vanessa originally. She had long, blonde hair and sharp green eyes. Her skin held a faint tan with an ethereal luminescence. It stung Leon's eyes at first, but he was slowly adjusting to the strange elven attribute.

Raven nodded with a smile, "Thank you, Fielan."

Fielan looked around the group and drew in a long breath only to release it, unsure of how to say what weighed on her mind. Drawing in another breath, the elf said, "The Allatari will call for you. Be sure to eat and rest while you can."

Leon's brows bent as he touched his ear and twitched his lips while in thought. "I think that oil was old. My barrier breaker oil seems to be fizzing out. The who will call for us?"

Raven leaned over in the Summoner's direction and stated plainly, "Your kind does not have a word that could surmise what the Allatari is. They are the parent of the people, a powerful being that is the final decider in all matters of the elves. The closest thing your tongue has to that is... a ruler, though I strongly advise against addressing them as such."

Leon came forward and bowed lightly. "Forgive my ignorance." He turned to face Fielan and bowed again. "Thank you for all that you have done for us. We shall take your advice."

The elf smiled and bowed in return. "Then I shall take my leave for now." With that, the elf turned and left the hut, shutting the door behind them.

Now that the hut was clear of anyone that wasn't Bobo, Raven, Leon, or the resting Vanessa, the three of them looked between each other before Bobo cleared his throat and piped up. "You don't seem a stranger to the way things work around here, though you are clearly not familiar with the city itself."

Raven drew her lips in and pressed down as she thought in silence on how to reply to that. "Are you asking me something or making an observation?"

"A bit of both," Bobo answered, his words deadpan.

"What can we expect?" Leon asked. "We don't have a lot of time to waste."

"Leon, even if they gave us the answer we are seeking, Vanessa wouldn't be able to move anytime soon. Our hands are tied on this one. Fate is dealing us a hand, my dear man. We need to just take a moment to breathe. We can carry on after she is better." The ogre stated while his hand searched his satchel for his book.

"But he isn't wrong, Bobo. I am aware of the way things are done here. I know what to expect. Alleviating your fears and doubts is about the only thing I can do that is useful while within this city." She sighed and grabbed a lock of hair, and slowly threaded it between her fingers repeatedly as she spoke. "The Allatari would be no different than the High Priest Council of your precious Coven," she stated matter-of-factly. "When you have an audience with them, they will have you take an oath to not lie within the city and then freely give your first name. While here, you have to accept their way of life and their customs. Most of the rules and etiquette can be bent and twisted. But you must never lie." She waited then for her words to sink in. "Once you are oath-bound, they will ask you why you are here. Hopefully, they give us a clear answer and we can be on our way."

No sooner had she finished the sentence, there was a knock at the door. Their food and water had arrived as promised. The trays of food carried by elves wearing soft pastel-colored robes came rolling through the door like a rush of swaying pale rainbows. Leon stared at them all curiously, not really taking note of the food even though he was hungry. One by one, they put the trays upon the table and any available surface, bowed, and stepped out of the hut.

Fielan bowed to them just outside the home as the last serving elf left. "Eat and rest, my friends. The Allatari announced that they will have an audience with you by the first light of dawn."

Raven and the others bowed in return and waited for the door to close before they would rise up. When all was quiet once more, Leon spoke first. "Is it just me or… is it really hard to discern which of them were—"

"Male or female?" Raven finished for him.

Leon turned with a perplexed look fixed upon his features. "Yeah," he breathed the word, feeling lost.

"That is because an elf does not have a gender for the first forty-five years of its life. They choose sometime after their forty-fifth completed year," Raven stated it like it was common knowledge, and Leon should have known.

"So… you just… don't have a gender?"

"We are a being regardless of the sex we choose. The idea of male or female doesn't change who we are or how we act. For the first forty-five years, we are obtaining knowledge, cultivating our power, and studying. After this, we choose what we think is the best path for us. Some don't think about it. They just evolve into a gender that is easiest for them to adjust to. Others go in knowing what they want to be. Then there are even some that choose to switch to a different gender later on in their life. And there are even a few that don't ever choose a gender at all. Though those cases are rare, but it does happen. "

"Hmm…" Leon hummed.

"Fascinating," Bobo whispered.

"Our kind understands that nature and magic are always there, but the forms are always changing. Long ago, we matched the world of Raen, and we mirrored the flow of magic. Magic, at the start, is neither good… nor evil. It simply *is*. Some of our kind forgot that…" she stated the last comment under her breath, barely audible to the two men in the group.

Bobo's stomach growled, and Raven's eyes grew as she darted her vision over to the beast. The ogre instantly blushed while Leon stifled a chuckle. "I do say. It has been some time since we last had a proper meal. Forgive my needs, but could we?" he motioned to the table with a longing stare.

Raven laughed and nodded. "Yes. Yes. Of course. Let us feast."

The food sprawled out on the multiple serving trays had many splendid dishes. All of them free of meat and mainly consisting of breads, fruits, cheeses, wonderfully flavored vegetables, and perfectly steamed rice. Large, edible leaves filled with a pasty cheese and cooked beans were rolled up and stacked near a pitcher of wine.

"I need a glass of that," Raven stated, pointing to the jug.

As Leon went to get her a glass, he noticed a small, pearl-sized, golden orb that rested on a tiny tray near the large spread of food. "What is… what is that?" Leon asked.

Raven stopped piling her plate to look in the man's direction. Seeing the item in question, she hummed knowingly. "Oh, yes. That is a nutrition pellet," she informed. "It is typically given to patients as they are easy to swallow."

"A nutrition pellet," Bobo repeated quietly.

Raven set her plate down and licked her fingers before speaking. "Yes. The best way to describe it is that it is a meal that has been refined and condensed by magic so patients can easily take it."

"Marvelous creation," Bobo confirmed.

"Oh, it is. However, the taste is most foul," she stated with a shudder.

Chuckling, Bobo finished making his plate and sat down at the table with Raven. "I say, Leon. Won't you be joining us?"

"Hmm? Oh, yeah. Just a minute," the Summoner announced. Before Leon joined the others to eat, he took the pellet to Vanessa and fed it to her.

After eating, they all settled in for the night. Even though they had slept back at the Altar of Offering, the need for rest was still strong. Running, fighting, spell casting had all taken their toll on them. So, feeling somewhat safer than they had since entering the Black Forest, they all settled in for the night.

As promised, by the first light of dawn, their door was being knocked on relentlessly. "Outsiders, your presence is requested before the Allatari. Ready yourselves, and we shall take you there within the hour," a new, unfamiliar guard's muffled voice rolled through the hut.

Leon cracked his back and groaned. "Rise and shine, everybody."

"I shall end you," Bobo grumbled.

"Hey, don't kill the messenger… but if you're going to," Leon motioned to the door. "He's on the other side of that."

Bobo muttered to himself as he sat up in his very tiny bed. The poor ogre had a most difficult time trying to become more accustomed to the furniture. They didn't exactly make these with creatures like Bobo in mind.

Raven looked apologetic. "Sorry…"

Waving the thought away, Bobo spoke while rubbing his face. "It is all right. It comes with the territory. Just tell me that you have a splendid coffee or breakfast tea and I won't be as grumpy."

"Promise?" Raven asked, raising a brow over one eye.

His hand lifted and the other lay over his heart. "On my honor, you have my word, my dear."

"Guard. Send word that we would like to have tea and cakes after our audience with the Allatari."

"Yes, m'lady," the guard barked back.

"Ah. An ogre could get used to this kind of treatment," Bobo said with a pleased sigh.

From across the room, Vanessa's bed creaked as she sat up, holding her head with one hand and steadying her weight on the bed with the other. "How long was I out this time?" she asked in a hoarse voice. Her brow creased, displaying how unhappy she was at the fact that she had been out of it… again.

Instantly, Raven dashed to get her a drink of water while Bobo and Leon rushed over to the witch's side. "Only a few hours," Bobo informed, his blue eyes searching her form for anything that would give hint that she was out of sorts. But he found nothing, and the gnawing worry melted away to display relief right before he threw his arms around her neck and squeezed her tight against his chest. "I'm so glad that you are well."

She tapped his forearms frantically as she strained to say, "I won't be if you keep squeezing me like that."

He flushed and released her quickly. "Oh. I do apologize for that…"

Leon pat the demon on the back. "Don't hold it against him. He was hugging you for all of us. We were worried, Vanessa. I'd be lying if I said otherwise."

Rubbing her neck, the Spellweaver looked from them to the floor and gave a slow nod. "I know." Her voice sounded weak.

The water was shoved in her face. Graciously, she took it from the adamant elf that refused to budge until the cup was taken and gulped it down. "Thank you," she said before wiping her mouth with her sleeve. "Did… did I hear correctly? We are going to speak with the elven lord?"

They all nodded in unison.

"Are you sure you're okay?" Leon asked.

She nodded. "I am. I just…" she looked around the room and she shook her head. "I'll talk about it later. Right now, we need to get ready. We've already wasted enough time."

The Summoner's brow knit as a collection of emotions washed over his face. "What's wrong?"

"Nothing," she tried to sound convincing, but there was no bite to her words. There was no irritation that she normally had when being defensive and closing him out. It was so bland and lifeless. And he didn't believe her for a second.

"Vanessa, we are not taking one step out of this hut until you tell me what is wrong," Leon growled. He was tired of her hiding. He was tired of her avoiding things because of silly reasons. If she was still not feeling well or if there was something wrong, they needed to know before they went to see the Allatari.

She sighed and threw her legs over the edge of the bed. "I'm sorry," Vanessa said softly.

Leaning over to Raven, Bobo whispered, "Might you have a means to take note? She apologized and… well, this is a rare occurrence, and I'd like to document it."

Vanessa looked upset, but also like she was about to laugh. Bobo had managed to turn a serious matter into a joke, and she was silently thankful for that. But it was also a joke at her expense, and she was not thrilled with that aspect. Fussing with her matted hair, the Spellweaver continued. "I keep getting us into these situations where

I'm teetering between life and death. I often almost deplete my magic because I'm not prepared or because I want to be stubborn. I thought… I thought I was getting better, but lately, I'm just realizing I haven't changed at all. I feel like I'm worse than I was before."

"You *are* trying. Did you think you were going to perfect yourself overnight, Vanessa?" Leon asked gently.

"I've been trying for months," she snapped.

"And we've been noticing," Leon countered.

Bobo nodded in agreement.

She pouted and looked away. "I just wanted to say I'm sorry. I know that… I'm realizing that, with every mistake, I'm learning." She raised her gaze and looked to her friends. "I'm going to get better. I'm going to get stronger, and you guys won't have to save me so much. But… I'm sorry that I'll still cause you trouble along the way. Because I still feel weak. I still don't feel like I'm anywhere near where I should be with my magic." She frowned as she traced the wood grain on the floor beneath her feet with her eyes.

Shaking his head, Leon reached out and touched the side of her chin, and guided her to look at him. "Vanessa. The world isn't full of beings so that we can battle things on our own. It's full of beings so that we have a tribe, an army, to armor up and fight alongside us when we feel weak. But you?" he smiled. "You're not weak. Maybe at one point in your life you were, but not anymore. You aren't perfect, and you're still learning. We all are. But when you do get stronger, you are going to be amazing and no one… No. One. Is going to be able to take that away from you because you will be your own army. And anyone with you on their side is going to win."

She smiled and threw herself at him. Leon almost tumbled back she had slammed into him so hard. "Thank you," she whispered in his ear, and her entangled arms constricted around the poor wizard without care of who was watching.

"You're welcome," he whispered back and wove his arms around her waist and hugged her like it would save her life.

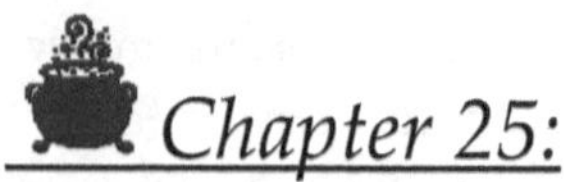 *Chapter 25:*

The grand hall was adorned in stone the shade of angel wings. It was seamless perfection that swept through from the main opening, down the hall, and up each and every step that led to the throne made of branches and woven vines that rested atop the high-raised pomp. Upon the ornate chair was a figure that Vanessa was still trying to figure out if he was a kind or cruel ruler. His face was free of emotion to the point that she could imagine him throwing her out to the wolves with an apple fixed between her teeth or gifting her with a thousand lost treasures. But the more she looked at him the more unsure she was of which he would do. As she watched him with his schooled features and piercing gaze, the Spellweaver was sure that he was going to decree them as a threat and end them right there.

She gulped.

Hopefully, no one heard that…

After she and the others had been oath-bound, they waited while two elves, Fielan and the female guardswoman from the entrance the night before, bowed before the Allatari.

The guardswoman spoke first, "Great One, these are the outsiders found by the main entrance."

The Allatari tilted his head as if peering around his subjects and eyed the group over with a scrutinizing glare. It was the kind of look that was slow, thoughtful, and picked apart every wrinkle on your clothing and strand of hair on your head, letting the way you appeared to tell the story your mouth may attempt to lie or hide from. When he spoke, it was not the thunderous tone Vanessa and the others had expected but a rather calm one. "Outsiders, what brings you to our city, and how did you come to find us?" the Allatari asked.

They all kneeled down, matching the elves in front of them. Vanessa took the lead. Though, she was silently fussing at herself for not letting Bobo speak for them. He was so much better at this sort of thing…

"Allatari," she started, licking her lips. "We performed a ritual at the Altar of Offerings within the Black Forest in hopes that the qilin would tell us how to reach the hidden elven city."

"And why were you trying to find us?" He didn't sound mad. He sounded curious, waiting to see what she would say and gauging her words appropriately.

Vanessa could feel the weight of every set of eyes in the throne room resting upon her form as she collected her courage. It didn't take long before she lifted her head and said, "I come to obtain all of what we have lost over a hundred years ago. The incantations your people had once taught us and the de-summoning spell to eradicate the feral demons that have plagued Aeristria for the past couple of months.

Now that earned a look of surprise that was quickly masked with curiosity once more. "All of what you have lost?" the Allatari repeated quizzically.

The witch locked eyes with him and nodded. "Yes. All that we have lost. We once lived together harmoniously. Your people aided us in the ways of magic. Long ago we have lost much of what you have given. I ask that you give us that knowledge once more. At the very least, I ask… I beg that you teach me the de-summoning spell so that many innocents can be saved."

The stiff branches woven to make the throne creaked as the Allatari sat back whispering, "All that you have lost," like he was bemused.

The guardswoman rose, heat lapping in her gaze as she tried to melt Vanessa and the others where they knelt. "How dare you come in here and make demands. You even bring that tainted creature here!" she barked, pointing a finger at Raven.

"Enough!" the Allatari's voice boomed through the throne room like the crack of a whip. "Eva, you may leave if you cannot set aside these ridiculous and archaic thoughts. They have never served us well, and they are doing us no favors now." He paused and rose from his throne. "Bend and ask for forgiveness," he ordered.

She spun and lowered herself, almost flattening her body against the ground, "Yes, Allatari!" Rising up, she remained on her knees and turned around to face Raven. Her mouth closed in a thin, angry line. Hands to the floor on either side, the guardswoman bowed, her forehead hovering over the white, marbled floors. "Forgive my rude behavior."

"Rise," Raven said with a thread of stately command woven into her tone. "I forgive you." The look that was plastered to the guardswoman's face didn't exactly say she felt the same.

"Now, back to the matter at hand," the Allatari began. "What are your names?"

Pointing to everyone in her party one by one, Vanessa listed everyone off. "Botobolbilian, Leon, Raven, and I am Vanessa."

The Allatari took a moment and sighed. "Do you know how you lost the knowledge of the elves?"

Vanessa nodded, "Yes. A fire burnt down the first Coven one-hundred years ago, destroying any documented information that we had gained from your people before communication was severed."

"And do you know who burned it?" he inquired.

She knit her brow and shook her head. "No. No one does."

"Hmmm." He started walking down the steps. "Quite sometime before your Coven burned down, the giant wolves showed up. My people had become scared. We chose to go into hiding to escape the wolves. Most agreed and stayed within the city while some chose to leave and live out in the woods where the monsters lurked."

"You cast out the Dark Elves!" Raven cried, standing up in a flash.

"Your kind chose to leave," the Allatari corrected. "But, I will admit, that the prejudice that we once had toward your kind did not make them feel welcomed. We know our faults now, and we cannot undo what has been done." He looked apologetically to Raven. "For your suffering, and the suffering of your kind, I am sorry."

Raven hit her knees and bowed her head. "It was before my time when it happened. The stories told to us were vague, and the elders were secretive. Forgive my anger."

"You are forgiven. Tell your people that they have a home here if they ever choose to re—"

Raven cut him short. "I am the only one left."

"Oh… I see…" He sighed, and silence impregnated the room. "You are still welcome to live here after the barrier is broken," he informed.

"The barrier needs to be broken?" Leon asked.

The Allatari returned his attention to the others. "Yes. It needs to be broken. After the wolves showed up and we, as a people, became divided, we decided to write important spells and information onto several sacred stone tablets and scattered them to ensure their safety. It just so happens that one of those tablets is in the Black Forest, and it holds the de-summoning spell that you seek. It is east of here, locked away inside a temple in a place known to us as the spirits' path."

Vanessa's eyes shined with hope, and a smile formed over her lips. They were so close. The de-summoning spell was so close.

The Allatari continued, "After the tablets were put into safeguarded temples, we created a barrier to protect ourselves from the threats lingering outside our city. But as the years passed, the wolves became stronger, and we continued to fortify the barrier until we sealed ourselves within the city."

"Are we stuck here now too?" Leon asked.

The Allatari shook his head. "No. You were not here when the spell was formed. You can come and go as you please. But, because of this, we need someone to gather the tablets and use them during the Wild Hunt spell. Surely that should be enough to start undoing all the wrongs we've committed."

"You sealed your people to protect them, I fail to see how that is a crime," Bobo stated, his eyes looking the Allatari over in a questionable manner.

The elven lord looked away as he spoke, "What we have done has caused there to be a break between the land and all beings. Because of us hiding away the sacred tablets, we have felt Raen being drained of power. Magic is dying…"

Everyone that had been present the day that High Priest Isolde and Dmitri betrayed the council had a brief flashback of what Dmitri spat at the Celestial.

"Don't you see? The magic of this land is fading. We need stronger members to keep the flow of magic from dying."

"Drained… of power," Bobo muttered. "What is the cause of it?"

"The tablets, no doubt. The temples that they have been sealed within are enchanted with time magic. It must be collecting magic but not giving it back. The flow of magic in all of Raen has been disrupted by it." The ruler descended a single step and drew in a slow, thoughtful breath before he let a long, drawn-out sigh escape his lips. "I fear that everything that we have done has endangered our people, placed a scar upon the land, and fed the hatred that the wolves seem to feast upon." He faced them all as he came to stand before them. "If you could venture to the temples, use the tablets in the next Wild Hunt ritual, we can be free of our self-made prison and order can be restored to the land. In turn, you will obtain the lost spells that you seek." He bowed to them, and the elves in the room all gasped at the Allatari's action. "Do I have your word that you exchange your aid to us for the stone tablets within the temples?"

Vanessa drew in a breath to speak, but the Allatari spoke up first. "Remember you are oath-bound and cannot lie. If you cheat us, the Wild Hunt will judge you and drag you back to that which is in between, where you will suffer greatly for your crimes."

The comment slammed into Vanessa like she had been punched in the chest. The Wild Hunt could do that? Her eyes searched the sea of expecting faces and noted their waning trust in them as she remained silent. Without thinking on the matter further, Vanessa rose from the floor, matched the Allatari's bow, and spoke clearly enough for all to hear. "You have my word that I give your people the aid that you seek in exchange for the stone tablets." She wasn't lying. She found relief in that after the words were spoken. But she could feel tiny, thorny vines of a spell entangling her. The metaphysical briars' presence surrounded the Allatari and her, binding the words with ancient magic. They were being oath-bound by their proclamations. It was an act that could not be undone without being true to their words or dying.

That much Vanessa was sure of.

When they both rose from their bow, there was a great cheer rising throughout the hall from countless onlookers. The joyful sound crashed in the throne room like a thousand waves upon a tired and forgotten shore.

"May it be," the Allatari said with a grin.

"May it be," Vanessa whispered in return.

"May we all survive this," Bobo mumbled.

And Vanessa silently hoped for the same…

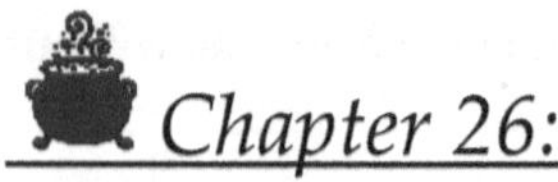 # Chapter 26:

After they left the throne room, all of the citizens gathered in the banquet hall to have a grand breakfast to see the outsiders off with good tidings and prayers of good fortune. Shortly after the morning feast, many of the elves collected near the exit to see the group off and give them gifts to aid them on their journey.

Early in the morning was the best time to leave. Or so the elves suggested. As the day went on, the wolves would become more of a threat, and as the night took over they would become more aggressive. It was best that they not linger in the city for long.

Vanessa had had enough of the wolves. She had had enough of the forest too, but they needed that tablet. Feeling replenished and their satchels full of rations and newly obtained treasures, they headed out before it got too late within the day.

Out on the road, Bobo was practically hugging the flask that Fielan had gifted him with a mad smile claiming his lips.

"You look silly doing that I hope you know," Vanessa teased.

"It is the most magnificent gift that I have been given. I don't care how I look holding this treasure," he retorted.

"It's a flask…" she muttered, unimpressed with the item.

"A flask that keeps all contents warm … forever. Forever, Vanessa. I can drink a nice cup of tea no matter the hour of the day. No matter the dangers you manage to get into, I will forever have a cup of warm tea in the waiting," he informed like he was trying to sell the container.

She rolled her eyes with a smile tugging at the corner of her lips. "Fine, it is a grand gift. But I wouldn't look at it like that around Lyx if I were you. She might get jealous."

He sputtered and coughed, and Leon and Vanessa could only laugh at his response. That is until Raven's voice broke through the cackling duo's symphony of unrestrained giggles.

"Who's Lyx?" she asked, blinking her black eyes curiously.

It was Leon who managed to get his giggle fit under control enough to answer. "My succubus partner."

Raven silently mouthed 'oh' while they continued to creep through the forest teeming with morning life. "Why is she not here?"

Again, Leon answered. "I-I wasn't concentrating when we rode on the waves of another caster's teleportation spell, and she was left behind."

"Ah. I see. Well," she turned her attention to Bobo. "I'm sorry that your heart-sworn was left behind. You shall meet up with her again soon, friend." She then slapped the ogre on the back, "No need to fret, for she will feel your embrace once more by day's end." She beamed at him happily.

All the while, Bobo tried not to drop his—newly—most treasured item and let his mouth unhinge wordlessly. His face paled and then tinges of pink flashed over his cheeks. He cleared his throat nervously. "She and I are not betrothed," he stated … finally.

"Oh…I, uhm. I'm sorry. I thought that you—" she floundered for a proper apology.

Bobo held up his hand. "It is quite all right. Our relationship is a bit complex," he admitted.

"I see," Raven whispered and pinched her brow while deep in thought.

Leon leaned over and whispered to the ogre, "Complex?"

The poor beast looked like his eyes were going to pop out of his skull. "Breathe a word and we will have one less body in this adventuring party."

The Summoner held up his hands with a mock grin. "Sure, sure. I heard nothing."

Vanessa was too focused on the map that the elves had gifted them to notice what they were all talking about. Her hazel hues scanned the thick paper and then rose to the surrounding wooded area in hopes that she'd find the landmarks listed. "A few hours walk should get us there in no time," she announced.

Raven was peering over Vanessa's shoulder when she started to speak to the young witch. "Which is good. We don't want to be caught out here another night with those wolves. Besides, tonight is the blood moon. It won't be pretty."

"Why is that?" Vanessa asked.

Leaning back flat on her two feet, Raven replied, "Because the wolves can change form during the full moon."

"Well, good thing we won't have to be out here another night to find out exactly what that means. By my calculations, the temple is barely two hours from here. After we get the tablet, we will only be a few hours from exiting the forest. From there, traveling from the Black Forest to Coven headquarters is a breeze. We'll be in Tolvade's town square before the moon hits its highest peak in the sky," the Spellweaver proclaimed happily.

Raven nodded her head and then changed the topic now that her fear of being caught out in the woods at night would not come to pass. "Vanessa, your new staff that you got from them, can I see it?"

The proud witch giggled gaily and held out the white staff to Raven, who had to half block the object before it hit her square in the nose. Excitedly, Vanessa spoke while Raven gently took the weapon from the young girl. "They said that it was Minathwa wood that had been soaked in the lunar pools during a lunar eclipse. Then their high priest prayed for seven days and seven nights while she etched runes with the chisel made from a unicorn's hoof." She was smiling so much that her cheeks were hurting. "I don't know what it is capable of doing in a battle, but it sure beats only having a wand to sling spells with."

Leon grunted to that, as he wasn't gifted with anything as nifty as a new weapon. His grumpy features were a testimony to that painful fact. He, unlike Vanessa, had been stuck with only a wand and premade spell pouches to protect himself with.

"Say, Leon. What did you get from the elves?" Vanessa asked curiously now that her attention was brought back to him.

"Hmm… oh, me? Nothing," he stated while averting his gaze.

Bobo gradually looked over in the direction of the Summoner. "Curious," he muttered. "Didn't they give you a small, wooden box before we left the city?"

Leon scratched the back of his head. But it was Raven who piped up next. "I got mana draining poisons," she exclaimed, a little too happy about her particular gift. She pulled out one of the vials and shoved it at Vanessa the same way the girl had presented her staff. The elf wore a mischievous grin that practically split her face in two. "Anytime I cut something or someone with my blade, I can drain small portions of their mana, er… uh, as you know it, magic, and turn it into my own magic to use." She pulled the vial back and shook the smoky green liquid therein from side to side. It swirled in a way that looked deadly even from behind the thick glass of the container holding it. It looked like a curse in a jar.

"Oh. That's so nice," Vanessa said with a smile, but her eyes betrayed her inner thoughts as they seemed to scream in horror at the sight of what the bottle contained. She sped up her pacing just a smidgen, as she didn't want to be close by if the vial were to drop and crack open. That substance made her skin crawl.

With a loud, satisfying, "Ah," Bobo withdrew his flask from his lips and chuckled. "It's still warm," he announced with a shake of his head. "Why have I not had one of these sooner? You know… we should get you one made in town, Vanessa."

Two hours later they arrived at the edge of the spirits' path. For as far as the eye could see, purple permeated through the land that lay beyond them. Hues of violet splashed over every inch of the forest that made up the spirits' path like the world, in this particular area, lacked any other color that Raen had to offer.

Lavender and plum-colored foliage mingled with mauve blades of grass. A sea of periwinkle moss lapped and climbed over the gray bark of the trees that were tinted with lilac tones. Amethyst-shaded bushes gently flowed with the spring breeze, their tiny branches scratching over orchid-dyed stones. The few flowers that had been brave enough to bloom this early in the season were an array of bright and cheerful heliotrope or deep and dark wine colors. Each blossom speckled the surrounding plant life and creeping moss like a beautiful disease.

Nestled just barely beyond the breach of where the spirits' path met with the Black Forest was the temple. The grays and blacks of the stone that were littered in deep green vines looked out of place amidst the vegetation that radiated with purple pigments.

Their walking had slowed to a crawl as they scoped out the building from afar. And for good reason. For outside the main—and only—entrance were two guards stationed. And, of course, they weren't just any plain guards that Aeristria had to offer. No, no. They were remnants of Fenrir.

Beings that had long ago dwindled in number and found homes alongside crumbling structures or places long forgotten. They guard the entrances to buildings appearing as intricately carved stone until someone nears the entryway. At that point, the stone carvings come to life and attempt to ward off the would-be intruders. With heads and claws of a wolf and the torso, legs, and arms of a man or woman, the Remnants of Fenrir were a strange mix of man and beast with a mentality that mirrored scroll-summoned spirits tasked with guarding a specific area. Their one and only purpose was to guard the entrance, only submitting to a master or chain spells. The problem with the chain spells was it was a temporary fix. Within a few hours, the chains would be broken and the guards would return to attacking the intruder. The only other, and safest way, of dealing with a Remnant of Fenrir was to run away or never approach to start with.

Vanessa peeled back a branch and grimaced at the two wolf-men that stood, unmoving, and proud with their spears in hand. Frowning hard, she sighed. From over her shoulder, Leon, too, sighed. Jolting from the unexpected appearance of the man, she stifled a squeak and narrowed her eyes at the Summoner. "What?" she snapped.

"They aren't going to be easy to pass," he grumbled.

She lost some of the tension in her shoulders and resumed eyeing the guards over. "Yeah," she whispered with a deep look of worry. "We should make two Gleipnir rope spells." She drew in her bottom lip between her teeth and chewed while formulating a plan.

"What are you thinking?" Leon asked.

"I'm thinking that I want to be fully prepared. Getting this tablet in our hands and making it back to the Coven take top priority. I don't want anything hindering us from returning home with it in our possession." Pausing for a moment, she turned her head so she could fully see Leon. "I'm tired of my mistakes putting myself and everyone I care about in danger."

He searched her eyes and their gazes became entangled. Dancing in his mind to an unheard song, Leon traveled through the past events that he had watched her go through and lead her to this defining point. "Okay," he whispered. "What is it that you want to do?"

Again, they resumed looking at the entrance. "I say we hit them before they know it's coming. Keep the second batch of Gleipnir rope spells at the ready just in case they break out before we can leave the building. I've never timed a Remnant of Fenrir breaking free from Gleipnir rope spells, and I am not too keen on trying to do that today."

"By the goddess, she can sound like she has some sense in her. I do wonder, what was in that food that the elves fed you?" Bobo teased his master.

"Shhh," Vanessa hissed. "Clear off that boulder so I can write out a few runes and prepare the spells," she ordered her pet.

"Such a demanding little thing," he griped.

While Vanessa and Leon prepared two Gleipnir rope spells, Raven and Bobo stood watching the guards. It didn't take long for them to complete the spells. After finishing, the young witch craned her head back to take note of the sun rising to reach its zenith in the sky. They might make it home before nightfall. The thought made her grin wildly. After all they had been through… that one thought brought her more comfort than she had expected it to.

Before they ventured closer, Vanessa took her new staff and waved it over the forest floor and then walked in a large circle around Raven, Leon, Bobo and closed the invisible circle as she stepped inside. "Whisper, my feet are like petals, hush, my body is weightless, quiet as we step along our way, hidden is our sound." Bobo stepped out of the circle and stomped on a twig covered by crisp leaves.

Silence stretched. Not a single sound from the wood splitting in two or the leaves turning to dust were heard. Only the distant sounds of the forest and the occasional sprite rushing by at breakneck speeds prevailed through the woodland. The spell wouldn't last long. They needed to act swiftly.

Leon and Vanessa both held a spell in hand and crept through the foliage, coming up behind Raven and Bobo as the Dark Elf and ogre took the lead. By the time they were a few feet away, no spell could hinder the Remnant of Fenrir from its task. Waking up, the amber orbs of the beast shot open and a snarling, "You shall not enter," ripped out from the two in unison with pure, territorial rage as they attempted to counter the unexpected attack.

Bobo barreled through, stomping his way as he stormed at the one on the left like he was an oversized, angry bull. The ax clashed with the spear in the guard's hands. The demon growled at the wolf as the Remnant of Fenrir went to bite at the ogre's arms. Bobo quickly kicked at the creature, sending it head over feet flying backward.

Meanwhile, Raven had raced out with the agility of a crafty fox with its prey in sight. She darted over the ground at a speed Vanessa could hardly keep up with and then vaulted into the air. Flipping, the elf twisted her body until she was swan diving back down over the head of the second guard. It hardly had enough time to register the attack when her blades sparked over the pole of the spear as the second guard held the vixen at bay. Twisting again, the bone blades whined over the metal as she pivoted just enough to land behind the creature, rested her weight on her hands, and kicked both feet out into the spine of the guard.

As the second guard flew, it slammed into the first guard that had picked itself up and was trying to race back to Bobo. The remnants of Fenrir collided with one another and slammed into the ground.

"Be still!" Vanessa screamed and threw her spell at the first guard while Leon yelled the same and threw his at the second.

They smiled and enjoyed the view of their handy work. Both guards thrashed about and tried to snap at the enchanted ropes as they wrapped around the beasts. They snarled unhappily as fierce, yellow eyes revered the ones responsible for their bindings.

"Mine," one snarled.

"You shall not enter," the other barked aggressively.

Leon and Vanessa gave each other slaps on the back and mad grins before they all raced into the building. The chain spells would not last forever and they needed to hurry. Soon after passing through the entrance, their bodies were engulfed in blackness, a cold licked over their skin like the shadows were a frozen blanket, and silence took over the sounds surrounding them.

"Oh no," Vanessa whined.

"It's spelled," Leon groaned.

"Why am I not surprised?" Bobo sighed.

Raven's voice sounded almost chipper in comparison to the other three. "You know. Just because it is spelled doesn't mean it's a bad thing."

No one in the party believed that even for a moment.

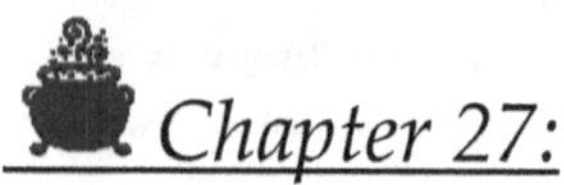 *Chapter 27:*

"Well, well. Would you look at what the griffin dragged in?" a high-pitched, feminine voice chimed through the darkness as the fog of the spell that had previously engulfed them all started to fade, and their vision slowly returned to normal.

Standing in front of them was a very lithe framed male wearing a long white and gold skirt and no shirt, which showed off his faintly blue-tinted and flawless skin. Endless numbers of bracelets and gold jewelry adorned the male's body. Minty-hued hair was styled with it being shaved on one side and long in the back and slowly tapering up the front. The bangs reached just past the male's chin. On his forehead, there was a symbol of three, connected, swirling circles drawn in a midnight blue. Bright magenta eyes stared at the group as their vision became clearer.

"Are you gonna say something, or am I gonna have to start guessing your names?" he asked, his wide eyes twinkling with interest. Flipping his seafoam green hair over his shoulder, he plucked at his skirt and smoothed it out over his waist.

Snapping his fingers at Vanessa, he rolled his wrist quickly, "Come on honey, just because we have forever doesn't mean we like to wait."

Double dip a candlestick; it was an undine… one of the sassiest creatures that the elemental world had to offer.

Bless her spell, how many years had it been since anyone saw one? Clearly, the Black Forest was a place for all lost, missing, and long since thought dead creatures to hang out in. Though, in Vanessa's opinion, it wasn't the best place to seek refuge at.

"Where are we?" Vanessa asked while looking over the building.

"Answering a question with another question. Ugh. You're one of *those*..." The water undine looked most displeased.

"You don't know the half of it," the ogre grumbled under his breath. "Let me handle the introductions," Bobo muttered to Vanessa while stepping forward. He awkwardly tugged at his shredded suit sleeves as he gave a light bow to the undine. "I am Botobolbilian, and what is your name, good sir?"

The undine spun on heel and stopped right before stumbling back with a hand lying dramatically over his chest. Gradually, magenta eyes crept over every magnificent inch of the demon as they scaled the ogre up and down completely unabashed. "Oh, well... hi there handsome." The undine cleared his throat and righted himself. Twirling a lock of vibrant seafoam hair around his slender finger, the blue-skinned being gave a flirtatious smile and finger wiggling wave to Bobo. "If I had been trapped in here to watch over that tablet with someone like you, I wouldn't have been so bored all these years," he stated with a dangerous gleam in his eyes.

Bobo stiffened while his darting eyes searched the others for a lifeline. "I assure you I'm not *that* sort of ogre."

"Hmmm... pity," the undine sighed with a pout.

Raven spoke up. "Now you're being rude. He gave a name and you said nothing."

The undine lightly slapped a hand on the side of his face and let his jaw unhinge. "Wha—I was getting ready to say it... I just got," his eyes trailed over to Bobo and the undine winked at the demon before he continued with, "...distracted. You just don't have any patience, honey."

Raven rolled her eyes and then pointed to each person left to be introduced in the tiny temple. "Vanessa, Leon," she then pointed to herself, "Raven." Her digit lopped over in the undine's direction. "And you are?"

The water spirit fussed with his clothing and jewelry before fluffing his hair and answering with, "Meladrious." There was a touch of sass in the undine's tone, but no one made mention of it.

"You say you've been trapped here, does that mean—" Leon began, but Meladrious cut him short with the answer.

"You can come and go as you please, as long as you don't get sliced in half by the two guarding the door. I, on the other hand, am stuck here until the tablet is taken and the spell is lifted from that stuck up elven city, Satviriya," the undine huffed. He gave a soft sigh while his gaze drifted thoughtfully, "But I suppose I will always have that glorious time in Satviriya two hundred years ago when the night was…"

Vanessa let her eyes wander about the tight enclosing while the undine prattled on. A small fountain of water trickled out from the mouth of a stone lion head mounted on the wall nearby. The tiny stream of liquid collected in a large, rocky basin resting on the ground. On the other side of the temple was a large pool of water that stretched from one end of the building to the other, and many other water spirits swam about the waters or perched near its edge while watching Meladrious interact with the newcomers. Each of the beings had skin tones that reminded the young witch of water. Their pale, pastel-colored hair of blues, greens, and purples fanned out in the depths of the water as a few of them twirled in the pool. Their bright, glowing eyes forever fixed on Vanessa and the others. Nervously, Vanessa averted her gaze from the limitless set of eyes staring silently in her direction. As her eyes drifted through what was left of the building, she noted two rows of pillars lined the center walkway up to a shrine-like area where blue flames flickered inside of the mounted wall sconces. The strange and calming glow of the fires washed over the tablet resting in a carved-out opening on the wall. Runes that were old and charred were along the edges and pulsing like a slow heartbeat. They glowed all around the opening. There were no windows lining the walls, and the ceiling was high, yet no skylight adorned the top. It felt like a cage. A large, dark, unforgiving, stone cage.

"You've been here… for two hundred years?" Vanessa whispered, her eyes still locked on the tablet on the far end of the temple.

"Oh, you bet I have. Not that I wanted to be. Those crafty little overgrown sprites *lied* to us. We've been stuck here watching over their tablet because they decided to throw a fit over magic and humans. Honey-child, let me just tell you, nothing good comes from an elf."

"Hey!" Raven cried.

Peering over to her, Meladrious cringed and mouthed 'sorry' before saying. "Okay. Well, at least those that sided with the ones that became the wolves."

"Whoa, whoa. I'm going to have you slow your casting for just a moment. The elves said that they were trying to lift the barrier on them and give us the tablets. They only did that to protect themselves from the wolves' attacks."

"Ha! So, their choices are biting them in their perfectly sculpted behinds, and they are finally realizing all that they've done has been one giant mistake. Ha, ha, ha. I knew this day would come. I told them it would too." The water spirit shook his head angrily and shut his eyes as he tried to calm the brewing anger within him. Opening them once more, he licked his lips and said, "They lied to you, sweetheart." Meladrious hooked his finger and beckoned them closer with it. "Let me tell you what really happened and not the half-baked lies the elves all fed you because they don't want to look like the bad guy."

Leon rolled a hand through his sandy locks and groaned, "This is going to be a long one. I can feel it."

"The elves and humans lived side by side, once. They even had children together. For years there was harmony and peace. That is, until the elves and humans started to search for other forms of magic. Thus, they stumbled onto dark magic. But the problem with dark magic is that it taints the caster… and anyone born from someone with dark magic running through their veins will be tainted as well. It is in the blood. It never goes away. These tainted signs can be as simple as black nails, hair, and eyes or as complex as the whole body being engulfed in black. The Light Elves didn't like it. They thought that those playing with the dark magic were soiling the gift that the goddess had bestowed upon them. While the tainted elves thought that all forms of magic were a gift from the goddess. However, it came to pass that the Light Elves called their brethren Dark Elves and treated them poorly because of their visual difference.

The Light Elf children weren't allowed to play with Dark Elf children for fear that just being near them would taint them as well. Their ignorance was the start of a long and ugly history. Soon after that, well, let me tell you… the humans started to speak up for the Dark Elves and they too were shut out from the city. Loved ones were cut off from each other or forced to make the choice of living within the purity and safety of the city or out within the woods."

"With the wolves," Vanessa asked, though, it sounded more like a statement.

Meladrious shook his head. "Girl, no. Not yet, at least. First, the elves shut out the humans. Blaming them for their brethren becoming what was now known as the Dark Elves. But when the Dark Elves chose to leave the city and live with the humans, that was when the insanity of the elders took over. Denmarius. He was the elf responsible for feeding into the fears of the elders. He told them to take all of the tablets that had information on spells, magic, and were needed for the ritual of the Wild Hunt, and told them to scatter them to the elemental shrines across the four points of Aeristria. Then, to ensure that the humans would not be able to keep the magic learned from the elves, the Light Elves burned down the Coven."

"Banish a banshee," Leon gasped.

"They didn't," Vanessa whispered.

The undine wagged a finger from side to side. "Oh, they did. And that wasn't the worst of it. The Dark Elves were still willing to teach the humans. So, you know what they did next?" Everyone shook their heads. "They tried to curse their own kind. But elves are immune to curses. Still, they tried. Thinking that they were impure, and therefore susceptible to curses, they conjured the evil spell and thrust it at their own kind. They were wrong, though. Instead of the mana-eating spell attacking the elves, it deflected from the targeted beings and sought after the humans, and then affected *all* beings with magic. Medusa's Kiss killed thousands within the first few weeks before it simmered down to only inhabiting a rare few every so often."

Vanessa balled her fists at her side. "What is wrong with them?" she snarled. They created Medusa's Kiss. They created the wolves. They hid away spells and precious magic, and they burned down the Coven. She thought back to the way that they acted when they had been in the city. So willing to give the tablets and aid them. Why? What the undine was saying had to be wrong… right?

"I'm not even done yet. The elders were so heated at the failure of the curse and that the Dark Elves had abandoned their people and wouldn't die that they did the one thing that means death for any elf."

"No," Raven whispered.

"Honey-child, yes. Yes, they did. Let momma tell you, they decided to give up their souls to the god."

"You mean goddess," Vanessa corrected.

The water spirit faced her and shook his head with a solemn look twisting his features. "No. I meant the god, Unsoul. He gave Denmarius and other the elves what they wanted. The ability to destroy their enemies. They turned themselves into the wolves to kill the Dark Elves. It is the only way an elf can kill another elf."

Raven covered her mouth and let a few tears drip down her face. "I … my parents never told me this. I always thought something was off, but I never thought…" she trailed off and hid her face from the rest of them. Rage and sadness boiled over inside her.

"We feasted with them. Swore to help them. But they should have been asking us for forgiveness and begging us to help them right their wrongs," Vanessa seethed.

"Indeed," Bobo growled.

Leon spat at the ground. "How deceitful."

The undine placed a hand on his hip. "After Denmarius and his followers turned into the wolves, they hunted down any Dark Elves and kept any Light Elves from trying to flee the city. Eventually, anything that came within the forest was attacked blindly by the wolves. Their hate and obsession with their race needing to be pure and flawless overruled any sensible way of thinking. Anything that entered the forest was a threat, and any elf brave enough to leave the city was a threat to them as well. That was when the elves that remained in Satviriya chose to throw up the barrier. They couldn't get the tablets to fix what they had done, and they were more content with sitting alone in cowardice within their perfect city … too afraid to sacrifice themselves further to right their wrongs and too proud to admit their mistakes. Even now, two-hundred years later, they couldn't bring themselves to tell you the whole truth. Honey, I've enough anger built up that I'll spew their whole mess to everyone on Raen if I get out of here. They'll think twice before trying to drag countless beings through hell for their own personal grudges."

"Okay, I have a question," Leon asked.

Eyeing over the Summoner, the undine stifled a moan and waggled his eyebrows at the wizard. "Your eyes remind me of the sky. It's been *so* long since I've seen it. Hold me and I'll tell you anything you want to know," Meladrious purred.

Without skipping a beat, Leon replied, "Never mind."

The water spirit pouted and made a whimpering sound. "You're no fun. Very well," the creature sighed and inspected his nails with a bored expression. "Ask me."

Leon gave the undine a blank stare before he shook his head and spoke. "You said that the tablets were needed for the Wild Hunt. Why?"

"Because all the magic collected throughout the year are held within them. Or years, in this case. When the spell is cast and you seek judgment for your ancestors and make your offerings, the magic is returned as a form of thanks for casting the spell."

"Seek judgment?" Bobo repeated in thought.

"Yeah, I'm with the big guy. What do you mean seek judgment for our ancestors, what do you mean the magic is given back?"

Raven raced over to stand in front of them and shrieked, "You've been doing the Wild Hunt spell *wrong*? For a hundred years!"

"I'm pretty sure that is a yes. Just look at their dumb expressions, honey. Girl… We. Are. Doomed," Meladrious said, fanning the Dark Elf's fears. The mischievous glint in the undine's eyes spoke in volumes of how he saw anything as entertainment within these four walls.

"I thought my magic felt weaker every year. I noticed it waning from the land but… I never thought…" She stared down at her hands and then her pained gaze looked up to Vanessa, Bobo, and Leon.

The undine tsked. "Look at how big this whole mess is that the Light Elves have made. And are they even cleaning it up?" He shook his head and giggled. "Nope. They hired a cleaning crew." He covered his mouth while he attempted to hide the insane giddy laughter he had bubbling to the surface. Clearing his throat, he swept the air with his hand, shooing them all toward the exit. "You better hurry up and take that tablet and then get the hex out of here. The sooner the better."

Vanessa didn't wait or ask while the others remained behind to speak with Meladrious, she raced over to retrieve the tablet from the wall.

Rubbing his chin in deep thought, Bobo cleared his throat. Instantly, the undine was near his side and batting his long lashes over his pink hues as he looked up longingly at the ogre. Caught a bit off guard, the demon took a step back and regained his bearings before stating, "As long as we get back before nightfall, we should be fine."

Pursing his lips to the side, Meladrious shook his head. "Well, considering that the ebb and flow of time in here is not the same, I'd tell you to hurry and watch your neck on the way out."

"That is what the spell was for. Not just trapping the undines here," Leon stated feeling enlightened.

The water spirit nodded. "Exactly."

"You may want to hurry up, my dear. The time we thought we had is no longer on the table," Bobo announced loud enough for Vanessa to hear.

She was racing for them, the stone in hand, as she said, "I just heard. As delightful as your company is, Meladrious, we have to go."

"Please, go. The faster you do your thing the sooner we are no longer held prisoner here, guarding a rock that should have never been placed here to start with. I'm so ready to be done with this drab place. I'm ready to see clear skies and dip my feet into ponds not surrounded by crusty, cold, stone walls." The undine shooed at them more aggressively. "Go, go, go."

Quickly, they raced back outside.

 *Chapter 28:*

Bobo and Raven went out first just in case the remnants of Fenrir had managed to free themselves. Indeed, their bindings had waned in their capabilities to keep the beings restrained. Metal on metal clashed as the one to Bobo's right tried to land a blow on the ogre. Raven immediately was ready for the attack that the other tried to slice through the gentleman-beast's back with. Her bone axes deflected the blow, and she pivoted her body before landing a sound kick to the guard's stomach. The creature attempted to sink its spear into the ground to stop it from sliding back, but the elf tucked and rolled out of the way, giving Leon enough clearance to throw the rope spell to the beast. Once more, it was bound and tied. Bobo slammed his head into the other guard, and it fell into a lump at his feet.

"Oh dear," the ogre gasped while looking at his unexpected handy work.

Leon chuckled and patted the demon's shoulder. "No problem, big guy. One less spell we need to use," he stated while his boot nudged at the guard suspiciously. It made no movement.

Having subdued the guards rather easily, Vanessa took the chance to look up and survey the hour by locating the sun's placement within the sky. They were greeted with twilight. An hour from now and the blood moon would be reaching its peak in the sky.

Wasting no time, they all said nothing of the dangers that lurked within the woods. They already knew them without saying it. Wordlessly, the adventurers raced for the edge of the forest, hoping to escape before more troubles would find them.

Their pace had slowed considerably since they had first emerged from the temple. The plan was to catch their breath and move on at swifter speeds as soon as possible. So, for now, they cautiously traversed through the greenery in silence. The hush had grown and stretched like ivy vines entangling the air and moments surrounding the group, strangling the words that they each wanted to say, and Raven slashed through every vine claiming them with a vengeance.

"For all these years, I thought something wasn't right. Now I know why," she seethed.

Leon looked like he wasn't a hundred percent sold on what the undine had said. "Yeah, but I'd still be a bit careful about how much you put into what Meladrious said. He seemed like someone who liked to stir up the cauldron, if you catch my drift."

Bobo grunted. "Indeed. Though, the information lines up rather well considering the circumstances, my good man. I think we need to realize that the Light Elves are the ones with darker shades of hearts."

"I think," Vanessa chimed in, "that they see the error of their ways. Although, they had to first suffer to actually understand just how wrong they were, but they are trying to fix it."

"All while lying about how it all came about. They were too proud and arrogant then and nothing has changed that in two-hundred years. They lied to us. They killed my people. I want a *real* apology," Raven growled.

"Understandable and within reason, my dear," Bobo sighed.

And he was right. It was understandable. As they walked, Leon and Vanessa kept looking up in the sky. The creeping blood moon had turned the once tranquil heavens into a horrific sight. Crimson light glowed around the full orb that steadily climbed toward its throne overhead. A bright ring of red adorned the celestial body as it washed the nightlife in hues of garnet that gave the forest an even more threatening aura.

"What an unsettling sight," Leon whispered.

"Yeah," Vanessa agreed. She shivered. Perhaps it was from the lingering winter chill that spring had unsuccessfully broken free from, or it was from the sense that they were being followed, and she was trying to ignore the sensation of being watched by multiple sets of angry eyes. Either way, she wanted to hurry up and get home.

After a few moments, Raven broke through the silence once more. "We may need to pause and let me do a quick stealth spell on all of us. Last thing we need is to be this close to freedom and get caught by, well… anything."

"No. Black magic is out of the question," Leon stated with heat lapping at every word.

"Excuse me?" Raven snapped back angrily.

"I said no black magic." The simplified reiteration fell from his mouth with not a care toward how the Dark Elf felt about his comment.

She stopped dead in her tracks just as they emerged from a thick collection of shrubbery and trees into a small clearing. The red from the moon painted over all of the scenery in pale reds and ominous shades of deep rose. Raven's starry-eyed gaze fixed on Leon's back with a glower that could melt rocks. "It isn't black magic," she snarled.

"Oh?" He sounded unbelieving as he continued to walk away. "If it isn't black magic, then, pray tell, what is it?"

Storming to stand toe to toe with the male, she corrected him with a peppery tone, "It is dark magic."

"Is there a difference?" Vanessa asked, though she sounded like she doubted that there was.

Onyx eyes shimmering with starlight shifted toward Vanessa's direction and rested on the witch. "Yes," Raven snipped. "There *is* a difference."

"Pardon me, but … perhaps we may not be educated properly. Might you enlighten us, my dear?" Bobo tried to quell the growing anger in the group with his comment.

It seemed to have worked some, as Raven let some of the tension in her shoulders dissolve and let the ice in her stare thaw a touch. A deep inhale was audibly heard before an explosive exhale escaped the woman while the Dark Elf steadied her nerve. "Black magic and dark magic are *not* the same. Dark magic is curses and spells that call upon darker elements of life. While black magic is the same thing, but the spirits without rest aid in the spell casting. Vengeful spirits answer. They taint the spell and everything it touches. The spirits demand a host, someone to do their bidding for the power that they give. They desire to seek vengeance for the wrongs done to them. That magic is dangerous. The spirits fog the mind, cloud the judgment, and they give enough power to a user that it causes the caster to get drunk off of it. It makes them crave it. Always inviting the spirits for another spell… until, one day, they are simply overtaken."

"Where did these vengeful spirits come from?" Vanessa asked, coming closer to Raven.

"My people. The elves that died in great pain after being rejected by their own kind. They demand recompense. They seek retribution for the atrocities committed against us." Raven reached up and held her arm with her other hand and squeezed. "We had been ostracized and then hunted. Never given a fair chance at life outside the city walls. For so long I never understood why. Today, everything made sense. The pieces to the puzzle all fit together, even the reason why the spirits seem more powerful and angry. Everything makes so much sense now… the shift in magic, the rise in the spirits' anger, how the wolves came to be." She stopped and cast her view to the ground as she tried to contain her growing emotions. "The magic is fading, and the spirits are becoming angrier because," her gaze rose to look at everyone, "… because you all haven't been doing the Wild Hunt spell right, they have not been laid to rest."

Vanessa, Bobo, and Leon looked between each other confused. "Wait. You mentioned that back at the temple," Vanessa interjected. "We perform the Wild Hunt spell every year." She attempted to defend herself, the Coven, but there was a lack of conviction in her tone.

Raising a brow over one eye, Raven smirked as if mocking the witch. "And you think that just because you perform a spell that you are doing it right?"

The Spellweaver's mouth opened to speak, but no words came out. Raven was right. Vanessa had no proof that they were casting the spell right. Saying anything further would just make her look ignorant and prideful. Instead, she huffed. "No," she admitted.

"The Wild Hunt was meant to judge the dead and give them peace. It was meant to allow the living a day to say goodbye to the dead. It was supposed to give back the magic that had been used that year… but you haven't been doing that. Of course, you haven't been. I was foolish to think that you had been. The Light Elves had made sure that your kind wouldn't be able to. Now they are regretting it because it isn't just killing your magic. It is killing theirs too. It is draining the very heart out of Aeristria." Raven stared at everyone and then pointed to the tablet in Vanessa's grasp. "That tablet has one-fourth of all the magic that has been given in prayer, spell, or casting within the past two-hundred years." She waited for the words to sink in. "We have to bring this back and mend the land. This tablet is just one of the keys to righting so many wrongs that have been done to our world," Raven cried.

Suddenly, the air smelled like rage. The kind of rage that had been building and brewing for ages. It was thicker than any tree trunk, and it saturated the air with a vow that someone was going to be the victim of its aggressive nature.

"Perspective is everything in the grand schemes of it all, you meddling elf!" The voice was dark and held even darker promises. The kind of promises that you hoped would not be kept.

Coal-shaded, lazy curls brushed over the male elf's shoulders as he stepped from the shadows of the forest. Tan pants clung to the man's long legs as he pushed past the shrubbery and became visible along the tree line. The V of his white tunic dipped dangerously low down the front, revealing a necklace with three shining crystals that dangled from around his neck. It swayed from side to side across his pale chest as he strode into the clearing. But the most mesmerizing feature of all was his eyes. His eyes were a cold and calculating slate color, and they reminded Vanessa of an enchanted blade. Beautiful and deadly.

"We have not watched and protected these woods for this long to have you four come along and mess it all up. This is for the greater good." His eyes lingered over each member of their party before resting on Vanessa and the tablet in her grasp. Instinctively, the witch slowly put the tablet into her spelled satchel. Her eyes remained ever fixed upon the evil creature disguised as an elf before her. "Come now. Be sensible," the dark-haired male's voice shifted. He sounded smooth and convincing.

"Denmarius," the Dark Elf hissed. "Don't listen to him," Raven warned as she stepped between Vanessa's line of sight and the male elf.

Leon came to one side, and Bobo was at the ready on the other. "Get that staff ready, and let us hope that it is for more than just looks," Bobo whispered to his master.

The Summoner's hand was inching down his hip, fingers getting ready to reach spell bag or wand, whichever would be needed first if a fight broke out. "Vanessa... if it comes down to it, I want you to make a run for it. You getting that tablet to headquarters means more than—"

"Don't," Vanessa snapped in a hoarse tone. "Don't say it. Because you're wrong, Leon. You mean more to me than this stupid rock." Her eyes shifted to Bobo. "You mean more to me than magic itself. Don't ask me to sacrifice you guys for this silly stone."

"Wise words," Denmarius practically purred. "You should heed these wise words of your friend there. Aren't your lives more meaningful than the need to have magic?"

Raven shot out angrily, "There are beings that are made up more of magic than any other element on Raen. Taking that away from them is setting them up for death. It is taking away a limb and way of life."

"Then let them die," he roared, his gaze turning menacing, and the weight of his stare bore down on her like the body of a slumbering rock troll.

"You can't do that. You are making choices for the land based off of your own selfish and narrow-minded views." Vanessa clipped off each word like she was firing off verbal enchants in his direction.

The male snarled. But it didn't sound like a man upset. No. It sounded like a beast. More accurately, it sounded like a wolf. The ghostly form of a giant wolf rose out of him like an angry spirit and narrowed its wolfish gaze at the group before it. "Watch your tongue, or I'll be sure to eat it," Denmarius growled the threat like he was ready to rip it from her mouth right then.

Vanessa took a step back. Her body screamed to run away from the dark and terrible creature before her. "He's one of the wolves," she whispered fearfully.

"Yeah," Leon gulped. "Kind of putting that together myself, there, Vanessa."

It was true. Denmarius had given his soul to Unsoul for the ability to change into a wolf. And during the full moon, they could shift back to their humanoid form. With that thought in mind, there was no way that she could look at the man and not see him with more savage, canine features. He was the embodiment of a wolf in elven skin.

"You are no match for me, little witch. Just hand over the tablet and I promise you, you and your friends are free to leave," Denmarius said, and his tone shifted and now sounded sweet and kind. But it reminded her that even venom could be drenched in the sticky, golden fingers of honey. Sweet and toxic and deadly.

She shook her head because she didn't trust her voice at the moment. There was no way that he would let them all go. Did the bad guy ever really mean it when they said that? No. She wasn't dumb enough to believe him either. They knew where the lost city of elves was, where the temple was, what the stone tablets were, and what using them could do for all of Aeristria. There was no way on Raen he was going to let them go.

"You are trying my patience. You've given me the slip already, I'll give you that, but you are not going to outrun us this time." From behind the trees encircling the small clearing, multiple yellow eyes pierced through the shadows. Guttural sounds that mimicked laughter emitted from the forest. "Just stop trying to prove you're something you're not and hand it over like a good girl."

"You can stop talking to me like I'm seven," Vanessa snapped. "I'm old enough to cast a spell that will have you begging me to end your life… and I'm strong enough to not think twice about complying with your pleas." She let every word drip with the warning she was giving him.

His face hardened as a scowl settled in. "My, my. We have ourselves a wannabe heroine…" He gave a quick snort of laughter at her expense. "Do you know what happens to heroes?"

"Yeah! They kick your a—" Vanessa started.

"They DIE!" he corrected fervently. The one word carried through the air like a verbal punch, and Vanessa jolted and took another step back.

Short, excited howls and yips enveloped the forest around them as the single word echoed through the clearing. The elf grinned maniacally. "Do I have your attention now? Hmmm?" His grin flattened into an expression that seemed bored with everything. "Now, hand over the tablet before I take drastic measures to obtain it."

Vanessa's eyes darted around. There was no end to the shadows or the dangers that lurked in them. She looked up to the moon, red as a gaping wound and perched at its highest peak in the sky like someone had stabbed heaven and was ready to bleed it dry. They had come so far and now, and now it felt like they had done it all for nothing. Denmarius took a step forward, and instinctively, Vanessa held out her staff, the bulbous tip pointing right at the wolf-elf's heart. "I never said I would hand it to you," she growled.

"I wasn't exactly giving you a choice," the elf snarled. His advance did not falter, it only inched closer. His slow approach was like a tidal wave about to devour a tiny ship on a stormy sea.

Her heartbeat quickened, and her blood roared in her ears like an angry manticore. The closer the elf got, the more frantic her mind tried to race and obtain one clear thought. Just one. Something that could stop the madness and get her and everyone else out of the forest unscathed. But nothing came to mind.

Her palm was sweaty, and it was hard to clutch the satchel where the tablet was safely tucked away and not lose grip of the staff in her weapon hand. Still, it was pointed at Denmarius, though her lack of courage had dispelled some of the threat that it once held. She just needed to be able to pull off a miracle and not get them all killed, and they would be good.

Bobo and Leon stepped a few feet in front of her, and Raven took a protective stance in front of Vanessa but remained behind the other two. Reluctantly, the Spellweaver lowered the weapon, not wanting to accidentally hit one of her friends.

"There is hope, Vanessa. But your friend is right," Raven whispered loud enough for only the witch to hear. "You are going to have to run," she advised.

There was no hiding the amount of displeasure Vanessa had while she heard those words spill from the Dark Elf's lips. "No," she whispered angrily. "I'm not leaving you guys behind."

"Then you are signing up countless innocent beings to be subjected to a magic-less life, and even death, if you stay here. If that stone doesn't make it back to the Coven then we've failed," Raven clipped back with heat lining her hoarse tone.

"Let me try," Vanessa whined. She hated this. Everyone was protecting her by putting their lives on the line. Was she not good enough to stay and fight?

As if reading her mind, Leon called back to her. "You are the only one that I trust to get that tablet back to headquarters, Vanessa. I don't even trust myself. This isn't about the strongest staying to fight and sending the weakest to the Coven; it is about sending the strongest back to headquarters because they are your last hope."

The comment hurt. It hurt more than it should have. Tears welled in her eyes and stung as they threatened to fall. "I can't," she declared. But the growing lump in her throat almost snuffed out the words that she struggled to produce.

"Of course you can't. Trying to run from us is just a foolish way to die. Your friends are setting you up for disaster. Run, and you all die. That is the simple truth. Give me the stone and there will be some shred of hope for you all yet," Denmarius stated with his usual smile. The one that wasn't real and never reached his eyes.

Vanessa's vision snapped to the assailant. He was closer than what she found to be comfortable and already the wolves were starting to slink out of the forest. There was saliva dripping from their jaws, tongues lolling as they panted excitedly, and eyes bearing down on the group like they were the beasts' next meal.

Nothing good was going to come from this.

The artifact that he wanted held a fraction of all the magic that had been stored away for hundreds of years. Even if Denmarius stored it back inside the temple and let them walk free, they would still die because they were oath-bound to the Light Elves in aiding them to break the barrier. If she ran, surely the wolves would rip through her friends and come for her soon after. They would all be shredded to ribbons before she'd see the edge of the forest. Giving the elf what he wanted… was that really the best option that they had?

Slowly, her hand reached inside the satchel at her hip. The wolfish elf's eyes grew wide with wonder, and his grin practically split his face in two. "Yes, yes!" he urged her while frantically waving for the Spellweaver to come closer.

Leon, Bobo, and Raven all turned to see what was making Denmarius so happy. That was when they realized that Vanessa was removing the stone from her bag.

"What are you doing?" Leon hissed.

"Do you really think that is wise, my dear?" Bobo added, his tone grave. His deep blue eyes searched his master for some sort of explanation, but the witch said nothing. She only took a step forward.

Her march forward was only stopped by Raven, who had grabbed a hold of the girl's arm and held her tightly in place. "And just where do you think you are going with that?" Raven asked with irritation scratching over her words.

"I'm trying to choose the option that doesn't get us all killed, Raven," Vanessa stated while jerking her arm back.

Raven's eyes narrowed. "If we choose to die so that you have a chance to live and save countless lives then let us do this. Don't take that glory away from us."

"Glory? Glory? You are saying that you are willing to die for a sliver of a chance that I escape."

"Yes, glory. Yes, a chance. There is glory in dying while protecting something you believe in. Do not look down on those that do. A warrior's death is the backbone of your peace and the foundation that your precious Coven is built upon. So, don't pretend like what we are doing right now isn't something worthy of the title glory."

Bobo added, "She is right. Don't give up, Vanessa. We believe that you can do it."

Vanessa forced a smile and took another step forward. "I know, Botobolbilian." To his full name, Bobo looked as if he was worried, and there was a look exchanged between her and the demon. A wordless second that held the weight of the world on its shoulders. "But I'm not willing to risk the chance that I would mess it up. Besides," she laid a hand on Leon's arm, gave him a soft smile, and took a step beyond her friends as she said, "I'm better at spell casting and fighting than I am at running."

Before the elf could react, Vanessa raised her staff and yelled, "Force push." As soon as the magic made impact, Denmarius went flying across the clearing and crashed clean through a bush. From all around them the wolves came running, a few even lunging toward the center where they were all collected. And one was coming down over Vanessa with its jaws open wide.

Raven quickly darted into the fray, and all the witch saw was the blur of a red cape as the Dark Elf leaped into the air. One of her bone blades went racing up the paw of the descending beast and bit deep into the skin as it sliced through its leg. Vanessa could hear the bone whine as it connected with the ax halfway up the limb. A yelp of pain escaped the beast. The other ax was swung underhandedly and connected with the creature's lower jaw. The blade sank deep into the flesh. The cry of pain was snuffed out by the gargling of blood filling its mouth right before the mongrel fell to the floor. The giant wolf's limbs twitched as it tried to run, but it couldn't move so it just sputtered in a circle on its side and flopped about, rubbing its face into the dirt as blood poured out in droves. The floor became soaked in thick, crimson liquid.

From beside them, another rushed over, and Bobo was more than happy to greet it. He ran at the creature head-on and buried his hand deep into the fur at the beast's neck. Using the momentum from him running and the force of the creature trying to jerk away from the ogre's grasp, the demon kicked off the ground and slammed onto the canine's back. Wrapping his legs around its neck, Bobo squeezed while he pulled his ax free from his hip, raised his hands over his head, and crashed a powerful blow into the beast's skull. There was a sickening crack, and the wolf instantly went limp and crashed into the forest floor. The whine of anguish escaped the animal like a mournful exhale.

"Enough!" Denmarius's voice was harsh and loud like the crack of a bullwhip on a silent night. The elf emerged from the bushes, pulling out leaves and twigs from his hair and fuming with rage. The wolves stopped their attack, but they were not happy about it. With a wave of his hand, the snarling monsters reseeded a few feet, but it was hardly enough room to give any real form of comfort to the adventurers. "I'm done with your games! I grow tired of these dances. No more. I'll ask you one last time. Give me the tablet or die," he roared.

"You don't scare me," Vanessa bellowed back.

The elf closed his fist, the appendage glowing blue before he flicked his wrist and a bolt blasted Leon square in the chest. The Summoner went flying, bounced off the floor, and rolled until a tree brought him to a sudden and painful stop. His cry pierced through the woods.

"STOP!" Vanessa begged.

Tilting his head, Denmarius played dumb. "You could kill two of my brethren, but you have the nerve to beg me to stop when all I've done is harm *one* of your friends?" He sneered.

Without warning, another spell came from the forest and hit Bobo in the back. The ogre dropped to his knees, but a volley of spells ripped through the shadows and the demon fell forward. "No, Bobo!"

One of the wolves placed a paw on the gentleman-monster's body, its snout dipping dangerously close to the demon's passed out form. While another sniffed and nipped at the cuff of Leon's pant leg.

But the male elf held up a hand and both wolves stopped. The creatures' yellow eyes glared at Vanessa as they snarled over the ogre and wizard, their teeth itching to sink into the flesh of the beings below them. Raven came closer until she was hip to hip with the witch. Both of her blades were out and at the ready as she turned this way and that while the multiple encroaching threats inched toward them.

Trapped.

No matter the way she looked at the situation, they were all trapped. If she ran, she would need the blessing of the goddess herself to escape the wolves. If she stayed, the chances of them all surviving the fight that would ensue were slim to none. If she returned the tablet to the temple, her oath to the Light Elves would kill her. If she broke the tablet, all of Aeristria would slowly be consumed by feral demons *and* she would die. Her eyes darted. Her mind raced. Her heartbeat choked her.

Every little idea and plan turned into a bloodbath or worse. Vanessa looked to Leon and then to Bobo and frowned hard. This all seemed so familiar. She could hear the screams echoing in her ears, she could still feel the blasts of magic whirling by her head, and her body heard the cries for help like she was there, during the blue cloak's battle, all over again. *Did she smell smoke?* Her head swam for a moment, and her lungs felt like they were vacant no matter how much air she sucked in. She remembered crying over Bobo and begging him to wake up. Her eyes pricked with the stinging warmth of tears on the edge of spilling over. They smeared her vision, and she heard a wolf yip out excitedly or perhaps it was the ghost of a scream from her haunted memories.

"*Stop!*" Vanessa screamed. The threads of distress woven within the fabric of her voice revealed a tapestry that displayed a memory of both pain and fear. Her russet eyes locked onto the scoundrel that held all the power in that moment. A power that needed to fall. But he held it just the same.

Raven looked at Vanessa like she was just as concerned as she was confused about the outburst. "Vanessa, are you all right?" she asked in a hushed tone.

The panic commanding her heart to pound at a painful beat and send blood rushing through her ears was louder than Raven, though. "Please, let them go." The Spellweaver sounded crushed as she spoke to Denmarius. "I'll …I'll give you it…Just don't hurt my friends anymore." She made the choice then. A dangerous choice. A choice she never thought that she'd have to make. Vanessa dropped her staff and held up her hands in defeat. "Please," she begged. "I will give it to you," she repeated and slowly shook her hands to show how she was without a weapon and no longer a threat.

Denmarius's face instantly went from menacing to full of glee as his vision swept over the broken forms scattered around the clearing. "Oh? You've finally come to see reason, have you? Very well…" With a snap of his fingers and a wave of his hand, the wolves went from pinning Leon and Bobo to circling them. "Come now," he motioned her closer as he spoke. "Bring it here."

"No," Leon croaked out from behind them. Vanessa turned to see his hand stretched out in her direction. A thin line of blood rolled out from the corner of Leon's mouth and dripped down his chin. The sight of it made Vanessa's stomach clench uneasily. She wanted nothing more than to run to him and mend him, gather up Bobo, and get the hex out of this cursed forest. She turned from him. She couldn't see him like this right now. Not with what she was about to do. They were willing to lay their lives on the line, but she wasn't willing to let them go like that. It was her turn to make a sacrifice.

"Please, Vanessa. Don't," his voice strained to say the words, but the emotion in them was so thick that it made her heart hurt.

"Forgive me," she whispered in a tone that was far from audible.

The wolves made their presence known as each growl rumbled over the forest floor and vibrated over her skin like a power that resonated with hate. Fear threatened to cripple her, but she managed to hide it. If Denmarius could fake kindness, then she could fake courage. She took hold of her emotions and faced him, straightened up to her full height, locked onto her target, and tilted her chin up. Though this was not the greatest idea she had ever come up with, she would walk the path she chose with pride.

"Vanessa," Raven sounded pained, and Vanessa couldn't make eye contact with the woman's starry-eyed gaze.

She drew in a breath, and it sounded like a sapling rustling in the winds of a storm. She hadn't intended it to. "Take care of them," she said quietly to the woman at her side, but her voice broke, almost betraying her.

Raven's hand reached for the witch as the Dark Elf gasped. If Raven knew what she was about to do, she didn't say a word, but she did try to reach out and turn the young girl around. She tried to bring Vanessa back from the hell she was willfully walking into. But at least that was the extent of her attempt to stop the Spellweaver because Vanessa was not about to be swayed from this.

One foot stepped forward and it was all it took to bring her out of Raven's reach. One step forward was all it took to drive Vanessa forward. One foot in front of the other, she marched. And with each step, she found a courage that she had hidden deep down. She was going to protect them. She was going to be the one to buy them time. She was going to get them out of this mess. She had not gone through everything that she had and become who she was today by sacrificing those that she loved. And she wasn't going to start a new habit of trying to today.

Her hand once more reached inside the bag as Denmarius came to meet her halfway. His grin was half-mad, and his eyes were twinkling with the victory. She could feel the dark intentions that he had for her and the others. There was no doubt in her mind that he didn't plan to make good on his promise. For a single moment, her heart sank. She wasn't ready for what was about to come next, but that wouldn't stop her.

The male elf's hand lay flat and awaiting. It all happened so fast. She didn't have time to even think of a single regret. In that one, perfect moment she let it all go. She let her free hand shoot out, like a snake attacking its unsuspecting prey, she let her fingers curl tightly around Denmarius's wrist and pull him dangerously close. She had used a touch of magic when she did. Her own strength was enough to throw him off balance, but the spell was to ensure that he would follow her tug. At the same time that she had grabbed him and pulled him toward her, Vanessa's other hand came out of the satchel. Yet, instead of the tablet being in her hand, there was a ghostly, turquoise blade that moved like liquid smoke within her grasp.

Thrusting it forward, Vanessa slammed the blade into Denmarius's body. Pain and sorrow melded together and swelled within her chest. She screamed in his face. Tears stung her eyes as she twisted the blade in the elf's stomach. He stiffened on the spot and looked down, his hands grasping pathetically at the weapon. The sneer on her face twisted into a frown as he looked back at her.

Adrenaline soaked her every nerve and drop of blood. With trembling hands that matched her voice, she spoke clearly to him, an anger that was laced in agony tinting every word that fell from her lips. "I just wanted to get close enough to see you realize that you picked the wrong witch to mess with."

Swiftly, she withdrew the blade, altered the angle up, and shoved it back in. A poor attempt stopped the blade when it had sunk in halfway. His hands fumbled over the grasp of her hand and the magical blade. Denmarius coughed up blood in her face and let one bloodied appendage snatch her by the back of the head. But she refused to cry out in pain as those red-drenched fingers knotted themselves in her hair.

"You'll all die," he rasped through crimson covered lips.

She shivered and took in a deep breath. A quiet quake rattled her voice as she spoke to him, "Not. Before. You." It was an undeniable promise that she had reserved herself to when she had taken that one step forward.

With all her might she shoved the blade further in, slicing through his hand as she did. The light was there. The one everyone says plays in the harbors of a being's eyes. She could see it as plain as she could see the moon in the sky. The same moon that mimicked the color that stained her hands and robes. The light was there one moment, and she watched it drift until the elf's body slunk to the ground gracelessly into a heap at her feet.

Swallowing hard, Vanessa tried to silence her scream, to dull the pain that rolled through her every limb as she looked down at the body and let the reality sink in. She had killed him. The shadow blade flicked in and out of existence, and her hand gripped the hilt tighter. A single tear streamed down her face with the same intensity of a burning sun.

"One," she announced, staring down at the motionless Denmarius.

A piercing cry erupted from the wolves, and they both turned from the injured bodies they guarded and flew for Vanessa. The shadow blade dissipated as her concentration slipped. One gray and one tawny wolf were rushing at her as she heard the forest erupt with mournful cries that threatened to rupture her ears.

"Raven!" Vanessa screamed.

The staff was thrown in her direction, and she caught it right as one of the wolves lunged at her. Quicker than she had ever recited a spell before, she channeled her magic and chanted, "By the goddess, I ask for protection from the evil that wishes me harm, by the land I ask for your aid, by my hand I let you work through me, by the law may it be," the other wolf lunged from behind her, and she stabbed the ground with the staff and stood tall, proud, and unmovable as she yelled, "… *threefold!*"

Both wolves crashed into an invisible force. Crackles of power exploded around the dome that protectively surrounded her. The little slivers of tiny bolts of lightning took shape, moulding into swords. The light blades zipped through the air and sliced without mercy. Suddenly scratches and wounds raced over the skin of the wolves, the blood quickly collecting on their coats and matting their fur. Yelps of pain shot out through the night right before they were slung with great force to the ground.

Removing her staff and wasting no time, Vanessa raced over to Bobo. She waved her mint glowing hands over his body as she poured a healing spell over him hastily. The ogre rolled over with a groan. "Don't fuss over me," he said and then coughed. "I'm well enough to still fight," he informed. Though he didn't look it.

A second later and Raven was close by while she aided the limping Leon. Pushing away from the Dark Elf, the Summoner took a few steps before his legs refused to hold up his weight any longer. Hitting his knees, he crawled the remaining distance to Vanessa. Leon reached out and forced the young witch to look at him, his hands searching for some sign of injury. When he saw the drying blood covering her face and hands, she touched his face gingerly, snapping his attention back to her emotionally chaotic orbs. "It isn't mine," she assured, but her voice lacked evenness.

His worried expression shifted into gratitude. "You are a crazy fool!" Leon shook his head. "But you are a brave, crazy fool." He crashed into her, holding her close.

"The wolves," Raven cried out with panic strangling her voice.

Leon shot up to fight them off and almost fell over. Shaking his head, he struggled to stand his ground. Raven's blades were out, glowing, and ready. The green poison was visible by the light of the eerie moon.

"This doesn't look good," Bobo rasped, scanning the tree line as the army of wolves emerged.

The witch's hand slid over the satchel protectively and then she paused. Looking down at the bag, she removed the tablet quickly and felt the power pulsing off of it. She either tried and failed or did nothing and died. Closing her eyes, Vanessa dug deep. To places forgotten and kept under lock and key.

"You gave more power than needed, Vanessa. For your generosity and for your ability to put selfish questions off to the side, I leave you with a gift." She remembered those words that the qilin had said to her, but it wasn't enough. She needed to find a way to touch on the magic.

"You are so in touch with magic, yet you fear it. I simply opened your mind and freed you from your shackles. The power that you have is not a burden, Vanessa. It is a gift. And gifts are meant to be shared. Fear not the power that you have. Fear not the magic you wield. You are the vessel of a lost world. It is my duty to see it flourish once more."

The voice of the qilin echoed in her mind as the first thrums of a power rumbled through the forest floor and raced for her tiny body. She called to it as her metaphysical self started to sift and search through thoughts and spells, visions and memories, frantically trying to find the one thing that would awaken her again. But that was when she heard the whisper caress her hearing. It was a sound that your ears didn't hear. It was a sound that you felt. Something that resonated within and echoed in your soul.

"Believe in yourself. Believe in your magic, daughter of Saellah."

Gasping, Vanessa opened her eyes.

Everything around her went quiet before her whole body felt like a tidal wave of power had slammed down on her and broke against her spirit. It was enough to crush her bones and rip her out of her physical form, but she willed herself to remain whole and unbroken. A single beat, like a forgotten heart awakening, pulsed inside of her entire being right before a song-like scream ripped out of her mouth and splendid yellow light exploded from her. Heat radiated off of her like she was a walking sun, and the magic prickled through her body like her blood had become static electricity. She illuminated the red-tinted darkness in a shower of golden light.

Leon and Raven had doubled back to her side.

"Vanessa, are you all right?" Bobo asked.

"It's happening again…" Leon whispered.

"*Cel'tos ali mahen,*" Raven stated in rushed astonishment. "She is touched by the goddess," she reiterated with mist forming in her black eyes.

Wasting no time, Leon reached out and caressed Vanessa's arm. "Can you do it? Can you teleport us out of here?"

Her hazel gaze held an otherworldly glow as she looked to the Summoner and replied with an echoic voice, "Yes."

Immediately after, she closed her eyes. The wolves started to close in. But when Vanessa opened her eyes again, she thrust out her arms, and a wave that looked like a giant sickle swept through the air and slammed into the approaching beasts. A few darted out of the way, watched it connect with their brethren who howled in pain, ensured it was the only attack, and then resumed their prowl toward the group.

Wordlessly, Vanessa took in a calming breath. Slowly, she spoke softly, without fear or care. "Fold the space, bend the time, bring me to another place, bring to that in which is mine."

The power enveloped them all before the sound of thunder boomed in the clearing. Golden lightning crackled over the space around the group before, in a glorious white storm cloud, they were consumed. The wolves pounced, and, when they landed, there was nothing there but grass and dirt and the remaining twinkles of a spell that had been cast.

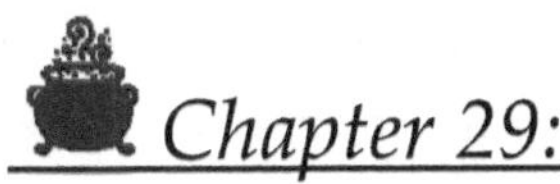 *Chapter 29:*

Lightning split the sky asunder and bolts lit up the night as the four of them landed on the banks of the Gentle Titan River that rested on the quieter side of the Vemeese district. They all landed with less grace than they would have desired. Black-tinged sand rubbed into their clothing, their hands sank deep into the soggy bank, and the waters lapped over the shore inches from their tired bodies.

From miles away they could still hear the relentless howling of the wolves. But Vanessa didn't care. All she wanted was to sleep. Her head lulled back, and she fell into the edge of the river, the freezing water waking her up instantly. Her head spun, and her vision swam as pain blossomed over her body like a spring of suffering.

She held her body and fought past the discomfort as she lifted from the river and half-crawled to the grassy hill near the sandy shores. Panting, she turned and fell backward to the ground. When she opened her eyes, Leon was hovering over her. "I'm all right," she said quietly.

He needed nothing further from her. As soon as the words left her mouth, Leon dipped down and collided with her lips. Hungrily, desperately, his mouth claimed hers as he poured every emotion that he had into that one, demanding kiss. It left her body tingling and her lungs starved for air, but she didn't fight it. In fact, she kissed him back while wrapping her arms around his neck. When their lungs felt like they were ablaze, they peeled away from one another, but their arms had become entangled around each other and refused to relent their hold on the other.

"Are you all right?" she asked breathily.

Leon smirked. "Yeah," he replied.

"I'm not!" Bobo whined while covering his eyes.

"Shush," Raven heatedly whispered at the ogre while slapping his shoulder. The demon grunted in pain, and she instantly inspected his wounds. "Sorry," she said with a light laugh.

They all laughed. Because it felt good to laugh and joke and just… be alive.

The undeniable sound of leathery wings flapping filled the air overhead right before a very angry, and very tired, Lyx landed with little grace. Twigs, leaves, and thorns were in her hair and attached to various buckles of her corset and boots. Dirt smudges adorned her usual pretty features, and her amber jeweled eyes lacked their usual luster. Deep purple and black circles lined the bags under the succubus's angry eyes. Her hair shifted from red to orange to a light blue color as she looked them all over. She attempted to slow her inhaling and exhaling, and her chest rose and fell frantically with her labored breathing.

"Do you have any idea how worried I was?" she bellowed her question. No hello. No happy reuniting. Just anger flickering in her goldenrod orbs and heat lacing every word she spat out. A perfectly broken nail pointed in the direction of the Black Forest. "Two days," she said breathlessly. "For two days I was circling that blasted-with-hellfire place looking for you all. For a sign of you. Anything. Any sign." Her lip quivered as she shouted. "Anything," she repeated in a high-pitch yell. "A spell. A sound. A crystal ball. A lingering piece of a cloak clinging to a tree branch." She drew in a breath to continue, "A dead body," her voice cracked. "Anything," she said again, and tears of blood fell from her eyes in uncontrollable droves.

Two, massive hands lay on her shoulder and spun the succubus around. Bobo stood there looking down at the distraught demoness and, without a word, he drew Lyx into his embrace. His large arms encircled her and squeezed her lightly within them.

"We are all here. We are all okay," he said, letting one hand draw her closer into the line of his body. The other hand cradled her head against his tattered button-up shirt. "Shhh. There, there, my dear. We are all fine. We are all right. You did enough. We are okay," he assured in a passionate whisper. "You did enough," he whispered one last time.

The bank of the Gentle Titan was filled with the grateful wails of a succubus reunited with everyone that she cared about. And the demoness let the emotions overtake every word she wanted to speak, and she just cried.

After everyone collected themselves, and long after Lyx's tears had dried up, they explained to the succubus what had transpired after they had been split up. They introduced her to Raven as well. It was evident that it was a lot of information to take in as quickly as it had been explained to the poor demoness.

Rubbing her nose with one of Bobo's handkerchiefs, Lyx cleared her throat softly and attempted to run a hand through her knotted hair. "We need to get you to the Coven quickly, then. And to the infirmary as well," she stated while looking them all over respectfully and yanked her long fingers out of her ensnaring mane.

They all agreed. Limping toward the Coven, they chattered over the events as they were explained more slowly and in far more detail.

The bubbles of cobblestone made the streets look like waterless rivers running through the city. Their natural tones held red hues from the light of the blood moon that was steadily coming down from on high. Lanterns were still lit along the sidewalks, making the void roads and blacked out shops lining the walkway seem a little less cold even though they were vacant.

Vanessa ached all over. Her staff had become her newfound blessing as she rested her weight upon it like she had aged a hundred years in a matter of hours. Dragging her sore legs, she willed them to rise and fall as she silently commanded them to carry her along. The desire to just stop and lie down on the path and fall asleep was strong. She had to constantly push herself to stay awake like she hadn't slept for days. Her eyelids drooped with their threat to force her body to shut down, to obey its command for rest.

"Are you really all right?" Leon questioned, his voice raspy.

Forcing a smile, Vanessa nodded while she replied. "Yes. I'm fine. I just felt like Tolvade was quieter than normal. It just felt like… something was off," she said.

Bobo grunted with a slight nod. "Though it would appear that way, I'm sure it is just the residual excitement of the hell that we've all been through these past few days, my dear," he assured.

"Yeah," Vanessa whispered. But there was still part of her that felt like something was not right in the grand city. Perhaps she was still on edge or—just maybe—she had been in far too many situations that she shouldn't have been able to walk away from and could smell the smoke that lingered from a disaster within the calm, crisp, night air.

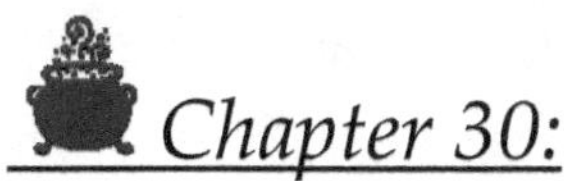 *Chapter 30:*

Coven headquarters never looked as good as it did at that moment. Their sluggish pace picked up speed as they knew behind its doors was safety and a place to rest. The comforts that they had always taken for granted were now a mere couple of feet away.

Practically falling in through the front doors, they scrambled over themselves as they headed for the main lobby. As they did, there was a strange, chaotic hush emitted from the countless bodies taking up the space. Hunter, Spellweaver, and Summoner alike all crowded the service desks and collected in small groupings throughout the room. Softly spoken tales of how two Coven members, Thea and Rafe, had just taken on a horde of blood mages and lived to tell the tale rode through the casters. Hearing the news of their impressive feat made Vanessa's eyes widen. It was going to be the hot topic of the Coven for a while, to say the least. Others whispered of a long-lost artifact. But it was the whispered gossip of the great orb blacking out that made Vanessa stop in her tracks.

The great orb was down?

"Vanessa, dear, let us make way to make our report and hand in that… Uhm…" He gestured with a clawed digit to the satchel that she clutched to just as desperately as her new staff.

Lyx's gentle touch helped the witch steady her weight as they walked. "I've got you, darling. Come on."

Nodding, she said nothing and limped for the desk that was the least swamped. A group of Coven members shifted off to the side as they started to fill out forms that had been handed out. Ell and a pixie aided the next in line while Vanessa and the others fell in behind them.

"Ah, Spellweaver Peterson," a voice called from amidst the throng of ebbing Coven members. If the bright, ginger-colored hair wasn't a dead giveaway to the owner, the battle scar running its jagged course along the side of his head was.

"Riker," Vanessa breathed his name.

The smile on his face was a cross between a smirk and something dark. It was hard to get a read on the man as he approached. "I seem to have good luck running into you," he stated and lifted a scroll. "I just received word that we are to be paired for your next mission."

"Y-you are what?" Leon gasped.

"Ah, and Summoner… or, rather, to-be Summoner Zvěrokruh, you are to finish up your final oath-taking and training this week so you can assume your new rank and role." He flashed a smile that lacked any real warmth at the man.

Leon looked torn and clamped his mouth shut. Vanessa cut in, "What sort of mission is it?'

Her inquiry was met with Riker stepping closer and touching the rolled-up parchment to her shoulder, "You," he stated and then pointed to himself with the scroll, "and I are to find the cause of the great orb blacking out. The details are being hashed out with the High Priest Council at the present moment. Once they have more information, I'll have a clearer mission scroll to share with you," he informed. His eyes suddenly trailed slowly over her body, and he looked to the rest in her party in a similar fashion. "It seems that you all just got back from a recent mission."

"You could say that, "Vanessa said under her breath. "Yes, we did," she stated louder for Riker to hear.

"Humph… I'll say," Lyx said with an agitated whip of her tail.

Riker stood poised and clasped his hands behind his back. "Ah, I see. Very well then, Spellweaver Peterson. Carry on with your mission report. As I said, we shall speak again when I have more information."

"All right. Thanks for letting me know," Vanessa replied.

"Rest up, Spellweaver Peterson," he threw in passing with a lazy wave rising and falling while he went to file his own report at a neighboring desk.

"Why do you need to be paired up with him?" Leon griped.

The witch rolled her eyes. "Oh, hush up. Someone's going to hear you and claim you are jealous."

"Nah, more like worried that you are going to be kicked out of the Coven by the day's end knowing you and your lack of respect for the handbook that Riker treats as a religious tome," Leon corrected.

Instantly, Bobo sputtered with laughter, and the ogre attempted to hide his giggles but failed. Raven was far too busy with her attention being pulled in various directions to be paying any mind to the conversations that were taking place. Her eyes trailed the floors and walls like they were masterpieces and she was a collector of fine art.

Angrily, Vanessa's mouth opened to make a witty comeback, but the soft voice of Ell called out to them, "Next!"

Choosing to ignore Leon and Bobo's quiet chuckling, Vanessa restrained her urge to scream and stormed up to the front desk with purpose after screwing her jaw shut.

"Oh my. You look terrible," Ell gasped at the witch.

"Yeah, I feel like it," Vanessa admitted. "I need to make a report on my recent missions, and I have to turn in this," she mentioned, placing the satchel up on the counter and lifting the flap to show the stone within its confines.

Ell's eyes widened more than Vanessa had expected them to before the girl quietly mused to herself, "Another one?"

"'Another one?'" Bobo shot out while stepping forward.

Ell nodded. "Yeah. Not too long before you guys came in, another pair of Coven members had brought in a stone that looked exactly the same. It's been a pretty big deal because not only is it a lost magical artifact, but that one has the Wild Hunt spell on it."

There was no way to mask the surprise scrolled across their faces. "This… this one has the de-summoning spell," Leon announced quietly while jabbing at the rocky tablet with his finger. Lyx nodded next to her master, agreeing silently.

"Oh. Oh, that is good news," Ell stated. "Let's go ahead and get you those forms so you all can go see a medic," she said with a smile.

Bending over to grab a few forms from the filing cabinet, Ell paused in mid-action and slowly rose. Her usual soft features scrunched as she narrowed her eyes at something. A moment later, they bulged. The few items she had gathered plummeted from her grasp and clattered against the desktop and floor below.

Jumping up on the counter, Ell swung her legs over the surface and leaped down on the other side. Without a word she stepped forward, her hands shaking, confusion consuming her face as she gently parted Bobo and Vanessa out of the way. "You," she hissed. "Wh-what are you doing back here?"

Raven immediately turned from her amazed inspection of the main lobby and rested her starry night gaze upon the freckled blonde in front of her.

"Ell?" Understanding registered over the Dark Elf's features as her eyes darted to Vanessa.

Ell nodded quickly as if answering a question that hadn't been asked aloud. A look swirled behind the receptionist's eyes as she watched the realization take hold of the Dark Elf.

Shocked, she stared at Vanessa as a sea of emotions scrolled themselves all over the elf's features. Raven gasped and whispered, "Then, that means… you… are…" Her hands clamped down over her mouth, and she looked like she was about to weep as black tears welled in her starry eyes. Raven's voice was faint and strained as she spoke, "You're her."

To be continued…